ROBIN HOOD

Robin Hood

HENRY GILBERT

WORDSWORTH CLASSICS

For my husband
ANTHONY JOHN RANSON
with love from your wife, the publisher.
Eternally grateful for your
unconditional love.

Readers who are interested in other titles from
Wordsworth Editions are invited to visit our website at
www.wordsworth-editions.com

Robin Hood first published as a Children's Classic
in 1994 by Wordsworth Editions Limited
8B East Street, Ware, Hertfordshire SG12 9ET

This edition first published in 2018

ISBN 978 1 84022 758 1

© Wordsworth Editions Limited 1994

Wordsworth® is a registered trademark
of Wordsworth Editions Limited,
the company founded in 1987 by

MICHAEL TRAYLER

Typeset in Great Britain by Antony Gray
Printed and bound by Clays Ltd, Elcograf S.p.A.

CONTENTS

PREFACE

Once upon a time the great mass of English people were unfree. They could not live where they chose, nor work for whom they pleased. Society in those feudal days was mainly divided into lords and peasants. The lords held the land from the king, and the peasants or villeins were looked upon as part of the soil, and had to cultivate it to support themselves and their masters. If John or Dick, thrall of a manor, did not like the way in which the lord or his steward treated him, he could not go to some other part of the country and get work under a kinder owner. If he tried to do this he was looked upon as a criminal, to be brought back and punished with the whip or the branding-iron, or cast into prison.

When the harvest was plenteous and his master was kind or careless, I do not think the peasant felt his serfdom to be so unbearable as at other times. When, however, hunger stalked through the land, and the villein and his family starved; or when the lord was of a stern or exacting nature, and the serf was called upon to do excessive labour, or was otherwise harshly treated, then, I think, the old Teutonic or Welsh blood in the English peasant grew hot, and he longed for freedom.

The silence and green peace of forest lands stood in those days along many a league where now the thick yellow corn grows, or the cows roam over the rich pastures, or even where today the bricky suburbs of towns straggle over the country. Such forests must have been places of terror and fascination for the poor villein who could see them from where he delved in his fields. In their quiet glades ran the king's deer, and in their dense thickets skulked the boar, creatures whose killing was reserved for the king and a few of his friends, the great nobles, and princes of the

Church. A poor man, yeoman or peasant, found slaying one of the royal beasts of the forest was cruelly maimed as a punishment. Or if he was not caught, he ran and hid deep in the forest and became an outlaw, a 'wolf's-head' as the term was, and then anyone might slay him that could.

It was in such conditions that Robin Hood lived, and did deeds of daring such as we read of in the ballads and traditions which have come down to us. Because his name is not to be found in the crabbed records of lawyers and such men, some people have doubted whether Robin Hood ever really existed. But I am sure that Robin was once very much alive. It may be that the unknown poets who made the ballads idealised him a little – that is, they described him as being more daring, more successful, more of a hero perhaps, than he really was; but that is what poets and writers are always expected to do.

The ballads which we have about Robin Hood and his band of outlaws number about forty. The oldest are the best, because they are the most natural and exciting. The majority of the later poems are very poor; many are tiresome repetitions of one or two incidents, while others are rough, doggerel rhymes, without spirit or imagination.

In the tales which I have told in this book, I have used a few of the best episodes related in the ballads; but I have also thought out other tales about Robin, and I have added incidents and events which have been invented so as to give a truthful picture of the times in which he lived.

HENRY GILBERT
London, July 1912

CHAPTER ONE

How Robin Became an Outlaw

It was high noon in summer-time, and the forest seemed to sleep. Hardly a breeze stirred the broad fans of the oak leaves, and the only sound was the low hum of insects which flew to and fro unceasingly in the cool twilight under the wide-spreading boughs.

So quiet did it seem and so lonely, that almost one might think that nothing but the wild red deer, or his fierce enemy the slinking wolf, had ever walked this way since the beginning of the world. There was a little path worn among the thick bushes of hazel, dogberry, and traveller's joy, but so narrow was it and so faint that it could well have been worn by the slender, fleeting feet of the doe, or even by the hares and rabbits which had their home in a great bank among the roots of a beech near by.

Few, indeed, were the folks that ever came this way, for it was in the loneliest part of Barnisdale Forest. Besides, who had any right to come here save it was the king's foresters keeping strict watch and ward over the king's deer? Nevertheless, the rabbits which should have been feeding before their holes, or playing their mad pranks, seemed to have bolted into their burrows as if scared by something which had passed that way. Only now, indeed, were one or two peeping out to see that things were quiet again. Then a venturesome bunny suddenly scampered out, and in a moment others trooped forth.

A little way beyond the bank where the rabbits were now nibbling or darting off in little mad rushes, the path made a bend, and then the giant trunks of the trees were fewer, and more light came through from the sky. Suddenly the trees ceased, and the little sly path ran into a wide glade where grass grew, and bushes of holly and hazel stood here and there.

A man stood close by the path, behind a tree, and looked out into the glade. He was dressed in a tunic made of a rough green cloth, open at the top, and showing a bronzed neck. Round his waist was a broad leathern girdle in which were stuck at one place a dagger, and at the other side three long arrows. Short breeches of soft leather covered his thighs, below which he wore hosen of green wool, which reached to his feet. The latter were encased in shoes of stout pig's leather.

His head of dark brown curls was covered by a velvet cap, at the side of which was stuck a short feather, pulled from the wing of a plover. His face, bronzed to a ruddy tan by wind and weather, was open and frank, his eye shone like a wild bird's, and was as fearless and as noble. Great of limb was he, and seemingly of a strength beyond his age, which was about twenty-five years. In one hand he carried a long-bow, while the other rested on the smooth bole of the beech before him.

He looked intently at some bushes which stood a little distance before him in the glade, and moved not a muscle while he watched. Sometimes he looked beyond far to the side of the glade where, on the edge of the shaw or wood, two or three deer were feeding under the trees, advancing towards where he stood.

Suddenly he saw the bushes move stealthily; an unkempt head issued between the leaves, and the haggard face of a man looked warily this way and that. Next moment, out of the bush where the hidden man lay, an arrow sped. Straight to the feeding deer it flew, and sank in the breast of the nearest doe. She ran a few feet and then fell; while the others, scared, ran off into the trees.

Not at once did the hidden man issue from his hiding-place to take up the animal he had slain. He waited patiently while one might count fifty, for he knew that, should there be a forester skulking near who should meet the scampering deer whose companion had been struck down, he would know from their frightened air that something wrongful had been done, and he would search for the doer.

The moments went slowly by and nothing moved; neither did the hidden man, nor he who watched him. Nor did a forester show himself on the edge of the shaw where the deer had fled. Feeling himself secure, therefore, the man came from the bush, but there was no bow and arrows in his hand, for these he had left secure in his hiding-place to be brought away another day.

He was dressed in the rough and ragged homespun of a villein, a rope round his brown tunic, and his lower limbs half covered with loose trousers of the same material as his tunic, but more holed and patched. Looking this way and that, he walked half-bent across to where the doe lay, and leaning over it, he snatched his knife from his belt and began almost feverishly to cut portions of the tenderest parts from the carcass.

As the man behind the tree saw him, he seemed to recognise him, and muttered, 'Poor lad!' The villein wrapped the deer's flesh in a rough piece of cloth, and then rose and disappeared between the trees. Then with swift and noiseless footsteps the watcher went back through the path and into the depths of the forest. A few moments later the villein, with wary eyes looking this way and that, was passing swiftly between the boles of the trees. Every now and then he stopped and rubbed his red hands in the long, moist grass, to remove the tell-tale stains of blood.

Suddenly, as he came from behind the giant trunk of an oak, the tall form of the man who had watched him stood in his pathway. Instantly his hand went to his knife, and he seemed about to spring upon the other.

'Man,' said he in the green tunic, 'what madness drives you to this?'

The villein recognised the speaker at once, and gave a fierce laugh.

'Madness!' he said. ' 'Tis not for myself this time, Master Robin. But my little lad is dying of hunger, and while there's deer in the greenwood he shall not starve.'

'Your little lad, Scarlet?' said Robin. 'Is your sister's son living with you now?'

'Ay,' replied Scarlet. 'You've been away these three weeks and cannot have heard.' He spoke in a hard voice, while the two continued their walk down a path so narrow that while Robin walked before, Scarlet was compelled to walk just behind.

'A sennight since,' Scarlet went on, 'my sister's husband, John a' Green, was taken ill and died. What did our lord's steward do? Said, "Out ye go, baggage, and fend for yourself. The holding is for a man who'll do due services for it." '

' 'Twas like Guy of Gisborne to do thus,' said Robin; 'the evil-hearted traitor!'

'Out she went, with no more than the rags which covered herself and the bairns,' said Scarlet fiercely. 'If I had been by I could not have kept my knife from his throat. She came to me; dazed she was and ill. She had the hunger-plague in truth, and sickened and died last week. The two little ones were taken in by neighbours, but I kept little Gilbert myself. I am a lonely man, and I love the lad, and if harm should happen to him I shall put my mark upon Guy of Gisborne for it.'

As Robin had listened to the short and tragic story of the wreck of a poor villein's home, his heart burned in rage against the steward, Sir Guy of Gisborne, who ruled the manor of Birkencar for the White Monks of St Mary's Abbey with so harsh a hand. But he knew that the steward did no more than the abbot and monks permitted him, and he cursed the whole brood of them, rich and proud as they were, given over to hunting and high living on the services and rents which they wrung from the poor villeins, who were looked upon merely as part of the soil of the manors which they tilled.

Robin, or Robert of Locksley, as he was known to the steward and the monks, was a freeman, or socman, as it was termed, and he was a young man of wealth as things went then. He had his own house and land, a farm of some hundred and sixty acres of the richest land on the verge of the manor, and he knew full well that the monks had long cast covetous eyes upon his little holding. It lay beside the forest, and was called the Outwoods. He and his ancestors had held this land for generations, first from the lords to whom the manor of Birkencar had been given by King William, and for the last generation or so from the Abbey of St Mary, to which the last owner, the Lord Guy de Wrothsley, had left it in his will.

Robin held his land at a rent, and so long as he paid this to the monks they could not legally oust him from his farm, much as they would have liked to do this. Robin was looked upon by the abbot as a discontented and malicious man. He had often bearded the abbot in his own monastery, and told him to his face how wickedly he and his stewards treated the villeins and poorer tenants of their manors. Such defiance in those days was reckoned to be almost unheard of, and the monks and Guy of Gisborne, their steward at Birkencar, hated Robin and his free speech as much as Robin hated them for their tyranny and oppression.

'Pity it is I was away,' said Robin in reply to Scarlet's last words. 'But you could have gone to Outwoods, and Scadlock would have given you food.'

'Ay, Master Robin,' said Scarlet, 'you have ever been the good and true friend of us all. But I, too, have been a freeman, and I cannot beg my bread. You have made enemies enough on our behalf as it is, and I would not live upon you to boot. No, while there is deer in the greenwood, I and the little lad shall not starve. Besides, Master Robin, you should look to yourself. If your unfriends had known how long you would be away they would – it hath been whispered – have proclaimed you an outlaw, and taken your land in your absence, and killed you when you returned.'

Robin laughed. 'Ay, I have heard of it while I was away.'

Scarlet looked at him in wonder. He thought he had been telling his friend a great and surprising secret.

'You have heard of it?' he replied; 'now that is passing strange.'

Robin made no answer. He knew well that his enemies were only looking out for an opportunity of thrusting him to ruin. Many a man going on a long journey had come back to find that in his absence his enemy had made oath to a justice that he had fled on account of some wrong-doing, and thus had caused him to be proclaimed an outlaw, whose head anyone could cut off.

Scarlet was silent, thinking of many strange tales which the villeins, when they sat together at ale after work, had spoken concerning their great friend Robin.

Suddenly, from a little way before them, came the sound as if a squirrel was scolding. Then there was silence for a space; and then the cry, a lonely sad cry it was, as of a wolf. Instantly Robin stopped, laid the long-bow he had in his hand at the root of a great oak, together with the arrows from his girdle. Then, turning to Scarlet, he said in a low stern voice:

'Place the deer's meat you have in your tunic beside these. Quick, man, ere the foresters see your bulging breast. You shall have it safely anon.'

Almost mechanically, at the commanding tones Scarlet took the rough piece of hempen cloth in which he had wrapped the flesh of the doe from the breast of his tunic and laid it beside the bow and arrows. Next moment Robin resumed his walk. When they had gone a few steps, Scarlet looked round at the place where they had placed the things. They were gone!

A cold chill seemed to grip his heart, and he almost stopped, but Robin's stern voice said: 'Step out, man, close behind!' Poor Scarlet, sure that he was in the presence of witchcraft, did as he was bidden; but crossed himself to fend off evil.

Next moment the narrow path before them was blocked by the forms of two burly foresters, with bows at their backs and long staves in their hands. Their hard eyes looked keenly at Robin and Scarlet, and for a moment it seemed that they meditated barring their way. But Robin's bold look as he advanced made them change their minds, and they let them pass.

'When freeman and villein are found together,' scoffed one, 'there's ill brewing for their lord.'

'And when two foresters are found together,' said Robin, with a short laugh, 'some poor man's life will be sworn away ere long.'

'I know ye, Robert of Locksley,' said the one who had first spoken, 'as your betters know ye, for a man whose tongue wags too fast.'

'And I know thee, Black Hugo,' replied Robin, 'for a man who swore his best friend to ruin to join his few poor acres to thine.'

The man's face darkened with rage, while the other forester laughed at his discomfiture. Black Hugo looked at Robin as if he would have thrown himself upon him; but Robin's fearless eyes overawed him, and he sullenly turned away without another word.

Robin and Scarlet resumed their walk, and in a little while had issued from the forest, and were tramping through the bush and thick undergrowth of the waste lands which divided the farms of the manor on this side from the forest.

At last they came to the top of an incline, and before them the land sloped down to the cultivated fields and the pasture which surrounded the little village of villeins' huts, with the manor-house at a distance beyond the village half-way up another slope. Scarlet looked keenly about him, to see if anyone in the fields had seen him coming from the forest; for he had run from his work of dyke building to shoot the deer, and wondered whether his absence had been discovered. If it had, he didn't care for the scourging-post and the whip on his bare back, which might be his portion tomorrow when the steward's men came round to find his work only half done. At any rate, his little lad, Gilbert of the White Hand, would have a king's supper that night.

Would he? He suddenly remembered, and again fear shook him. Where had Robin's bow and arrows and his venison disappeared? Had some goblin or elf snatched them up, or had he really looked in the wrong place, and had the foresters found them by now? He clenched his jaw and looked back, his hand upon his knife, almost expecting to see the two foresters coming after him.

'Hallo,' said Robin carelessly, 'there are my bow and arrows and your venison, lad.'

Turning, Scarlet saw the things lying beside a tussock of grass at a little distance, where he was certain he had looked a moment before and seen nothing!

'Master,' he said in an awed voice, 'this is sheer wizardry. I – I – fear for you if unfriends learn you are helped by the evil spirits that dwell in the woods.'

'Scarlet,' said Robin, 'I thought thou wert a wiser man, but, like the rest, thou seemest to be no more than a fool. Have no fear for me. My friends of the woods are quite harmless, and are no worse than thou or I.'

'Master,' said Scarlet, sorry for his hasty speech, 'I crave pardon for my fool's words. My tongue ran before my thoughts, for the sight of those things where nothing had been a moment before affrighted me. But I know there cannot be worse things in the woods than there are in strong castles and abbots' palaces whose masters oppress and maim poor villeins. Say, master, is that which has helped us but now – is it a brownie, as men call it – a troll?'

Robin looked quietly into Scarlet's face for a moment or two without speaking.

'Scarlet,' he said, 'I think I see a time before us when thou and I will be much together in the greenwood. Then I will show thee my friends there. But until then, Scarlet, not a word of what has passed today. Thou swearest it?'

'By the gentle Virgin!' said Scarlet, throwing up his hand as he took the oath.

'Amen!' replied Robin, doffing his cap and bending his head at the name. 'Now,' he went on, 'take thy meat and hand me my bow and arrows. For I must back to the greenwood. And tell thy little man, Gilbert, that Robin wishes him to get well quickly, for I would go shooting with him again on the uplands at the plovers.'

'Ay,' said Scarlet, and his haggard, hungry face shone with a gentle look as he spoke, 'the little lad hath ever loved to speak of you since you took such note of him. Your words will hearten him bravely.'

When the two men had parted, Robin turned and plunged into the thick undergrowth, but in a different direction from that in which he had come with Scarlet. He looked up at the sun and quickened his pace, for he saw it was two hours past noon. Soon he had reached the trees, and threading his way unerringly among them, he struck southwards towards the road that ran for many a mile through the forest from Barnisdale into Nottinghamshire.

With a quick and eager step did Robin pass through the glades, for he was going to see the lady he loved best in all the world. Fair Marian was she called, the daughter of Richard FitzWalter of Malaset. Ever since when, as a boy, Robin had shot and sported in Locksley Chase, near where he had been born, Marian had been his playmate, and though she was an earl's daughter, and Robin was but a yeoman and not rich, they had loved each other dearly, and sworn that neither would marry anyone else.

This day she was to journey from her father's castle at Malaset to Linden Lea, near by Nottingham, to stay a while at the castle of her uncle, Sir Richard at Lee, and Robin had promised to guard her through the forest.

Soon he reached a broad trackway, carpeted with thick grass and with deep wheel-holes here and there in the boggy hollows. He walked rapidly along this, and did not rest till he had covered some five miles. Then, coming to where another road crossed it, he paused, looked about him keenly, and then disappeared among some hazel bushes that crowned a bank beside the four ways.

Proceeding for some distance, he at length gained a hollow where the ground was clear of bushes. On one side was a bare place where the sand showed, and to this Robin walked straightway. On the bare ground were a few broken twigs which to the ordinary eye would have seemed to have been blown there by the wind; but with hands on knees Robin bent and scanned them keenly.

'One bent at the head and eight straight twigs,' he said under his breath; 'a knight on horseback, that will mean, with eight knaves afoot. They are halted on the western road not far from here. Now what means that?'

He stood up, and turning away, quickly crossed the road by which he had come, and dived into the forest which skirted the right-hand road. Very cautiously he made his way between the trees, taking care not to step on a twig as he walked rapidly over the grass, his quick eyes meanwhile bent in every direction, trying to pierce the twilight of the thick forest round about.

Suddenly he dropped on his knees, and began working away farther into the trees. He had heard the tiniest noise of a jingling bridle before him. In a little while, peering from between the branches of a young yew tree, he saw, drawn up into the deepest shadow of the trees, a band of armed men, with a knight in chain mail on horseback in their midst.

Eagerly he scanned each, in the endeavour to learn to what lord they belonged; but the men on foot were dressed in plain jerkins, and the knight bore a blank shield, kite-shaped. For some moments he was baffled in his attempt to learn who these men were, and why they lay hid in the wood as if about to set on some travellers whom they expected to pass by. Then the knight swept his glance round the forest, and with a gesture of impatience and an oath quieted his restive horse.

At the sound of his voice Robin recognised him, and his face went stern, and a fierce light came into his eyes.

'So, Roger de Longchamp,' he said to himself, 'you would seize by force my lady, whose favour you cannot get by fair means!'

For this Sir Roger was a proud and tyrannical knight, who had asked for the hand of Fair Marian, but her father had refused him. FitzWalter loved his daughter, and though he laughed at her for her love of Robin, he would not give her to a man with so evil a fame as Roger de Longchamp, brother of that proud prelate the Bishop of Fécamp, and favourite of Duke Richard.

Often, when Robin had thought how Sir Roger de Longchamp
or any other man, however evil he was, could visit Sir Richard
FitzWalter and speak openly with Marian, he became moody,
and wondered whether indeed there was any truth in the tales
which old Stephen of Gamwell, his uncle, had told him concerning his noble lineage. He had said that, three generations before,
Robin's ancestors had owned broad lands and many manors, and
had been lords of Huntingdon town. But that, for having taken
part in some revolt of the English against the Norman con-
queror, their lands had been seized by the king, the earl slain,
and his kinsmen hunted this way and that into obscurity.

Everyone knew now, that the earldom and lands of Huntingdon
were in the hands of the king himself, and that the title had been
given to David, brother of the Scottish king. But Robin had
often wondered whether he could regain something of the
former honours and rank of his family. If so, then he would go
and claim Marian boldly, and take no denial.

A movement among the lurking men before him caused him to
cease his thinking. A man came running through the trees
towards them, and going up to the knight, said in a low voice:

'They are coming! The lady and one varlet are on horseback,
the others are walking. There are nine in all, and they are mere
house-churls.'

'Good!' said the knight. 'When they come near I will ride
against them and seize the lady's bridle. Should the churl who is
riding seek to follow me, do you knock him down.'

Robin smiled grimly as he listened, and slipped an arrow from
its fastening at his belt. Almost immediately the voices of men
were heard coming along the grassy road, with the beat of
horses' hooves, and in a little while Robin's heart warmed as he
saw through the leaves the gentle womanly figure of Marian on a
horse, with her hood thrown back from her face. She was
conversing with Walter, the steward of her father's house, who
rode beside her.

Next moment the knight had burst through the trees, followed
by his men. The brave Walter instantly pushed his horse before
that of his mistress, and with a stout staff which he carried
prepared to defend her, while the others of her guards also ran
before her. Sir Roger struck at the steward with his sword, which

sliced a huge splinter from the staff which the other held. With a quick turn of the staff, however, Walter beat on the knight's sword hand, and so shrewd was the blow that the weapon fell from the knight's fingers. It was hung by a strap at his wrist, however, and with a furious cry he regained the haft again.

In a second more the sword would have pierced the body of the brave steward, but suddenly he was jerked from his horse by one of Sir Roger's men, and fell senseless on the ground. The struggle between Marian's men and those of the knight was now becoming hot, but the poor villeins with their staffs or short spears had little chance against the swords of the robbers.

Already the hand of Sir Roger was on the reins in Marian's fingers, and with flashing eyes she was trying to back her horse away, when suddenly there came a sound like a great bee, and as she looked at the bars of the knight's visor she was aware that something flew into them, and next moment she saw the long yellow shaft of an arrow quivering before them.

The knight gave a deep groan, swayed, and then fell from his horse. Instantly his men ceased fighting; one, the chief among them, ran to the dead knight, drew the ruddily tipped arrow from his master's eye, and then all looked swiftly up and down the broad track and at the dense green forest at their sides.

' 'Tis but one man!' said one of them. 'It came from the left side here.'

'Ay, but I know the bolt! It is – ' began he that still held the arrow, but he never ended his words. Again came a swift sound through the air, but this time like the low whistling of a forest bird, and he sank to the ground with a small black arrow-shaft jutting from his breast. The bolt had been shot from the right side, showing that more than one bowman observed them.

Instantly the others scattered and ran into the forest, but ere the last could reach its shade an arrow, no larger than a birding bolt, issued from the trees on the right and sank into the shoulder of the last fugitive, who shrieked, but still ran on.

Next moment Marian saw Robin, with cap in hand, issue from the wood beside her. He came to her side, and with flushing cheeks she bent to him and said:

'Sweet Robin, I knew thou wouldst not fail me. That was a brave shot of thine which struck down that felon knight. But, dear heart of mine, if he be he whom I think he is, his death will work thee much harm.'

She gave him her hand, and fondly Robin kissed it.

'He is Roger de Longchamp, sweetheart,' replied Robin; 'but if it had been King Henry himself lurking thus to do you harm, I would not have saved my bolt.'

'But, Robin dear,' went on Marian, and her eyes were soft yet proud, 'the bishop his brother will pursue thee and outlaw thee for this. And thou wilt lose lands and name for my sake! O Robin! Robin! But I will take counsel of Sir Richard at Lee, who loves thee dearly, how best to get thee pardon from the bishop.'

'Sweet Marian,' said Robin, and very stern was his look and voice, 'I will have no pardon from any proud prelate for any ill I do the evil brood of priests. Come soon, come late, I knew that ere long I should do some deed against the doers of evil who sit in strong castles or loll in soft abbeys and oppress and wrong poor or weaker folk. It is done at last, and I am content. Trouble not for me, dear heart. But now, let us get thee to a safe place ere those runaway rogues raise the hue and cry after me. Walter,' said Robin to the poor steward, who, dazed and faint, was now sitting up in the road, 'gather thy wits together, brave man, and see to thy mistress. Lads,' he said to the villeins, most of whom were wounded, 'think no more of thy wounds till thy lady be safe. The knight that is slain hath friends as evil as he, and they may be down upon us ere long, and then you may not escape so lightly. And now trot forward to where the roads fork, and I will join thee anon.'

Robin helped Walter on his horse, and Fair Marian and her faithful villeins went forward. When they had passed, Robin pulled the dead knight out of the track and far into the forest, then raised the visor of the helm, placed the dead man's sword-hilt on his breast, and folded the limp arms over it, so that it seemed as if the dead were kissing the cross of the sword. Then, with bared head, kneeling, he said a short prayer for the repose of the knight's soul. He did the same with the dead body of the marauder who had been slain by the second arrow, and then, picking up both his own bolt and the smaller arrow, he slashed the knight's horse across the loins and saw it go flying down a forest drive that would lead it quite away from the spot. All this

The death of Sir Roger de Longchamp

he did so as to put pursuers off the track as long as possible.

Then, going a few steps into the forest in the direction in which the knight's men had fled, he put a horn to his lips and blew a long shrill blast with strange broken notes at the end. Afterwards he hastened to rejoin Fair Marian, and with his hand upon the bridle of her horse he led the way from the beaten track, and passing by secret ways and tiny paths only half visible, he rapidly pushed on, and very soon they were in the deeps of the forest where none who were with him had ever passed before.

Fair Marian, content to know that Robin was with her, saw nothing to fear in the silence and sombre shadows about them; but many of the villeins, as they walked in single file along the narrow way made by the hooves of the horses, often crossed themselves as they passed along some gloomy grove of trees, or wound across the solitary glades where everything was so silent and grey that it seemed as if no life had stirred there since the beginning of the world.

To their simple minds they were risking the loss not only of their lives, but of their immortal souls, by venturing into these wild places, the haunts of wood demons, trolls, and witches. They kept close together, the last man in the line looking ever behind him in dread; while all glanced furtively this way and that between the close trunks of the mossy trees, expecting every moment to see the evil eyes of elves gleaming out at them, or dreading that warlocks or witches, with red grinning mouths, would dart from behind some great screen of ivy or dodder which hung from some of the old trees.

The only sounds to be heard were the soft padding of their own footsteps over the thick grass or the snap of a twig here and there. Sometimes far up through the dense leaves above their heads they could hear the cry of a bird, or from a thicket here and there would come a strange, uncanny cheep! cheep! but nothing could be seen. Once or twice they heard the murmur of water, and they would come upon a little lonely brooklet half hidden beneath the undergrowth.

Once they passed through a wide glade, and in the middle thereof were two green mounds close to each other, and at the sight of them the poor churls were exceeding afraid.

'Trolls' houses!' they whispered to each other, and pointed and hurried on.

'I doubt we 'scape with our souls this day,' said one in a half whisper.

'Why doth he that leads us bring us by those places of dread?' growled another. 'The trolls will spy us as we pass, and work some wizardry upon us, and the bones of all of us will be left to whiten in this unholy forest till the crack of doom.'

So closely, in their terror, did they press upon the haunches of Walter's horse that he had to warn them.

'Keep back, thou fellows,' he said. 'Thou knowest my horse is mettlesome, and if he lash out at thee, thy heads, though thick, will not be thick enough to withstand his hoof.'

By this time the light from the sky showed that the afternoon was drawing to even. Little had Robin spoken since he began the swift flight through the forest, but now he turned to Marian, and with a smile said:

'Forgive me, sweet lady, for my seeming churlishness. But Roger de Longchamp's friends at his castle of Evil Hold are men not to be despised. Their cruel deeds are not fit for thy ears, and I have hastened to escape them speedily. Have I taxed thee beyond thy strength?'

'Nay, nay, Robin dear,' said Marian, with a sweet look. 'I knew what was in thy heart, and therefore I troubled thee not with talk. But what mean you by the Evil Hold? I knew not Roger de Longchamp's castle of Wrangby was so named.'

'That is how it is named by the poor folk who own him lord,' replied Robin, 'because of the nameless deeds that are committed there by him and his boon comrades, Isenbart de Belame, Niger le Grym, Hamo de Mortain, Ivo de Raby, and others.'

Marian shuddered and paled at the names.

'I have heard of them,' she said in a low voice. 'Let us push on,' she continued. 'I am not tired, Robin, and I would fain see thee safe in Sir Richard's castle.'

'Have no fear for me,' laughed Robin. 'While I have my good bow, and the greenwood stands to shelter me, I can laugh at all who wish me ill. In a little while now you shall be greeting your uncle, and safe within his strong walls.'

Suddenly from somewhere in the twilight forest before them

came a scream as of some animal or bird in the talons of a hawk. Robin stopped and peered forward. Then there came the lonely cry of a wolf, causing the villeins behind to shudder as they, too, strained their eyes into the murky depths of the trees.

Robin stepped forward, and as he did so he gave a cry as if a blackcock called his mate; then he led Marian's horse forward at a slow pace. In a little while they came to rising ground, and approaching the top they saw the sinking sun gleaming redly through the trees. At the summit they found the trees gave place to a gentle slope of greensward, and before them, beyond some meadows, lay a castle, and on a trackway not far from the forest were two riders passing towards the castle.

'I think,' said Robin, 'that yonder horsemen are Sir Richard and his kinsman, Sir Huon de Bulwell.'

'It is in truth they,' replied Marian; 'I think they have been to meet me by the highway, and are no doubt wondering what hath befallen me. Give them a call, dear Robin, and do you, Walter, ride forward and tell them that, thanks to my friend, Robert of Locksley, I am safe and well.'

Robin blew a blast on his horn. The horsemen turned their heads at the sound, and Marian, pushing her horse away from the trees, waved a kerchief at them. Instantly they recognised her, and waving their hands in greeting, began to ride towards the party.

'Tell me, Robin,' said Marian as, having dismounted to rest her stiffened limbs, she walked beside her lover, 'what meant those cries we heard but now? It was as if someone signalled and you answered them.'

'It meant, sweetheart,' replied Robin, 'that a friend of mine in the greenwood there saw these horsemen and thought they might be our enemies. But I guessed they could not have reached this spot so quickly as we, and that they whom he saw were some of Sir Richard's meinie [followers] come to look for thee. Then I warned him that I thought all was well, and so came on.'

'Who are these friends who guard you thus when you pass through the forest?' she asked. 'Is it the same who shot those smaller arrows at Sir Roger's men?'

'I will tell thee, sweeting,' replied Robin. 'They are dwellers in the forest whom once I rescued from a fearful death at the hands of evil and cruel men. And ever since they have been my dear friends, to guard and watch for me when I am in the greenwood.'

'I am glad thou hast such friends, dear Robin,' said Marian. 'It lightens my heart to think thou hast such faithful watchers. For I fear me that thou wilt have need of such ere long.'

But now Sir Richard at Lee and his kinsman had come up, and great was their joy to find Fair Marian was safe, for they had been much troubled to find no sign of her upon the road by which she usually came; and were riding back to the castle to collect a body of retainers to search the forest roads for her.

When Sir Richard and Sir Huon were told of Sir Roger's attempt to kidnap Marian, and of how Robin had slain him, they looked grave, and Sir Huon shook his head. But Sir Richard, a grey-haired man with a noble countenance, turned to Robin and shook him by the hand heartily.

'Thou hast rid the earth of a vile oppressor and a felon knight,' he cried, 'and I for one thank thee heartily. The evil that he hath done to poor folks, the robbery of orphans, the cruelties to women – all his crimes have cried long to heaven for vengeance. And I rejoice that your good bolt hath pierced his evil brain.'

'Ye say truth,' said Sir Huon gravely, 'but I think me of what Robin may suffer. The bishop will not let his brother go unavenged, nor will the comrades of Roger rest in their efforts to capture Robin and take him to their crucet-house [torture-house], which men rightly call the Evil Hold.'

'Fear not for me,' said Robin, with a quiet yet firm voice. 'I doubt not I shall escape all their traps and snares. But do you and the father of my dear lady take care that, in despite, those evil knights do not capture Fair Marian and wreak their vengeance upon her. As for me, I will do all I may to shield her.'

'Ye say truth,' said Sir Richard. 'I had not thought on that, but of a surety Isenbart de Belame and Niger le Grym will wish to seize our fair niece as a prize. God and Our Lady forfend us all from their evil wiles.'

'Amen,' said Robin; 'and meanwhile I will keep a watch upon Castle Wrangby and its villainous lords.'

For the next three days Robin and Marian, with Sir Richard and the Lady Alice, his wife, spent the time merrily together, hunting with hawks along the leas, or hunting the wild boar in the woods. At night in hall they played hoodman blind, or danced to the

viols, or sat at draughts or chess, or heard minstrels sing to them
or tell them tales of Arthur's knights, of Roland, and of Oliver his
dear friend, or of Ogier the Dane, or Graelent, and how they had
all vanished away into the realms of the Fairy Queen.

But on the fourth day Robin went into the forest to shoot
small birds, and as he sat on a bank he heard the tapping as of a
woodpecker. Looking up into the limbs of the wych-elm above
him, he saw a little man's face peeping out through the leaves.

'Come down, Ket the Trow,' said Robin, 'and tell me thy
news, lad.'

Next moment the little man had dropped from the tree and
stood before Robin. Ket was no taller than a medium-sized lad
of fourteen, but he was a man full grown, with great breadth of
chest, long hairy arms and legs, the muscles on which stood up
like iron bands. His hair was black, thick, and curly; he had no
shoes on his feet, and the only covering he wore was a stout
leather jacket laced in front, and close-fitting breeches of doeskin that reached to his knees. His face, broad and good-natured,
was lit up with a smile as he returned Robin's kindly gaze, and
his eyes, bright and keen, yet gentle as those of a fawn, rested on
Robin's face with a look of respect that was almost reverence.

'You followed the men that fled. Where went they?' asked
Robin.

'Through the forest north by west went they, till they came to
the burn,' answered Ket. 'They forded it at the Stakes and
crossed the moor to the Ridgeway. Through Hag's Wood they
wended, and through Thicket Hollow, and then I knew where
they would go; by the Hoar Tree and the Cwelm stone, over
Gallows Hill and by the Mark Oak, till they came to the Dead
Man's Hill, and so by the lane of the Red Stones to the Evil
Hold. All night I watched in the Mark Oak, and at dawn I saw
three knights ride from the castle. One went south by east, and
with him on horses were two of the knaves I had followed. Two
went east, and these I followed. They had ten horsed knaves with
them. They went through Barnisdale Wood, and I left them on
the wide road which leads to Doncaster.'

'You did well, Ket,' replied Robin. 'And then?'

'I went to thy house, Outwoods, by Barnisdale Wood,' replied
Ket, and Scadlock thy man I met in Old Nick's Piece, and sad

was he, for he said that he saw Guy of Gisborne and two monks riding by thy land the day before, and they spoke together, and stopped and pointed at thy fields. And he thinks the curse of that Judas, Sir Guy, is on thy land, and that ruin cometh quickly to thee, and full was he of woe, and much he longed to see thy face.'

Robin was silent for a while, and he was sunk in thought.

'Heard you aught else? What of Scarlet and the little lad?'

'I saw them not, but at night I crept down to the village and stole beside the cot with the bush before the door [the village alehouse], and leaned my ear against a crack and listened. And much woe and anger was in the mouths of the villeins, so that they drank little.'

'What said they?' asked Robin. 'How many think you were there?'

Ket lifted up both hands and showed ten, then he dropped one hand and showed five fingers, and then two more.

'Were they the young men or the older?'

'Most were full of fiery words, and therefore young I guess,' went on Ket. 'They that had the sorest backs spoke most bitterly. Cruel had been the beatings at the post that day, it seems; one was yet in the pit, too sore to move; one had been burned that day with the branding-iron because the steward swore he was a thief – and he was most fierce of all; and many said their lives were too bitter to be borne. The work they must do on the lord's land was more than was due from them, and their own fields were left untilled, and therefore they starved. Some said they would run away to the town, where, if they could hide for a year and a day, they would be free men; others said the plague and pestilence could be got in a village cot as easily as in a town hovel, and they would prefer to live on the king's deer in the greenwood.'

'Ay!' said Robin, in a bitter voice, 'poor folks have no friends in these days. The king's own sons rebel and war upon their father, the lords and monks fight for power and wider lands, and grind the faces of their villeins to the soil which they delve and dig, and squeeze from them rents and services against all rightful custom. Ket!' he said, rising, 'I will go home this day. Find Hob, your brother, and when I have said farewell to my friends I will come anon.'

Saying these words, Robin picked up the birds he had shot and went back to the castle of Sir Richard, to say farewell to Marian. Ket the Trow or Troll glided among the trees and disappeared.

That day, when the shadows of the trees cast by the sinking sun lay far over the fields, and in the warmth and quiet of the departing day there seemed no room in the peaceful world except for happy thoughts, Robin with quick soft steps came to the edge of Barnisdale Forest where it marched with his own land.

The forest side was on high ground, which then sank gently away to his fields. Long and earnestly he looked at his house, and beyond to the cots of the five villeins who were part of his land. His own house, and the garth or yard in the low quickset hedge about it, seemed quite peaceful, as indeed it should be at that time. Perhaps Scadlock, his bailiff, was inside, but the villeins must still be at work in the fields. Then it struck him that perhaps it was too quiet. There were no children tumbling and playing about in the dusty space before the villeins' cottages, but every door was fast closed, and no life stirred.

He was about to continue his walk under the trees to gain the footpath which led to the front of his house, when he saw a woman, a serf's wife, steal from the door of her hovel and creep along to the end of the hedge. There she stood, and seemed to watch for someone coming across the fields on the other side of the house. Suddenly he saw her with both hands gesticulating, as if signing to someone to keep away. For a long time she stood thus, but from where Robin stood he could not see who it was to whom she made her signal.

At length the woman, having apparently succeeded in giving her warning, stole cautiously back into her house and quietly closed the door.

Something was wrong. Of that Robin was certain now. Glancing warily this way and that, he went farther among the trees, and approached the head of the footpath with every care. Suddenly as he looked from behind a tree he dodged down again. A man-at-arms stood beneath the next tree, which threw its broad branches over the footpath.

From behind the beech trunk Robin keenly observed the man, whose back was towards him. He had evidently been put there to guard the approach from the forest. From where he stood the soldier could see the front of the house, and something that was happening there seemed to hold his attention. Sometimes he gave a laugh or a grunt of satisfaction.

Robin's eyes went hard of look. He knew the man by his tunic of red cloth and his helm to be one of the guard of armed retainers which the abbot of St Mary's, lord of the manor, had formed for his own dignity and to add to his retinue of lazy and oppressive menials. Very cautiously Robin crept along between the two trees, keeping himself hidden by the trunk against which the man leaned.

With the stealthiness and quietness of a wild-cat, Robin covered the space, until only the trunk of the tree separated him from the unsuspecting soldier. He rose to his full height, but as he did so his leg snapped a twig jutting from the tree. The man half swung round at the noise, but next moment Robin's fingers were about his throat, and in that grip of iron he was powerless.

The man swooned, and then, laying him down, Robin quickly bound his hands and feet and placed a rough gag in his mouth, so that when he revived, as he would shortly, he would be unable to do any harm.

When Robin turned to see what had drawn the man's attention so much, a groan burst from his lips. Tied to posts in front of the house were Scadlock and three of the poor villeins. Their backs were bare, and before each stood a burly soldier with a long knotted strap in his hand.

A little way from them stood others of the men-at-arms and their chief, Hubert of Lynn, a man whom for his brutal insolence and cruelty Robin had long hated. In the still air of the afternoon Robin's keen ears could catch the laughter which came from Hubert and his men. At length, when all seemed ready, the voice of the leader rang out:

'A hundred lashes first for these dogs that would resist the servants of their lord, and then an arrow for each. Now – go!'

Almost as if one man moved the four whips, they rose in the air and came down upon the bare backs which, since Robin had been their lord, had never been wealed by the cruel whip.

Robin, under the beechen boughs, picked up his longbow and the long deer-bolts or arrows, which he had laid down when he had prepared to creep upon the man at the top of the path. He twanged his bowstring, saw that it was well set to the bow, and laid each arrow apart before him.

Then kneeling on one knee, he whispered a prayer to Our Lady.

'The light is bad, fair and sweet Mother of Christ,' he said, 'but do thou guide my arrows to the evil hearts of these men. Six bolts have I, and out of the pity I have for my poor, folk I would slay first him with the bitterest heart, Hubert of Lynn, and then those four with whips. Hear me, O our sweet Lady, for the sake of thy Son who was so stern against wrong, and pitiful for weak folk. Amen.'

Then he notched the first shaft, and aimed it at the breast of Hubert. Singing its deep song as if in exultation, the great arrow leaped through the air upon its way. When it was but half-way across the field, another, with as triumphant a song, was humming behind it.

With a cry, Hubert sank on one knee to the ground, the shaft jutting from his breast. Feebly he tried to pluck it forth, but his life was already gone. He fell over on his side, dead. At the same time the place seemed full of great bees. First one man dropped his whip, spun round with his hands upon a bolt in his side, and then fell. Another sank to the ground without a murmur; a second leaped in the air like a shot rabbit; and the other, with one arm pinned to his side by an arrow, ran across the field swaying this way and that, until he dropped in a furrow and lay still.

There were four who remained untouched, but filled with such consternation were they, that they broke and fled in all directions. So dazed was one that he came flying up the field path at the head of which Robin still kneeled, terrible in his wrath, with his last bolt notched upon his string. The fellow ran with open arms, terror in his eyes, thinking not at all of whither he was going.

He pulled up when he came within a few yards of Robin, and yelled:

'O master, be you fiend or man, shoot not! Thy witch bolts spoke as they came through the air. I yield me! I yield me!'

The man fell before Robin, crying: 'I will be your man, lord. I was an honest man two days ago, and the son of an honest man, and my heart rose against the evil work I was in.'

Robin rose to his feet, and the man clutched his hands and placed his head between in token of fealty.

'See to it,' said Robin sternly, 'that you forget not your plighted word. How long have you been with Hubert and his men?'

'But two days, lord,' said the man, whose simple and honest eyes were now less wide with terror. 'I am Dudda or Dodd, son of Alstan, a good villein at Blythe, and forasmuch as my lord beat me without justice I fled to the woods. But I starved, and for need of food I crept out and lay at the abbey door and begged for bread. And they fed me, and seeing I was strong of my limbs said I should bear arms. And I rejoiced for a time till the cruel deeds they boasted of as done upon poor villeins like myself made me hate them.'

'Get up, Dodd,' said Robin. 'Remember thy villein blood henceforth, and do no wrong to thy kind. Come with me.'

Robin went down to the garth of his farm, released poor Scadlock and his other men, then entered the house and found salves wherewith he anointed their wealed and broken backs.

' 'Twas but yesterday, master,' said Scadlock, in reply to Robin's question as to what had happened, 'that they proclaimed you an outlaw from the steps of the cross at Pontefract, and this morning Hubert of Lynn came to possess your lands for the lord abbot. We here – Ward, Godard, Dunn, and John – could not abear to see this wrong done, and so, like poor fools, with sticks and forks we tried to beat them back.'

'Ay, poor lads, foolish and faithful, ye had like to have paid with your lives for it,' said Robin. 'But now, come in and feed, and I will take counsel what must needs be done.'

By this time it was dark. One of the women was called in from the serfs' cottages, a fire was lit in the centre of the one large room which formed Robin's manor-house, and soon bowls of good hot food were being emptied, and spirits were reviving. Even the captured man-at-arms was not forgotten; he was brought in and fed, and then lodged securely in a strong outhouse for the night.

'Master,' said Scadlock, as he and Robin were returning to the house from this task, 'what is in your mind to do? Must it be the woods and the houseless life of an outlaw for you?'

'There is no other way,' said Robin, with a hard laugh. 'And glad I shall be, for in the greenwood I may try to do what I may to give the rich and the proud some taste of what they give to the poor men whom they rule.'

'And I will go with you, master, with a very glad heart,' said Scadlock. 'And so will the others, for after this day they can expect no mercy from Guy of Gisborne.'

Suddenly they heard across the fields towards the village the sound of many voices, and listening intently, they could hear the tramp of feet.

'It is Guy of Gisborne and his men-at-arms!' said Scadlock. 'Master, we must fly to the woods at once.'

'Nay, nay,' said Robin, 'think you Guy of Gisborne would come cackling like so many geese to warn me of his approach? They are the villeins of the manor, though what they do abroad so late is more than I may say. They will smart for it tomorrow, I ween, when the steward learns of it.'

'Nay, master,' came a voice from the darkness at their elbow; 'here'll be no tomorrow for them in bondage if you will but lead us.'

It was the voice of one of the older villeins, who had stolen up before the crowd. It was Will of the Stuteley, generally called Will the Bowman – a quiet, thoughtful man, whom Robin had always liked. He had been reeve or head villein in his time.

'What, Will,' said Robin, 'what would they with me? Where should I lead them?'

'Give them a hearing, Master Robert,' said Will. 'Their hearts are overfull, but their stomachs are nigh empty, so driven and stressed beyond fair duty have they been this winter and summer. First the failure of harvest, then a hard winter, a hungry summer, and a grasping lord who skins us. I tell thee I can bear no more, old as I am.'

'Well, well, Will, here they are,' replied Robin, as a crowd of dark forms came into the yard. 'Now, lads, what is it you want of me?' he cried.

'We would run to the greenwood, master,' some cried. 'Sick and sore are we of our hard lot, and we can bear no more,' cried others.

Unused to much speaking, they could not explain their

feelings any more, and so waited, hoping that he who was so much wiser, yet so kind, would be able to understand all the bitterness that was in their hearts.

'Well,' said Robin earnestly, 'and if you run to the woods, what of your wives and children?'

'No harm can come to them,' was the reply. 'Our going will give them more worth in the eyes of the lord and his steward. We do not own them. They are the chattels of the lord, body and soul. There will be more food for them if we go.'

There was some truth in this, as Robin knew. The lord and his steward would not visit their vengeance upon the women and children of those villeins who ran away. The work on the manor lands must go on, and the women and children helped in this. Some of the older women held plots of land, which were tilled by their sons or by poorer men in the hamlet who held no land, and who for their day's food were happy to work for anyone who would feed and shelter them.

'How many of ye are there?' asked Robin. 'Are there any old men among ye?'

'There are thirty of us. Most of us are young and wiser than our fathers,' growled one man. 'Or we will put up with less these days,' added another.

'So you will let the work of the manor and the due services ye owe to the lord fall on the shoulders of the old men, the women, and the youngsters?' said Robin, who was resolved that if these men broke from their lord they should know all the consequences. 'Come, lads, is it manly to save our own skins and let the moil and toil and swinking labour light on the backs of those less able to bear the heat of the noonday sun, the beat of the winter rain?'

Many had come hot from the fierce talk of the wilder men among them as they sat in the alehouse, and now in the darkness and the chill air of the night their courage was oozing, and they glanced this way and that, as if looking how to get back to their huts, where wife and children were sleeping.

But others, of sterner stuff, who had suffered more or felt more keenly, were not to be put off. Some said they were not married, others that they would bear no more the harsh rule of Guy of Gisborne.

Suddenly flying steps were heard coming towards them, and all listened, holding their breath. The fainter-hearted, even at the sound, edged out of the crowd and crept away.

A little man crashed through the hedge and lit almost at the feet of Robin.

' 'Tis time ye ceased your talking,' he said, his voice panting and a strange catch in it.

' 'Tis Much, the Miller's son!' said they all, and waited. They felt that something of dread had happened, for he was a fearless little man, and not easily moved.

' 'Tis time ye ceased plotting, lads,' he said, with a curious break in his voice. 'Ye are but serfs, of no more worth than the cattle ye clean or the grey swine ye feed – written down on the lawyers' parchments with the ploughs, the mattocks, the carts, and the hovels ye lie in, and to be sold at the lord's will as freely!'

Tears were in his voice, so great was his passion, so deeply did his knowledge move him.

'I tell thee thou shouldst creep back to the sties in which ye live,' he went on, 'and not pretend that ye have voice or wish in what shall befall ye. For the lord is sick of his unruly serfs, and tomorrow – tomorrow he will sell thee off his land!'

A great breath of surprise and rage rose from the men before him. 'Sell us?' they cried. 'He will sell us?'

'Ay, he will sell some ten of thee. The parchment is already written which shall pass thee to Lord Arnald of Shotley Hawe.'

'That fiend in the flesh!' said Robin, 'and enemy of God – that flayer of poor peasants' skins! But, lads, to sell thee! Oh, vile!'

A great roar, like the roar of maddened oxen, rose from the throats of the villeins. Oh, it was true that, in strict law, the poor villeins could be sold like cattle, but on this manor never had it been known to be done. They held their little roods of land by due services rendered, and custom ruled that son should inherit after father, and all things should be done according to what the older men said was the custom of the manor.

But now, to be rooted out of the place they and their folk had known for generations, and sold like cattle in a market-place! Oh, it was not to be borne!

'Man,' said one, 'where got you this evil news?'

'From Rafe, man to Lord Arnald's steward,' replied Much. 'I

met him at the alehouse in Blythe, and he told it me with a laugh, saying that Guy of Gisborne had told the steward we were an unruly and saucy lot of knaves whom he knew it would be a pleasure for his lordship to tame.'

'Ye say there are ten of us to be sold?' asked a timid voice in the rear. 'Do ye know who these be?'

'What matter?' roared one man. 'It touches us all. For me, by the holy rood, I will run to the woods, but I will put my mark on the steward ere I go.'

'Rafe knew not the names of any,' said Much. 'What matter, as Hugh of the Forde says. There are ten of ye. They are those who have given the hardest words to Guy of Gisborne, and have felt the whip most often across their backs at the post.'

'How many of us are here, lads?' said Will the Bowman in a hard voice.

'We were thirty a while ago,' said one with a harsh laugh. 'But now we are but fourteen, counting Much.'

'Where is Scarlet and his little lad?' asked Robin. He had suddenly remembered that his friend was not among these others – yet Scarlet had been the boldest in opposing the unjust demands and oppressive exactions of the steward.

'Will Scarlet lies in the pit!' said Much, 'nigh dead with a hundred lashes. Tomorrow he will be taken to Doncaster, where the king's justice sits, to lose his right hand for shooting the king's deer.'

'By the Virgin!' cried Robin, 'that shall not be. For I will take him from the pit this night.' He started off, but many hands held him back.

'Master, we will go with thee!' cried the others.

'See here, Master Robin,' said Will the Bowman, speaking quietly, but with a hard ring in his voice. 'We be fourteen men who are wearied of the ill we suffer daily. If we do naught now against the evil lord who grinds us beneath his power we shall be for ever slaves. I for one will rather starve in the greenwood than suffer toil and wrongful ruling any more. What say you, lads all?'

'Yea, yea! We will go to the greenwood!' they cried. 'Whether Master Robin leads us or not, we will go!'

Robin's resolution was quickly taken.

'Lads,' he cried, 'I will be one with you. Already have I done a deed which I knew would be done ere long, and I am doubly outlaw and wolf's-head. The abbot's men-at-arms came hither while I was away and claimed my lands. Scadlock and my good lads resisted them, and were like to suffer death for doing so. With my good bow I shot five of the lord's men, and their bodies lie in a row beneath that wall.'

'I saw them as I entered,' said Will the Bowman, 'and a goodly sight it was. Had you not slain Hubert of Lynn, I had an arrow blessed by a goodly hermit for his evil heart, for the ill he caused my dear dead lad Christopher. Now, lads, hold up each your hand and swear to be true and faithful till your death day to our brave leader, Robert of Locksley.'

All held up their hands, and in solemn tones took the oath.

'Now, lads, quickly follow,' said Robin.

In a few moments the garth was empty, and the dark forms of Robin and his men were to be seen passing over the fields under the starlit sky.

There was not one backward look as the men passed through Fangthief Wood and came out on the wold behind the village. From here they could dimly see the little group of hovels lying huddled beside the church, the dull water of the river gleaming farther still, and the burble and roar of the stream as it flowed through the mill-race came faintly up to their ears.

In those days, whenever the villein raised his bended back from the furrows, and his eyes, sore with the sun-glare or the driving rain, sought the hut he called home with thoughts of warmth and food, he was also reminded that for any offence which he might commit, his lord or the steward had speedy means of punishment. For, raised on a hill as near as possible to the huts of the serfs, was the gaunt gallows, and, near by, lay the pit. Gallows or Galley Hill is still the name which clings to a green hill beside many a pretty village, though the dreadful tree which bore such evil fruit has long since rotted or been hewn down. In the village street itself were the stocks, so that he who was fastened therein should escape none of the scorn, laughter, or abuse of his familiars.

It was thus with the village of Birkencar. On the wold to the north were the gallows and the pit, only a few yards from the manor-house, in the parlour of which Guy of Gisborne dealt forth what he was pleased to term 'justice'. The manor-house

Robin Hood

was now dark and silent; doubtless Guy was sleeping on the good stroke of business he had done in getting rid of his most unruly, stiff-necked serfs.

Over the thick grass of the grazing fields the steps of Robin and his men made no noise, and, having arrived at a little distance from where the gallows stood, Robin bade the others wait until he should give them a sign. Then, passing on as quietly as a ghost, Robin approached the prison built under-ground, in which serfs were confined when they awaited even sterner justice than that which the lord of the manor could give.

The prison was entered by a door at the foot of a flight of steps dug out of the soil. Robin crept to the top of the steps and looked down. He did not expect to find any guard at the door, since the steward would not dream that anyone would have so much hardihood as to attempt a rescue from the lord's prison.

As Robin scanned keenly the dark hole below him, down which the starlight filtered faintly, he was surprised to see a small figure crouching at the door. He heard a groan come from within the prison, and the form beneath him seemed to start and cling closer to the door.

'O uncle,' said a soft voice, which he knew was that of little Gilbert of the White Hand, 'I thought thou didst sleep awhile, and that thy wounds did not grieve thee so much. Therefore I kept quiet and did not cry. Oh, if Master Robin were but here!'

'Laddie, thou must go home,' came the weak tones of Scarlet from within the prison. 'If Guy or his men catch thee here they will beat thee. That I could not bear. Laddie, dear laddie, go and hide thee somewhere.'

'O Uncle Will, I can't,' wailed the little lad. 'It would break my heart to leave thee here – to think thou wert lying here in the dark with thy poor back all broken and hurt, and no one near to say a kind word. Uncle, I have prayed so much this night for thee – I am sure help must come soon. Surely the dear sweet Virgin and good Saint Christopher will not turn deaf ears to a poor lad's prayers?'

'But, laddie mine, thou art sick thyself,' came Scarlet's voice. 'To stay there all night will cause thee great ill, and – '

'Oh, what will it matter if thou art taken from me,' cried the little boy, all his fortitude breaking down. He wept bitterly, and pressed with his hands at the unyielding door. 'If they slay thee, I will make them slay me too, for my life will be all forlorn without thee, dear, dear Uncle Will!'

'Hallo, laddie, what's all this coil about?' cried Robin in a hearty voice, as he rose and began to descend the steps.

Little Gilbert started up half in terror; then, as he realised who it was, he rushed towards Robin, and seizing his hands covered them with kisses. Then, darting back to the door, he put his lips to a crack and cried delightedly:

'I said so! I said so! God and His dear Saints and the Virgin have heard me. Here is Robin come to take you out.'

'Have they scored thee badly, Will?' asked Robin.

'Ay, Robin, dear man,' came the answer with a faint laugh; 'worse than a housewife scores her sucking pig.'

'Bide quiet a bit, lad,' replied Robin, 'and I'll see if what axe has done axe can't undo.'

With keen eyes he examined the staples through which the ring-bolt passed. Then with two deft blows with his axe and a wrench with his dagger he had broken the bolt and pulled open the door. The little lad rushed in at once, and with a knife began carefully to cut his uncle's bonds.

Robin gave the cry of a plover, and Scadlock with two of his own villeins hurried up.

'Quick, lads,' he said. 'Bring out Will Scarlet; we must take him to Outwoods and bathe and salve his wounds.'

In a few moments, as gently as was possible, they brought poor Scarlet forth and laid him on the grass. A hearty but silent hand-grip passed between him and Robin, while little Gilbert, his eyes bright, but his lips dumb with a great gratitude, kissed Robin's hand again and again.

'Where are the others?' asked Robin of Scadlock, when two of the men had raised Scarlet on their shoulders and were tramping downhill.

'I know not,' said Scadlock. 'They were whispering much among themselves when you had gone, and suddenly I looked round and they were not there. I thought some wizard had spirited them away for the moment, but soon I saw some of them against the stars as they ran bending over the hill.'

'Whither went they?' asked Robin, a suspicion in his mind.

'Towards the manor-house,' was the reply.

'Go ye to Outwoods,' Robin commanded. Do all that is needed for Scarlet, and await me there.'

With rapid strides Robin mounted the down, while the others with their burden wended their way towards Fangthief Wood. When Robin reached the top of the down the manor-house stood up before him all black against the stars. He ran forward to the high bank which surrounded it, and met no one. Then he found the great gate, which was open, and he went into the garth and a few steps along the broad way leading up to the door.

Suddenly a form sprang up before him – that of Much, the Miller's son.

'Ay, 'tis Master Robin,' he said in a low voice, as if to others, and from behind a tree came Will Stuteley and Kit the Smith.

'What's toward, lads?' asked Robin. 'Think ye to break in and slay Guy? I tell ye the manor-house can withstand a siege from an armed troop, and ye have no weapons but staves and your knives.'

'Master Robin,' said Will the Bowman, 'I would that ye stood by and did naught in this matter. 'Tis a villein deed for villein fowk to do. 'Tis our right and our deed; in the morn when we're in the greenwood we'll do thy biddin' and look to no one else.'

A flame suddenly shot up from a heap of dried brush laid against a post of the house before them, then another near it, and still another. The sun had been shining fiercely the past two weeks, and everything was as dry as tinder. Built mainly of wood, the manor-house would fall an easy prey to the flames.

'But at least ye must call out the women,' urged Robin. 'There is the old dame, Makin, and the serving-wench – would ye burn innocent women as well?'

Already the inmates were aware of their danger. A face appeared at a window shutter. It was that of Guy. A stone hit the frame as he looked out, and just missed him as he dodged back.

Huge piles of brushwood had been heaped round the house, and these were burning furiously in many places, and the planks of the walls had caught fire, and were crackling and burning fiercely.

'Guy of Gisborne!' came the strong voice of Will the Bowman, 'thy days are ended. We have thee set, like a tod [fox] in his hole. But we've no call to burn the women folk. Send 'em out, then, but none o' thy tricks.'

They heard screams, and soon the front door was flung open and two women stood in the blazing entrance. One of the men with a long pole raked the blazing brushwood away to give them space to come out. They ran forward and the door closed. Next moment it had opened again, and a spear came from it. It struck the villein with the pole full in the throat, and without a groan he fell.

A yell of fury rose from the others who were standing by, and some were for rushing forward to beat down the door.

'Ha' done and keep back!' came the stern level tones of Will the Bowman. 'There's nobbut the steward in the house and he'll burn. Heap up the wood, and keep a keen watch on the back door and the windows.'

An arrow came from an upper window and stuck in a tree near which Will was standing. Will plucked out the quivering shaft and looked at it coolly.

'Say, Makin,' he said to the old woman who had come from the house, 'are there any of the abbot's archers in th' house?'

'Noa,' replied the old housekeeper; 'nobbut the maister.'

'I thought 'twas so,' replied Will. 'Yet he should shoot a bolt better than that.'

'You're no doomed to die by an arrow,' said the old dame, and laughed, showing her yellow toothless gums.

'No, maybe so,' replied Will, 'and maybe not. I lay no store by thy silly talk, Makin.'

'Nor will the maister die by the fire ye've kindled so fine for un,' went on the old woman, and laughed again.

Will the Bowman looked at the fiercely burning walls of the house and made no answer. But he smiled grimly. Who could escape alive from this mass of twisting and whirling flames?

Suddenly from the rear of the house came cries of terror. Robin, followed by Will, quickly ran round, and in the light of the burning house they saw the villeins on that side with scared faces looking and pointing to a distance. They turned in the direction indicated, and saw what seemed to be a brown horse running away over the croft.

Glancing back they saw that the door of a storehouse which adjoined the manor-house was open, though its wood and frame were burning. With a cry of rage Will the Bowman suddenly started running towards the horse.

'Come back! come back!' cried the villeins in terrified voices. ' 'Tis the Spectre Beast! 'Twill tear thee to pieces!'

But he still ran on, and as he ran they could see him trying to notch an arrow to the bow he held in his hand.

'Whence did it come?' asked Robin of the villeins.

'It burst on a sudden from the house, with a mane all of fire and its eyes flashing red and its terrible mouth open,' was the reply. It ran at Bat the Coalman there, and I thought he was doomed to be torn to pieces, but the Bargast turned and dashed away over the croft.'

'I think Guy has escaped you,' said Robin, who suspected what had happened.

'How mean'st tha?' asked Bat the Charcoal-Burner.

'I doubt not that Guy of Gisborne has wrapped himself in some disguise and frightened you, and has now got clear away,' replied Robin.

'But 'twas the Spectre Mare!' the villeins asserted. 'We saw its mane all afire, and its red flashing eyes and its terrible jaws all agape.'

Robin did not answer. He knew it was in vain to fight against the superstition of the poor villeins. Instead, he went back to where he had left Makin, the old woman.

'Makin,' he said, 'did thy master flay a brown horse but lately?'

'Ay, but two days agone.'

'And where was the hide?'

'In th' store beyond the house.'

'Thou saidst thy master should not die by fire, Makin?'

'Ay,' replied the old woman, and her small black eyes in a weazened yellow face looked narrowly into Robin's.

'Will the Bowman hath gone to shoot thy master,' went on Robin; 'but I think he will not catch him. I think thou shouldst not bide here till Will comes back, Makin. He will be hot and angry, and will strike blindly if he guesses.'

The old woman smiled, and gave a little soft laugh. Then, with a sudden anger and her eyes flashing, she turned upon Robin, and in a low voice said:

'And could I do aught else? A hard man he's been and a hard man he'll be to his last day – as hard to me as to a stranger. But these arms nursed him when he was but a wee poor bairn. 'Twas I told him what to do wi' the hide of the old mare. Could I do aught else?'

'Ay,' said Robin, 'I know thou'st been mother to a man who has but a wolf's heart. But now, get thee gone ere Will of Stuteley comes.'

Without another word, the old woman turned and hurried away in the darkness.

A little while later Will the Bowman returned, and full of rage was he.

'The dolterheads!' he cried. 'Had ye no more sense in thy silly heads as not to know that so wily a man would be full of tricks? Spectre in truth and in deed! Old women ye are, and only fitten to tend cows and be sold like cows! Could ye not see his legs beneath the hide of the horse which he'd thrown over himself? – wolf in horse's skin that he is. Go back to thy villein chores; ye're no worthy to go to the greenwood to be free men.'

He went off in great anger, and would say no word to anyone.

It was only later that he told Robin that he had run after the horse-like figure, and had distinctly seen the human legs beneath the hide. He had tried a shot at it, but had missed, and the figure ran forward to the horse pasture on the moor. There his suspicions had been proved to be true, for he had seen Guy of Gisborne pull the hide off himself, and jump on one of the horses in the field and ride away, taking the hide with him.

'Now, lads,' said Robin to the villeins, ' 'tis no use wasting time here. The wolf hath stolen away, and soon will rouse the country against us. You must to the greenwood, for you have done such a deed this night as never hath been done by villeins against their lord's steward as far back as the memory of man goeth.'

'Thou'rt right, maister,' they said. ' 'Tis for our necks now we must run. But great doltheads we be, as Will said truly, to let the evil man slip out of our hands by a trick!'

No more, however, was said. All made haste to leave the burning manor-house, most of which was now a blackening or smouldering ruin. Rapidly they ran downhill, and having picked up Scadlock and the other villeins with Scarlet and the little lad, Robin led the way under the waning stars to the deep dark line of forest which rose beside his fields.

CHAPTER TWO

How Little John Stole the Forester's Dinner,
and of His Meeting with Robin Hood

'Ay, lads, but this be bliss indeed!'

The speaker was Much, the Miller's son. He gave a great sigh of satisfaction, and rolled himself over on the grass to make himself even more comfortable than he was. Grunts or sighs of satisfaction answered him from others of the twenty forms lying at full length under the deep shadow of the trees. Some, however, answered with snores, for the buck they had eaten had been a fine one, and the quarterstaff play that morning had been hard, and for ringing heads slumber is the best medicine.

It was in a small glade deep in the heart of Barnisdale Forest where the outlaws lay, and was known to them as the Stané Lea or Stanley. At one side of it a little rivulet gurgled over its pebbles, and at the other end stood a great standing stone, green with moss, where, doubtless, ages before, the skin-clad warriors of the forest had come with their prayers to the spirit of the great chief who was buried beneath it. Beside the brook knelt Scadlock and his fellow cook, cleaning the wooden platters which had just been used, by the simple process of rubbing them with sand in the clear running water.

The sunlight of the hot July day fell on the water through spaces between the slowly bending leaves, and in the deep green gloom the rays shone like bars of gold. Most of the villeins lay on their backs, feeling pure enjoyment in looking up into the weaving masses of leaves above their heads, through which, like flaming spear-heads, the sunlight slid now and then as the gentle summer breeze stirred the deeps of the trees. After a full meal, and with the soft air blowing upon their cheeks, these poor outlaws tasted such happiness as had never before been their lot.

Little Gilbert, his cheek now ruddy with health, sat beside Scarlet shaping arrows with a knife.

Seated with his back against the trunk of a fallen elm was Robin, his bearing as bold, his eye as keen and fearless and his look as noble now as when a short month ago he was not an outlaw, a 'wolf's-head' as the phrase was, whom any law-abiding man could slay and get a reward for his head.

Strict had been his rule of these twenty men who had come to the greenwood with him and had chosen him as their leader. Slow of step and of movement they were, but he knew that the lives of all of them depended upon their learning quickly the use of the quarterstaff, the sword, and the longbow. Every day, therefore, he had made them go through set tasks. Chapped and hard with toil at the plough, the mattock, and the hedge knife, their hands took slowly to the more delicate play with sword, quarterstaff, and bow; but most of them were but young men, and he had hopes that very soon they would gain quickness of eye and deftness of hand, besides the lore that would tell them how to track the red deer, and to face and overcome the fierce wolf and the white-tusked boar in his wrath.

'What should us be doin' now,' murmured Dickon the Carpenter, 'if we were still bondsmen and back in the village?'

'I should be feeding the lord's grey swine or ploughing his domain lands,' said Long Peter, 'while my own fields grew rank with weeds'

'I,' said Will Stuteley bitterly, 'should be cursing the evil abbot who broke my poor lad's heart. When I feel I should be happiest, I think and grieve of him the most. Oh, that he were here!'

No one spoke for a few moments. All felt that although all had suffered, Will the Bowman had suffered most bitterly from the heartlessness of the lord abbot of St Mary's and Sir Guy of Gisborne's treacherous dealing. Will had had a son, a villein, of course, like himself. But the lad had run away to Grimsby, had lived there for a year and a day in the service of a shipman, and thus had got his freedom. Then he had saved all he could, toiling manfully day and night, to get sufficient money to buy his father's freedom. He had scraped and starved to win the twenty marks that meant the end of his father's serfdom. At length he had saved the amount, and then had gone to the lord abbot and offered it for his father's freedom. The abbot had seized him and cast him into prison, and taken the money from him. Then witnesses were found to swear in the manor court that the young man had been seen in his father's hut during the year and a day, and by this the abbot claimed him as his serf. As to the money he had saved – 'All that a serf got was got for his lord' was an old law that none could deny. The young man, broken in health and spirit, had been released, had worked in the manor fields dumb and dazed with sorrow, and at length one night had been found dead on his pallet of straw.

'And I,' said Scarlet, leaning on his left elbow and raising his clenched right hand in the air, 'I should be reaping the lord's wheat, and with every stroke of my sickle I should be hungering for the day when I should sink my knife in the evil heart of Guy of Gisborne, who made me a serf who was once a socman, because of the poverty which came upon me.'

This, too, was true. Scarlet had been a freeman, but harvests had failed, the lord's steward had forced him to do labour which it had never been the custom for a freeman to do, and gradually his fields had run to waste, and Scarlet had lost his land, and sunk to the level of a common serf.

'Master,' said Much, the Miller's son, 'it seemeth to me that we be all poor men who have suffered evil from those who have power. Surely now that we are outlaws thou shouldst give us some rule whereby we may know whom we shall beat and bind, and whom we shall let go free? Shall we not let the rich and the lordly know somewhat of the poor man's aching limbs and poverty?'

'It was in my mind to speak to you of such things,' said Robin. 'First, I will have you hurt no woman, nor any company in which a woman is found. I remember the sweet Virgin, and will ever pray for her favour and protection, and I will, therefore, that you shield all women. Look to it, also, that ye do not any harm to any honest peasant who tilleth his soil in peace, nor to good yeomen, wherever you meet them. Knights, also, and squires who are not proud, but who are good fellows, ye shall treat with all kindness. But I tell thee this, and bear it well in mind – abbots and bishops, priors, and canons, and monks – ye may do all your will upon them. When ye rob them of their gold or their rich stuffs, ye are taking only that which they have squeezed and reived from the poor. Therefore, take your fill of their wealth, and spare not your staves on their backs. They speak the teaching of the blessed Jesus with their mouths, but their fat bodies and their black hearts deny Him every hour.'

'Yea, yea!' shouted the outlaws, moved by the fire which had been in Robin's voice and in his eyes. 'We will take toll of all such who pass through our greenwood roads.'

'And now, lads,' went on Robin, 'though we be outlaws, and beyond men's laws, we are still within God's mercy. Therefore I would have you go with me to hear mass. We will go to Campsall, and there the mass-priest shall hear our confessions, and preach from God's book to us.'

In a little while the outlaws in single file were following their leader through the leafy ways of the forest, winding in and out beside the giant trees, across the fern-spread glades whence the red deer and the couching doe sprang away in affright, wading across brooks and streams, skirting some high cliff or rocky dell; but yet, though the way was devious and to most unknown, all felt confidence in the leadership of Robin.

Suddenly Much, who walked beside Robin, stopped as they entered a small glade.

'Look!' he said, pointing to the other side. ' 'Tis an elf – a brownie! I saw it step forth for a moment. 'Tis no bigger than a boy. It is hiding behind that fern. But this bolt shall find it if 'tis still there!'

He raised his bow and notched an arrow, but Robin struck down his wrist, and the arrow shot into the earth a few yards ahead of them.

'The brownies are my friends,' said Robin, laughing, 'and will be yours too, if you deserve such friendship. Hark you, Much, and all my merry fellows. Shoot nothing in the forest which shows no desire to hurt thee, unless it is for food. So shall ye win the service of all good spirits and powers that harbour here or in heaven.'

The men wondered what Robin meant, and during the remainder of their walk they kept a keen look-out for a sight of Much's brownie. But never a glimpse did they get of it, and at length they began to chaff Much, saying he had eaten too much venison, and took spots before his eyes to be fairies. But he persisted in asserting that he had seen a little man, 'dark of face and hair, no bigger than a child. A sun-ray struck him as he moved,' he said, 'and I saw the hairy arm of him with the sunlight on him.'

' 'Twas no more than a squirrel!' said one; 'and Much took his brush for a man's arm.'

'Or else Much is bewitched,' said another. 'I said he slept in a fairy ring the other night.'

'I tell thee it was Puck himself, or Puck's brother!' said Much with a laugh, who now began almost to doubt his own eyes, and so stopped their chaffing by joining in the laughter himself.

At the little forest village, set in its clearing in the midst of giant elms and oaks, the men went one by one and made confession to the simple old parish priest, and when this was done, at Robin's request the mass service was said. Before he knelt, Robin looked around the little wooden church, and saw a young and handsome man kneeling behind him, dressed in a light hauberk. In one hand he held a steel cap, and a sword hung by his side. He was tall and graceful, yet strongly built, and was evidently a young squire of good family. Robin looked at him keenly, and liked the frank gaze that met his eyes.

Mass was but half done when into the church came a little man, slight of form, dark of face. With quick looks his eyes swept the dim space, and then, almost as by instinct, they rested on Robin, where in the front row of his men he knelt before the priest. Swiftly and with the stealthy softness of a cat, the little man crept along the aisle past the kneeling outlaws. As their bent eyes caught the lithe form stealing by, they looked up, some with wonder in their eyes, while others gazed almost with terror on the uncanny dwarfish figure.

They watched it creep up to Robin and touch his elbow. Then their master bent his head, and the little man whispered a few quick words into his ear.

'Two of the four grim knights have followed thee, Maister,' were the words he said. 'They are within a bowshot of the kirk door. A churl hath spied upon thee these last days. There are twenty men-at-arms with the knights.'

'Go and keep watch at the door,' said Robin in a whisper. 'Evil men must wait till God's service be done.'

The little man turned and crept quietly back the way he had come, and the outlaws nudged each other as he passed, and gazed at him in wonder. Much, the Miller's son, smiled with triumph.

The mass went on, and the outlaws responded in due manner to the words of the priest; the last words were said, and the men were just rising from their knees, when, with a hum like a huge drone, an arrow came through one of the narrow window slits, and speeding across the church, twanged as it struck on the wall at the opposite side.

'Saint Nicholas shield us!' said the priest in affright, and shuffled away through a door at the back of the church.

'Now, lads,' said Robin, 'today will prove whether ye have at heart those daily lessons with the longbow. To the window slits with you! The knights of the Evil Hold have run us down, and would dearly like to have our bodies to torture in their crucet-house.'

The faces of the outlaws went grim at the words. Throughout the length and breadth of the Barnisdale and Peak lands the tales of the cruelties and tortures of the robber lords of Wrangby had been spread by wandering beggars, jugglers, and palmers. The blood of the villeins and poor folk whom the evil knights had hurt, maimed, or slain had long cried out for vengeance. The outlaws flew to the window slits, while Robin and Scarlet, having shut the big oaken door, kept their eyes to the arrow slits in the thick oak panels. Every church in those hard days was as much a fortress as a place of worship, and Robin saw that this little wooden building could be held for some hours against all ordinary enemies save fire.

The young squire went up to Robin, and said:

'Who are these folk, good woodman, who wish thee harm?'

'They are lords of high degree,' replied Robin, 'but with the manners of cut-purses and tavern knifers. Niger le Grym, Hamo de Mortain –'

'What!' interrupted the knight hotly; 'the evil crew of Isenbart de Belame, grandson of the fiend of Tickhill?'

'The same,' said Robin.

'Then, good forester,' said the young man, and eager was his speech, 'I pray thee let me aid thee in this. Isenbart de Belame is the most felon knight that ever slew honest man or oppressed weak women. He is my most bitter enemy, and much would I give to slay him.'

'Of a truth,' replied Robin, 'ye may help me as you may, seeing your anger is so great. Who may ye be?'

'I am Alan de Tranmire, squire to my father Sir Herbrand de Tranmire,' replied the other. 'But I love most to be called by the name which my friends give me – Alan-a-Dale.'

While he talked, the outlaw had kept one eye on the arrow slit before him, and saw how the men-at-arms on the borders of the forest were forming in a body, headed by two knights on horseback, to make a dash at the door of the church to beat it down.

'I hope, young sir,' said Robin, 'that thy sword may not be needed. For I hope with my good fellows to keep those rascals from coming so near as to let them use their swords, of which, I admit, my men are as yet but sorry masters'

'But I love the bow,' said Alan, 'and in the forest near my father's manor I have shot many a good bolt.'

'Good!' said Robin, and his eyes showed that his appreciation of the young squire was increased by what he had said. 'Ho, there, Kit the Smith! Give this gentleman, Alan-a-Dale here, one of the spare bows thou hast, and a bunch of arrows. Now,' went on the outlaw, when this had been done, 'do you all, my lads, stand at the arrow slits which command that group of rascals there at the woodside. They plot to beat down this door, thinking we are but poor runagate serfs with no knowledge of weapons, whom they can butcher as a terrier doth rats in a pit. Prove yourselves this day to be men of the good yew-bow. Mark each your man as they advance, and let them not reach the door.'

Eagerly the outlaws crowded to the arrow slits which commanded the place where, in the shade of the shaw, the men-at-arms seemed busy about something. At length they could be seen to lift some weight from the ground, and then their purpose was seen. They had felled a young oak, which, having lopped off its branches, they intended to use as a battering-ram wherewith to beat down the door.

Soon they were seen advancing, some dozen of the twenty ranged beside the trunk which they bore. Two outlaws stood at each window slit, a short man in front and a tall man behind, and each man squinted through the slit with a grim light in his eyes, and held his arrow notched on the string with the eagerness of dogs held in leash who see the quarry just before them.

'Much, Scadlock, Dickon, and you twelve fellows to the right, mark each your man at the tree,' came the low stern tones of Robin, 'and see that you do not miss. You other eight, let your arrows point at the breasts of the others. By the rood!' he exclaimed, marking how confidently the knights' men advanced over the open ground, 'they think the hunting of runaway serfs is like hunting rabbits. Hold your bolts till I give the word!' he said. 'Ye will forgive me this day the sweating I ha' given thee, good lads, when I made thee shoot at the mark nigh day-long these last weeks.'

'O master!' cried one man, quivering with excitement, 'a murrain on this waiting! If I shoot not soon, the arrow will leap from my hand.'

'Shoot not till I say!' said Robin sternly. 'Forty paces is all I trust thee for, but not eight of the rascals should be standing then. Steady, lads!'

For one tremendous moment all nerves were taut as they waited for the word. The men-at-arms, coming now at a trot, seemed almost at the door when Robin said 'Shoot!'

Twenty-one arrows leaped from the slits in the wooden walls, and hummed across the space of some sixty feet. To the men in the church peering out, bated of breath, the effect seemed almost one of wizardry. They saw eight of the men who ran with the tree-trunk suddenly check, stagger, and then fall. Of the others, three dashed to the ground, one got up and ran away, and two others, turning, pulled arrows from their arms as they too fled back to the wood. One of the horses of the knights came to the ground with a clatter and a thud, throwing his master, who got up, and, dazed with the blow or the utterly unexpected warmth of the defence, gazed for a moment or two at the church.

The other knight, who was untouched, yelled something at him, and fiercely pulling his horse round, rode swiftly back to the shelter of the forest, whither all the men who could run had already fled. Suddenly the unhorsed knight seemed to wake up, and then turning, ran as swiftly as his armour would allow him towards the forest. An arrow came speeding after him, but missed him, and soon he had disappeared.

On the worn grass before the church lay ten motionless forms and the dead horse, who had been struck to the heart by an arrow.

'Now, lads,' said Robin, 'to the forest with you quickly, and follow them.'

Quickly the door was unbarred, and the outlaws gained the forest at the spot where their attackers had disappeared. The traces of their hurried flight were easily picked up as the outlaws pushed forward. Alan-a-Dale came with them, and Robin thanked him for the aid he had given them.

'If at any time,' said Robin, 'you should stand in need of a few good bowmen, forget not to send word to Robert of Locksley, or Robin of Barnisdale, for by either name men know me.'

'I thank thee, Robin of Barnisdale,' said Alan, 'and it may be that I may ask thy help at some future time.'

'What!' said Robin with a laugh, 'has so young and gallant a squire as thou seemest already an enemy?'

'Ay,' replied Alan, and his handsome face was gloomy. 'And little chance as yet do I see of outwitting my enemy, for he is powerful and oppressive.'

'Tell me thy tale,' said Robin, 'for I would be thy friend, and aid thee all I can.'

'I thank thee, good Robin,' replied Alan. 'It is thus with me. I love a fair and sweet maiden whose father has lands beside Sherwood Forest. Her name is Alice de Beauforest. Her father holds his manor from that great robber and oppressor, Isenbart de Belame, who wishes him to marry the fair Alice to an old and rich knight who is as evil a man as Isenbart himself. The knight of Beauforest would rather wed his daughter to myself, whom she hath chosen for the love I bear to her; but the lord of Belame threatens that if he doth not that which he commands, he will bring fire and ruin upon him and his lands. Therefore I know not what to do to win my dear lady. Brave is she as she is fair, and would face any ill for my sake, but she loveth her father, who is past his fighting days and desires to live in peace. Therefore her loyalty to him fights against her love for me.'

'Is any time fixed for this marriage?' asked Robin.

'Belame swears that if it be not done within a year, Beauforest shall cook his goose by the fire of his own manor-house,' was the reply.

'There is time enow,' said Robin. 'Who knows? Between this

Fast and furious was that fight

and then much may happen. I am sure thou art brave. Thou must also have patience. I shall be faring south to merry Sherwood ere long, and I will acquaint myself of this matter more fully, and we shall meet anon and speak of this matter again. But see, who are these – knight and churl, who speak so privily together?'

Robin and Alan had separated from the main body of outlaws, and were about to enter a little glade, when at the mouth of a ride at the other end they saw a man in armour, on foot, speaking to a low-browed, sinister-looking man in the rough tunic of a villein – his only dress, except for the untanned shoes upon his feet. As Robin spoke, the knight turned and saw them, and they instantly recognised him as the man who had been unhorsed before the church. The churl pointed at them, and said something to the knight.

'Ha, knaves!' said the latter, advancing into the glade towards them. 'Thou art two of those company of run slaves, as I guess.'

'Run slaves we may be,' said Robin, notching an arrow to his string, 'but, sir knight, they made you and your men run in a way you in no whit expected.'

'By Our Lady,' said the knight, with a harsh laugh, 'thou speakest saucily, thou masterless rascal. But who have we here,' he said, glancing at Alan; 'a saucy squire who would be the better of a beating, as I think.'

Alan-a-Dale had already dressed his shield, which hitherto had hung by a strap on his back, and drawing his sword, he stepped quickly towards the other.

'I know thee, Ivo le Ravener,' he said, in a clear ringing voice, 'for a false knight – a robber of lonely folk, an oppressor of women, and a reiver of merchants' goods. God and Our Lady aiding me, thou shalt get a fall from me this day.'

'Thou saucy knave!' cried the other in a rage; and with great fury he sprang towards Alan, and the clash of steel, as stroke came upon guard or shield, arose in the quiet glade.

Fast and furious was that fight, and they thrust at each other like boars or stags in deadly combat. Alan was the nimbler, for the other was a man of a foul life, who loved wine and rich food; and though he was the older man and the more cunning in sword-craft, yet the younger man's swiftness of limb, keenness of eye, and strength of stroke were of more avail. Alan avoided or guarded his opponent's more deadly strokes, and by feinting and leaping back, sought to weary the other. Yet he did not escape without wounds. He had but a light hauberk on his body, and on his head a steel cap with a nasal piece, while the other had a shirt of heavy mail and a visored helm laced to his hauberk.

At last Sir Ivo's shield arm drooped, for all his efforts to keep it before him, and his sword strokes waxed fainter, and his breath could be heard to come hoarsely. Suddenly Alan leaped in upon him, and with an upward thrust drove his sword into the evil knight's throat.

At the same moment Robin, who had been watching intently the fight between Alan and the knight, heard the hiss as of a snake before him and then a footstep behind him. He stepped swiftly aside, and a knife-blade flashed beside him. Turning, he saw the churl who had been speaking with the knight almost fall to the ground with the force of the blow he had aimed at Robin's back. Then the man, quickly recovering, dashed away towards the trees.

As he did so, a little dark form seemed to start up from the bracken before him. Over the churl tripped and fell heavily, with the small, pixie-like figure gripping him. For a moment they seemed to struggle in a deadly embrace, then suddenly the big body of the churl fell away like a log, the brownie rose, shook himself, and wiped a dagger blade upon a bracken leaf.

'I thank thee, Hob o' the Hill, both for the snake's warning and thy ready blow,' said Robin. 'I should have kept my eyes about me. Who is the fellow, Hob?'

' 'Tis Grull, the churl from the Evil Hold,' said Hob. 'He hath haunted the forest by the Stane Lea where was thy camp these three days past. I thought he was a serf that craved his freedom, but he was a spy.'

Hob o' the Hill was brother to Ket the Trow or Troll, but in build or look he differed greatly. He was no taller than his bigger brother, but all his form was in a more delicate mould. Slender of limb, he had a pale face, which set off the uncanny blackness of his eyes, black curly hair, and short beard. His arms were long, and the hands, as refined almost as a girl's, were yet strong and rounded. He, too, was dressed in a laced leather tunic and breeches of doeskin that reached the ankles, while on his feet were stout shoes.

Robin went to Alan, whom he found seated on the ground
beside his dead enemy. He was weary and faint from a wound in
his shoulder. This Robin bound up with cloth torn from Alan's
shirt of fine linen, after which the outlaw asked him what he
would do now.

'I think I will take me home to Werrisdale,' said Alan. 'I am
staying at Forest Hold, the house of my foster-brother, Piers the
Lucky, but there will be hue and cry raised against me ere long
for the slaying of this rascal knight, and I would not that harm
should happen to my brother for my fault.'

'I have heard of Piers,' said Robin, who knew indeed something of everyone who dwelt in or near the wide forests which he
loved, 'and I think he would not wish thee to avoid him if he
could help thee.'

'I know it,' said Alan, 'but I would not that Belame and his evil
crew should burn my foster-brother in his bed one night in
revenge upon me. Nay, I will get me home if I can come at my
horse, which I left at a forester's hut a mile from here.'

Together Robin and Alan went on their way towards the hut
of the forester.

While the events just described had been taking place, a man
had been passing along a path in a part of the forest some mile
and a half distant. He was a tall man, with great limbs, which
gave evidence of enormous strength, and he was dressed in the
rough homespun garb of a peasant. He seemed very light-
hearted. Sometimes he twirled a great quarterstaff which he held
in his hands, and again he would start whistling, or begin trolling
a song at the top of a loud voice.

'John, John,' he said suddenly, apostrophising himself, 'what a
fool thou art! Thou shouldst be as mum as a fish, and shouldst
creep like a footpad from bush to bush. Thou singest like a
freeman, fool, whereas thou art but a runaway serf into whose
silly body the free air of the free forest has entered like wine. But
twenty short miles separate thee from the stocks and whipping-
post of old Lord Mumblemouth and his bailiff, and here thou art
trolling songs or whistling as if a forester may not challenge thee
from the next brake and seize thee for the chance of a reward
from thy lord. Peace, fool, look to thy ways and – Saints! what a
right sweet smell!' He broke off, and lifting up his head, sniffed

the sunlit air of the forest, casting his bright brown eyes humorously this way and that. 'Sure,' he went on, 'I have hit upon the kitchen of some fat abbot! What a waste, to let so fat a smell be spent up in the air. Holy Virgin, how hungry I am! Let me seek out the causer of this most savoury odour. Maybe he will have compassion upon a poor wayfarer and give me some little of his plenty.'

Saying this, John pushed aside the bushes and stole in the direction of the smell. He had not gone far before he found himself peering into a glade, in the midst of which was a tree, to which was tethered a horse, while not far from the bushes where he stood was a hut of wood, its roof formed of turves in which grew bunches of wallflower, stitchwort, and ragged robin. Before the door of this abode a fire was burning brightly without flame, and on skewers stuck in the ground beside it were cutlets of meat. These spluttered and sizzled in the genial heat of the fire, and gave forth the savoury smell which had made John feel suddenly that he was a very hungry man, and had walked far without food.

John eyed the juicy steaks, and his mouth watered. For a moment he thought no one watched the spluttering morsels, and he was thinking that for a hungry man to take one or even two of them would be no sin; but as he was thinking thus a man came from the hut, and bending down, turned two of the skewers so that the meat upon them should be better done.

John's face gloomed. The man was one of the king's rangers of the forest, as was shown by his tunic of green and his hose of brown, and the silver badge of a hunting-horn upon his hat. Moreover, his face was surly and sour – the face of a man who would sooner see a poor man starve than grant him a portion of his meal. It was Black Hugo, the forester who had accosted Robin and Scarlet in so surly a manner when he had met them in the forest.

John thought for a few moments, and then, backing gently away so that he made no noise, he reached a spot at some distance from the glade. Then, casting caution aside, he tramped forward again, and reaching the glade, burst into it, and then stopped, as if surprised at what he saw before him. He had dropped his quarterstaff in the bushes before he issued from them.

The surly forester glared at him from the other side of the fire.

'How now?' said he; 'thou lumbering dolt! Who art thou to go breaking down the bushes like some hog? Hast thou no fear of the king's justice on all who disturb his deer?'

'I pray your pardon, master ranger,' said John, pulling a forelock of his hair, and pretending to be no more than a rough oaf. 'I knew not whither I was going, but I smelt the good smell of your meat, and thought it might be that some good company of monks or a lord's equipage was preparing their midday meal, and might spare a morsel for a poor wayfarer who hath eaten naught since dawn.'

'Go thy ways, churl,' said the ranger, and his face looked more surly than ever when he heard John ask for a portion of his meat. 'Thou seest I am no monk or lord, but I prepare my own meal. So get thee gone to the highway ere I kick thee there. Knowest thou that thou hast no right to leave the road? Get thee gone, I say!'

Black Hugo spoke in angry tones, looked fiercely at the apparently abashed churl, and started forward as if about to put his threat into action. John, pulling his lock again, retreated hurriedly as if thoroughly frightened. Black Hugo stood listening for a few moments to the peasant's heavy footsteps as he crashed through the bushes towards the highway again, and then, turning to the hut, drew from a chest a huge piece of bread, from which he cut a thick slice. Then, going to the fire, he bent down and took up one of the skewers, and pushed off the meat with a knife on the slice. He did the same to the second, and then bent to the third.

Suddenly a small pole seemed to leap like a lance from the bush nearest to him, and flying across the space to the fire, one end caught the bending forester a sounding thwack on the side of the head. He fell sideways almost into the fire, stunned, and the skewer with the meat upon it flew up into the air.

John, leaping from the bush, caught the skewer as it fell, saying: 'I like not dust on my food, surly ranger.'

He deposited the meat on the bread beside the others and then, going to the prostrate ranger, turned him over and looked at the place where the pole had struck him.

' 'Twas a shrewd blow!' said John, with a chuckle, 'and hit the very spot! An inch lower would have slain him, perhaps, and an inch higher would have cracked his curmudgeon skull. As 'tis, he'll get his wits again in the turn of a fat man's head, just in time to see me eating *my* dinner.'

He lifted the forester as easily as if he were a child, and propping him in a sitting position against one of the posts of the hut, he lashed him securely to it with a rope which he found inside. Then, with his quarterstaff beside him, he sat down beside the fire and began demolishing the three juicy venison steaks.

In a few moments Black Hugo with a great sigh, opened his eyes, lifted his head, and looked in a dazed manner before him. At sight of John biting huge mouthfuls out of the bread, all his wits returned to him.

'Thou runagate rogue!' he said, and his face flushed with rage. He strove to pull his hands from the rope, but in vain. 'I will mark thee, thou burly robber. Thou shalt smart for this, and I will make thee repent that thou didst ever lay me low with thy dirty staff. I will crop thy ears for thee, and swear thy life away, thou hedge-robber and cut-purse!'

'Rant not so, thou black-faced old ram!' said John, with a laugh, 'but think thee how sweeter a man thou wouldst have been hadst thou shared thy meat with me. See now, surly old dog of the woods, thou hast lost all because thou didst crave to keep all. Thy cutlets are done to a turn; thou'rt a good cook – a better cook, I trow, than a forester; and see, here is the last morsel. Look!'

Saying which, John perched the remaining piece of meat on the last piece of bread, and opening his huge mouth popped them both in, and gave a great laugh as he saw the black looks in the other's eyes.

'I thank thee, forester, for the good dinner thou didst cook for me,' went on John. 'I feel kindly to thee, though thou dost look but sourly upon me. I doubt not thou dost ache to get at me, and I would like to try a bout with thee. Say, wilt thou have a turn with the quarterstaff?'

'Ay,' said Black Hugo, his eyes gleaming with rage. 'Let me have at thee, thou masterless rogue, and I will not leave one sound bone in thy evil carcass.'

'By Saint Peter!' said John, with a laugh, 'art thou so great with the quarterstaff? Man, I shall love to see thy play. Come, then, we will set to.'

Rising, John approached the ranger for the purpose of unloosing his bonds, when the sound of voices was borne to him through the forest. He stopped and listened, while the eyes of Black Hugo glared at him in triumph. Doubtless, if, as was probable, the travellers who were approaching were law abiding, he would soon be released, and could wreak his vengeance on this rogue. The sounds of steps and voices came nearer, until from the bushes midway on one side of the glade there issued Alan-a-Dale and Robin, who looked at the tall form of the serf and then at the ranger tied to the post.

John bent and took up his staff, and turning to Black Hugo, said:

'I doubt thy honesty, good ranger, if, as thy evil face seems to say, these are thy friends. But fear not I shall forget. We will have that bout together ere long. Thanks for thy dinner again.'

Saying this, John disappeared among the bushes and noiselessly stole away.

Robin and Alan-a-Dale came up, and could not forbear laughing when they saw the sour looks of Black Hugo.

'What is this?' asked Robin. 'The king's forester bound to a post by some wandering rogue! What, man, and has he taken thy dinner too!'

The gloomy silence of the forester confirmed what they had gathered from the parting words of the big churl, and both Robin and Alan laughed aloud at the discomfiture of the ranger, who writhed in his bonds.

'Have done with thy laughter, thou wolf's-head!' he cried to Robin.

But Robin laughed the more, until the glade re-echoed.

'Unloose me,' cried Black Hugo, in a rage, 'and I will let thee know what 'tis to laugh at a king's forester thou broken knave and runagate rascal!'

Still Robin laughed at the futile anger of the ranger, whose face was flushed as he stormed.

'I think, friend,' said Alan gently, in the midst of his laughter, 'thou dost foolishly to threaten this bold woodman whilst thou art in bonds. 'Twere more manly to stay thy threats till thou art free. Thou'rt over bold, friend.'

'Knowest thou not who this rogue is?' cried Hugo. 'He is the leader of a pack of escaped serfs, and for their crimes of firing their lord's house and slaying their lord's men they are food for the gallows or for any good man's sword who can hack their wolves' heads from their shoulders.'

'Whatever you may say of this my friend,' said Alan coldly, 'I can say that both he and his men are bold and true men, and if they have fled from a tyrant lord I blame them not.'

Alan, with a haughty look, went towards his horse. Robin ceased his laughter, and now addressed the forester.

'My heart warms to that long-limbed rascal who tied thee up and ate thy dinner,' he said. 'Thou, who with others of thy sort live on poorer folk by extortion and threats, hast now had a taste of what thou givest to those unable to withstand thee. I will give thee time to think over thy sins and thy punishment. Bide there in thy bonds until the owl hoots this night.'

Together Robin and Alan-a-Dale moved from the glade, and the forester was left to cool his anger. The sun poured down its heat upon his naked head, and the more he strained at his bonds the more the flies settled upon him and tormented him. Then he shouted for help, hoping that one of his fellow-foresters might be near, or that some traveller on the highway would hear and come and release him.

But no one came, and he grew tired of shouting. The sunlight burned through his hose, his tongue and throat were dry, and his arms, pinioned to his side and bound by ropes, were almost senseless. The forest about him seemed sunk in silence. Sometimes across the glade a flash of jewel-like light would come. It was a dragon fly, and in the rays of the sun it would hover and swerve before the bushes, like a point of living flame. Then birds came down and hopped and pecked among the embers of his fire, and even at his feet, or from a hole beneath a tree a ferret would peep forth, and encouraged by the silence would steal forth and across the glade, running from cover to cover, until he disappeared in the forest beyond.

The afternoon wore to a close, the sun went behind the trees on the western verge of the glade, and the shadows stretched along until the grey light lay everywhere. Then the forest seemed to wake up. Bird called to bird across the cool deeps of the trees, the evening wind rustled the leaves, and a great stir seemed to thrill through the woods.

The blue of the sky became slowly grey, the darkness deepened under the trees, and strange things seemed to be moving in the gloom. There came a great bird flying with noiseless wings, and hovered over the glade. Then it sank, and a sudden shriek rose for a moment as of something from which life was being torn. Then came the weird cry of 'To whee – to whee – to whoo!'

The ranger shivered. Somehow the cry seemed like that of a fiend; besides, the cold air was creeping along the ground. He pulled at his arms, which seemed almost dead, and to his wonder his bonds fell away and he found that he was free. He looked behind and inside the hut, but he could see no one. Then with lifeless fingers he picked up the rope which had bound him to the post, and found that it had been cut by a keen knife.

He looked round affrighted, and crossed himself. Robin the Outlaw had said he should be free when the owl hooted, but who had crept up and cut his bonds so that he had not been aware of it?

Black Hugo shook his head and wondered. He believed in brownies as much as he believed in his own existence, but hitherto he had not thought that brownies used knives. He shook his head again, and began to chafe his cold limbs, and as the blood began to run through them again he could have cried aloud with the pain.

He decided that someday ere long he would be revenged upon that seven-foot rascal who had stolen his dinner and tied him up. As for Robin the Outlaw, he would earn four marks by cutting off his head and taking it to the king's chief justice in London.

Meanwhile, Robin and Alan-a-Dale had pursued their way, discoursing on many things. Both found that they loved the forest, and that never did they find more delight than when, with bow in hand, they chased the king's deer, or with brave dogs routed the fierce boar from his lair. Robin put Alan upon a short route to his home in Werrisdale, and when they parted they shook hands, and each promised the other that soon they would meet again.

Then Robin turned back towards the meeting-place at the Stane Lea, where he knew his men would be waiting for him after their chase of the men-at-arms, to share the evening meal together.

Robin was almost near the end of his journey when he came to the brook which, farther up-stream, ran beside the very glade where his men would be busy round a big fire cooking their evening meal. At this place, however, the stream was broad, with a rapid current, and the forest path was carried across it on a single narrow beam of oak. It was only wide enough for one man to cross at a time, and of course had no railing.

Mounting the two wooden steps to it, Robin had walked some two or three feet along it, when on the other bank a tall man appeared, and jumping on the bridge, also began to cross it. Robin recognised him at once, by his height, as the fellow who had tied the forester to his door-post and stolen his dinner. He would have been content to hail the big man as one he would like to know, but that he had a very stubborn air as he walked towards him, as one who would say: 'Get out of my way, little man, or I will walk over thee.'

Robin was some twelve or fourteen inches shorter than the other, and being generally reckoned to be tall, and strong withal, he deeply resented the other's inches and his bragging air.

They stopped and looked frowningly at each other when they were but some ten feet apart.

'Where are thy manners, fellow?' said Robin haughtily. 'Sawest thou not that I was already on the bridge when thou didst place thy great splay feet on it?'

'Splay feet yourself jackanapes,' retorted the other. 'The small jack should ever give way to the big pot.'

'Thou'rt a stranger in these parts, thou uplandish chucklehead!' said Robin; 'thy currish tongue betrayeth thee. I'll give thee a good Barnisdale lesson, if thou dost not retreat and let me pass.'

Saying which, Robin drew an arrow from his girdle and notched it on his string. 'Twas a stout bow and long, and one that few men could bend, and the tall man, with a half-angry, half-humorous twinkle in his eye, glanced at it.

'If thou dost touch thy string,' he said, 'I'll leather thy hide to rights.'

'Thou ass,' said Robin, 'how couldst thou leather anyone if this grey goose quill were sticking in thy stupid carcass?'

'If this is thy Barnisdale teaching,' rejoined John, 'then 'tis the teaching of cowards. Here art thou, with a good bow in thy hand, making ready to shoot me, who hath naught but this quarterstaff.'

Robin paused. He was downright angry with the stranger, but there was something honest and manly and good-natured about the giant which he liked.

'Have it thy way, then,' he said. 'We Barnisdale men are not cowards, as thou shalt see ere long. I will e'en lay aside my bow and cut me a staff. Then will I test thy manhood, and if I baste thee not till thou dost smoke like a fire, may the nicker who lives in this stream seize me.'

So saying, Robin turned back and went to the bank, and with his knife he cut a stout staff from as fine a ground oak as could be found anywhere in Barnisdale. Having trimmed this to the weight and length he desired, he ran back on the bridge where the stranger was still waiting for him.

'Now,' said Robin, 'we will have a little play together. Whoever is knocked from the bridge into the stream shall lose the battle. So now, go!'

With the first twirl of Robin's staff the stranger could see that he had no novice to deal with, and as their staves clanged together as they feinted or guarded he felt that the aim of Robin had a strength that was almost if not quite equal to his own.

Long time their staves whirled like the arms of a windmill, and the cracks of the wood as staff kissed staff were tossed to and fro between the trees on either side of the stream. Suddenly the stranger feinted twice. Quickly as Robin guarded, he could not save the third stroke, and the giant's staff came with a smart rap on Robin's skull.

'First blood to thee!' cried Robin, as he felt the warmth trickle down his face.

'Second blood to thee!' said the giant, with a good-natured laugh.

Robin, thoroughly angry now, beat with his staff as if it were a flail. Quick as lightning his blows descended, now here, now there, and all the quickness of eye of his opponent could not save him from getting such blows that his very bones rattled.

Both men were at the great disadvantage of having to keep their footing on the narrow bridge. Every step made forward or backward had to be taken with every care, and the very power

Robin meeets with Little John

with which they struck or guarded almost threw them over one side or the other.

Great as was the strength of the big man, Robin's quickness of hand and eye were getting the better of him. He was indeed beginning to 'smoke', and the sweat gathered on his face and ran down in great drops. Suddenly Robin got a blow in on the big man's crown; but next moment, with a furious stroke, the stranger struck Robin off his balance, and with a mighty splash the outlaw dived into the water.

For a moment John seemed surprised to find no enemy before him; then, wiping the sweat from his eyes, he cried:

'Hallo, good laddie, where art thou now?'

He bent down anxiously, and peered into the water flowing rapidly beneath the bridge. 'By Saint Peter!' he said, 'I hope the bold man is not hurt!'

'Faith!' came a voice from the bank a little farther down, here 'I am, big fellow, as right as a trivet. Thou'st got the day,' Robin went on with a laugh, 'and I shall not need to cross the bridge.'

Robin pulled himself up the bank, and, kneeling down, laved his head and face in the water. When he arose, he found the big stranger almost beside him, dashing the water over his own head and face.

'What!' cried Robin, 'hast not gone forward on thy journey? Thou wert in so pesty a hurry to cross the bridge just now that thou wouldst not budge for me, and now thou'st come back.'

'Scorn me not, good fellow,' said the big man, with a sheepish laugh. 'I have no whither to go that I wot of. I am but a serf who hath run from his manor, and tonight, instead of my warm nest [hut], I shall have to find a bush or a brake that's not too draughty. But I would like to shake hands with thee ere I wend, for thou'rt as true and good a fighter as ever I met.'

Robin's hand was on the other's big fingers at once, and they gave a handshake of mutual respect and liking. Then John turned away, and was for crossing the bridge.

'Stay awhile,' said Robin; 'perhaps thou wouldst like supper ere thou goest a-wandering.'

With these words, Robin placed his horn to his lips and blew a blast that woke the echoes, made the blackbirds fly shrieking away from the bushes, and every animal that lurked in the underwood to dive for the nearest cover. The stranger looked on marvelling, and Robin stood waiting and listening. Soon in the distance could be heard sounds as if deer or does were hurrying through the bushes, and in a little while between the trees could be seen the forms of men running towards them.

Will Stuteley the Bowman was the first to reach the bank where Robin stood.

'Why, good master,' said he, 'what hath happened to thee? Thou'rt wet to the skin!'

Will looked at the stranger, and glared angrily at him.

' 'Tis no matter at all,' laughed Robin. 'You see that tall lad there. We fought on the bridge with staves, and he tumbled me in.'

By this time Much, the Miller's son, Scarlet, and the others had reached the bank, and at Robin's words Scarlet dashed at the stranger, and by a quick play with foot and hand tripped up the big man. Then the others threw themselves upon the stranger, and seizing him cried:

'Swing him up and out, lads! Duck him well!'

'Nay, nay,' shouted Robin, laughing. 'Forbear, lads. I have no ill-will – I've put my hand in his, for he's a good fellow and a bold. Get up, lad,' he said to the stranger, who had been powerless in the hands of so many, and would next moment have been swung far out into the stream. 'Hark ye, seven footer,' said Robin. 'We are outlaws, brave lads who have run from evil lords. There are twenty-two of us. If thou wilt join us, thou shalt share and share with us, both in hard knocks, good cheer, and the best that we can reive from the rich snuffling priests, proud prelates, evil lords, and hard-hearted merchants who venture through the greenwood. Thou'rt a good hand at the staff: I'll make thee a better hand at the longbow. Now, speak up, jolly blade!'

'By earth and water, I'll be thy man,' cried the stranger, coming eagerly forward and holding out his hand, which Robin seized and wrung. 'Never heard I sweeter words than those you have said, and with all my heart will I serve thee and thy fellowship.'

'What is thy name, good man?' asked Robin.

'John o' the Stubbs,' replied the other; 'but' – with a great laugh – 'men call me John the Little.'

'Ha! ha! ha!' laughed the others, and crowded round shaking hands with him and crying out: 'John, little man, give me thy great hand!'

'His name shall be altered,' said stout Will the Bowman, 'and we will baptise him in good brown ale. Now, shall we not be back to camp, master, and make a feast on't?'

'Ay, lads,' replied Robin, 'we will be merry this night. We have a new fellow to our company, and will e'en bless him with good ale and fat venison.'

They raced back to camp, where over the fire Scadlock had a great cauldron, from whence arose the most appetising odours for men grown hungry in greenwood air. Robin changed his garments for dry ones, which were taken from a secret store-place in a cave near by, and then, standing round John the Little, who overtopped them all, the outlaws held each his wooden mug filled to the brim with good brown ale.

'Now, lads,' said Stuteley, 'we will baptise our new comrade into our good free company of forest lads. He has hitherto been called John the Little, and a sweet pretty babe he is. But from now on he shall be called Little John. Three cheers, lads, for Little John!'

How they made the twilight ring! The leaves overhead quivered with the shouts. Then they tossed off their mugs of ale, and gathering round the cauldron they dipped their pannikins into the rich stew and fell to feasting.

Afterwards Little John told them of his meeting with the forester, and how he had tied him up and ate up his dinner before his eyes. They laughed hugely over this, for all bore some grudge against Black Hugo and the other foresters for their treacherous oppression of poor peasants living on the forest borders. They voted John a brave and hefty lad, and said that if they could get fifty such as he they would be strong enough to pull down the Evil Hold of Wrangby, or the robbers' castle on Hagthorn Waste.

Then Robin continued Little John's tale, and told how he left the ranger in his bonds 'to think over his sins till the owl hooted.'

'What mean you, master?' said Little John. 'Did you go back and cut the rogue loose?'

It was dark now, and only the flicker of the firelight lit up the strong brown faces of the men as they lay or squatted.

'Nay, I cut not the rogue loose! But he is free by now, and, I doubt not, crying o'er his aching limbs, and breathing vengeance against us both.'

'How, then, master?' said Little John, gaping with wonder; while the others also listened, marvelling at their leader's talk.

'I have friends in the greenwood,' said Robin, 'who aid me in many things. Yet they are shy of strangers, and will not willingly show themselves until they know ye better. Hob o' the Hill, show thyself, lad!'

Then, to the terror of them all, from a dark patch near Robin's feet there rose a little man whose long face shone pale in the firelight, and whose black eyes gleamed like sloes. Some of the men, keeping their eyes on him, dragged themselves away; others crossed themselves; and Much, the Miller's son, took off his tunic and turned it inside out.

'Holy Peter!' he murmured, 'shield us from the power of evil spirits!'

'Out upon thee all!' cried Robin in a stern voice. 'Hob is no evil spirit, but a man as thou art, with but smaller limbs, maybe, but keener wits.'

' 'Tis a boggart, good maister,' said one of the outlaws; 'a troll or lubberfiend, such as they tell on. He leads men into bogs, or makes them wander all night on the moors.'

' 'Tis such as he,' said Rafe the Carter, 'who used to plait my horses' manes in the night, and drove them mad.'

'And,' said another,' his evil fowk do make the green rings in the meadows, in which, if beasts feed, they be poisoned.'

'Speak not to the elf,' said another, crossing his finger before his face to protect himself from the 'evil eye' of the troll, 'or you will surely die.'

'Old women, all of ye,' said Robin, with scorn. 'Hob is a man, I tell thee, who can suffer as thou canst suffer – hath the same blood to spill, the same limbs to suffer torture or feel the hurt of fire. Listen,' and his voice was full of a hard anger. 'Hob hath a brother whose name is Ket. They are both my very dear friends. Many times have they aided me, and often have they saved my life. I charge you all to harbour no evil or harm against them.'

'Why, good master, are they friends of thine?' asked Little John, who smiled good-humouredly at Hob. 'How came ye to win their love?'

'I will tell thee,' went on Robin. ' 'Twas two summers ago, and I walked in the heart of the forest here, and came to a lonely glade where never do ye see the foresters go, for they say 'tis haunted, and the boldest keep far from it. In that glade are two green mounds or hillocks. I passed them, and saw three knights on foot and two lying dead. And the three knights fought with two trolls – this man and his brother. Hob here was gravely wounded, and his brother also, and the knights overpowered them. Then I marvelled what they would do, and I saw them make a great fire, and creeping nearer I heard them say they would see whether these trolls would burn, as their father had burned on Hagthorn Waste, or whether they were fiends of the fire, and would fly away in the smoke. Then as they dragged the two men to the fire I saw a door of green sods open in the side of one of the hills, and from it rushed three women – one old and halt, but the other two young, and, though small, they were beautiful. They flung themselves at the feet of the knights, and prayed for pity on their brothers, and the old woman offered to be burned in place of her sons. The felon knights were struck dumb at first with the marvel of such a sight, and then they seized the three women and swore they should burn with their brother trolls. Then I could suffer to see no more, and with three arrows from my belt I slew those evil knights. I pulled the two poor hill folk from the fires, and ever since they and their kin have been the dearest friends I have in the greenwood.'

'Master,' said Little John soberly, ' 'twas bravely done of thee, and truly hast thou proved that no man ever suffers from an honest and kindly deed.'

He rose and bent his giant form down to Little Hob, and held out his hand.

'Laddie,' he said, 'give me thy hand, for I would be friend to all who love good Master Robin.'

'And I also,' said brave Will Stuteley and Scarlet, who had come forward at the same moment.

The little man gave his hand to each in turn, looking keenly into each face as he did so.

'Hob o' the Hill would be brother to all who are brothers of Robin o' the Hood,' said he.

'Listen, friends all,' went on Robin. 'Just as ye have suffered from the oppression and malice of evil lords, so hath suffered our friend here and his brother. The five knights whom they and

I slew were of that wicked crew that haunt Hagthorn Waste, and hold all the lands in those parts in fear and evil custom. I know there was some cruel deed which was done by Ranulf of the Waste upon the father of these friends of ours, and someday before long it may be that we may be able to help Hob and his brother to have vengeance upon that evil lord for the tortures which their father suffered. What sayest thou, Hob, wilt thou have our aid if needs be?'

'If needs be, ay,' replied Hob, whose eyes had become fierce, and whose voice was thick and low, 'but we men of the Underworld would liefer have our vengeance to ourselves. In our own time will we take it, and in full measure. Yet I thank thee, Robin, and these thy fellows, for the aid thou dost offer.'

The little man spoke with dignity, as if he thanked an equal.

Then came little Gilbert, and put his hand in the strong clasp of the mound man, and after him Much, the Miller's son; and all the others, putting off their dread of the uncanny, seeing that Robin and Little John and the others were not afraid, came up also and passed the word of friendship with Hob o' the Hill.

'Now,' said Robin, 'we are all brothers to the free folk of the wood. Never more need any of ye dread to step beyond the gleam of fire at night, and in the loneliest glade shall ye not fear to tread by day. Ye are free of the forest, and all its parts, and sib to all its folks.'

'So say I,' said Hob, 'I – whose people once ruled through all this land. Broken are we now, the Little People, half feared and half scorned; we and our harmless deeds made into silly tales told by foolish women and frightened bairns around their fires by night. But I give to ye who are the brothers of my brother the old word of peace and brotherhood, which, ere the tall fair men ravened through our land, we, the Little People, gave to those who aided us and were our friends. I whose kin were once Lords of the Underworld and of the Overworld, of the Mound Folk, the Stone Folk, and the Tree Folk, give to you, my brothers, equal part and share in the earth, the wood, the water, and the air of the greenwood and the moorland.'

With these words the little dark man glided from the circle of the firelight, and seemed suddenly to become part of the gloom of the trees.

CHAPTER THREE

How Robin Fought the Beggar-Spy
and Caught the Sheriff

Winter was gone, the weak spring sunlight struck its rays deep through the bare brown trees of Sherwood, the soft wind dangled the catkins on the hazel, the willow, and the poplar; and the thrush, who had lived in the glade for five winters, sat high on the top of the tallest elm, and shouted to all who chose to listen that he could not see snow anywhere, that the buds on all the trees were growing as fast as they could, that the worms were beginning to peep through the mould, and, indeed, that food and life and love were come again into a world which for long weeks had seemed to be dead, and wrapped in its winding-sheet for evermore.

A wide glade, strangely clear of all bushes, lay far down before him, and on one side of it were two great green hillocks, nearly side by side. One rose well out in the glade, but the shadows from the fringe of the forest lay on the heaving swell of the other.

There seemed no sign of human life anywhere in the vast glade. Certainly a faint path seemed to start from a particular spot on the green side of the farther mound and lead towards the forest; but that might easily be the track of a couple of hares who had made their home in the hill, and who, as is well known, always race along one beaten track to their feeding-ground.

Suddenly from the forest on the wider side of the glade the figure of a small man ran out into the open. As swiftly as a hare he raced over the grass, breasted the nearest mound, and reaching the top, seemed suddenly to sink into the ground. It was Hob o' the Hill. A few moments later, and on that side of the mound which faced the nearer forest, a portion of the green turf seemed suddenly to fall in, and the two small forms of Hob o' the Hill and Ket his brother came out. They looked keenly round, the turf behind them closed again, and with swift steps they ran along the little path. Every now and then they glanced behind to see that they kept the bulk of the mound between them and prying eyes in the forest at the point whence Hob had issued.

In a little while they gained the nearer verge of the forest, and ran forward through its shady aisles under the bare brown trees. For a space of time wherein a man might count twenty there was no movement in the glade. But then, at that part of the forest whence Hob had first run, came the sound of hooves, the flash of arms, and along a narrow path there came eight riders who, issuing from the trees into the glade stopped and gazed forward.

The foremost of these was a man of fine, almost courtly, bearing, with handsome features. On his head was a steel cap, his broad breast was covered with a hauberk, and in his right hand was a lance. Beside him on a palfrey rode a man of mild and gentle countenance, who looked like a chaplain, for he was clothed in the semi-monkish robe of a clerk. Behind them rode six men, each with lance, hauberk, and steel cap, quivers at their back, and bows slung within easy reach at their saddle-bows. They had the frank, open look of freemen, and were evidently a bodyguard of freeholding tenants.

'Well, Master Gammell,' said the clerk, looking this way and that, 'which is the way now? In this wilderness of trees and glades and downs it passes me to know where thou canst hope to find this runagate kinsman of thine.'

' 'Tis as clear as noonday,' said Master Gammell, with a laugh. ' "Beyond the two howes", was the word of the good churl at Outwoods, "through the wood for a mile till you come to the lithe. Then search the scar of Clumber cliffs beyond the stream, and – " ' Master Gammell laughed good-humouredly ' " – belike an arrow in your ribs from Lord knows where will tell you that your man has seen you, even though you have not seen a sign of him." The way is clear, therefore, good Simon,' he ended, 'to the place where Robin has wintered, so let us push forward.'

Putting spurs to his horse, the leader, Alfred of Gammell, or Gamwell, pushed forward into the glade, followed by the clerk and the six archers.

'Let us not pass too close to those green hills,' said Simon. 'Men say that fiends dwell within them, and may work wizardry upon us if we pass within the circuit of their power.'

'Thou art no countryman,' laughed Master Gammell. 'There be many such mounds scattered up and down the country hereabouts, and no man ever got hurt from them that I know of. Indeed, one was upon my waste land at Locksley, and though I remember my villeins came and begged me not to dig it up, I said I could not let it cumber land that could be brought into good ploughland, and therefore I had it digged up, and naught ill was found in it but a hollow in the midst and an old jar with a few burned bones therein, and some elf-bolts and bits of stone. Such things are but ancient graves.'

'Yet have I read,' went on the clerk, 'that it is within such high mounds in lonely places that one enters into entrancing lands of green twilight, where lovely fiends do dwell, and dreadful wizards work their soul-snatching wiles and enchantment.'

'I fear me,' said Gammell, 'that such tales are of no greater truth than the songs and stories of lying jongleurs, which serve but to pass an empty hour or two, but are not worth the credence of wise men.'

Nevertheless, the clerk kept a keen eye on the green hills as they rode beside them, as if every moment he expected something of mysterious evil to issue from them and whelm them in the chains of some strange enchantment. When they entered the forest beyond, he still kept his glance continually moving through the dim ways. Simon, indeed, loved not the dark woods. He was a man who had lived much in towns, and thought that there was no sweeter sound than the shouts of men and women chaffering in the market-place, nor more pleasant sight than the street with its narrow sky blocked out by high pent roofs.

They had ridden about half a mile through the wood, when suddenly a shrill call resounded above their heads. 'Twas like the cry of a bird in the talons of a hawk, and, almost without knowing it, all lifted their eyes to see the kill. As they did so a great voice shouted:

'Stand, travellers, and stir not!'

At these words their eyes were swiftly brought down, and looking round, they saw that where they had seen only the dark trunks of trees were now some twenty men in dark brown tunic, hose and hood, each with a great bow stretched taut, and his hand upon the feather of an arrow drawn to his very ear.

One or two of the men-at-arms riding behind their master cursed in their beards and glared fiercely about, as if to seek for a way of escape. But looking closely they perceived that the bowmen surrounded them on all sides. Their dark tunics and hose, being of the colour of the trees, made them so like the very trunks themselves that some had thought for a moment that they looked at a gnarled thorn or a young oak, until the glint of light on the keen arrow point had shown them their error.

Alfred of Gammell bit his lip, and his eyes flashed in anger; but his good-humour conquering his chagrin, he said:

'Well, good fellows, what want ye of me?'

'Throw down thy weapons,' came the answer from a tall and powerful man standing beside the trunk of an oak just before them.

Very glumly the six archers did as the robber bade them, and when all their weapons were lying on the ground, came the command:

'Ride forward ten paces!' When this had been done, the speaker gave orders to three of his men to pick up the weapons.

'Now,' said he to Master Gammell, 'thou shalt come away and see our master who rules in these shaws.'

'Who may your master be, tall man?' asked Gammell angrily, as the man seized his horse's bridle and drew him forward.

'That's for him to say,' said the robber. 'But 'tis to be hoped thy purse is well lined, for though he will dine thee and thy company well, thou wilt have to pay thy shot.'

Master Gammell was prevented from replying by a shout which came from among the trees before them. Looking in that direction, they were aware of a tall man coming towards them, with two little men walking beside him. The tall man was dressed in green, with a cloak or capote which reached to his knees, while his head was covered and his face concealed by a hood.

The robber who held the bridle checked Gammell's horse as the man in green approached, and said:

'Master, here be a party of foolish armed men blundering

through thy woods as if they had the word of peace from thee that the king himself hath not got. Wilt thou dine them, or shall we take toll of their purses and let them gang their way lighter and wiser than they came?'

For a moment the man in green stood in silence looking up at the face of the first horseman. Then, with a frank laugh, he approached with outstretched hand, and throwing off the hood so that his face was seen, he said:

'Thy hand, cousin, and thy forgiveness for my men's rough ways.'

With a start, Gammell looked keenly at the face of Robin Hood, for he was the man in green; then, clasping the outstretched hand of the outlaw, he laughingly said:

'Robin, Robin, thou rascal! I should have known that these were thy faithful fellows. Thou art the man of all men I came hither to see.'

Gammell leaped from his horse, and the two men embraced, kissing each other on both cheeks. Then Gammell held Robin at arm's length and looked at him, scanning with half-laughing, half-admiring eyes the tanned face with the fearless bright eyes, the head of dark brown hair, and the length and strength of limb.

'By the shrine of Walsingham!' said Gammell, 'I should hardly have known thee, so large of limb thou hast grown since we parted five years ago at Locksley. Robin, sorry was I to hear thou hadst been forced to flee to the greenwood – pity 'tis thou wert ever so free of speech and quick of action!'

'Now, lad,' replied Robin soberly, 'naught of that. We could never agree on it. Thou hast found it pay thee best to court the strong lord whose lands lie by thine, and to shut thy eyes to many things which I must speak and fight against. Now, tell me, coz, why camest thou here?'

'To see thee, Robin, and to thank thee,' was the reply, 'and also to warn thee!'

'To thank me?'

'Ay, for that noble deed of thine at Havelond!' said Gammell. ' 'Twas but justice that thou didst give to those traitors and robbers of our poor cousin, after she had in vain besought justice of the king's court – indeed, at his very seat!'

This indeed had been an act which, almost as much as his first flight after slaying the lord abbot's men-at-arms, had made Robin's fame spread wide through the lands of Yorkshire, Derby, and Nottingham which lay beside the great rolling forests. It had happened in the late autumn, just before winter with its iron hand had locked the land in ice and snow. Robin had a cousin, a lady named Alice of Havelond, who had married Bennett, a well-to-do yeoman who dwelled in Scaurdale in Yorkshire. Two years before, the plundering Scots and fiendish Galloway men, wild and fierce and cruel as mountain cats, had come from the north ravaging and burning. A Scottish knight had taken Bennett and held him to ransom, and shut him in prison until his ransom should be paid. In his absence Thomas of Patherley and Robert of Prestbury, neighbours of his wife's, had seized on his fields at Havelond, divided them between themselves, and pulled down the houses, even throwing Alice his wife out of the house in which she dwelled.

No justice had the poor lady been able to get, neither from the king's justices nor from the steward of the lord from whom the land was held. Then, when he had lain a year in prison, she was able to pay her husband's ransom. He returned, and full of anger on hearing of the robbery of his lands, had entered on the same lands as the rightful owner. His enemies lay in wait, and beat him so greatly that barely was he left alive. His wife went to the king's court, and after long and weary waiting was told that Bennett must make his appeal in person – though the poor man was so ill from his beating that he would be sick and maimed for life. It seemed, therefore, that Thomas of Patherley and Robert of Prestbury, having shown themselves to be strong and unscrupulous, would be left in undisturbed possession of the lands which they had robbed.

Then Alice had bethought herself of her kinsmen. She had gone to Alfred of Gammell, and he had promised to take the case again to the king's court, but the lady despaired of justice in that way. Then she had taken horse, and, with one serving-girl and a villein, had sought the greenwood where her bold kinsman, Robin Hood, was said to lurk, and after many toils had found him and told him all her trouble, and begged his help.

Robin had sent her away comforted, but she had kept word of her visit to him very secret. A few days had passed, and then one night men in Scaurdale had seen two houses burning far away on the wolds, and knew that somehow vengeance had fallen on the two robbers. Next day all knew and rejoiced in the bold deed – that Robin o' the Hood had come and slain both Thomas of Patherley and Robert of Prestbury, and thus had given back to Bennett of Havelond the fields which the evil men had wrested from him.

'I tell thee,' said Alfred of Gammell, his admiration breaking through his well-bred dislike of violent deeds, 'that deed of thine made all high-handed men dwelling beside the forests bethink themselves that if they oppress too cruelly their turn might come next.'

'I hope they think thus,' said Robin, and his face was grim. 'If men let such a wrong go unpunished and unrighted as was suffered by Bennett and our cousin, to whom can those who are oppressed look to for succour? Not to thy soft priests, cousin, who squeeze poor men as evilly as any robber baron, and who fill their purses with money wrung from poor yeomen. But tell me, against whom wouldst thou warn me?'

'Against Sir Guy of Gisborne and his evil plots,' replied Gammell. 'I was yesterday at Outwoods, which now the king's bailiff holds, until a year and a day from when thou wert made outlaw. There I sought out Cripps, the old reeve, whom I knew was thy friend, and he told me that Sir Guy hath his discomfiture by thee and thy fellows keenly at heart. A bitter man he was before thou didst burn him from his house, but now he is still more evil-minded and harsh. And he hath sworn by dreadful oaths to have thee taken or slain.'

'What plots did old Cripps speak of?'

'He hath become hand in glove with Ralph Murdach, the sheriff of Nottinghamshire, and the villeins say that wandering men have told them that, together, Sir Guy and Master Murdach are bribing evil men to dress as beggars, palmers, and hucksters to wander through the forests to find thy secret places, so that one day they may gather their men-at-arms and fall upon thee.'

'I thank thee for thy counsel,' said Robin, appearing not to treat it, however, as of any special importance; 'but now thou and thy men shall dine with me this day.'

They had by this time reached a secret place in some tree-clad hills which rose steeply up beside a river in the forest, and in a cave a feast was already spread, at which all now sat down to do full justice.

Robin and his men inquired of Gammell whether Sir Guy now treated the villeins of the manor more harshly than before.

'Men say that he does not,' was the reply; 'and for a good reason. It is said that when Abbot Robert of St Mary's heard of thy slaying the men-at-arms and of the flight of thy fellows, he was exceeding wroth with Sir Guy, and told him that he had overdriven the people of his manor, and must look to his conduct, or he would not suffer him to rule the manor. So that the folk are not so harshly overborne as formerly, yet that Sir Guy is the more hateful of them.'

'A miracle!' said Scarlet scornfully, when he heard this, 'a word of mercy from the thick-jowled, proud-lipped Abbot of St Mary's!'

'Maybe, uncle,' said little Gilbert of the White Hand, who had ever wanted to be a priest and to learn to read, 'maybe the abbot never told Sir Guy to oppress the manor folk, but that Sir Guy did it from his own heart as a tyrant.'

And this, indeed, was what many of the outlaws deemed in their hearts, and thought not so harshly of the abbot thereafter.

Soon after this, Master Gammell and his men took their departure, and Robin Hood and some of the outlaws went with him to the edge of the forest, and put him on his way towards Locksley village, which lay south-west beyond the little town of Sheffield.

Now it happened one afternoon some three days afterwards that Robin was walking along beside the broad highway which led from Pontefract through the forest to Ollerton and Nottingham. He was thinking of what his cousin had said concerning Sir Guy of Gisborne's plots to capture him, dead or alive, and as he walked beneath the trees he heard the shuffle of footsteps, and looking up, saw a beggar coming down the road.

Robin, from among the trees, could see the man, while he himself was unobserved, and as he saw the beggar stamping along with a great pikestaff in his hand, he wondered whether indeed this man was a genuine beggar, or one of the spies whom Guy of Gisborne had set to watch for him.

The man's cloak was patched in fifty places, so that it seemed more like a collection of many cloaks than one; his legs were encased in ragged hose, and great tanned boots were on his feet. Round his body, slung from his neck by a great wide thong, was his bag of meal, and in a girdle about him was stuck a long knife in a leathern sheath. On his head was a wide low hat, which was so thick and unwieldy that it looked as if three hats had been stitched together to make it.

Robin's suspicions were aroused, for the man seemed to be dressed for the part, and not to be a real beggar. Moreover, his eyes continually glanced from side to side in the wood as he walked along the uneven track.

By this time the beggar had gone past the place where Robin stood, and the outlaw shouted to him:

'Stand, beggar! why in such haste to get on?'

The beggar answered nothing, but hurried his steps. Robin ran up to him, and the man turned angrily and flourished his staff. He was a man of an evil countenance, with a scar from brow to cheek on one side.

'What want you with me, woodman?' he cried. 'Cannot a man fare peacefully along the king's highway without every loose wastrel crying out upon him?'

'Thou'rt surly, beggar,' said Robin. 'I'll tell thee why I bade thee stop. Thou must pay toll ere thou goest farther through the forest.'

'Toll!' cried the other, with a great laugh; 'if you wait till I pay you toll, thou landloper, thou'lt not stir from that spot for a year.'

'Come, come,' said Robin; 'unloose thy cloak, man, and show what thy purse holds. By thy clothes thou'rt a rich beggar – if such thou truly art, and not a rogue in the guise of an honest beggar.'

The man scowled and glanced suspiciously at Robin, and gripped his staff.

'Nay, lad,' said Robin good-naturedly, 'grip not thy staff so fiercely. Surely thou hast a broad penny in thy purse which thou canst pay a poor woodman for toll.'

'Get thy own money, thou reiving rascal,' growled the beggar. 'Thou gettest none from me. I fear not thy arrow sticks, and I

'What want you with me, woodman?'

would be blithe to see thee hanging from the gallows-tree – as, indeed, I hope to see thee ere long.'

'And doubtless,' said Robin, 'if thou couldst earn dirty coin by treachery thou wouldst not stop at any evil work. I thought thou lookest like an honest beggar! Rogue and traitor are written all over thy evil face. Now listen to me! I know thee for a traitor in the pay of an evil man, but I'll not be baulked of my toll. Throw thy purse on the ground, or I will drive a broad arrow through thee!'

Even as he spoke, Robin prepared to notch an arrow to the string of his bow. His fingers missed the string, and he bent his eyes down to see what he was doing. That moment was fatal. With a bound like that of a wild-cat the beggar leapt forward, and at the same instant he swung his pikestaff round and dashed the bow and arrow from Robin's hand.

The outlaw leaped back and drew his sword, but quick as thought the beggar beat upon him and caught him a great swinging blow beside the head. Robin fell to the ground in a swoon, just as shouts were heard among the trees beside the way. The beggar looked this way and that, his hand went to the haft of the keen knife in his belt, and for a moment he crouched as if he would leap upon the prostrate outlaw and slay him outright.

A man in brown jumped from some bushes a few yards away, and then two others. They looked at the beggar, who had instantly assumed an air of unconcern and began to walk forward, and a bend in the narrow track among the trees soon hid him from their sight.

Two of the men were young recruits of the outlaw band, and the other was Dodd, the man-at-arms who had yielded to Robin when the latter had slain Hugo of Lynn. As they began walking along the road, suddenly Dodd espied the bow and arrow which had been dashed from Robin's hand, and he stopped.

'Ay, ay,' he said; 'what's been doing here? 'Tis our master's bow. I know it by its size, for no other hath the hand to draw it.'

'Look! look!' cried one of the others, pushing behind a bush where Robin had fallen; 'here is a wounded man – by the Virgin, 'tis our master! Now, by Saint Peter, who hath done this evil deed?'

Swiftly Dodd knelt beside his leader, and pushed his hand into his doublet to feel whether his heart still moved. Then he cried:

'Lads, thanks be to the Saints, he's alive. Run to the brook beside the white thorn there and bring water in thy cap.'

The water being thrown upon the outlaw's face, he quickly revived. He sighed heavily, his hand went up to his aching head, and he opened his eyes.

'O master,' said Dodd, 'tell us who hath treated thee so evilly. Surely 'twas done by treachery. How many were they who set upon thee?'

Robin smiled wanly upon the three eager faces bending above him, and in a little while was sufficiently recovered to sit up.

'There was no more than one who set upon me,' said Robin, 'and he was a sturdy rogue dressed like a beggar. With his great pikestaff he dashed upon me as I fitted an arrow to my string, and ere I could defend myself he knocked me down in a swoon.'

'Now, by my faith,' said Dodd, ' 'twas that rascal beggar whom we saw as we came to the road – so innocent he looked! Go you, lads,' he said, turning to the other two men, 'show yourselves keen lads, and capture him and bring him back, so that our master may slay him if he will.'

'But,' said Robin, 'use stealth in the way you approach the rogue. 'Twas my foolishness to get too near his long staff that was my undoing. If ye let him use his great beam, he'll maim ye.'

The two young fellows promised to creep upon the beggar warily, and set off eagerly, while Dodd stayed by Robin until the latter felt strong enough to stand up and be assisted towards the camp of the outlaws.

Meanwhile, the two young outlaws, knowing the beggar must keep to the only road through the forest, swiftly ran to catch him up. But presently one of them, Bat or Bart by name, suggested that they should go by a nearer way through the trees, which would enable them to lie in ambush for the beggar at a narrow part of the road. The other agreed, and accordingly they pushed through the forest. Strong of limb they were, and if their wits had only been as keen as were their senses, all would have gone well with them. But they were only three weeks from the plough, and from the hard and exhausting labour in the fields of their lord, and they were not as sharp as they would soon become when the dangers of the greenwood had been about them a little longer.

On they ran between the trees, through the glades and the boggy bottoms, flinching at neither mire nor pool, and baulking at neither hillock nor howe. At length they reached the highway through the forest again at a place where the road ran through a dell. At the bottom was a thick piece of wood through which the road narrowed, and here they took up their place, each hiding behind a tree on opposite sides of the way.

Soon, as they crouched waiting, they heard the shuffle and tramp of footsteps coming down the hill, and peering forth, they saw it was the beggar man whom they had seen near where their master lay in a swoon.

As he came to the part of the road between them they both dashed out upon him, and before he could think of fleeing, one had snatched the pikestaff from his hand, and the other had caught his dagger from his girdle and was holding it at his breast.

'Traitor churl!' said the outlaw, 'struggle not, or I'll be thy priest and send thee out of life.'

The beggar's evil face went dark with rage as he glared from one to the other, and then looked about for a way of escape. But there was no chance of escape that he could see, and therefore he determined on craftiness to get him out of his trouble.

'Kind sirs,' he said humbly, 'grant me my life! Hold away that keen and ugly knife, or I shall surely die for fright of it. What have I done to thee that thou shouldst seek to slay me? And what profit will thou get from my rags if thou killest and robbest a poor old beggar?'

'Thou liest, false knave!' cried Bat fiercely. 'I think 'twould be better if I thrust this knife at once between thy evil ribs. Thou hast near slain the gentlest man and the bravest in all Sherwood and Barnisdale. And back again thou shalt be taken, fast bound and trussed, and he will judge whether thou shalt be slain, as a mark for our arrows, or be hung from a tree as not worthy to have good arrows stuck in thy evil carcass.'

'Kind sirs,' said the beggar whiningly, 'is it that woodman whom I struck but now that I have nearly slain? Oh, by the rood, but 'twas only in defence of myself that I struck him. Sorry I am that my awkward stroke hath near slain him.'

'Out upon thee, thou hast not slain him!' cried Bat. 'Think you his good life is to be put out by thy dirty staff. He'll live to do thee skaith [harm] within the next hour, as thou shalt see. Now, Michael,' Bat said to his comrade, 'let us truss this rogue up with his own rope girdle and push him along to our master. Thou art ugly enough now, rogue,' Bat went on, 'but thou'lt look uglier still when thou art swinging and grinning through a noose.'

The beggar saw that Bat was a determined man, and that if he thought not speedily of some wile wherewith to escape from their hands, it would fare ill with him.

'O brave gentlemen,' he said in a shaking voice, 'be kind, and spare a poor old beggar. Sorry I am if I have done any ill to the brave nobleman, your leader. But I am very willing to make a good recompense for any ill I have done him. Set me free, and I will give thee twenty marks which I have in my poke [bag] here, as well as odd bits of silver which I have hidden among my rags.'

At these words the eyes of both Bat and Michael glistened. They had never had money in their lives before, and the chance of getting ten marks each – a fabulous sum to them – was too much for their loyalty to their master.

'Show us thy money, old rogue,' said Bat. 'I believe thou liest. But show it to us!'

They let the beggar loose, and he untied his cloak and laid it on the ground. The wind was blowing gustily now as the twilight was descending, and he stood with his back towards it. Then he took off two big bags which they supposed contained meal and meat and bread, and placed them on the ground before him.

Finally he took the great belt from his neck which supported another bag by his side.

'In this,' he said, 'I hide my money for greater safety. 'Tis full of old clouts with which to stuff my clothes against the bitter wind, and my shoon to keep my feet warm.'

As he was lifting the belt over his head Bat saw that immediately under his left arm was a little pouch slung by a thin strap. This seemed so artfully hidden that the outlaw thought that it must contain something of great value, and he almost suspected that the beggar, with all the clumsy preparations he was making, must be intending to keep the richest pelf from them.

He leaned forward, gripped the thin strap, and with a quick turn of his knife cut it, and the purse came away in his hand. The beggar tried to snatch it, but he was encumbered by the great bag he had in his hands. He struggled to seize it, but both outlaws held their knives against his breast.

'Cease, ugly knave!' cried Bat, 'or we'll let out thy life and have thy booty as well. And see thou playest no tricks, or 'twill go ill with thee.'

The beggar saw that Bat was becoming suspicious, and stayed his attempts to snatch at the purse which the outlaw had now crammed into the breast of his tunic. With black looks and glowering eyes the beggar rested his big bag on the ground, and bent to undo it, the outlaws also stooping to see that he played no tricks.

He pushed his hands into the bag, and then suddenly dashed in their faces a great cloud of meal. The two outlaws were blinded at once and retreated, howling imprecations and threats upon the beggar, though they could not see a whit where he was.

Next moment, however, they felt the weight of his pikestaff upon their heads, for he had quickly seized his stick, and with fierce blows attacked them. Bat, his eyes still smarting with the meal in them, felt the beggar's hand tear at his tunic, but he slashed it with his dagger, which he still held, and dimly he saw the beggar retreat for a moment with a gory hand, and make ready to bring his pole down on Bat's head with a deadly blow.

The outlaw knew then that the purse held something of value. He dashed away just as the staff fell with a blow that, had it alighted on his head, at which it was aimed, would have cracked his skull. Bat looked no more behind, but ran as fast as he could go, followed by his comrade. For some time the beggar followed them, but he was burdened by his heavy clothes, and soon gave up the chase.

It was now almost dark, and very ruefully the two outlaws made their way back to the camp.

'We are two great fools,' said Bat, 'and I will give my back willingly to Master Robin's scourge.'

'My bones ache so sorely,' said Michael, 'from the brute beast's cudgel that I crave no more basting for a time. I think I will hide me till I be a little less sore and master's anger hath cooled.'

'Flee then, ass,' said Bat, angry with himself and his companion, 'and starve in the woods as thou surely wouldst, or run back to thy manor, thou run serf, and be basted by thy lord's steward.'

But Michael was too fearful both of the lonely woods and of the strong arm of his lord's scourging man, and chose after all to go with Bat and take what punishment Robin chose to mete out to them.

They reached the camp just as the outlaws were about to sit to their supper, and Bat told everything with a frankness which showed how ashamed he was of himself. Robin heard them patiently, and then said:

'Hast thou still the purse which thou didst take from the rogue?'

Bat had thought no more of the purse, but feeling in his tunic found it was still there, and, drawing it forth, gave it to Robin. The outlaw bade Bat bring a torch to light him while he examined the contents of the purse.

First he drew out three rose nobles wrapped in a piece of rag, then a ring with a design engraved upon it, and lastly, from the bottom of the purse, he drew out a piece of parchment folded small. This he opened and smoothed out upon his knee, and read – slowly, 'tis true, since Robin, though he had been taught to read his Latin when a lad in his uncle's house at Locksley, had had little use for reading since he had reached man's estate.

Slowly he read the Latin words, and as he grasped their meaning his face became grim and hard. The words, translated, were these:

'To the worshipful Master Ralph Murdach, Sheriff of the Shires of Nottingham and Derby, these with greeting. Know ye that the Bearer of these, Richard Malbête, is he of whom I spoke to thee, who hath been commended to me by my friend, Sir Niger le Grym. He is a man of a bold and crafty mind, stinting no labour for good pay, and blinking not at any desperate deed: of a cunning mind, ready in wit and wile and ambuscades. But keep him from the wine, or he is of no avail. This is he who will aid thee to lay such plans and plots as will gain us that savage wolf's-head, Robin, and root out that growing brood of robbers who go with him. I hope to hear much good done in a little while.'

The letter was not signed, for in those days men did not sign their letters with their names, but with their seals, and this was sealed on a piece of blue wax with the signet of Sir Guy of Gisborne, which was a wild man's head, below which was a sword.

Robin looked at Bat and Michael, who, with heads bent, seemed filled with shame, and as if expecting some punishment.

'Ye are not fit to be outlaws,' he said sternly. 'Ye are but common reivers and cutters [cut-purses], and shouldst run to the town and lurk by taverns and rob men when they are full of wine and cannot help themselves. When I send ye to do a thing that thing thou shalt do, whatever temptation is placed before ye. But as ye are but fresh from the plough, I will overlook it this time. Go,' he ended in gentler tones, 'get your supper, and remember that I shall expect ye to be keen and good lads henceforth.'

Bat had never before known a kind word from a superior, and his heart was greatly moved at Robin's words.

'Master,' he said, bending on one knee, 'I have been a fool and I deserve the scourge. But if you will not give me that, give me some hard task to do, so that I may wipe the thought of my doltishness from my memory.'

'And let me go with him, good master,' said Michael, 'for I would serve you manfully.'

Robin looked at them for a moment, and smiled at their eagerness.

'Go get your suppers now, lads,' he said at length. 'It may be I will set thee a task ere long.'

When the meal was ended, Robin called Little John to his side and said:

'John, hath the proud potter of Wentbridge set out on his journey yet?'

'Ay, master,' replied John, 'he went through but yesterday, with horse and cart laden with his pots and pans. A brisk man is he, and as soon as the snows are gone he is not one to play Lob-lie-by-the-fire.'

Robin asked where the potter would be lodging that night, and John told him. Then Robin called Bat and Michael to him.

'Thou didst ask for a task,' he said, 'and I will give thee one. It may be a hard one, but 'tis one thou must do by hook or by crook. Thou knowest well the ways of the forest from here to Mansfield, for thou hast both fled from thy lord at Warsop. Now I will that ye go to Mansfield for me this night and seek the proud potter of Wentbridge. Tell him that I crave a fellowship of him. I wish him to let me have his clothes, his pots, his cart and his horse, for I will go to Nottingham market disguised.'

'This will we do right gladly, master,' said Bat. 'We will take our staves and our swords and bucklers and start on our way forthwith.'

Little John began to laugh heartily.

'Ye speak as if thou thinkest it will be no more than to say "bo!" to a goose,' he said. 'But if thou knowest not the proud potter of Wentbridge, that lacking he will soon make up in thee by the aid of his good quarterstaff.'

'I know, Little John,' said Bat with a laugh, 'that he hath given thee that lesson.'

'Ye say truly,' said honest John; 'evil befell me when I bade him pay toll to the outlaws last harvest time, for he gave me three strokes that I shall never forget.'

'All Sherwood heard of them,' said Bat; 'but the proud potter is a full courteous man, as I have heard tell. Nevertheless, whether he liketh it or not, he shall yield Master Robin his wish.'

'Then I will meet thee at the Forest Herne where the roads fork beyond Mansfield,' said Robin, 'an hour after dawn tomorrow.'

'We will fail not to be there with all that thou wishest,' replied Bat, and together he and Michael set out under the starlight on the way to Mansfield.

Next day, into the market-place of Nottingham drove a well-fed little brown pony, drawing a potter's cart, filled with pots and pans of good Wentbridge ware. The potter, a man stout of limb, plump of body, and red of face, wore a rusty brown tunic and cloak, patched in several places, and his hair seemed to have rare acquaintance with a comb. Robin indeed was well disguised.

Farmers, hucksters, merchants, and butchers were crowded in the market-place, some having already set up their booths or stalls, while others were busy unloading their carts or the panniers on their stout nags. The potter set his crocks beside his cart, after having given his horse oats and hay, and then began to cry his wares.

He had taken up a place not five steps from the door of the sheriff's house, which, built of wood and adorned with quaint designs, occupied a prominent place on one side of the

market-place; and the potter's eyes were constantly turned on
the door of the house, which now was open, and people having
business with the sheriff rode or walked up and entered.

'Good pots for sale!' cried the potter. 'Buy of my pots! Pots
and pans! Cheap and good today. Come, wives and maidens! Set
up your kitchens with my good ware!'

So lustily did he call that soon a crowd of country people who
had come to the market to buy stood about him and began to
chaffer with him. But he did not stay to bargain; he let each have
the pot or pan at the price they offered. The noise of the
cheapness of the pots soon got abroad, and very soon there were
but half a dozen pots left.

'He is an ass,' said one woman, 'and not a potter. He may
make good pots, but he knoweth naught of bargaining. He'll
never thrive in his trade.'

Robin called a serving-maid who came just then from the
sheriff's house, and begged her to go to the sheriff's wife, with
the best respects of the potter of Wentbridge, and ask whether
the dame would accept his remaining pots as a gift. In a few
minutes Dame Margaret herself came out.

'Gramercy for thy pots, good chapman,' she said, and she had
a merry eye, and spoke in a very friendly manner. 'I am full fain
to have them, for they be good pots and sound. When thou
comest to this town again, good potter, let me know of it and I
will buy of thy wares.'

'Madam,' said Robin, doffing his hat and bowing in a yeomanly
manner, 'thou shalt have of the best in my cart. I'll give thee no
cracked wares, nor any with flaws in them, by the Mass, but every
one shall ring with a true honest note when thou knock'st it.'

The sheriff's wife thought the potter was a full courteous and
bowerly man, and began to talk with him. Then a great bell rang
throughout the house, and the dame said:

'Come into the house if thou wilt, good chapman. Come sit
with me and the sheriff at the market table.'

This was what Robin desired. He thanked the dame, and was
led by her into the bower where her maidens sat at their sewing.
Just then the door opened and the sheriff came in. Robin looked
keenly at the man, whom he had only seen once before. He knew
that the sheriff, Ralph Murdach, was a rich cordwainer who had

bought his office from the grasping Bishop of Ely for a great price, and to repay himself he squeezed all he could out of the people.

'Look what this master potter hath given us,' said Dame Margaret, showing the pots on a stool beside her. 'Six pots of excellent ware, as good as any made in the Low Countries.'

The sheriff, a tall spare man of a sour and surly look glanced at Robin, who bowed to him.

'May the good chapman dine with us, sheriff?' asked the dame.

'He is welcome,' said the sheriff crossly, for he was hungry, and had just been outwitted, moreover, in a piece of business in the market-place. 'Let us wash and go to meat.'

They went into the hall of the house, where some twenty men were waiting for the sheriff and his lady. Some were officers and men of the sheriff, others were rich chapmen from the market.

When the sheriff and his wife took their seats at the high table, all the company sat down, Robin being shown a seat midway down the lower table. A spoon of horn was placed on the table where each sat, and a huge slice of bread, called a trencher! but for drinking purposes there was only one pewter cup between each two neighbours. Then the scullions from the sheriff's kitchen brought in roasted meat on silver skewers, and these being handed to the various guests, each would take his knife from his girdle, rub it on his leg to clean it a little, and then cut what he wanted from the skewer, laying his portion on the thick slice of bread. Then, using his fingers as a fork, the guest would eat his dinner, cutting off and eating pieces of his trencher with his meat, or saving it till all the meat was eaten.

On the rush-covered floor of the hall dogs and cats fought for the meat or bones thrown to them, and at the door beggars looked in, crying out for alms or broken meat. Sometimes a guest at the lower end of the table would throw a bone at a beggar, intending to hit him hard, but the beggar would deftly catch it and begin gnawing it. When, as sometimes happened, the beggars became too bold and ventured almost up to the table, a serving-man would dart among them with his staff and thump and kick them pell-mell out through the door.

Suddenly, a sturdy beggar came forthright into the hall and walked up among the sprawling dogs towards the high seat.

Instantly a serving-man dashed at him and caught hold of him to throw him out.

'I crave to speak with the sheriff,' cried the beggar, struggling with the man. 'I come with a message from a knight.'

But the serving-man would not listen, and began to drag the beggar to the door. The noise of their struggle drew the attention of all the guests, and Robin, looking up, recognised the beggar. It was Sir Guy's spy, whom he had met but yesterday, and who had outwitted the two outlaws whom Robin had sent to take him – Richard Malbête, or, as the English would call him, Illbeast.

The beggar fought fiercely to free himself, but the serving-man was a powerful fellow, and Malbête's struggles were in vain. Suddenly he cried:

'A boon, Sir Sheriff! I have a message from Sir Guy of Gisborne!'

The sheriff looked up and saw the struggling pair.

'Let the rogue speak,' he cried. The servitor ceased the struggle, but still held the beggar, and both men stood panting, while Richard Illbeast glared murderously at the man beside him.

'Speak, rogue, as his worship commands,' said the servitor, 'and cut not my throat with thy evil looks, thou scarecrow.'

'I come from Sir Guy of Gisborne,' said the beggar, turning to the high table, 'and I have a message for thy private ear, Sir Sheriff.'

The sheriff looked at him suspiciously.

'Tell me thy message, rogue,' said the sheriff harshly.

The beggar looked desperately round at the faces of the guests, all of which were turned to him. Some laughed at his hesitation, others sneered.

'He hath a private message for thy ear, sheriff,' cried one burly farmer with a laugh, 'and light fingers for thy jewels.'

'Or,' added another amid the laughter, 'a snickersnee [small dagger] for thyself.'

'Give some proof that you bear word from him you prate of,' commanded the sheriff angrily, 'or I will have thee beaten from the town.'

'A dozen cut-purses set upon me in the forest,' said Richard Illbeast, 'and robbed me of the purse in which was Sir Guy's letter to thee!'

A roar of laughter arose from all the guests. This was a likely tale, they thought, and japes and jokes were bandied about between them.

'What sent he thee to me for, knave?' shouted the sheriff. 'A likely tale thou tellest.'

'He sent me to aid thee in seizing that thieving outlaw, Robin Hood!' cried Richard Illbeast, beside himself with rage at the laughter and sneers of the guests, and losing his head in his anger.

Men roared and rocked with laughter as they heard him.

'Ha! ha! ha!' they cried. 'This is too good! The thief-taker spoiled by thieves! The fox mobbed by the hares he would catch!'

'Thrust him forth,' shouted the sheriff, red with rage. 'Beat the lying knave out of the town!'

'I am no knave!' cried Richard. 'I have fought in the Crusade! I have – '

But he was not suffered to say further what he had done: a dozen men-servants hurled themselves upon him. Next moment he was out in the market-place, his cloak was torn from his back and his bags ripped from him. Staves and sticks seemed to spring up on all sides, and amidst a hail of blows the wretch, whose heart was as cruel as any in that cruel time, and whose hands had been dyed by many a dreadful deed, was beaten mercilessly from the town along the road to the forest.

For a little time the guests at the sheriff's table continued to laugh over the beggar's joke, and then the talk turned on a contest which was to be held after dinner at the butts outside the town between the men who formed the officers of the sheriff, for a prize of forty shillings given by their master.

When the meal was ended, therefore, most of the guests betook themselves to the shooting, where the sheriff's men shot each in his turn. Robin, of course, was an eager onlooker at the sport; and he saw that not one of the sheriff's men could shoot nearer to the mark than by the length of half a long arrow.

'By the rood!' he said, 'though I be but a potter now I was a good bowman once, and e'en now I love the twang of my string and the flight of my arrow. Will you let a stranger try a shot or two, Sir Sheriff?'

'Ay, thou mayst try,' said the sheriff, 'for thou seemest a stalwart and strong fellow, though by thy red face thou seemest too fond of raising thy own pots to thy lips with good liquor in them.'

Robin laughed with the crowd at the joke thus made against him, and the sheriff commanded a yeoman to bring three bows. Robin chose one of these, the strongest and largest, and tried it with his hands.

'Thou'rt but poor wood, I fear,' he said, as he pushed the bow from him and pulled the string to his ear. 'It whineth with the strain already,' he went on, 'so weak is the gear.'

He picked out an arrow from the quiver of one of the sheriff's men and set it on the string. Then, pulling the string to its fullest extent, he let the bolt fly. Men looked keenly forward, and a shout from the chapmen went up when they saw that his bolt was within a foot of the mark, and nearer by six inches than any of the others.

'Shoot another round,' said the sheriff to his men, 'and let the potter shoot with thee.'

Another round was accordingly shot, and each man strove to better his previous record. But none got nearer than the potter had done, and when the last of them had shot his bolt they stood aside with glum faces, looking at the chapman as he stepped forward and notched his arrow upon the string.

He seemed to take less pains this time than before. The bolt snored away, and in the stillness with which the onlookers gazed, the thud, as it struck the broad target, two hundred yards away, was distinctly heard. For a moment men could not believe what their keen eyes told them. It had hit the centre of the bull's eye, or very close thereto.

The target-man, who stood near by the butt to report exactly on each shot, was seen to approach the target and then to start running excitedly towards the archers.

'It hath cleft the peg in three!' he shouted.

The peg was the piece of wood which stood in the very centre of the bull's eye. A great shout from all the bystanders rose up and shook the tassels on the tall poplars above their heads, and many of the chapmen gripped Robin by the hand or clapped him on the back.

'By the rood!' one said, 'thou'rt a fool of a chapman, but as a bowman thou'rt as good as any forester.'

'Or as Robin o' th' Hood himself, that king of archers, wolf's-head though he be,' said another, a jolly miller of the town.

The sheriff's men had black looks as they realised that they had been worsted by a plump potter, but the sheriff laughed at them, and coming to Robin, said:

'Potter, thou'rt a man indeed. Thou'rt worthy to bear a bow wherever thou mayest choose to go.'

'I ha' loved the bow from my toddling days,' said the potter, 'when I would shoot at small birds, ay, and bring them down. I ha' shot with many a good bowman, and in my cart I have a bow which I got from that rogue Robin Hood, with whom I ha' shot many a turn.'

'What!' said the sheriff, and his face was hard and his eyes full of suspicion. 'Thou hast shot with that false rascal? Knowest thou the place in the forest where he lurketh now, potter?'

'I think 'tis at Witch Wood,' said the potter easily. 'He hath wintered there, I ha' heard tell as I came down the road. But he stopped me last autumn and demanded toll of me. I told him I gave no toll on the king's highway except to the king, and I said I would e'en fight him with quarterstaff or shoot a round of twenty bolts with him to see if I were not a truer archer than he. And the rogue shot four rounds with me, and said that for my courtesy I should be free of the forest so long as my wheels went round.'

This was indeed the fact, and it was this friendship between Robin and the proud potter which had made Bat's task of obtaining the potter's clothes and gear for Robin an easy one.

'I would give a hundred pounds, potter,' said the sheriff gloomily, 'that the false outlaw stood by me!'

'Well,' said the potter, 'if thou wilt do after my rede [advice], Sir Sheriff, and go with me in the morning, thee and thy men, I will lead thee to a place where, as I ha' heard, the rascal hath dwelled through the winter.'

'By my faith,' said the sheriff, 'I will pay thee well if thou wilt do that. Thou art a brave man and a stalwart.'

'But I must e'en tell thee, sheriff,' said the potter, 'that thy pay must be good, for if Robin knows I ha' led the dogs to his hole, the wolf will rend me, and it would not be with a whole skin that I should go through the forest again.'

'Thou shalt be well paid,' said the sheriff, on my word as the king's officer.'

But he knew, and the potter knew also, that the sheriff's promise was of little worth, for the sheriff loved his money too well. But the potter made as if he was satisfied. When the sheriff offered him the forty shillings which was the prize for winning at the shooting, the potter refused it, and so won all the hearts of the sheriff's men.

'Nay, nay,' said the potter; 'let him that shot the best bolt among your men have it. It may be that 'twas by a flaw of wind that my arrow struck the peg.'

The potter had supper with the sheriff and his men, all of whom drank to the potter as a worthy comrade and a good fellow. A merry evening was passed, and then Robin was given a bed in a warm corner of the hall, and all retired to rest.

Next morning, before it was light, all were afoot again. A jug of ale was quaffed by each, and a manchet of rye bread eaten. Then the horses were brought round, together with the potter's pony and cart, and with the sheriff and ten of his men the potter led the way into the forest.

Deep into the heart of the greenwood the potter went, by lonely glades and narrow deer-drives by which not one of the sheriff's men had gone before. In many places where an ambuscade could easily be laid the sheriff and his men looked fearfully around them, and wondered whether they would win through that day with whole skins.

'Thou art sure thou knowest the way, potter?' said the sheriff more than once.

'Know the road, forsooth!' laughed the potter. 'I ha' not wended my way up and down Sherwood these twenty years without knowing my way. Belike you think I lead you into fearsome lonely places. But do you think a rascally wolf's-head will make his lair by the highway where every lurching dog can smell him out?'

'How dost thou know that the false outlaw hath wintered in the place you named?' asked the sheriff, with suspicion in his eyes.

'So the peasants tell me in the villages I have passed on my way from Wentbridge,' replied the potter. 'I will take thee to within half a mile of the Witch Wood, and then thou must make thy own plans for talking the rogue.'

'What manner of place is Witch Wood?' asked the sheriff.

' 'Tis a fearsome place, as I ha' heard tell,' said the potter. ' 'Tis the haunt of a dreadful witch, and is filled with dead men's bones. Outside 'tis fresh and fair with trees, but there are caves and cliffs within, where the witch and her evil spirits dwell among the grisly bones, and the churls say that Robin o' th' Hood is close kin to her, and that while he is in the greenwood he is within her protection and naught can harm him.'

'How so?' asked the sheriff, and the ten men glanced fearfully around and closed up together.

'They say that she is the spirit of the forest, and that by her secret power she can slay any man who comes beneath the trees, or lock him up alive in a living trunk of a tree, or cast him into a wizard's sleep.'

'What be those things there?' asked the sheriff, pointing in front of him. They had now come to an opening in the forest, where the trees gave way to a piece of open rising ground covered with low bushes. On a ridge in its midst was a great oak, its broad limbs covering a great space of ground, and beneath its shade were three tall upright stones, leaning towards each other as if they whispered.

' 'Tis the Three Stane Rigg,' said the potter. 'Men say that they be great grey stones as thou seest by daylight, but when owls hoot and the night wind stirs in the bushes, they turn into witch hags which ride about like the wind, doing the bidding of the great witch of the forest – bringing murrain or plague, cursing the standing corn, or doing other ill to men.'

Men looked in each other's eyes, and then turned their heads swiftly away, for they were half ashamed to see the fear in them, and to know that dread was in their own. All men in those days believed in wizards and witches, even the king and his wisest statesmen.

'I think,' said the sheriff gruffly, 'thou shouldst have told us these things ere we set out, and I would have brought a priest with us. As it is – '

Shrieks of eldritch laughter rang out in the dark trees beside them. So sudden and so fearful were the cries, that the horses stopped and trembled as they stood, while their riders crossed themselves and looked peeringly into the gloom of the forest. 'Let us ride back!' cried some, while one or two turned their horses in the narrow path and began to retreat.

Again the mad laughter rang out. It seemed to come from all parts of the dark earthy wood about them. More of the men put spurs to their horses, and in spite of the cries of the sheriff bidding them to stay, all were soon riding helter-skelter away from the spot.

The potter, standing up in his cart, and the sheriff, dark of look, listened as the sound of the thudding hooves became fainter and fainter in the distance.

'The craven dolts!' cried the sheriff, grinding his teeth. Yet, for all his bravery, he himself was afraid, and kept looking this way and that into the trees.

Suddenly the potter cracked his whip. Instantly the clear notes of a horn sounded away in the open glade, and next moment there came some twenty men in brown, who seemed to rise from the ground and to issue from the trunks of the trees. Some even dropped to the ground from boughs just above where the sheriff stood.

'How now, master potter,' said one tall fellow, bearded and bare-headed, 'how have you fared in Nottingham? Have you sold your ware?'

'Ay, by my troth,' said the potter. I have sold all, and got a great price for it. Look you, Little John, I have brought the sheriff himself for it all.'

'By my faith, master, he is welcome,' cried Little John, and gave a great hearty laugh, which was echoed by all the outlaws standing around when they saw the angry wonder on the sheriff's face.

'Thou false rogue!' cried he, and his face beneath his steel cap went red with shame and chagrin. 'If I had but known who thou wert!'

'I thank good Mary thou didst not,' said Robin, taking off the potter's cloak and then the tunic, which had been stuffed with rags to make him look the stouter.

' 'Tis a fearsome place, as I ha' heard tell'

'But now that thou art here, sheriff, thou shalt dine with us off the king's fat deer. And then, to pay thy toll, thou shalt leave thy horse and thy armour and other gear with me.'

And thus was it done. The sheriff, willy-nilly, had to dine off a steak cut from a prime buck, and washed down his meal with good sack, and having been hungry, he felt the better for it.

Then, when he had left his horse and all his arms with Robin Hood, and was preparing to return home on foot, the outlaw ordered a palfrey to be led forward, and bade the sheriff mount it.

'Wend thy way home, sheriff,' he said, 'and greet thy wife from me. Thy dame is as courteous and kind as thou art sour and gruff. That palfrey is a present from me to thy lady wife, and I trust that she will think kindly of the potter, though I cannot hope that thou thyself wilt think well of me.'

Without a word the sheriff departed. He waited till it was dark ere he rode up to the gate of Nottingham and demanded to be let in. The gateman wondered at the sheriff's strange return, riding on a lady's palfrey, without so much as a weapon in his belt or a steel cap on his head. The tale of the shamefaced men who had returned earlier had been wormed out of them by the wondering citizens, and the sheriff, hoping to creep home unobserved, was disagreeably surprised to find the streets full of gaping people. To all their questions he returned cross answers, but as he alighted at his own door he heard a laugh begin to arise, in cackling bursts, among the crowd before his house, and when he was inside he heard the full roar of laughter rise from a thousand throats.

Next day there was never a man so full of anger as Sheriff Murdach. The whole town was agrin, from the proud constable of the castle with his hundred knights, to the little horseboys in the stables – all smiled to think how the sheriff had gone with his posse to capture the outlaw Robin, led by a false potter who was the rogue Robin himself, and had been captured and spoiled.

CHAPTER FOUR

How Robin Hood Met Father Tuck

It was full summer again, and life was very pleasant in the greenwood. However fiercely the sun burned in the open fields where the poor serfs swinked and sweated, it was always cool and shady in the woods, and under the trees the gentle breezes blew, and the flies, swinging to and fro in their perpetual dance, kept up a soft drone that seemed to invite one to slumber.

Many a poor villein as he bent over the digging or the reaping in the hot sun, thought of the cool shadows in the shaws, and raising his aching back would look far away to the dark line of tossing trees and think of the men who had escaped from serfdom, and now were ranging there free from toil and tax and hard usage. Many such wondered whether they, too, could ever be so bold as to break away from the habits and routine of years, and put themselves outside the law, and rob their lords of a valuable piece of farming stock, which was the true description of a villein in the eyes of the law of those hard times.

For many miles up and down the country bordering on the broad forest lands, the fame of Robin Hood and his men had spread. Wandering pedlars, jugglers, and beggars told tales of his daring deeds, and minstrels already, when they found a knot-of villeins in a village alehouse, would compose rough rhymes about him – how he did no evil to poor men, but took from rich, proud prelates, merchants, and knights.

Then, when times were hard, when the labours of sowing, reaping, or digging imposed upon the poor villeins seemed beyond all bearing, as they were already beyond all custom, one or two in a manor would find that their thoughts shaped for freedom, and taking the opportunity they would creep away from their village of little mean hovels and run to the greenwood.

It was thus that Robin Hood's band, which at first had numbered but twenty, had gradually grown until the runaway villeins in it numbered thirty-five, though he had only taken to the forest a full year. But there was another way in which Robin obtained good men of their hands. Wherever he heard of a man who was a good bowman, or one who could wield the quarterstaff well, or was a skilful swordsman, he would go and seek this man out and challenge him to fight.

Most times Robin conquered, but several times he came across men who were more skilful than he, or more lucky in their strokes. But, whatever the result, Robin's manliness and courtesy generally won them to become his comrades, and to join him and his band under the greenwood tree.

In this way he won over that valiant pinder or pound-keeper, Sim of Wakefield, with whom, as says the song which was made by Jocelyn the minstrel, he fought –

A summer's day so long,
Till that their swords on their broad bucklers
Were broke almost into their hands,

when Robin had to confess that he had had enough, and craved of the pinder that he would join him in the greenwood. The pinder was quite willing, but being a man of honesty, he said that he had been elected by his fellow villeins to the office of pound-keeper until next Michaelmas, when he would receive his fee for his work.

'Then, good Robin,' said he, as he shook hands with the outlaw, 'I'll take my blue blade all in my hand and plod to the greenwood with thee.'

In the same way Robin fought a stout battle with Arthur-a-Bland of Nottingham, who was a famous man with the quarterstaff. In this case it was a drawn fight, and they agreed to be friends, and Arthur joined the band of outlaws. He was a cousin of Little John's, and the two kinsmen greeted each other right joyfully when they met. Ever afterwards they were almost inseparable in all their exploits, and so tall were they and skilful with staff and bow, that it was reckoned that together they were the equal of ten men.

When Robin Hood first went to the greenwood, he found

there were many bands of robbers in it – men who had been made outlaws for crimes of murder or robbery; and these had recruited their bands from runaway serfs and poor townsmen and other masterless men who were not really vicious themselves, but had had to seek the woods to escape from punishment.

Robin had had a very short way with these marauding bands of robbers, who made no distinction between rich and poor, but would as soon rob a poor serf of his last piece of salted pork or bag of meal as a rich priest of his purse of gold. Whenever Robin learned of the hiding-place of a band such as these, he would go there secretly with his men, and surprise them before they could lay hand to weapon. Then, while everyone was covered by a yard-long arrow, he would say:

'I am Robin Hood, whom ye know, and I give ye this choice. Cease your evil pilferings, wherein ye respect neither the poor nor the needy, and join my band and take our oath, or fight with me to the death, and put the choice to the ordeal by combat.'

Generally the robbers would give in, and joined Robin's band, taking the oath which all had sworn – to do harm to no poor man, honest yeoman, or courteous knight or squire, and to do no ill to any woman or any company which included a woman; but to help the poor and needy, and succour them whenever it was in their power. One or two of the robber leaders, however, had defied Robin, and had fought with him. Three of these he had slain, while four others had yielded to him and became his men.

By all these means his band, that had first been no more than twenty, now numbered fifty-five. All were dressed in Lincoln green while the leaves were on the trees, but when the leaves began to turn russet and to fall, and the forest to be filled with the sombre light of autumn, all the men assumed their tunics, hoods, and hose of brown, or long-hooded capotes of the same colour, so that they passed among the trees unseen by many of the travellers from whom they were about to take toll.

One day in July Robin and many of his band were passing the time in their caves in Barnisdale. Outside all was wet and stormy, for the rain beat down like great grey spears. Every leaf dripped like a spout, the forest ways were sodden, and the dark mist hung sombrely in the hollows and moved but slowly down the long forest drives. None that could help themselves were out on the highroads, which were no more than rivers of mud, but every beggar, pedlar, quack-doctor, pilgrim, juggler, or other traveller had fled to the village alehouse, or to the inn that at rare places could be found at the side of the highway.

In their caves on Elfwood Scar, Robin and his band sat dry and cosy, telling tales to each other, or listening to the travels of a pilgrim whom Will Scarlet had found that morning with a swollen foot, limping on his way. Gilbert of the White Hand had washed the wound and salved it, and now for payment the grateful pilgrim, a brown-faced, simple man, told of his marvellous experiences and the sights which he had seen on the long road to Rome, and the terrible days spent on the sea from Venice to Jaffa.

There were other wayfarers with them. One was a quack-doctor, a merry, wizened rogue, with a wise look which he often forgot to wear in the midst of his solemn talk. He had a much-worn velvet cloak trimmed with fur which had almost worn off, and on his hat were cabalistic signs which he asserted only the very wisest of men could read, including himself. He had with him, he asserted, a little of the very elixir which had given Hercules his godlike strength, and some of the powder which had made Helen of Troy so beautiful.

' 'Tis a marvel thou takest not some of Hercules his liquor thyself,' said Little John, laughing, 'for thy wizened frame was no good to thee when that great rogue at the Goose Fair at Nottingham downed thee with his fist for saying thy salve would cure his red nose.'

'I need not strength of arm,' said the quack; his little black eyes lit up merrily. 'Confess, now, thou big man, did not my tongue scorch him up? Did not my talk cause the sheriff's man to hustle the big fellow away with great speed! Why do I need strength of limb when I have that which is greater than the strongest thews – ' he tapped his forehead ' – the brains that can outwit brute strength?'

'Yet I doubt if thy wit availed thee much,' said a voice in a far corner of the cave, 'when thou camest across the curtal hermit of Fountains Dale. Tell this good company what befell thee that day.'

The little quack's face darkened angrily, whereat the speaker, a pale-faced man in pilgrim's robes, laughed, but not with ill-nature.

'Tell us the tale, doctor!' cried the outlaws, enjoying the quack's discomfiture, while others besought the pilgrim to relate it. But to all their appeals the quack turned a deaf ear, his face red with anger, and his mouth filled with muttered curses on the loose tongue of the pilgrim-rogue and on the curtal hermit.

'Tell us, good pilgrim,' commanded Little John, whereat the quack snapped out:

'That rogue is no pilgrim! I know the gallows face of him. He is a run thrall of the abbot of Newstead, and I could get a mark for my pains if I put the abbot's bailiff on his track.'

All looked at the pilgrim. He was big of body and limbs, but by his face he looked as if he had suffered some illness.

'Ay, he speaks truth,' said the man; 'I am Nicholas, cottar and smith of my lord, the abbot of Newstead. But,' and his voice became hard and resonant, 'I will not be taken back alive to the serfdom in which I served until yesterday's blessed morn. I seek only to work in freedom under a master who will give me due wage for good work done. I can do any smith's work well and honestly – I can make and mend ploughs, rivet wheels and make harrows, and I have even made swords of no mean workmanship. But because I fell ill and could not work, my lord's bailiff thrust my poor mother out of her holding and her land, ay, with blows and evil words he thrust her out, and while I was on my pallet of straw too weak to move, they bore me out to the wayside, and the sturdy villein whom they put in our place jeered at us with evil words. And thus against all right and custom were we cast out!'

'A foul deed, by the Virgin!' cried Robin. 'But, poor lad, thou canst not expect aught else of priests and prelates and their servants. Their hearts are but stones. And so thou hast run. 'Twas well done. But what of thy mother?'

'She is out of it all, thanks be to God,' said Nicholas solemnly, 'and under the turf of the churchyard, where no lord's bailiff can harm her more.'

'Lad, if thou wantest work in freedom,' said Robin, 'stay with me and thou shalt have it, and thy due wage every Michaelmas. Many's the brown bill or sword blade we want mended. Wilt thou come with us?'

'Ay, master, willingly,' said Nicholas. Coming forward, he put his hand in Robin's, and they grasped each other's hands in sign of agreement. Then the smith took off his palmer's robe, and his great frame in rough jerkin and hose seemed thin and worn.

'Thou'rt fallen away a bit, lad,' said Robin with a smile, 'but I can see good thews are there, and in a month our forest air, our cream and venison and good ale will fill thee out till I can see thee o'ertopping Little John here.'

Little John smiled good-naturedly, and nodded in friendly wise to the new recruit.

'But now, tell us, good Nick,' said Robin, 'who is this hermit of Fountains Dale, and how served he our friend here, Peter the Doctor?'

'Oh,' said Nick with a smile, 'I meant no ill-will to Peter. Often hath his pills cured our villeins when they ate too much pork, and my mother – rest her soul – said that naught under the sun was like his lectuary of Saint Evremond.'

'Thou hearest, good folks!' cried the little quack, restored to good-humour by the smith's friendly speech. 'I deserve well of all my patients, but – ' and his eyes flashed ' – that great swineheaded oaf of a hermit monk – Tuck by name, and would that I could tuck him in the deepest, darkest hole in Windleswisp Marsh! – that great ox-brained man beguiled me into telling him of all my good specifics. With his eyes as wide and soft as a cow's he looked as innocent as a mawkin [maiden], and asked me this and that about the cures which I had made, and ever he seemed the more to marvel and to gape at my wisdom and my power. The porcine serpent! He did but spin his web the closer about me to my own undoing and destruction. When I had told him all, and was hopeful that he would buy a phial of serpent's oil of Jasper – a sure and certain specific, my good freemen, against ague and stiffness – for he said the winter rains did begin to rust his joints a little, the vile rogue did seize me by the neck and take my box of medicaments. Then he tied my limbs to the tree outside his vile abode, and from my store he took my most precious medicines, sovereign waters and lectuaries, and did force me to swallow them all. Ugh, the splay-footed limb of Satan! He said that I was too unselfish – that I gave all away and obtained none of the blessings myself, and that when he had done with me I should be as strong and as big as Hercules, as fair as Venus, as wise as Solomon, as handsome as Paris, and as subtle as Ulysses. Then, too, did he stick hot plasters upon my body, making me to suffer great pain and travail. In a word, if it had not been that I always keep the most potent and valuable of my medicines in a secret purse, I should not only have been killed but ruined, for – '

Further words were drowned by the burst of uncontrollable laughter which greeted his unconscious 'bull'.

He was plied with many questions as to the effects which this commingling of the whole of his potent wares had had upon him, to all of which the little quack replied in good humour.

'But now tell us,' said Robin Hood, 'who is this hermit who treated thee to so complete a course of thy own medicines? Where doth he dwell?'

'I will tell thee,' replied Peter the quack. 'I have heard it said of thee that since thou hast come to the greenwood thou dost allow no one to rob and reive and fight and oppress poor folks. Well, this runaway priest is one who doth not own thee master. He is a man who shoots the king's own deer, if it were known, with a great longbow; he is such a hand with the quarterstaff that he hath knocked down robbers as great as himself. He liveth a wicked and luxurious life. He hath great dogs to defend him, who I believe are but shapes of evil fiends. He is a great spoiler of men, and would as lief fight thee, Robin Hood, as a lesser man.'

'This is not the truth which Peter saith,' said Nick the Smith angrily. 'Father Tuck is no false hermit; he liveth not a wicked life as other false hermits do. He ever comes and solaces the poor in our village, and any good he can do if one is sick, that he doth for no payment. He is great of limb, and can fight well with the bow, the staff, or the sword, but he is no robber. He is humble and kind in heart, but he can be as fierce as a lion to any that would do ill to a poor man or woman. Evil wandering knights have sometimes striven to thrust him from his hold, but with the aid of his great ban-dogs and his own strong arms he hath so prevailed that neither knight nor other lord or robber hath made him yield.'

'He is a strong and a masterless rogue, this curtal monk,' repeated Peter, 'a man that will not confess that anyone is his better. 'Tis said that he was thrust forth from the brotherhood of Fountains Abbey to the north by reason of his evil and tumultuous living, and hath come into this forest to hide. If thou art truly master of the greenwood, Sir Robin,' he said, 'thou hadst best look to this proud and truculent hermit and cut his comb for him.'

Little more was said about the hermit then, and in a little while, when the rain had ceased and the sun shone out, making every leaf dazzle as if hung with a priceless pearl, the wayfarers went on the road again, and the outlaws separated to their various tasks. Some made arrows and bows, others cut cloth for new tunics, or stitched up hose which had been torn by brambles. Others, again, took up their position among the trees along the highroad to watch for a rich convoy of the Bishop of York which they heard was on its way from Kirkstall to Ollerton, for they were lacking many good things both of food and clothing and other gear, which they could only replenish from some rich prelate's store.

It was some days before Robin found an opportunity of faring south to seek the hermit of whom Peter and the runaway workman had spoken. The boldness and independence of the hermit, Father Tuck, had excited his curiosity, and Robin was eager to put the skill of the fellow to the test. He therefore gave the word to Little John and some dozen or so of the others to follow him in the space of an hour, and then betook his way towards Newstead Abbey, near where he had learned was the 'hold' or strong dwelling-place of Father Tuck.

To make greater speed Robin was mounted, and, moreover, he wore his thick jerkin of tanned leather. A cap of steel was on his head, and at his side were sword and buckler. Robin never moved a step without his good yew-bow, and this was slung across his body, while a sheaf of arrows in a loose quiver hung from his girdle.

The sun was nearly overhead when Robin set out, and he travelled for some hours through the fair forest roads before he began to approach the neighbourhood of the curtal monk's abode. At length he reached the silent solitudes of Lindhurst Wood. As he was riding through the trees a sound made him check his horse and listen. He looked about him, peering under the giant branches flung out by the grey monarchs of the forest. All about him they stood, trunk after trunk, stretching out their gnarled and knotted arms, hung with grey moss like giant beards. In the green twilight he could see nothing moving, yet he felt conscious that something watched him. He turned his horse aside into a dim alley which seemed to lead to an opening among the trees. His horse's feet sank noiselessly into a depth of moss and leaves, the growth of ages. He reached the opening among the great grey trees, and whether it was a flicker of waving leaves or the form of a skulking wolf he was not sure, but he believed that away in the dark under the trees to his left, something had passed, as silent as a shadow, as swift as a spirit.

He turned back upon his proper path, looking keenly this way and that. At length he came to where the trees grew less thickly, and he knew that he was approaching the stream near which the hermit's hold was situated. Dismounting, he tied his horse to a tree and then gave a long, low bird's note. Twice he had to give this before a similar note answered him from a place away to the right of him. He waited a few moments, and then a squirrel churred in the thick leaves of the oak above his head. Without turning to look, Robin said:

'Sawest thou, Ket, anyone in the wood but now as I came down by the Eldritch Oaks?'

For a moment there was silence, then from the leaves above Ket answered:

'Naught but a charcoal-burner's lad, belike.'

'Art sure 'twas not someone that spied on me?'

'Nay, sure am I 'twas no one that meant thee hurt.'

This was not a direct reply, and for a moment Robin hesitated. But he did not know any reason for thinking that anyone knew of his presence in Lindurst, and therefore he questioned Ket no more.

'Keep thy eye on my horse, Ket,' said Robin; and began to walk towards the stream. Soon the trees opened out, and he saw the water gleaming in the sunlight. Looking up and down, he saw where a small low house stood beside the stream to the left. It was made of thick balks of timber, old and black with age. A wide, deep moat surrounded it on three sides, and before a low-browed door stretched a wide plank which was the means by which the inmate of the house gained the land. This plank had chains fixed to it whereby it could be raised up, thus effectually cutting off the dwelling from attack or assault by all who had not boats.

'A snug hermit's hold, by my troth,' said Robin; 'more like the dwelling of some forest freebooter than the cell of an austere monk who whips his thin body by day, and fasts and prays all night. Where, now, is the humble hermit himself?'

He looked more closely by the trees, and saw where a little path came down through the trees to the water as if to a ford, and on the opposite bank he saw where it issued again from the stream and went like a tunnel through the trees that there came down to the water's edge. Sitting, as if in meditation, by a tree beside the path on this side of the stream was a man in the rough homespun garb of a monk. He seemed big and broad of body, and his arms were thick and strong.

'A sturdy monk, in faith!' exclaimed Robin. 'He seems deep in thought just now, as if the holy man were meditating on his sins. By the rood, but I will test his humility at the point of a good clothyard arrow!'

Robin silently approached the monk, who seemed sunk in thought or slumber. Drawing an arrow, and notching it upon the string of his longbow, Robin advanced and said:

'Ho, there, holy man, I have business t'other side of the stream. Up and take me on thy broad back, lest I wet my feet.'

The big monk stirred slowly, lifted his face, and looked stolidly at Robin for a moment as if he hardly understood what was said. Robin laughed at the simple look upon his face.

'Up, oaf,' he cried; 'ferry me over the stream on thy lazy back, or this arrow shall tickle thy ribs!'

Without a word the monk rose, and bent his back before Robin, who got upon it. Then slowly the monk stepped into the stream and walked as slowly across the paved ford till he came to the other side. He paused for a moment there as if to take breath. Then he stepped up to the bank, and Robin prepared to leap off. But next moment he felt his left leg seized in an iron grip, while on his right side he received a great blow on the ribs. He was swung round, and fell backwards upon the bank, and the monk, pressing him down with one knee, placed great fingers upon his throat, and said:

Robin carries Father Tuck over the stream

'Now, my fine fellow, carry me back again to the place whence I came, or thou shalt suffer for it.'

Robin was full of rage at his own trick being turned upon him in this way, and tried to snatch at his dagger, but the monk caught his wrist and twisted it in a grasp so powerful that Robin knew that in strength, at least, the monk was his master.

'Take thy beating quietly, lad,' said the monk, with a slow smile. 'Thou'rt a saucy one, but thou hast not reached thy full strength yet. Now, then, up with thee and carry me back.'

The monk released him, and Robin, in spite of his rage, wondered at this. Why had he not beaten him senseless, or even slain him, when he had him in his power? Most other men would have done this, and none would have blamed them. Already in his heart Robin regretted that he had treated the monk with so high a hand. He saw now that it was in his ignorance that he had scorned Father Tuck.

Without a word, therefore, he bent his back, and the monk slowly straddled upon it and clasped his hands round Robin's neck, not tightly, but just enough to make him understand that if he tried to play another trick the monk was ready for him. When he reached the middle of the stream, where it ran most deeply and swiftly, Robin would greatly have liked to have tipped the monk in the water; but as the odds were too much against him he went on.

When he was nearing the bank he suddenly heard a laugh come from the hermit's hold, and looking up he saw at a little window hole which looked upon the stream the face of a lady. It had a wimple about it, and she was very pretty. As he looked up the face swiftly disappeared. He did not know who the lady might be, but the thought that he was made to appear so foolish in her eyes made Robin almost mad with rage. He reached the bank, and when the monk had got from his back he turned to him and said:

'This is not the last thou shalt see of me, thou false hermit and strong knave. The next time we meet thou shalt have a shaft in thy great carcass.'

'Come when thou likest,' said the monk with a jolly laugh. 'I have ever a venison pasty and a bottle or two of Malvoisie for good friends. As to thy bow shafts, keep them for the king's deer, my pretty man. Pay good heed to thy wits, young sir, and try not thy jokes on men until thou knowest they go beyond thy strength or not.'

So enraged was Robin at the monk's saucy answer that next moment he had dashed at him, and in an instant they were struggling fiercely, each striving to throw the other into the stream. The end of it was that both slipped on the soft bank, and both, still clutching each other, rolled into the stream.

They crawled out quickly, and Robin, still blinded with rage, ran to his bow and arrows, which he had dropped on the bank, and notching a bolt, he turned and looked for the monk The latter had disappeared, but next moment he came from behind a tree with a buckler in one hand and a sword in the other, while on his head was a steel cap. Robin drew the string to his ear, and the arrow twanged as it sped from the bow. He looked to see it pierce the great body of his enemy, but instead, with a laugh, the monk caught it on his buckler, and it glanced off and stuck in the ground, where it stood and shook for a moment like a strange stiff kind of plant moved by the wind.

Three more arrows Robin shot at him, but each was deftly caught by the monk upon his shield, and the outlaw was in a rage to see that by no means could he get the better of this redoubtable monk.

'Shoot on, my pretty fellow,' cried the monk. 'If you wish to stand shooting all day I'll be thy mark, if it gives thee joy to waste thy arrows.'

'I have but to blow my horn,' returned Robin angrily, 'and I should have those beside me who should stick so many arrows in thy carcass that thou wouldst look like a dead hedgehog.'

'And I, thou braggart,' said the monk, 'have but to give three whistles upon my fingers to have thee torn to pieces by my dogs.'

As the monk spoke, Robin was aware of a noise in the trees beside him. He looked, and saw a slim youth running towards him, with a hood round his head so that his face was almost concealed, a bow slung on his back, and a staff in his hand. Robin thought the youth was about to attack him, and therefore brought his buckler up and drew his sword. At the same time came other sounds from the woods as of men dashing through the undergrowth. There came a shrill whistle, and then Robin heard a scream as of an animal or bird in the talons of a hawk.

Robin recognised it at once as the danger-signal of Ket the Trow, and knew that enemies were upon him.

He thought the slim youth who had paused for a moment at the sound of the whistle was some spy of Guy of Gisborne's who was leading an ambush upon him. Robin lifted his sword and rushed upon the youth. He was but the space of a yard from the other, and noticed how he stood panting and spent as with running. The youth raised his head, and Robin caught a glimpse of the face in the shadow of the hood.

'Marian!' he cried, for it was his sweetheart. 'What is this? What – '

'Robin,' she panted, and her face flushed as she looked at him, and laid one fair hand on his arm, 'sound thy horn for thy men, or thou art lost indeed.'

Instantly she turned and ran to the monk and said some rapid words to him. The notes of Robin's horn rang out clear and shrill, and reverberated through the dim leafy alleys. Almost at the same moment the monk raised two fingers, and putting them in his mouth, blew so shrill a whistle as almost to split the ear. As he did so, men came running from the trees, and Robin knew them for the men-at-arms of the abbot of St Mary's.

'Quick, Marian!' cried Robin, 'get thee to the monk's hold. There is still time!'

Swiftly Robin looked about for some point of vantage whence he could defend himself, and saw a spit of land where it jutted into the stream. He notched an arrow on his bowstring, shot the first man down, then ran to the spit, and notched another arrow as he ran. Marian and the monk reached it as soon as he.

'Nay, nay,' repeated Robin, 'go ye across the bridge to the monk's hold. If my fellows are not near 'twill go hard with me, and I would not have thee harmed, sweetheart.' He notched a third arrow.

'Nay, Robin,' cried Marian. 'I can bend a bow, as thou well knowest, and the good monk Tuck will aid us. Look, here are the dogs!'

The men-at-arms by this time were but some ten yards away, and already Robin had sent three arrows among them, wounding two and killing one man.

Black Hugo was leading them, and cried:

'Lads, we must get together and rush him. If he can hold us at distance with his arrows we shall all be shot down.'

Even as he spoke, the long snore of an arrow suddenly stopped, and the man beside him fell with the clothyard wand sticking through his throat. The men began to egg each other on, but the great arrows made them wary. While they hesitated, suddenly they heard a baying, and before they were aware of the cause ten great ban-dogs had leaped upon them. Fierce brutes they were, of the size of bloodhounds, with great collars about their necks in which were set keen spikes.

The men fought blindly with sword and dagger against these strange and terrible foes. Suddenly a shrill whistle sounded, a giant man in monk's form, bearing a buckler, came towards them, crying upon the dogs by name to cease. Five hounds lay wounded or dead, but the others at the sound of their master's voice ceased and drew back, licking their wounds

Black Hugo wiped the sweat from his swarthy face, and looked about him, and his face went suddenly white. Across the lea or open field, which was on the side of the monk's hold, were the forms of a score of men in green running towards them as fast as they could, and each was notching an arrow to his bow even as he ran.

'Save thyselves!' cried Black Hugo; 'here come more rogues than we can face.'

The men gave a swift look across the lea, and then, turning, they dashed for the cover of the trees. The outlaws paused for a moment, and a flight of arrows droned through the air, cutting the fans of leaves, and disappearing into the bushes. Three were slain by these bolts, but the others rushed madly on in the green twilight of the old trees, scattering as they ran, to make pursuit more difficult.

When the last of the outlaws had disappeared after the fleeing men-at-arms, Robin turned to Marian, who, with heightened colour and quick breath, tried to forestall the anger which she feared her lover would have against her.

'Be not angry with me, Robin,' she said, 'but I have feared for thee so much that I had to come to the greenwood to learn how it fared with thee. You know how many a time and often we have shot and hunted on Locksley Chase when we were boy and girl together. Why should I not do that now?'

'Why shouldst thou not, sweetheart?' answered Robin. 'Because I am an outlaw, and thou art a lording's daughter. My head is for anyone to take who may, and those who aid me run the same danger. But tell me, Marian, how long is it since thou hast donned the clothes that make thee so sweet-looking a lad, and how dost thou know this rascal monk?'

'He is no rascal, Robin, but a good man,' answered Marian. 'He is Sir Richard at Lee's good friend, and hath ever spoken well of thee, and cheered me greatly when I have sorrowed for thee. And when at last I resolved to don these clothes and come to the greenwood to learn, if I might, how thou didst live, I spoke to Father Tuck, and he promised to aid me. For he hath friends throughout the forest, and thus I got to know thy friends the trolls. And I watched thee in the forest as thou didst ride hither, and Ket knew I was there.'

While Marian had been talking, she had led Robin across the drawbridge, and they were now in the dwelling of the monk. It was a room which partook of the character of kitchen, oratory, and hall. A crucifix with a praying-stool before it stood in one corner; on another wall were coats of chain-mail, steel headpieces, a double-handed sword, two or three bright bills, and a sheaf of arrows, together with a great bow. Along a third wall were ranged rough shelves on which were bags of meal and two or three pieces of salted ham or venison. In the centre of the room was a table.

As they entered, a lady rose from a seat, and Marian ran to her with hands outstretched, and drew her impulsively forward.

'Alice, this is my Robin,' she said.

Robin recognised the lady's face. She it was who had seen him carrying the monk across the river, and had laughed at him. The lady had a bright and merry face, and looked at him with a twinkle in her eye. Then she put forth her hand and said:

'So you are that bold outlaw whose head Sir Ranulf de Greasby swears every night ere he goes tipsy to bed shall yet be hung on the walls of Hagthorn Castle.'

She gave so merry a laugh, and her eyes spoke her admiration of the handsome outlaw so eloquently, that Robin's heart was completely won. He bent his knee and kissed the lady's hand very gallantly.

'I am Robert or Robin Hood, as men call me,' he said, 'and I think you must be Mistress Alice de Beauforest, whom Alan-a-Dale loves so well.'

The lady's face flushed for a moment and then went pale, and a look of pain came into her eyes. She turned away, and Marian went to her with a tender look and put her arm about her neck.

Just then the monk entered. 'By my faith,' he said, 'but thou'rt a wasteful fellow to aid. Four of my poor hounds have barked their last bark and gnawed their last bone on thy account.'

'Good hermit,' said Robin, going up to him with outstretched hand, 'I hear thou hast been a true friend to the lady I love best in the world, and I would that thou wert my friend also.'

'Robin, lad,' replied Father Tuck with a smile on his broad good-humoured face, 'I ha' been thy well-wisher since I heard how thou didst help burn Sir Guy's house about his ears. I think we are not enemies at heart, lad, you and I. Since I ha' kept this hold these seven years with the help of my good friend, Sir Richard at Lee, I ha' never heard of a man whose doings I liked to hear o' so well as thine. How thou didst put the surly sheriff o' Nottingham to scorn! I never laughed so much since the day I trundled my holy brothers into the fish-stews at Fountains Abbey and got my wicked self expelled for the deed!'

The monk caught Robin's hand and gave it a squeeze that would have crushed a weak man's bones. But Robin's grip was almost as strong, and Father Tuck smiled admiringly.

Thereafter there was much talk between them all. Marian told how Father Tuck had been her guide through the forest ways during the summer, teaching her woodcraft, and giving her much knowledge of herbs and cures. She told him that she had also made friends with Ket the Trow and Hob o' the Hill and their mother and sisters, and through them had been kept informed of all that had befallen Robin and his men.

'Robin,' said Father Tuck, 'a proud man thou shouldst be to think so fair a maid should do all this for love of thee.'

'Proud I am,' said Robin, 'and yet I have sorrow in my heart to think that I am an outlawed man, and can offer her, who hath ever known the softest ways of living, only the bare and houseless life of the wild forest. I would not change my life for anything the king could offer me, but for my nut-brown maid here to wish to wed me against her kinsmen's wishes would be to doom herself to a life that I would not – nay, that I cannot ask her to share.'

'Robin,' said Marian, 'I love but you alone, and I will wed none but thee. I love the woodland life even as thou dost, and I should be happy, though I forsook all my kindred. You think doubtless that I should repine when the leaves fall from the trees, when the wind snarls down the black ways or the snow-wreaths dance in the bitter winter. But my heart would be warm having thee to turn to, and I would never repent leaving the thick walls of my father's castle. He is kind to me, but he scorns me and daily rails at me for my love of thee, and though I would leave him with sorrow, I will come to thee swiftly if and when thou hast need of me.'

There was a little shake in her gentle voice as she ended, and tears were in the brave eyes. Robin took her hands and, raising them to his lips, kissed them fervently.

'Almost you persuade me, sweetheart mine,' he said. 'I know thou lovest but me alone, but it is not right that a maid should run to the wood with an outlaw, to live in dread, watching day and night lest their enemies approach. But this I promise thee, Marian, that if at any time ye are in peril from those that wish ye ill, and are alone and pursued by evil men, then do ye send to me and I will come, and we will be wed by this good monk here, and then together we will suffer whatever fortune doth betide us.'

'Well said, Robin Hood,' said the monk heartily, 'and well advised ye be. I see thou art an honourable man, as indeed I knew aforetime. And indeed I think it not unlikely that ere much more water floweth under Wentbridge, the fair young maid will have need of thy strong arm and the love of a good man strong enough to protect her from evil wishers.'

The monk said this knowing that Marian's father was but sickly, and that if he should die many powerful and evil barons or prelates, desiring the lands and riches of the lady Marian, would plot to get her into their power, so that they could profit from her wealth, and sell her to a husband who would give them a good price for her rich dower.

A horn sounded from the forest outside, and going to the door, Robin espied Little John and the other outlaws. Little John reported that the abbot's men and the king's rangers had been chased to the highway beyond Harlow Wood, several having been wounded. That then two knights, who seemed to be waiting for them, had striven to rally the men-at-arms, but that the arrows of the outlaws had put them all to the rout, one of the knights riding away with an arrow in his side.

'Was there aught to show who they were?' asked Robin.

'One had a blank shield, the other had a red tower on his,' replied Little John

'The red tower was a man I did not know,' said Scarlet, 'but he with the white shield was one of those whom we beat back last year at the church at Campsall.'

'Scarlet speaks truth,' said Will the Bowman, 'he is Niger le Grym, and I think the other, by the snarl in his voice and the fire of his curses, was no other than the fiend Isenbart de Belame himself.'

'I doubt it not,' said Robin. 'It shows that their spies watch us continually. Go into the forest and keep within sound of my horn. There are two ladies here within whom we must guard to their homes.'

Within, Father Tuck was preparing a woodland meal, and Marian having changed into her proper attire, they all sat to eat. Afterwards two horses were brought forward from their hiding-place in the forest, and the ladies, having mounted, bade goodbye to the monk and set off with Robin to the castle of Sir Richard at Lee, where both were dwelling for a time.

As they rode along down the sunny forest ways, Robin saw that the lady Alice still seemed sad and thoughtful, and he asked Marian why his words had caused such sorrow in her.

'Because,' said Marian, 'she can no longer save herself from wedding the old and evil lord, Sir Ranulf de Greasby. The day of marriage is set, and her lover, Alan-a-Dale, is outlawed, and is hiding in the wild hills of Lancaster.'

'I heard not of that,' said Robin. 'Why is the young squire outlawed?'

'Sir Isenbart de Belame got him proclaimed outlaw because he slew Ivo le Ravener,' was the reply. 'Moreover, he hath got a heavy fine placed on the lands of Alan's father, Sir Herbrand, and it is likely that Sir Herbrand will be ruined and his son slain ere long. Therefore, for the misery that she suffers because of this, my dear friend Alice is sad.'

'He did in truth slay Ivo le Ravener,' said Robin, 'but 'twas in fair fight, for I was by them when they fought; but I know not how the report could have been made that Alan slew him, because there was no one of his party near him, except a churl whom Ket the Trow slew.'

Robin related what had happened at the fight in the forest between Alan and Ivo le Ravener.

'I remember now,' said Marian, 'that Sir Richard told me that word was given by a forester that on the day when the knight was found slain, Alan-a-Dale came to him for a horse which he had left in his charge, and he had a sore wound on his shoulder.'

'That was Black Hugo,' said Robin, 'who was with the men-at-arms today. Said he aught else? Said he anything of who was with Alan when he came for his horse, or of the plight in which Hugo was himself?'

'Nay, I think not.'

Robin told Marian of how they had found Black Hugo tied up to his own door-post, while a big man was seated before him eating the toasted collops which the forester had prepared for his own dinner. Marian laughed heartily at this, and said that Sir Richard would be hugely delighted to hear so merry a tale.

'See you that tall fellow there?' said Robin, pointing to where the fine athletic figure of Little John, supple and wiry, strode before them, glancing keenly here and there into the forest beside them. 'He is the villein who tied up the forester, and a jollier comrade and a finer fighter I ne'er wish to meet.'

Marian thereupon wished to speak to Little John, who was called up by his leader, and soon Little John, his face flushing, was speaking to the first lady he had ever met in his life. Yet he bore himself with the dignity of a freeman, for in the frank life of the forest and the open air, the awkward and loutish manners of a serf quickly dropped away from manly natures.

While they spoke thus together, Marian asking Little John many questions concerning the life of the outlaws under the greenwood tree, Robin rode forward to the lady Alice where she rode with her woman beside her.

'Lady Alice,' said the outlaw, 'sorry am I that those words of mine caused your sad thoughts to rise. But tell me, for I have known young Alan, and a bolder, braver squire I never met, nor one more courteous in speech and kindly in manner – how soon is it appointed that thou shalt wed the old knight whom those tyrants of Wrangby wish to be thy husband?'

'Sir Outlaw,' said the lady, and her dark eyes glowed, 'I thank thee for thy kind words concerning him I love. He hath written of thee in his few letters which I have received since, a year ago, he fled an outlaw to the woods and wilds, and ever he spoke warmly of thy friendship. My hateful marriage is fixed for three days hence on the feast of Saint James, at the church of Cromwell. My poor father can no longer resist the wicked demands of Sir Isenbart, who threatens fire and sword if he submit not to his will and weds me to the old tyrant, Sir Ranulf. And we have no great and powerful friends to whom we may appeal for protection, and my lover is outlawed and cannot save me.'

Tears were falling from the brave eyes, and they went to Robin's heart. His brow was dark with anger as he thought for some moments deeply. Then he said:

'Take heart, dear lady. There may be hope in a few strong arms and stout hearts, though the time is but short. Hast thou anyone who could take a message to thy lover from me?'

'Thanks for thy great cheer, good Robin,' replied the lady, and smiled through her tears. 'There is a serf of my father's who knoweth my lover's hiding-place and hath taken four messages from me, though the way is fearsome and long for a poor untravelled villein. Yet he is brave, and loves to do my behests.'

'How is he named, and where doth he live?'

'He is named John or Jack, son of Wilkin, and dwelleth by the Hoar Thorn at Cromwell.'

'Give me something which he will know for thine,' said Robin, 'for I will send one of my fellows to him ere the vesper bell rings tonight.'

Lady Alice took a ring from one slender finger and put it in Robin's hand.

'This will he know as from me, and he will do whatsoever the bearer telleth him to do gladly,' she said, 'for my sake.'

The waiting-woman riding beside her now put out her hand, holding a thick silver ring between her fingers.

'Bold outlaw,' said the girl, a dark-haired, rosy-cheeked and pretty lass with a high look, 'let thy man take this also to Jack, and bid him from me, whom he saith he loves, that if he do not what you tell him and that speedily, then there is his ring back again, and when I see him again he shall have the rough side of my tongue and my malison besides. For if he'll not bestir his great carcass for the love of my lady who is in such a strait, then he is no man for Netta o' the Meering.'

'I will do thy bidding, fair lass,' said Robin with a smile. 'And as I doubt not he is a brave man indeed from whom thou hast accepted this ring, I have no fear that all will go well.'

In a little while they had reached Sir Richard's castle, and the ladies were safely in hall again. By this time the afternoon light was softening to evening, and Robin knew that no time was to be lost. He called Will the Bowman to him, and giving him the two rings, entrusted him with the mission he had planned. A few moments later, on Robin's own swift horse, Will was galloping with loose rein along the forest drives that led eastward to the waters of the Trent.

CHAPTER FIVE

How by the Help of Robin Hood and Jack, Son of Wilkin, Alan-a-Dale Was Wed to the Lady Alice

Jack, son of Wilkin, as he stood in the wood, tying the last bundle of faggots on a rough cart, which he had made himself, little thought that there was hastening to him a message that would have a very great effect on all his future life. Jack was a well-built, sturdy youth of about twenty, good-looking, with quick brown eyes and freckled skin. His head of curly brown hair never knew a covering, except when snow was falling or the east wind blew shrill in the frosts of winter.

He was a villein of the manor of Cromwell, and his lord was Sir Walter de Beauforest, father of the lady Alice. The lord hardly knew that Jack existed; sometimes he saw the lad when he himself was going hawking or coming from the chase, but he did not trouble to acknowledge the pull of the front lock which Jack gave him. John the Thinne, however, steward of the lord, knew Jack as one of the most willing of the younger workers on the manor. Once on a while indeed, when Jack was a boy of twelve, the steward had looked rather sourly upon him, because the boy had been noticed by the lady Alice, then a girl of but a year or two older, and she had made the boy one of her falconers. When, however, Jack's father had died, the lad had been compelled to do his work in return for the hovel and the few square rods of land which supported his mother and himself, and Jack had seen less of the lady Alice, for whose smile or kind word he would have gone through fire or water.

On the great parchment roll of the manor, which the steward kept, and which contained the pedigrees of all the serfs on the

land of the lord, Jack was entered as John, Wilkin's son. His
father's name was Will, and as he was a little man he had been
called Wilkin, which means Little Will. But Jack's surname was
not a fixed thing, because villeins and poor folk did not usually
own them in those days. Sometimes, indeed, he was called Jack
Will's son, or, because an old hawthorn leaned beside his hovel,
Jack-a-thorn, or from his mother's name Jack Alice's son, or as
we should call it, Alison; but being a cheerful fellow and quick,
Jack usually knew when he was being called, and therefore did
not stand on strict ceremony.

Jack loved horses and dogs and hawks. He knew the name of
every horse on the manor, and many a day had he spent with
them when he went a-lea or afield, driving the long straight
furrow across the strip of the lord's land which he had to plough.
Many a happy day, too, had he spent with the lady Alice on the
wild open lands, hunting with merlin or peregrine, tiercel or
kestrel.

Every little cur in the village was on speaking terms with Jack,
but there were no large dogs, such as mastiffs, hounds, or setters,
for the village was too near the king's forest where the red deer
roamed, and all large dogs were either slain by the foresters, or
their forepaws were maimed, so that they should not be used for
hunting.

Jack's great ambition was to obtain his freedom. To be a
freeman and to work his own land, like Nicholas o' the Cliffe
did, or Simon the Fletcher, seemed to him to be the greatest
happiness a man could possess. Not that his lord was a hard one,
or that John the Steward was oppressive, but nevertheless Jack
would prefer to be free than bound to the soil as he was. His
mother explained this strange desire by saying that, four generations before, in the peaceful time of the blessed king, Edward the
Confessor, when the land had known no fierce lords and violent
robber-barons, Jack's forefathers had been free people, but that
when the evil Normans had come they had enslaved them all.

To Jack it seemed a great injustice that when his father had
died, his mother had had to give the steward the finest beast they
had, Moolie the cow, a splendid milker, besides the best
cauldron in the house and the soundest stool. These were said to
be payment to the lord for letting them still 'sit' in the land and

in the hovel which they and their forbears had possessed for generations.

Until some ten months ago, the world outside Jack's village had seemed to him to be a dark, terrible, and mysterious region. He knew the country for quite three miles from the church in the centre of the village, but far into the forest to the west he had never dared to penetrate. He had suspected all strangers, and when he had met with any coming towards the village he had hidden until they had passed.

The forest he had heard was a place of dread, for the other villeins had told terrible tales. Of monsters who flew by night and hid in dark thickets by day to snap up unwary travellers; of hills from whose tops at night the glow of fire shone forth, and within which little dark elves or spirits dwelled. Indeed, the fear of little malicious fiends was never very distant from Jack's mind in those times. These evil things might take any shape, and they dwelled in the spring or the stream, in the wood beside the road, and in the tufts of grass in the field which he was ploughing or mowing. The whole village, and thousands of villages up and down broad Britain, believed in such wicked sprites, and therefore Jack was no worse than his fellows, or, indeed, than men who were famed for their learning in those days, and sat at the council boards of kings.

That sooty old crow flapping over the furrows, or the raven who came and sat on a clod and cocked his beady eye at Jack as he was ploughing, might be a witch or wizard come to see if he could do some evil trick – not a wild bird looking for the worms or the leather-jackets which the plough turned up. Therefore Jack had to cross two fingers when he passed the bird of ill-omen and say a paternoster. In the same way, if Jack saw floating in the stream a stout piece of bough which, when dried, would boil the pot, he did not pull it out thoughtlessly, as a boy of today would do. Nay; before he touched it he made the sign of the cross over it, lest some evil water nicker might be hiding beneath it, ready to clutch him down, if he did not disarm it by means of the sacred sign.

To find a cast horse-shoe or to get hold of one which was too worn to be of further use was a great piece of good luck. Jack had a horse-shoe over the door of his hovel, to keep witches and wizards from entering his abode, and another over the window-shutter. And Jack knew which was the proper way to hang the shoe. On All Souls' Eve, a time when evil things are moving much about, Jack wore a sprig of rowan in his belt.

He had never seen an elf or brownie himself, but he knew that they lived in hollows in the hills or in secret places in the forest. The tale went, indeed, that long ago a man named Sturt of Norwell, a serf, had heard someone crying in a wood that he had lost his pick. Going to see who it was that cried, Sturt found it was a brownie. Frightened though he was, Sturt sought for and found the pick, and the fairy had then invited him home to dinner. Afterwards Sturt often went to the green hill in the forest, and in a year married the fairy's daughter, and thrived all his life. His children still lived at Norwell, and one was a freeman, and all were lively little fellows, welcomed wherever they went for their songs and jolly ways.

Such had been Jack's manner of thinking of the world and things generally until some few months before; and then one day the lady Alice, like a vision from heaven for beauty and graciousness, had met him in a lonely place, and giving him a parchment wrapped in silk, had begged him to take it to her lover, who lay hid at a certain place in the forests of Lancaster. He was the only man she could trust, she had said, and her words had seemed to make Jack's heart swell in his breast.

Jack was a brave lad, but that first journey through the great forest, bearing his precious message, was an experience which, for dread, he would never forget. But for sheer worship of the fair Alice, whose love for Alan-a-Dale was known to all the manor, his loyalty had overcome all his fear, and he had performed his mission well and faithfully.

Three times since then he had done the journey, and every time his dread of the strange roads and the wild waste country, which lies between Sherwood and Werrisdale, had returned to him, but his pluck and his shrewdness had carried him safely through the various adventures he had met with.

He had never seen an outlaw or real robber of the woods. Pedlars and lusty beggar men or saucy minstrels had tried to frighten or defraud him out of his few poor possessions or his bag of food; but never had he seen any of those terrible men who had fled from their rightful lords, forsaking land and home and the daily customs of their forefathers. He had often wondered what reckless and desperate men they must be, how quick they must be to slay or injure.

That evening, as he stood tying the last faggot on the little cart, he was wondering what he should have done had one dashed upon him from the thicket on one of his journeys, and demanded the precious thing which the lady Alice had entrusted to him. He would have fought to the death rather than give it up.

He clicked his tongue to the rough pony which drew the cart, and led it down the track out of the wood. He looked west, and saw far away over the shaggy line of the forest the upper limb of the huge red sun in whose light the tree stems around him shone blood red. The light dazzled his eyes. He heard a twig break beside him, a man stepped from behind the trunk of a tree and stood barring his passage.

'Art thou Jack, son of Wilkin?' said the stranger, in a sharp commanding tone.

Jack stepped back, and his hand fell to the haft of the knife stuck in his belt. He looked keenly at the man, who was short and sturdy. He was dressed in green tunic and hose, much worn in places and torn here and there as if by brambles. A bow was slung across his back, and a bunch of arrows were tied to his girdle beside a serviceable sword.

Jack wondered, as he scowled at the stranger, who he might be. He looked by his clothes to be some lord's woodman, and his face, covered with a great grizzled beard, seemed honest though stern. Yet there was an air about the man that seemed to say that he owned no one lord but himself. The stamp of the freeman was in his keen eyes, in the straight look, and the stiff poise of the head.

These thoughts took but a moment to pass through Jack's mind; then he said:

'What's that to thee who I be?'

'It's much to thee who ye be,' said the stranger with a laugh. 'Look 'ee, lad, I mean thee no harm.'

There was an honest ring in the other's laugh which pleased Jack. The stranger's left hand went to his pouch and drew something from it. Then he pulled forth his dagger and upon the point of it he slipped two rings – one of gold, the other of

silver – and held the weapon up to the light. The dying rays of
the sun struck a diamond in the tiny hoop of gold, so that it
dazzled and glowed like a fairy light in the darkening wood.

'Do ye know aught of these, lad?' asked the man.

'Where got ye them?' asked Jack, his face dark with anger.
'Ha' ye robbed them from those who wore them? If 'tis so, then
thou'lt never leave this place alive.'

'Soft, brave lad,' replied the other, watching keenly the
involuntary crouching movement which Jack made as if he was
preparing to spring upon the other. 'My master got them from
the hands of their fair owners, with these words. The lady Alice,
thy mistress, said: "Jack is brave, and loves to do my behests. He
will know this is from me, and he will do whatsoever the bearer
telleth him to do gladly, for my sake." '

'Said the lady Alice those words?' asked Jack. His face was
flushed, the blood seemed suddenly to have swept hotly into his
heart, and he glowed with the pleasure of hearing his lady's
praise even by the mouth of this rugged old woodman. 'And
what,' he went on, 'what would my lady wish me to do?'

'Go with me and lead me to Alan-a-Dale,' said Will the
Bowman.

For a moment Jack hesitated. Go with this stranger through
the wild forest and the lonely lands of the Peak! But his loyalty
suffered no question of what he would do.

'I will do this, friend,' replied Jack. 'Tell me thy name and who
thou art.'

'I am called Will the Bowman,' was the reply. 'Robin Hood is
my master'

'What!' said Jack, and started back. 'Thou art an outlaw! One
of Robin Hood's men?'

'That am I,' replied Will, 'and proud to serve so brave and
wise a master.'

Jack looked in wonder for a moment. This was no desperate
and reckless cut-throat, such as he had imagined; but a man with
a homely face, with eyes that could be stern, but which could
also smile. Jack put out his hand on an impulse, and the other
gripped it.

'Thou art the first outlaw I have seen,' said Jack with a hearty
laugh, 'and if thy master and thy fellows are like thee, then my

heart tells me that thou art honest and good fellows. And Robin Hood will befriend my lady?'

'Ay, that will he,' said Will, 'but now let's chatter no more, but get to the forest ere the light is wholly gone.'

No more words were said. Jack led the horse and cart to the rough track which led to the village, and then gave a slash to the horse and knew as it cantered off that it would soon reach home in safety. Before sending it off, however, he tore a strip of traveller's joy from the hedge and twined it round the pony's head. By this his mother would know that again he had set off suddenly at the bidding of the lady Alice.

When the two men had left the wood a mile behind them, Will said:

'Ye asked not what message came with the silver ring, lad.'

Jack laughed. 'Nay, I did not. First, because my lady's message drove it from my head, and second, because I doubt not 'twas no soft message.'

' 'Twas a maid's message,' replied Will, 'and that's half bitter and half sweet, as doubtless ye know. Then I guess the maid Netta o' the Meering flouts thee as often as she speaks kind words?'

'Ye are older than I,' said Jack with a little awkward laugh, 'and doubtless ye know the ways of girls better than I. What was the message she sent me?'

Will told him, and Jack's face reddened at the telling. 'I needed not her rough tongue,' he said with some shade of haughtiness in his voice, 'to make me stir myself for my lady's sake.'

Thereafter he would say no more, but Will noticed that he quickened his pace and seemed very full of thought. By the time the last faint light had died from the clear sky, they were deep in the forest ways. They rested and ate food from their scrip until the moon arose, and then by its gentle light they threaded the paths of the greenwood, looking like demons as their dark forms passed through the inky blackness, and like fairies covered with magic sheen when they stepped silently across some open glade.

Two days later, in the morning, the villeins of Cromwell village stood in groups about their hovels talking of the sad fate that was to befall their beloved young mistress that morning. All knew that she had given her heart to Alan-a-Dale, but that some hard destiny which ruled the lives of knights and ladies was forcing her to wed old Ranulf de Greasby, a white-haired, evil old lord who lived in the fenlands to the east.

Some of the villeins stood in the churchyard, in the church of which the ceremony was to take place. They often looked along the road to the north, for it was from thence that the wedding party would come. Already the priest had been seen ambling along towards the manor-house, from whence he would probably accompany the bride to the church.

'He goes to take comfort to her to whom he can give none,' said one young woman with a baby in her arms. 'Poor lady!' she went on, 'why should he be denied her whom she loves best in all the world?'

' 'Twould be at the price of his head if he came here this day,' said a man near her. 'Outlaw he is, and a broken man.'

'Nay, I fear there's no help for the young lass!' said a younger man. 'She'll eat her heart out when she's wed, and never be the same bright winsome maid she has ever been among us.'

'Oh, 'tis a foul wrong!' cried a young girl. 'Is there no one of all her kin who would save her?'

'Her kin are a weak people, Mawkin,' said an old wrinkled woman, 'and they would be like mice in the jaws of Isenbart de Belame if they stood against his will.'

Just then there came the sound of horses' hooves along the rough road coming from the north, and ten mounted men-at-arms rode up wearing the livery of Ranulf de Greasby. Men of hard, coarse looks they were, and without a word they rode their horses into the gate and up to the church porch, scattering the poor villeins, who got out of the way of the horses as quickly as they could. The horsemen ranged themselves five on each side of the porch, and, dismounting, each stood by his horse and glared insolently at the villeins, who were now huddled together by the gate.

'Is it from such rubbish as these that the old man fears a rescue?' asked one man-at-arms.

The others laughed at the joke. 'Our old lord hath been flouted so long by the pretty young jade,' said another, 'that now she's almost in his hand he fears some evil hap may snatch her from him.'

'Ay, she hath flouted him overlong,' said another. 'I'd not give much for her flouts once she's in his castle by Hagthorn Waste. There be ways he hath of taming the fiercest maid, as his last wife knew, so they say.'

'Ay, she that went in a handsome, dark-eyed lass with a look like a sword one minute and as sweet as a child's the next,' said another.

'I remember her,' said the first speaker. 'She lived two years. She 'scaped from him one winter's night, and was found at the dawn in Grimley Mere frozen stiff.'

'Ye are cheerful bridesmen, by the rood,' said he who was evidently the leader. 'Let us have that minstrel to give us a rousing song more fitting for a wedding. Hi, there, varlet!'

A tall minstrel, wearing a gaudy striped doublet and patched hose, had strolled from the village up to the group of villeins, and was laughing with them, while he twanged the harp which he wore round his neck by a soiled ribbon. At the call of the soldier, the minstrel stepped to the gate, and taking off his velvet cap, swept it before him with a bow.

'What would you, noble squires? A song of war and booty, or one of the bower and loving maidens, or one which tells of the chase of the good red deer?'

'Sing what thou likest, so it be a jolly song,' commanded the chief man-at-arms.

Whereupon, with a few preliminary twangings and a clearing of the throat, the minstrel gave them a popular song called 'The Woodstock Rose'. He had a rich tenor voice, and the ditty was a rollicking one, with a chorus in which all took part. Afterwards the minstrel sang them a ballad about a wedding, which pleased them mightily. When the minstrel appeared wishful to depart, the leader said:

'Stay, jolly fellow, for I think we shall have need of thee. We are like to have a sad-faced bride here soon, and thy lively songs may brighten her, so that my lord may take cheer of her gay looks. If thou pleasest our lord this day thou shalt have good reward, I doubt not.'

The minstrel was not unwilling to stay, and was preparing to sing another lay, when four horsemen were seen riding swiftly towards the church. The tallest one was Sir Ranulf de Greasby, an old grey knight with a red and ugly face. His lips were cruel, and his red eyes were small and fierce. He was dressed in a rich cloak of red silk, his belt was encrusted with diamonds, and his sword-hilt blazed with jewels. The three men with him were younger knights, of a reckless air, well dressed but slovenly in bearing. One of them was Sir Ranulf's nephew, Sir Ector of the Harelip, a ruffianly-looking man, whose fame for cruelty was as great as that of his uncle's.

The old knight drove through the gate furiously as if in a great hurry.

'Hath the lady come yet?' he cried in a hoarse voice to the men-at-arms, and his red, foxy eyes gleamed suspiciously from one to the other.

'Nay, lord,' replied the leader.

'Plague on it!' the old knight rapped out, and turning in his saddle he glanced sourly up and down the road, then at the crowd of villeins and the hovels beyond. 'She keeps me waiting still,' he muttered into his beard, while they could hear his teeth grind and could see the fierce red eyes close to slits through which came an evil light. 'It shall be hers to wait, anon, if she speak not fair to me!'

'Who art thou, knave?' he said, suddenly glancing down at the minstrel who stood beside his horse.

'I am Jocelyn, the minstrel, Sir Knight,' replied the man, and twanged his harp.

'Thou hast a knave's face,' said Sir Ranulf suspiciously; 'thou'rt not sleek enough for a gleeman.'

'Nevertheless, Sir Knight, I am a poor gleeman come to give your highness pleasure with my simple song, if ye will have it,' said the minstrel, and twanged his harp again.

'Sing then, rascal, and let thy song be apt, or thou'lt get but a basting.'

The gleeman screwed up two strings of his harp, and began:

> 'Though lord of lands I sadly strayed,
> I long despised my knightly fame,
> And wakeful sighed the night hours through!
> A thrall was I to that fair dame,
> To whom long time in vain I prayed –
>   The haughty lady Alysoun.

Blow, northern wind,
Send me my sweeting,
Blow, northern wind, blow, blow, blow.'

As he finished the last line, a scornful laugh, strangely shrill, rang out. Men looked this way and that, but could see naught. It seemed to come from above their heads, but there was nothing to be seen except the wooden front of the church tower. Round this a few daws were flying and crying, and in and out of the arrow-slits swallows were passing to and from their nests.

The gleeman sang another verse:

'Ah, how her cruel looks tortured me –
How like two swords her eyes of gold –
Until my cheeks waxed wan with woe!
But, happy me, though I am old,
Ah, now, she, winsome, smiles on me,
    My lady fair, my Alysoun.

Blow, northern wind,
Send me my sweeting,
Blow, northern wind, blow, blow, blow.'

Again the laugh rang out, this time with a more mocking note in it. Sir Ranulf looked at the gleeman.

'Who made that noise, knave?' he said, anger in his voice. 'Hast thou any fellow with thee?'

'No one is with me, lord,' the minstrel replied.

'Belike, lord,' said one of the men, who had fear in his eyes, 'it is a nixie in the church tower.'

'Belike, fool,' roared Sir Ranulf, 'thou shalt have a strong whipping when thou art home again. Go ye round the church in opposite ways and see if no churl is hiding. And if any be there, bring him here and I will cut his tongue from his mouth. I'll teach aught to fleer at me!'

Four of the men went round the church, while others went among the graves, lest someone was hiding behind the low wooden slabs raised over some of the burial-places; but both parties returned saying they had seen nobody. The knight was in a furious rage by now, and sending five of his men, he commanded them to scatter the villeins who stood by the churchyard gate, marvelling at the strange happening. The villagers did not wait for the blows of the soldiers, but fled among their hovels.

'Now, rogue,' cried Sir Ranulf to the gleeman, 'sing another verse of thy song, and if another laugh be heard I shall know it to be caused by thyself. Think ye that I know not the wizard tricks of thy juggling tribe?'

'As I hope to be saved,' said the jongleur gravely, 'it is not I who do make that laughter. Nevertheless, I will sing another verse and stand to the issue thereof.'

Thereupon, making his harp to accompany his tune, he sang.

> 'A gracious fate to me is sent,
> Methinks it is by Heaven lent!
> Ah now as mate she will me take,
> For ever, sweet, to be thy thrall,
> While life shall last, my all in all,
>   My gentle, laughing Alysoun.
>
> Blow, northern wind,
> Send me my sweeting,
> Blow, northern wind, blow, blow, blow.'

A shout of mocking laughter, so fierce and grim as to startle all, sounded immediately above the heads of the listeners, so that all involuntarily looked up, but there was nothing to be seen. The noise ceased for a moment; then a croaking laugh came from over the road, as if that which caused the sound was slowly passing away. Then the sound came nearer for a moment, and all heard distinctly words uttered with a fierce and threatening cry.

'Colman Grey! Colman Grey!'

At the sound of these words Sir Ranulf started back and fiercely pulled his horse so that he leaned against the very church door, at which he beat with clenched fists, and cried out: 'Avaunt! Avaunt! Keep him from me! Call the priest! Call the priest! 'Tis an evil spirit – keep it from me!'

He seemed in mortal terror. His face that had been red was now white; his lips twitched and gibbered, and while with one hand he crossed himself repeatedly, with the other he now seemed to push something from him and sometimes covered his eyes. The men standing about marvelled to see him, and stood gaping with open mouths at their lord distraught.

At length he came to himself: he saw the wonder in the eyes about him, and recovering his spirit somewhat, though he still trembled, he drove his horse forward among his men-at-arms.

'What gape ye at, ye knaves and fools!' he cried violently, and raising the whip which hung on his saddle, he slashed it at the men. They gave way before him; he charged them to stand still, but they would not, and in a mad fury he dashed his horse this way and that, beating at them, where they stood among their horses. The animals reared and began to bite and tear at each other, and an almost inextricable confusion arose. Suddenly his nephew, Sir Ector, caught the arm of the mad old lord and cried:

'Sir Ranulf, the lady comes! Cease!'

The furious man looked up the northern road and saw a party of riders coming towards the church. Instantly he dropped the whip, set his hat straight, and righted his tunic. Then he bade his sullen men mount their horses and prepare to receive the lady. Already the priest and the sacristan had entered the church by a side door, and now the great doors behind them swung open, and the darkness of the church yawned.

Sir Ranulf, seeing that all was now in order, cast a fierce eye around for the minstrel. He was nowhere to be seen.

'Where went that rogue the juggler?' he asked one of his companion knights.

'I know not,' said the other. 'I kept my eye upon him till thou didst begin to whip thy knaves, and then in the confusion he crept off, for I saw him not again!'

'Good Sir Philip,' said Sir Ranulf, 'do thou do me the greatest favour, and go search for that varlet. I shall not be happy till I have him in my hands and see him under torture. Then will I learn what the knave knows and – and – what – what – meant that cry. Thou canst take two of my men with thee, but seek him out, and when thou hast seized him take him to Hagthorn Waste, and lodge him in my hold there.'

'I will do this for thee, Greasby,' said the young knight, with an insolent laugh, 'but if I bring him to thee, thou must give me thy hound Alisaundre and thy merlin hawks, Grip and Fang.'

'Thou churlish knight!' said Sir Ranulf, in a fierce undertone; 'they are those I love best. But I must have that juggler. Go ye, and I will give thee what thou askest. Quickly go, or the varlet will be in hiding.'

A few words to two of the men-at-arms, and they and the knight rode out of the churchyard just as Sir Walter de Beauforest and a friend of his, with the lady Alice between them, rode up, accompanied by a house villein and the lady Alice's maid, both on horseback behind them. The old knight, Sir Ranulf, his crafty face all smiles now, stood at the churchyard gate doffing his hat, and with his hand on his heart, bowed to the lady Alice, greeting her. The lady Alice, with face pale and sad, hardly looked at him. She was clad in a rich dress of white silk, ropes of pearls were about her neck, her light summer cloak was sewn with pearls, and her wimple cloth was richly embroidered with gold; but this richness only showed up the dreadful pallor of her face, and her eyes that looked as if they strained to weep but would not.

Sir Walter, her father, looked no more wretched than he felt. He was a proud knight, and hated to think that he had to submit to the commands of a tyrant lord, and to marry his only daughter to a knight with the evil fame which Sir Ranulf de Greasby had possessed so long. Robbery on the highways and cruel tyranny of poor folk for the sake of their meagre hoards or their lands were the least of the crimes which report laid to the guilt of Sir Ranulf. Tales there were of a tortured wife, and of poor men and women put to cruel torment in the dungeons of his castle on Hagthorn Waste.

All rode up to the church door and then dismounted. Netta, whose eyes were red, went to her mistress, and under pretence of arranging her cloak whispered words of cheer to her while for sorrow she could hardly keep herself from weeping. Then Sir Walter, taking his daughter by the hand, led her into the church and up the dim aisle towards the altar, where already the priest stood ready to perform the ceremony.

Four of the men-at-arms stood without the church with the horses, the other four went in with Sir Ranulf and his two knights, of whom Sir Ector acted as his best man. Together they approached the altar, and then, while the others kept back, Sir Walter Beauforest placed his daughter's hand in the hand of Sir Ranulf who immediately led her up to the priest.

The old priest was as sad as any of the poor villeins who now crept into the church and sat in the back benches. He had known the lady Alice when she was brought to the font to be baptised, he had taught her to read and to write, and had loved her for her graciousness and kindness. Moreover, Sir Walter had always been a good friend to the poor priest. Nevertheless, he had to do his duty, and now, opening his service-book, he prepared to read the words that should make these two man and wife.

Suddenly from the gloom along the wall of the church came a movement, and a man stepped forth into the light of the candles which stood upon the altar. It was the minstrel, but now in his hand he bore a longbow, and his harp was carried by a fair young man – Gilbert of the White Hand.

'This is an evil and unfitting match,' he cried in a loud, stern voice. 'Sir Ranulf of the Waste, get thee gone lest ill and death befall thee. Sir Priest, this maiden shall wed him she loveth best, at a more fitting time.'

All eyes were turned to the tall figure in green. The lady Alice, her eyes bright and a flush in her cheeks, had torn her hand from the fingers of Sir Ranulf, and stood trembling, her hands clasped together.

Sir Ranulf, his face dark with passion, looked from the lady to the minstrel. He was almost too furious to speak.

'So!' he said mockingly. 'Who is this? Is this the wolf's-head, the broken fool for whom this maiden here hath flouted me and put me off this year and more?'

None answered. Sir Walter peered at the minstrel and shook his head. Sir Ranulf, with a gesture of rage, drew his sword, and made a step forward.

'Who art thou, knave, to dare to withstand me?' he cried.

From the darkness of the roof above their heads came a croaking voice:

'Colman Grey! Colman Grey!'

Sir Ranulf faltered at the name and looked up, his face white with terror. As he did so, the hum as of a bee was heard, and a short black arrow shot down and pierced his throat. Without a cry he fell heavily to the ground, twitched a little, and lay still.

The knights and men-at-arms who looked on stood motionless, too surprised to do or say aught. The minstrel placed a horn to his lips and blew a shrill blast which filled the church with echoes.

Instantly, as if the sound awoke him from his stupor, Sir Ector drew his sword and with a yell of rage dashed at Robin Hood, for he was of course the minstrel. Hardly had Robin time to draw his own sword, and soon he and Sir Ector were fighting fiercely in the gloom. At the sound of the horn, also, there came the sound of clashing weapons at the door, and the men-at-arms, who had hitherto stood too amazed to move, now seized their swords and ran towards the door, only to be stayed by three of their fellows who ran into the church, pursued by a flight of arrows which poured in like a horde of angry wasps. Two men fell dead, and another tottered away sorely wounded. Next moment into the church came some half-score men in green. The five remaining men-at-arms, knowing the hatred with which any men of Sir Ranulf's were looked upon, dashed against the bowmen and strove to cut their way through, for they knew that no quarter would be given them. The fight raged furiously at the door, the men in green striving to thrust them back, and the Greasby men struggling to win through to the open.

Suddenly a scream rang through the church. Looking quickly around, Sir Walter saw the second knight who had been with Sir Ranulf rushing towards the priest's side door, and in his arms was the lady Alice, struggling to free herself from his powerful grasp.

Behind him ran Netta the maid, screaming, and tearing at the knight's garments; but as he reached the door he turned and struck the girl a blow which laid her senseless. Next moment he had disappeared through the arras which hid the door.

At the same moment Robin Hood, after a fierce struggle with Sir Ector, slew him, though wounded himself, and then swiftly made for the door through which the other knight had dashed with the lady Alice. Looking out, he saw nobody in sight, and guessed that the knight had rushed forward to the horses which stood before the church.

This was indeed the truth. Still clutching his struggling burden, the knight reckoned on seizing a horse and escaping before anyone would recover from the confusion. When he reached the front of the church he found two men in deadly combat. One was the knight who had gone off in pursuit of the minstrel, the other was a stranger. But at sight of the latter the lady Alice, breathless and panting, cried out:

The rescue of the lady Alice

'Alan! Alan! Save me!'

Her cry was almost the death-knell of her lover, for, surprised at the voice of his sweetheart crying so near him, Alan turned his head, and the knight struck at him a deadly blow, which would most surely have sheared his head from his shoulders had not Jack, son of Wilkin, who was standing near, seen the danger, and with his staff struck a shrewd blow at the knight's shoulder. This saved Alan's life and gave him time to turn. Furiously he strove to beat down his foe, knowing that he must slay this one before he could turn upon the knight who was bearing off his lady.

But the knight, Sir Philip, was a stout and crafty fighter, and meanwhile the knight who bore the lady had reached a horse, had thrown her across the saddle, and had swung himself into the seat. Next moment he had dashed towards the churchyard gate, cutting down two poor brave villeins who, seeing their lady thus used, hoped with their staves to check the robber knight. With a yell of exultation the knight saw his way clear before him, he put spurs to the steed, and spoke mockingly to the now unconscious form of the lady lying across the horse before him.

Suddenly he felt someone leap on the haunches of the animal behind him. Ere he could think what to do, a long knife flashed in the sun before his eyes. He felt a thud on his breast and a keen pain like fire, then blackness swept down upon him. He rocked in his seat, the reins were caught from his hands, and Jack, son of Wilkin, heaving the dead knight from before him, checked the frightened horse, brought it to a standstill, and lifted the unconscious body of his mistress tenderly to the ground.

By this time Alan-a-Dale had leaped in under the guard of his adversary and by a swift blow had dispatched him, and instantly had run to the side of his mistress, for whom already Jack, Wilkin's son, had brought water. Soon she revived and sat up, and hearing who was her rescuer, gave her hand to Jack, who kneeled and reverently kissed it.

'Jack,' she said, smiling sweetly though wanly, 'for this great service thou shalt be a free man, and my father shall give thee free land.'

Jack glowed with gladness, but was too tongue-tied to say aught but 'Thank you, my lady!'

By now, too, Netta, a little dazed, came forward and tended

her mistress. Robin Hood, going into the church to fetch Sir Walter, found that of his own men two had been slain in the fierce encounter with the men-at-arms, of whom but one of all the ten had escaped alive by rushing away through the side door.

'Sir Walter,' said Robin, when father and daughter had embraced each other, 'this hath been a red bridal, and I have meddled in thy affairs to some purpose.'

'I cannot be ungrateful to you, Sir Outlaw,' said Sir Walter, who, proud and stiff as he was, knew a brave leader from a paltry one, and honoured courage, whether found in earl or churl, villein or freeman; 'I thank thee from my heart for saving my daughter from this ill-starred and unhappy match. I must stand the issue of it, for the knights you have slain have powerful aiders, and I doubt not their vengeance will be heavy upon us all.'

'You speak of Belame and the Wrangby lords?' said Robin, and his brow was dark and his voice stern.

'They are the rulers of these parts in these present unhappy times,' replied the knight. 'While the king's own sons plunge the country in civil war and wretchedness, weak men have to submit to the gross tyranny of stronger neighbours.'

'Ranulf of Greasby and Ector Harelip are two the less,' said Robin grimly. 'Mark me, Sir Walter,' he went on, 'the lords of Wrangby have already filled the cup of suffering beyond men's bearing. As I hope to be saved, by the Virgin's dear word, I swear it here and now, that ere long they shall lie as low as do these robber knights, and when I pull them down, I will root out their nest, so that not one evil stone shall stand upon another.'

Sir Walter looked at the dark glowing eye of the outlaw, and remembered the deeds of wild justice which already had spread the fame of Robin throughout the forest lands from Pontefract to Nottingham, and from the desolate lands of the Peak to the flat fen marshes of Lincolnshire.

'I will help thee all I may, Sir Outlaw,' said the knight, 'and when the time comes thou mayest call on me to give thee all aid. Meanwhile, what's to be done?'

'This shall be done, Sir Walter,' replied Robin. 'Thy daughter and the man she loves shall dwell with me in the greenwood, and when they have been thrice called in a church they shall be wedded. If thou fearest assault by the robber baron, de Belame, thou canst leave thy house and live with us also; but if thou wouldst liefer stay beneath thy own roof, twenty of my men shall stay to guard and watch with thee. Dost thou agree?'

'I will liefer stay in my own house, good Robin,' said Sir Walter, 'if thy brave fellows will aid me to repel attack. And when times of peace return to this unhappy England, I trust my daughter and brave Alan, her husband, will live with me also.'

It was thus agreed. Within the next three weeks Father Tuck, in a church near by his cell, had published the banns of marriage between Alan and Alice, and it was the valiant monk himself who married the lovers, thus making them happy once for all.

On the day when Robin thus saved Alice from wedding the evil Sir Ranulf, the cruel lord, Isenbart de Belame, sat in the high seat of his castle at Wrangby, which just men called Evil Hold, and waited for his supper. About the board sat others as evil as himself, as Sir Niger le Grym, Hamo de Mortain, Sir Baldwin the Killer, Sir Roger of Doncaster, and many others.

'Plague take him!' at length cried de Belame, 'I'll wait no longer for him. Is Ranulf so jealous of his pretty bride that he fears to bring her here for us to give her our good wishes?'

The others laughed and made jeering jests.

'And where are Ector, Philip and Bertran?' said Sir Niger. 'They were to go with the bridegroom to give the shy fellow heart and courage in the ordeal.'

'Ho! scullions,' roared de Belame, 'serve the meats! And when Ranulf comes, we'll make such game of him and his bride that he'll be – '

Whang! Something had seemed to snore through the air from above their heads, and lo! here, sticking in the board before Sir Isenbart, was a black arrow, with a piece of parchment tied to it. Only for a moment de Belame lost his presence of mind. He looked up to the ceiling of the high hall and shouted:

' 'Twas shot from the spy hole! Ho, there, knaves, up and search the castle for him that shot this!' He rose himself and hurried away, while the men-at-arms from the lower table scattered throughout the castle.

Niger le Grym drew the arrow from the wood and looked at the parchment, on which were names in red and black. But being no scholar he could read naught of them. In a while came back de

Belame, red with rage, cursing his knaves and their non-success.

'What means it?' said de Mortain. 'There are names on the scroll here?'

De Belame had been a monk in his early youth, and could read. He looked at the slip of parchment, and his face went fierce and dark with fury.

'Look you,' he said, 'there are strange powers against us! Ranulf, Ector, and the others have been done to death this day. Written in blood upon this parchment are the names of all who once made our full company and are now dead. Thus, here are the names of Roger de Longchamp and Ivo le Ravener, and now there appear those of Ranulf de Greasby, Ector de Malstane, Philip de Scrooby, and Bertran le Noir – all written in blood!'

'This is passing strange!' said some. Others looked with whitened faces at one another, while one or two even crossed themselves.

'Also,' went on de Belame, 'our own names, the names of us still living, are written in black, but underneath each is a red line!'

He laughed hoarsely, and his bloodshot eyes glared at the faces beside him. He picked up the arrow, a short, stout bolt, the shaft and feathers being a jet black.

'This is a trick of that saucy knave, Robin Hood,' he said. 'He thinks to frighten us, the braggart fool. He would do justice, as he terms it, upon me – lord of Wrangby, grandson of Roger de Belame, at whose name the lords of forty castles shuddered when he lived. I have been too mild with this pretty outlaw! I will cut his claws! I will cut his claws! Lads, we will lay our snares, and when we have him in the crucet-house below, we will tame him of his sauciness!'

But in spite of de Belame's fierce and violent laughter, supper was eaten but moodily.

Next day, strange tales began to spread about the country-side. The noise of the fight at the church spread far and wide. It was said that when Robin and the priest went to bring out the dead from the church, the body of Sir Ranulf could not be found. Men said that the Evil One himself had carried him off, just as it must have been some fiend at whose call he had shown fear, and by whose black arrow he had been slain.

Then a villein raced home late the same night from a village near Hagthorn Waste and said that in the twilight he had seen, across the marsh, a dead man being borne by things that had no bodies but only legs – demons of the fen, no doubt, who were taking home the body of their evil master.

But strangest thing of all was that late that night, the moon being full, the men-at-arms on Hagthorn Castle, watching for the return of their master and his bride, had suddenly heard shrieks of fiendish joy sound far off in the waste, and looking closely they seemed to see where a flickering light danced to and fro, and small black forms that heaped up a great fire. Whereat, fearing they knew not what, they crossed themselves, but said that something fell and evil stalked abroad through the sedgy pools and stony wilderness that lay about them. Closely did they keep watch throughout the night, but at the darkest hour before the dawn a strange drowsiness fell upon those that watched, so that all within the castle slept heavily.

They woke again with fierce flames beating upon their faces, the thick reek of smoke blinding their eyes and choking them. Dashing to and fro, they sought for ways of escape, but found that every door was locked, every egress barred either by flame or by stout iron-studded doors. Then did these men who had never shown mercy cry for it to the red reaching hands of the flames, but found none. They who had tortured the poor and the weak were tortured and tormented in their turn, and all their prayers were unheard.

When dawn broke, the grey light shone wanly over a red and glowing ruin. Men and women from neighbouring villages came and stood marvelling to see it. Thin and poor, with wolfish, famished faces, they looked, and could scarce believe that at length the evil thing was brought to ruin – that the cruel power which had oppressed them and theirs so long was lifted from their backs, that no longer had it power to cripple their limbs, starve their bodies, and stunt their souls.

Far and near, when just men heard of the strange end of Sir Ranulf, slain by an unseen hand, and his castle brought low in fire lit by some mysterious power, they were glad at heart, and said that justice still lived. When Sir Isenbart de Belame and his evil crew heard of the deed they said naught openly, but their brows blackened with anger, though fear sat in their hearts.

They gave great heed to the watch which they set at night in the castle, and looked this way and that when they rode forth, and most of them avoided the forest ways. Then when King Henry died and his son Richard of the Lion Heart was anointed king and went upon his Crusade, some of them fared to the East with him. But de Belame stayed behind, biding his time.

Meanwhile, there was no happier, cheerier man in all England than Jack, Wilkin's son. For was he not now a freeman, and reaped his own free land? Jack whistled and sang about his work all day, a great thankfulness in his heart, both at his own good fortune and at the thought that he had brought happiness to his own fair lady, in helping to wed her to the man she loved best in all the world.

CHAPTER SIX

How Robin Gave Aid to Sir Herbrand

Robin Hood sat in his bower in Barnisdale Forest, and his men were waiting for their dinner. In the glade where they lay the crackle of fires under the pots and the bubbling of the stews in the cauldrons made pleasant sounds, and the smell of cooked venison and crusty pies when the cooks opened the earth-ovens put a keen edge on every man's appetite.

But Robin would not give the signal to dine, for they had had no adventure that morning. The men who had been lying in wait along the roads for travellers had reported that there seemed to be no one moving, and that day Robin had felt that he had no desire to dine until he had a stranger to sit and make cheer with him.

'John,' said he at length to his lieutenant, who was lying on the grass near him honing the point of an arrow, 'go you, lad, with Will and Much, the Miller's son, and wend ye to the Sayles by Ermin Street. From that place, since it lies high, ye may chance to see some wayfarer. If it be so, bring him to me, be he earl or baron, abbot or knight, or the king's justice himself.'

Cheerfully Little John rose from his place, and taking his bow and arrows, called Will Stuteley and Much, and together they went through the forest-ways until they came to where the land lay high. Here, in clearings of the forest, were two little stone houses, ruined now and deserted. Ten years ago they had been dwelt in by freemen, who had farmed their few acres of land and fed their swine in the forest. But the evil lord of Wrangby had passed that way, had demanded of Woolgar and Thurstan, the freeholding dwellers, to own that they held their lands from the Wrangby lord. The farmers had been men of Danish blood, who could not brook such tyranny, and had defied the evil Sir Isenbart, with result that by force they had been dragged from their holdings, their crops destroyed, and their houses fired and broken down. Woolgar had been slain defending his home, and his wife and children had become serfs at Wrangby. Thurstan had taken to the woods with his two boys, and had fled away, as men said, vowing that someday he would come back and help to burn down the Evil Hold and slay its lords.

'Remember Woolgar and Thurstan,' said Little John, as they passed the broken houses, with tall weeds nodding from the windows.

'Aye, aye,' said Much and Will, 'they are two of the poor broken men for whom we will strike a big blow someday.'

Passing through leafy paths the three outlaws at length reached the highway, where their feet beat on the high-crowned road that had been built by Roman hands eight hundred years before.

They came at last to where five roads met. The ground was high here, and there was a wide space where the forest-ways ran into each other. On all sides the ground sloped down, and they could see far over the tossing heads of the great forest which stretched away on all sides. They looked east and they looked west, but no man could they see. Then they looked north into the deep hollow of Barnisdale, and they were aware of a rider coming slowly along a narrow track between the trees to the left, which led from the town of Pontefract some seven miles away.

The horseman was a knight in mail, with a lance in his right hand, and he rode with bent head as if in deep thought. As he came nearer they could see that his face was grave, almost sad; and so dispirited was he that while one foot stood in the stirrup the other swung free, with the stirrup beating against it.

Little John hastened forward to meet the knight, and bending on one knee before him, said:

'Welcome, Sir Knight, to the greenwood. For these three hours hath my master been expecting you, and hath fasted until you came.'

'Thy master hath expected me?' said the knight, looking with surprise at the kneeling outlaw. 'Who is thy master, good woodman?'

'He is Robin Hood,' replied Little John, 'and he craves that you should dine with him this day.'

'I have heard of him,' said the knight, 'for a good fellow and a brave and just man. I will willingly take meat with him, though I had thought to have pushed on to Blythe or Doncaster before I dined. But how mean ye that thy master hath been awaiting me, since I know him not?'

'Our master will not dine today unless he have some wayfarer to keep him company,' replied Little John. ' 'Tis a habit which our master hath at times.'

'I fear me,' said the knight, 'I shall be but poor cheer for thy good leader.'

In a little while the knight and the three outlaws stood before the bower of branches and leaves in which Robin Hood was seated. The outlaw rose and looked keenly in the face of the knight, and said:

'Welcome be ye, Sir Knight. I would have thee dine with me this day.'

'I thank thee, good Robin,' replied the knight. 'God save thee and all thy men!'

Then bowls of water and a napkin were brought, and after Robin and the knight had washed their hands, they sat down to dinner. There was bread and wine, venison pies, fish, roast duck and partridges, besides stewed kale or cabbage, and the knight appeared to relish the rich repast laid before him. Robin did not ask the knight who he was, for it was not his custom to ask this of his guests until they had eaten. When at length the repast was finished and they had washed their hands again, Robin said laughingly:

'Now, Sir Knight, I hope you have dined well?'

'That I have, good Robin,' was the reply. 'Such a dinner, in faith, have I not had these three weeks.'

'Well, now,' went on Robin, smiling; ' 'tis unheard of that a yeoman should pay for a knight. I must ask toll of thee ere thou wendest farther through these woods.'

'My good Robin,' said the knight with a sad smile, 'I have naught in my purse that is worth thy accepting.'

'Come, come,' replied Robin, 'thou art a knight with a knight's lands. Tell me truth now. What hast thou ill thy saddle-bag?'

'I have no more than ten shillings,' said the knight, and sighed heavily.

'Ho, there!' cried Robin. 'Little John, go to this knight's horse and search his saddle-bag and see what he hath therein.' Little John went off at once to do his master's command.

Robin turned to the knight, and said: 'If indeed thou speakest truth I will not touch one penny thereof, and if thou hast need of more I will lend it to thee.'

In a few moments Little John came back, and said: 'Master, I find but this half a pound in the saddle-bag,' and he held out the silver coin in one broad brown palm.

'Fill up thy beaker to the brim,' said Robin to the knight; 'thou'rt a true man of thy word.' Robin and the knight drank to their mutual health and safekeeping.

' 'Tis a marvel,' said Robin, 'to see how thin is thy clothing. Never have I seen a knight so poor-seeming as thou art. Tell me truly, and I will not tell it to any man. Art thou a knight by birth, or wert thou made a knight by force for some brave deed, while thy means could not keep thee in dignity; or hast thou muddled thy wealth away, or been a brawler and a waster? How dost thou come to such a sorry pass?'

'None of those things which thou speakest of is the cause of my poverty and lowness,' said the knight gravely. 'For a hundred winters have my ancestors lived upon our land at home, and ever have they kept up the dignity of our name. But often it befalls, Robin, as thou must know, that a man falls into misfortune not by his own act, and only God who sitteth in the heavens may amend his state. Within the last two years, as my friends and neighbours know, I had four hundred pounds of money which I could spend, but now I have naught in all the world but my wife, and my lands that soon I must lose.'

'How is it thou hast fallen into such dire need?' asked Robin.

'Because of my son, who slew a man,' replied the knight. ' 'Twas done in fair fight, but the kin of the slain man did oppress me, and it was their evil purpose to ruin me because of my son's deed. I have paid them much money, but they demanded more, and therefore I have had to pledge my lands to the abbot of St Mary's. And in my heart I believe mine enemies will do all they may to gain my land, and would fain see me beg my living along the wayside, for they are most bitter against me, and have so worked by fear and threats on all my neighbours that no one will lend me the money wherewith to pay the abbot.'

'Now by my troth,' said Robin, and beat his knee with his clenched hand, 'shall we never be done with hearing of the evil deeds and crafty ways of the fat abbot of St Mary's? Tell me, now,' he said to the knight, 'what is the sum that thou owest?'

'Four hundred pounds,' replied the knight sadly. 'Four hundred have I already paid mine enemies, and they did demand four hundred more, which I was compelled to borrow from the abbot. And as I cannot pay it to the abbot tomorrow, I shall lose all I possess.'

'Now, if you lose your land,' asked Robin, 'what have ye in mind to do?'

'I will busk me and go to the Crusade,' said the knight, 'but first I go to the abbey of St Mary's to tell the abbot that I have not the money.' He rose from his seat as if there was no more to be said.

'But, Sir Knight,' urged Robin, 'have ye no friends who will aid thee?'

'Friends!' said the knight bitterly. 'While I was rich, friends boasted how they loved me, but as soon as they knew I was in need, and that powerful were mine enemies, they fled this way and that for fear that I should beg help of them.'

Pity was in the eyes of Little John and Will the Bowman, and little Much the Miller's son, turned away to hide a tear. The knight looked so noble and was so sad that the little man felt he would have done anything to help him.

'Go not away yet,' said Robin to the knight, who reached for his sword to buckle it to his side; 'fill thy beaker once more. Now, say, Sir Knight, if one should lend thee this money to save thy land, hast thou no one who will be a surety for the repayment?'

'Nay, by my faith,' said the knight reverently, 'I have no friend but Him that created me.'

'Jape me no japes!' replied Robin. 'I ask thee if thou hast not thine own friend – not one of the saints, who are friends to all of us, but who cannot pay thy debts.'

'Good outlaw,' said the knight, 'I tell thee truly, I have no friend who would answer for such a debt except Jesus and His Mother, the sweet Virgin!'

'By the rood!' cried Robin, and beat his knee again; 'now thou speakest to the point. If thou didst seek all England through, thou couldst not find a surety better to my mind than the blessed Virgin, who hath never failed me since I first called upon her. Come now, John,' he went on, turning to Little John, 'go thou to my treasury and pay out four hundred pounds, and let each coin ring true and sound and be unclipped and uncut. The tale of money must be truly the amount which the evil abbot will take, so that he may not be able to throw back a single bad coin and thus seize the land of our friend.'

Little John, with Much the Miller's son and Will Stuteley, went together to the secret place where Robin kept his chest of gold, and together they told out four hundred golden pounds, and wrapping them in a cloth which they tied up, Little John brought the money to Robin.

'Now here, Sir Knight,' said Robin, untying the cloth and showing the gold to the knight, 'are four hundred gold pounds. I lend it to thee on the surety of our dear Lady the Virgin, and by her blessing thou shalt pay me this money within a year and a day from now.'

The tears ran down the knight's thin cheeks as he took the money from Robin's hand.

'Sir outlaw,' said he, 'never did I think that any man was so noble of mind as to lend me on such a security. Good Robin, I thank thee, and I will see to it that thou shalt not suffer the loss of a single penny of this money, but in a year and a day will I return with the full sum. And now I will tell thee, that though I had heard thee well and nobly spoken of by my son who loves thee, little did I think I should find that his words spoke less than all the truth.'

'Who is thy son, Sir Knight?' asked Robin, 'and where hath he met me?'

'My son is Alan-a-Dale, ' replied the knight, 'whom thou hast aided more than once, and chief of all, for whom thou didst gain him the lady he loves best.'

'Now this is a goodly meeting,' said Robin, 'as he and the knight clasped each other's hands. 'Alan hath spoken to me of his grief concerning thee, and how he had not the wherewithal to save thee and thy land from the clutches of the crafty monk. But little did I guess that thou wert Sir Herbrand de Tranmire himself. Glad am I indeed, Sir Herbrand, to be able to aid thee, for I love thy son Alan, and would do all I could to bring joy to him and to the father whom he loves. Now thou art another whom those evil lords of Wrangby have oppressed and wronged. Tell me, wilt thou in good time aid me to pull down that Evil Hold of theirs, and scatter the vipers in that nest?'

'That will I most gladly,' said Sir Herbrand, and his voice was stern and hard. 'Not only for my own sake will I do this, but for the many tyrannies and evils which they have done to poor folks, as I know, in the lands which run from their castle in the Peak to the marches of Lancaster. Much would it gladden me to aid thee, and I promise to give thee all help in this matter when and as thou wilt.'

Then Robin Hood, from among his store of rich garments, took a knightly dress of fine array and donned it upon the knight, and it became him well. Also he gave him new spurs and boots, and afterwards, when the knight had to continue upon his journey, he gave him a stronger and better horse than his own.

When he was about to set out, after the knight had thanked Robin with tears in his eyes for all the kindness he had shown him, Robin said:

'It is a great shame for a knight to ride alone, without page or squire. I will lend thee a little page of mine own to attend thee to the abbey of St Mary's, so that he may wait on thee, and afterwards bring me word how things befall. John,' he called to his big lieutenant, 'do thou take horse and ride with Sir Herbrand, and do all that is squire-like, and bring me back word of how the abbot and his crafty crew do receive him.'

'I thank thee, good Robin,' said Sir Herbrand with a smile, 'for the little page thou sendest with me. And here I promise, by the sweet Virgin who hath never failed me, to bring to thee within a year and a day the money thou hast so nobly lent me, together with gifts to repay thee for those thou hast given me.'

'Fare thee well, Sir Herbrand,' said Robin as he shook hands with the knight, 'and send me back my little page when thou hast no longer need of him.'

As Little John rode off behind the knight there was much laughter and many jokes about the little page, and the knight was advised not to spare the rod, 'for,' many said, 'he was a saucy lad and needed frequent whipping'.

For some time the knight and Little John rode on along the lonely forest roads, and the talk between them was of Robin Hood and the many deeds of goodness which he had done.

'I fear me,' said the knight at length, 'though I will bring all the men I may to aid him, that he will find when the time comes that to pull down that evil nest of Wrangby will be beyond our strength. Isenbart de Belame is a crafty and skilful fighter, and I fear your master hath little knowledge of warfare and of how to take a strong castle such as Wrangby.'

'I have no fear of it,' said Little John with a laugh. 'My master is as wise a man as that limb of Satan. Besides, he hath right on his side, and is under the special care of Our Sweet Lady, and he that hath her blessing, who may avail against him?'

' 'Tis true,' replied the knight, 'the Blessed Virgin is worth a strong company of men-at-arms. But so far and wide do the evil plots of Belame and the Wrangby robbers spread, and so fearful are men to incur their displeasure, that from here to Doncaster on the east and to the marches of Lancaster on the west, I doubt if justice and right are ever allowed to be done if it comes to the ears of those evil men.'

'Ay,' said Little John sadly, 'they have laid the fear of death or torture on all who wish to live in peace, but, as I hope to be saved, I believe their wicked days are numbered. In every village lives some maimed wretch who bears the marks of their torture, in every manor-house or castle dwells some lord or lady, knight or dame, who hath been put to shame, or suffered ill by their ruffian deeds. And it is in my mind that, were my master once to rise against the evil crew, every peaceful man from here to Lancaster would rise also, and never lay aside his weapons until the cruel band were utterly wiped out.'

'May the Virgin grant that it be so!' said the knight. 'But what are those that follow after that man? It would seem that they have it in mind to rob or injure him.'

A little way before them was a group of some five or six men, walking in the middle of the road, and as the knight and Little

John approached them they could see that each of the five men behind bore a naked sword in his hand, while the man in front held a cross before him and was almost naked.

' 'Tis some felon who hath sworn to leave the country for some murder or other villainy,' said Little John, 'and those armed men are those whose kin he hath wronged, and who see that he go not out of the king's highway. And by the rood, he that holds the cross hath a right evil look.'

When they reached the group the knight asked courteously what crime the felon had committed. The man with the cross was ungirt, unshod, bareheaded and barefooted, and was clothed merely in a shirt, as if he were about to be hanged on a gallows. His look was black and evil, and across one cheek was the weal of an old wound. The five men who followed with swords drawn were well-to-do townsmen, or burgesses as they were called. One, by his dress, and by a certain authoritative look about him, was a man of power and influence, and he it was who replied.

'This evil wretch here whom we follow is a murderous knave, by name Richard Malbête,' he said. 'Our father was an old and doting man who, because he had ever dwelled in peace and quiet in his shop in Mercers Row, in our town of Pontefract, loved to hear tales of travel, and to speak to men who had fought and done warlike deeds. He fell in with this wretch here, who told many tales of his great adventures. Our father, John le Marchant, took this loose rascal into his house, much against the will and advice of us his sons. This Malbête, or Illbeast, as he rightly names himself, did slay our father, in a right subtle and wicked manner, and then fled with much gold upon him. We raised the hue and cry after him, and he took sanctuary in St Michael's church, and afterwards he did swear before the coroner to abjure and leave this realm, and to go to the port of Grimsby and there take ship. And we follow to see that he escape not.'

By the looks the five brothers gave the murderer it was evident that they would almost welcome any attempt he might make to escape, for then they would be justified, if he went but a step off the highway, in slaying him out of hand. There was nothing, really, to prevent them doing that now, for he was unarmed and there was no one by to protect him, but being law-abiding citizens they reverenced the oath which the murderer had taken.

Little John had not seen the robber when he had been disguised as a beggar and had fallen in with Robin, so that he did not recognise him. He looked at the brutal face of the man keenly, and noted the cruel and crafty glances which Malbête cast at the five brothers.

'I would counsel thee to take close heed of this rascal,' said Little John to the sons of John le Marchant. 'That evil face of his, I doubt not, hideth a brain that is full of guile and wile. Take heed lest by a trick he escape ye even now.'

The eldest brother, who had previously spoken, was a man unused to take advice, and resented the counsel of a man who looked to he no better than a woodman.

'I need no counsel to know what to do with a rogue,' he said stiffly. 'This felon shall have his life let from him ere he can hoodwink us.'

Little John laughed and said no more. When he and the knight had gone a little farther the latter said:

'I have seen that robber and murderer once before. He was taken up at Gisors for robbing in the very house where King Henry was sleeping. The camp provost condemned him to be hung forthwith, but I heard that by a trick he had escaped the hands of the camp marshals and got clean away. He is a man of a most evil life, and his mind is full of plots and crafty contrivings.'

'I knew it by his sly face,' said John, 'and I doubt not that one or more of the stiff-necked merchants behind him will pay with their lives for his escape.'

Nothing further happened to the two wayfarers until they reached the town of York just as daylight was dying from the skies. They were among the last to enter the city as the guard was shutting the huge gates. They went to a decent inn which the knight knew, where they supped and slept that night.

Next morning, in the chapter-house of St Mary's Abbey, were gathered the chief officers of the house. There was Abbot Robert, with proud curved lips, double chin, and fierce red face, and beside him on the bench was the prior, who was second in authority. He was a mild, good man, and did as much by kindness as the abbot did by his ways of harshness and tyranny.

Before them on a table were many parchments, for this was the day when tenants came to pay their rents or dues, and others

came to appear in answer to some charge or demand made by
the abbot. At the table were two monks who acted as clerks. On
the right of the abbot sat one of the king's justices, who was
travelling in that part of the kingdom, trying cases in the king's
name. There were one or two knights also sitting there, together
with the sheriff of York.

Many came in and paid their rents either in money or in
goods; others came and complained of the way in which the
abbot's bailiffs or stewards had oppressed them, and it was a
wonder to hear how many manors held by the abbey seemed to
have harsh bailiffs to rule them in the name of the abbot. To all
such complaining the abbot gave little heed, though the good
prior tried to make inquiry into the worse wrongs of which the
poor freemen or villeins complained.

'They are all a pack of grumbling rascals,' said the abbot
angrily at length. 'Save thy breath, prior, to say thy prayers, for I
would rather leave my bailiffs to do as they think needful than
meddle in matters of which I know little.'

'Nevertheless, when such great wrongs are charged against the
stewards of the abbey,' said the prior, 'methinks that for the
honour of the abbey and for the grace of the Holy Virgin after
whom our house is named, strict inquiry should be made, and if
our servants be shown to have acted without mercy they should
be punished.'

'If things were left to thee, prior,' said the abbot mockingly,
'we should all go bare to give the rascally villeins all that they
craved. Have done, and say no more. I am abbot, and while I am
chief of this house I will do as it seems to me fit.'

Just then into the chapter-house strode a tall and fierce-looking
man. He was dressed in half armour, having a hauberk on his
body, with a sword slung by a belt about his middle. On his head
of rough black hair was a hat of velvet, which he doffed as he
entered. Behind him came his squire, bearing his helmet and a
heavy mace. The abbot rose in his seat.

'Ha, Sir Niger,' he said with a laugh, 'so thou hast come as
thou didst promise. Dost thou think the knight of Werrisdale
will baulk us on this his last day of grace?'

'I think we may see him beg his bread of us today,' replied Sir
Niger le Grym with a cruel laugh. 'We will see to it that he pays

heavily for harbouring his rascal son, Alan-a-Dale, and if we cannot get at that wretched squire himself, we will make the father suffer in his stead.'

'I hear that his son hath joined that villainous robber and murderer, Robin Hood,' said the justice. 'Sheriff,' he went on, turning to that officer, 'you must take strong measures to root out that band of vipers who haunt Barnisdale. He hath not only, as I hear, slain Sir Ranulf of the Waste, but he hath burnt down his castle also.'

'Far be it from me, Sir Justice,' said the prior boldly, 'to take the part of so great a robber, but what he hath done hath been done by barons and lords of our county within this last year, and none of them ever received punishment from thee or from any of the king's justices.'

Sir Niger glared fiercely at the prior and muttered something under his red beard. The king's justice looked angrily at the speaker and could find nothing to say, for he knew it was true that when powerful knights such as de Belame and Sir Niger did evil, their wealth and their influence shielded them from punishment.

'This I know,' said the abbot hastily, 'that if Sir Herbrand of Werrisdale doth not come with four hundred pounds ere this day be done, he loses his land and is utterly disinherited.'

'It is still very early,' said the prior, 'for the day hath but half gone. It is a great pity that he should lose his land. His son slew the knight, Sir Ivo, in fair fight, and ye do Sir Herbrand much wrong so to oppress him. He is but a poor man, with no powerful friends to aid him.'

'Thou art ever against me, thou quarrelsome man,' said the abbot, and his heavy face went red with anger. 'I never say aught but thou dost contradict me.'

'I would have no more than justice done against high and low, knight or villein,' said the prior sturdily.

Just then there came in the high cellarer, the officer who looked to the provisions which had to be supplied to the abbey. He was so corpulent in body and red in face that it almost seemed that he partook more than was good of the food and drink over which he had control.

Ha! ha!' he said, and laughed in a fat wheezy way; 'this is the day when Sir Herbrand de Tranmire must lose his land if he pay us not four hundred pounds. I'll dare swear that he is dead or hanged, and will not come hither, and so we'll have his land.'

'I dare well undertake with thee,' said the justice, 'that the knight will not come today. And as I did lend thee some of the four hundred pounds, I count that I gain more than I sent thee, seeing that the knight's lands are worth much more than what they are pledged for.'

'Ye say right,' said the abbot. 'We be all sharers in the land of the knight except Sir Niger, and he seeks revenge alone.'

'Come you now to meat,' said the cellarer, and he led the way to the wide hall, where all the company sat down to a rich meal, served on silver platters by pages in fine attire. They laughed and jested as they ate, for they felt sure that the knight could not pay the money he owed, and therefore they would all make a great profit out of his land.

In the middle of their feasting there came the knight himself into the hall. He looked sad and sorrowful, and was dressed not in the rich clothes which Robin had given him, but in his old and worn garments. Behind him came Little John, clothed like a poor squire, in patched and sailed jerkin and ragged hose.

'God save you all!' said the knight, kneeling with one knee on the floor.

The abbot looked at him, and gladdened to see how mean and poor he looked. 'I have come on the day thou didst fix for me, father,' went on the knight.

'Hast thou brought my money?' asked the abbot in a harsh voice.

'Not one penny,' said the knight, and shook his head sadly.

The abbot laughed. 'Thou art an unlucky fellow!' he said, mocking him. Then raising his flagon of wine, he said to the justice:

'Sir Justice, drink to me, for I think we shall have all we hoped to get.'

Then, having drained the flagon, the abbot turned and said to the knight:

'What dost thou do here, then, if thou hast not brought my money?'

'To pray you, father, for a little further time,' said the knight in a sad voice. 'I have striven hard to find the money, and if thou wouldst give me but four more months, I shall be able to make up the sum due to thee.'

'The time is over, my man,' said the justice in a scornful voice. 'As thou hast not the money, thou wilt no longer have thy land.'

'Oh, for sweet charity's sake,' prayed the knight, 'do thou be my friend, Sir Justice, and shield me from these that would strip me to see me starve.'

'I am a friend of the abbot's,' said the justice coldly, 'and I will see naught but justice done between thee. If thou hast not the money, thou must lose thy land. 'Tis the law, and I will see it fulfilled, hark ye!'

Then the knight turned to the sheriff. 'Good Sir Sheriff,' he said, 'do ye plead with the abbot on my behalf to grant me a little longer time.'

'Nay,' said the sheriff, 'I will not – I may not.'

At length the knight, still kneeling, turned to the abbot.

'I pray thee, good Sir Abbot,' he pleaded, 'be my friend and grant me grace. Hold ye my land until I make up the amount which is due to thee. I will be true man to thee in all things, and serve thee rightfully.'

'Now by the rood,' said the abbot, and he was furiously angry, 'thou art wasting thy breath to ask such foolish prayers. I tell thee thou mayest get other land where thou wilt, but thy land is mine now, and never more shalt thou possess it.'

'By my faith,' replied the knight, 'and he laughed bitterly; 'thus is tested indeed the friendship which thou didst once profess to me!' The abbot looked evilly upon the knight, for he did not like to be reminded of such things in the presence of the enemies of Sir Herbrand.

'Out upon thee, traitorous and cozening man!' he cried. 'Thou didst make the bond to pay me on this day, and thou hast not the money. Out! thou false Knight! Speed thou out of my hall!'

'Thou liest, abbot!' cried the good knight, and got up from his knees. 'I was never a false knight, but ever a man of honour. In many lands have I fought, and in jousts and tournaments have I borne a lance before King Henry and the kings of France and Germany. And ever in all places did I get praise until I came hither in thy hall, Sir Abbot!'

The justice was moved at the noble knight's words, and he

thought the abbot had been harsh and oppressive. Therefore he turned to Abbot Robert and said:

'What wilt thou give him beyond the four hundred pounds so that he release all claim on his land to thee?'

Sir Niger looked black, and growled at the justice in his beard. 'Give him naught!' he said in a low tone to the abbot.

'I'll give him a hundred pounds!' said the abbot.

'Nay, 'tis worth two hundred – six hundred pounds in all,' urged the justice.

'Nay, by the rood!' cried the knight, and came to the foot of the table, and with flashing eyes he looked forward from one to other of his enemies. 'I know thy plots against me,' he went on. 'Ye foul-living monks desire my land, for thou art ever yearning to add acre to acre, and to grind down the souls and bodies of thy poor villeins to get more wealth from them. Thou, Sir Niger, wouldst revenge thyself of the death of thy kinsman, whom my brave son slew in fair and open combat. But chiefly thou desirest to have vengeance upon me because thou art not bold enough to seek for Robin Hood, who aided my son against thee. Therefore thou wouldst ruin and oppress me who cannot fight against the evil power of your Wrangby lords. But I tell thee, have a care how far thou goest. As for thee, Sir Abbot, here are thy four hundred pounds!'

With that he drew a bag from his breast, untied the mouth, and emptied the golden coins upon the table.

'Have thy gold, abbot,' he said mockingly, 'and much good may it do thy immortal soul.'

The prior came forward with two monks, and having counted the gold and found it was the proper amount, the prior made out a quittance and handed it to the knight. Meanwhile the abbot sat still, dumbfounded and full of shame, and would eat no more. The faces of the others also showed how bitterly they felt the way in which the knight had turned the tables upon them. Sir Niger le Grym, with a red and angry face, chewed his nether lip and darted fierce glances at the knight, who stood boldly meeting his gaze.

'Sir Abbot,' said the knight, waving the receipt in their faces, 'now have I kept my word, and I have paid ye to the full. Now shall I have my land again for aught that ye can say or do.'

'I pray thee, good Sir Abbot, be my friend'

With that he turned and strode out of the door, followed by Little John. Getting on their horses, they went back to their inn, where they changed their clothes, and having dined, rode out of the town and took the road toward the west, for the knight desired much to reach home swiftly, to tell his dear wife how well he had sped, thanks to the noble kindness of Robin Hood.

'Sir Knight,' said Little John, as they rode together through the forest-ways a few miles from York, 'I liked not the evil look upon that knight's face who sat at table with the abbot. 'Twere well to take heed against a sudden onfall or an ambush in a secret place.'

'I fear not Sir Niger le Grym,' replied the knight, 'nor any other knight so he come against me singly. But the Wrangby knights are full of treachery, and seldom fight except in twos or threes. Therefore thy words are wise and I will take heed. Do thou leave me now, good woodman, for I would not take thee so far out of thy way.'

'Nay,' said Little John, 'I may not leave thee in the forest. My master said I was to be thy squire, and I would stay with thee in case thou needest me until thou hast reached thy own lands.'

'Thou art a faithful fellow,' said Sir Herbrand, 'and I would that I could reward thee. But as thou knowest, I am bare of money and jewels.'

'I need no such rewards, I thank thee, Sir Knight,' replied Little John. 'I was ever ready to go out of my way for the chance of a good fight, and I think we shall have a few knocks ere we have gone far, or I know not a murderous look in a man's eyes.'

Little John felt sure that Sir Niger le Grym had meditated treachery when Sir Herbrand had put down the money, and he did not doubt that at some likely spot the knight would be set upon and perhaps killed in revenge.

As they rode along both kept a sharp look-out when the road narrowed and ran through thick woods, but they cleared the forest, and towards the end of the afternoon they found themselves upon the desolate moors, and there had as yet been no sign of their enemy. But now they were in the wild country, where the power of Sir Isenbart, Sir Niger, and their evil companions was strongest, and the two riders pushed on swiftly, hoping to reach the town of Stanmore before nightfall.

In this solitary country they met few people except a shepherd or two, or a couple of villeins now and then passing homewards from some errand. Once they saw a hawking-party in the distance, and another time they met a band of merchants with their baggage ponies. At length they began to mount a long and steep ascent towards a high ridge called Cold Kitchen Rigg, at the top of which was a clump of fir trees, their heads all bent one way by the strong wind which seemed always to blow up there.

As they pushed their jaded horses up the last few yards, suddenly from between the bushes beside the trees came the sound of a whizzing arrow, and next moment a bolt rattled harmlessly against Little John's buckler, which hung beside his knee, and then fell to the ground. Glancing down at it, he saw it had a short black shaft, and knew at once who it was that thus warned him. He called to the knight, who rode a few paces before him, ' 'Ware the trees, Sir Knight!' But even as he spoke, out from the firs came a horseman in mail armour, with lance set, and rushed at Sir Herbrand. At the same time, from the other side of the narrow road, another horsed knight dashed out with a huge mace in his hand and came towards Little John. The road was steep, and they thought that the speed with which they came down the track would without doubt dash the two riders to the ground. But both the knight and John were prepared in a measure for the attack. Sir Herbrand had drawn his sword as he heard the arrow whiz from the bush, and now dressed his shield, so that when the first knight sped against him he parried the lance with his buckler, and as his opponent, foiled of his blow, swept helplessly by him, he brought his sword down upon the other's neck with such force that the man rolled from the saddle. The horse careered madly down the hill, and the knight's spur catching in the stirrup, he was dragged along the road, his body leaping and bumping over the rough places.

Next moment, however, a third knight had come swiftly from among the trees, and had attacked Sir Herbrand with his sword so fiercely that, on the steep road, it required all the good knight's strength to keep his horse from falling, and at the same time to ward off his enemy's shrewd blows.

As for Little John, he was in hard case. So fiercely had the second knight dashed at him that John scarcely had time to dress his buckler, and half the blow from the descending mace was received upon his arm, numbing it so that it seemed almost powerless. With drawn sword, however, John did his best to defend himself; but the stranger being mounted on a stronger horse, as well as being protected by full armour, John could but just hold his own, while he could do little hurt to his opponent. Fiercely the blows from the heavy mace came down upon the yeoman's buckler, and the stranger pressed his horse so violently against the weaker animal which John bestrode, that John knew that it would be but a matter of a few moments before he would be overthrown upon the sloping road.

Suddenly the knight checked in his assault and seemed to shiver; a hollow groan came from the headpiece, the mace fell from the lifted hand, and the mailed figure swayed in the saddle. John looked and saw the end of a short black arrow jutting from the armpit of his enemy. At such close range had it been shot that it stood deep in the flesh. Little John looked around and saw a hazel bush beside the way, and from among its leaves the round, tanned face of Ket the Trow looked out, its usual good-nature now masked by a terribly savage look of triumph.

With a clatter the knight pitched to the ground, and his horse stood shaking beside the corpse of its master. Seeing the fall of his comrade, the third knight, who was fighting with Sir Herbrand, suddenly put spurs to his horse and dashed away through the trees. Rushing down the slope beyond, he could be seen riding swiftly over the moor in the direction of Wrangby Castle. Sir Herbrand, who was wounded, forbore to pursue his enemy.

Not so Ket the Trow. With a stealthy movement he ran across the road and was swallowed up in the tall bracken fronds.

'Who is that?' cried Sir Herbrand. 'Is it one of the men of these felon knights who have attacked us?'

'Nay,' said Little John; 'it is one to whom I owe my life today, for if his arrow had not ended this rogue's life here, I think I should have been overborne.'

'Who is this knight?' said Sir Herbrand, and getting off his horse he went and lifted the dead man's visor. 'By Holy Mary!' said the knight, 'it is Sir Niger himself!'

'Then there is one less of that evil crew,' said John, 'or perhaps two, for I doubt not that he on whose neck thou didst beat is dead by now, for if he was alive when he fell, his horse hath killed him by now.'

'Do you ride back, John,' said Sir Herbrand, 'and if the knight and his horse are to be found, bring them back, for I would give him proper burial. Moreover, by all the laws of combat, his harness and his horse are mine.'

John did as the knight bade him, and having retraced his steps about half a mile he found the horse quietly cropping the grass by the wayside, the body of its rider being a few yards away, the spur having become loosened when the horse had ceased its wild running. He lifted the dead man on the horse, and went back to Sir Herbrand, and leading the two captured horses, each with its dead master on its back, the knight and Little John pursued their way, and in an hour came to a wayside chapel. There they entered in, but the hermit who was its guardian was absent. Having stripped the armour from the two dead knights, Sir Herbrand laid the bodies decently before the altar, and then with Little John kneeled down and said a prayer.

Afterwards, taking the two horses with the armour piled upon them, they pursued their way to their night's lodging-place, and the next day Sir Herbrand reached his home, and was fondly welcomed by his wife and by all his people. When he had told them how he had been befriended by Robin Hood, his dame and her household made much of Little John, and wished him to stay with them for many days. But on the second day John said he must return to his master, and finding that he would not longer stay, Dame Judith made him up a good bag of meat and gave him a gold ring, and the knight made him a present of a strong horse, and gave him in gold the value of Sir Niger's horse and armour, which he said belonged by right to Little John. Thereafter the good outlaw bade farewell, and Sir Herbrand, at parting, shook his hand and said:

'Little John, thou and thy master have been good friends to me and my son, and may evil betide me if ever I forget thy good fellowship and aid. Tell thy master that within a year and a day, God willing, I will seek him and bring the money he hath so nobly lent me on the surety of Our Lady, and with that money will I bring a present. And tell him, also, from me, that if, as I think is likely, evil days come upon our dear land through the wrong and despite which Duke John beareth to his brother King Richard of the Lion Heart, there will be need for a few good and valiant men like thy master. And if he should at any time require my aid, tell him I can arm a hundred brave fellows to follow me.'

John promised to give the message faithfully, and so departed and reached Barnisdale without mishap.

Now, on the evening of the day on which the knights had set upon Sir Herbrand and Little John, the third knight, sorely faint and wounded, rode up to the gate of Wrangby Castle, which poor men called Evil Hold, and in a weak voice shouted to the gate-guard to lower the bridge across the moat. When this had been done he rode into the courtyard. Without dismounting he rode forward into the very hall where Sir Isenbart and his fellows were at their wine.

' 'Tis Sir Bernard of the Brake!' said the knights, looking up amazed at the swaying figure on horseback which came up to the very verge of the high seat.

'Where are Sir Niger and Sir Peter?' thundered Sir Isenbart, his fear of the truth making him rage.

'Dead!' said the knight, and they could see the white face within the helm. Give me wine – I – I am spent.'

A goblet of wine was handed to him, while men unloosed his helm and took it from off his head. Then they could see how he had been sorely wounded, but his great strength had kept him up. He drank off the wine and held out the vessel for more.

'The knight slew Sir Peter,' went on Bernard of the Brake, 'and the knave, I suppose, slew Sir Niger, for I saw him fall to the ground.'

All the knights looked gloomily at each other, and said no word.

Just then a man-at-arms from the gate-guard came running into the hall. In his hand he bore an arrow, which he laid on the table before Sir Isenbart.

'This, lord, hath just been shot through the bars of the portcullis, and narrowly missed my head. We could not see who shot it in.'

Sir Isenbart glanced at the short black arrow and his face went dark with rage. Along its shaft were notches, seven in number, which were stained red.

'Quick!' shouted Sir Isenbart, 'the wretch that shot it cannot have gone far. Out with you and search for him and bring him to me.'

There was bustle and noise for a few moments as some score of men-at-arms seized their weapons, and knights donned their armour and rode out, thundering over the drawbridge. There was a cleared space of a great extent before the gate, so that it was a marvel that anyone could have crept up unobserved by the men on watch at the slits over the drawbridge. The horsemen and footmen scoured the country for half a mile round, but not a sight or sound could they see of any lurking bowmen.

Darkness soon put an end to their search, and by ones and twos they returned to report their non-success. When the last had straggled across the drawbridge, the latter, with many creakings and shrieks as the rusty chains came over the beam, was hauled up for the night, and the portcullis ran down with a clang that shook the tower. Then, from beneath a little bush that overhung the outer edge of the ditch near the gate crept a small, lithe form. Slowly and with great care it drew itself out of the water, so that no splash could be heard by the men in the room of the gate-guard. It was Ket the Trow, who had been set by Robin Hood to keep watch on the Evil Hold. His bow and arrows he had kept dry by holding them in the bush above him.

He looked up at the black mass of the castle rising high and wide on the other side of the ditch. Light from cressets or torches shone out from the arrow slits here and there, and the gleam of a headpiece flashed up as a man-at-arms passed or repassed, walking on his watch. For some time Ket gazed, an arrow notched to his taut string, hoping that some face would come to look out from some near aperture, at which he might get another shot; But time passed, and no opportunity offered. He loosened his string, and turned reluctantly away.

'Seven have gone,' he muttered, 'but many are left. As they slew, so shall they be slain – without ruth, without pity.'

He trotted slowly away, looking back now and then at the dark bulk with little points of light here and there. For a mile he thus half ran until he came to where the forest began. Then in the darkness he passed through the deep gloom between the great trees until he came to one which was a giant among giants. With the stealth of a wild animal he looked about him and listened for a long time; then with an almost incredible swiftness he climbed up the trunk by means of tiny projections of knot and bark here and there until he disappeared in the massy leaves overhead. Higher and higher he mounted into a world where there was nothing but dark masses of leaves which murmured in the night wind, which was purer and stronger the higher he mounted. At length he reached a place where three great limbs jutted from the trunk, and in their midst was a space heaped with sweet-smelling fern fronds. Ket turned and looked forth to the way by which he had come. He was over the tops of all the other trees below him, which swayed and whispered like softly moving waves as the wind stirred them. Looking forth from among the leaves of the giant oak from where he sat in his lair, Ket could see far away the dark mass of the Evil Hold rising against the black sky behind it. A few lights still gleamed here and there, but every moment these were becoming fewer.

Casting off his wet clothes, Ket hung them securely on a limb to dry; then he wriggled deep into the great heap of fern, and having drawn food and drink from a hiding-place in the tree he munched and drank, his eyes never leaving the castle. When all the lights but those over the gate were darkened, he curled himself up in the scented fronds and fell to sleep instantly, and the murmur with which the wind strained through the leaves all about him was a lullaby that softly sang through the short summer night.

How Robin Hood Rescued Will Stuteley and Did Justice on Richard Illbeast, the Beggar-Spy

It was daybreak. A bitter wind blew down the forest ways, tearing the few remaining leaves from the wintry trees, and driving those upon the ground in great wreaths and eddies into nooks and corners. The dawn came with dull, low light over the forest, and seemed never to penetrate some of the deeper places, where the thickets of holly grew closer, or the bearded grey moss on giant oaks grew long.

Will of Stuteley, as he walked along a path, looked keenly this way and that into the gloomy tunnels on either side, for during the last three days he had seen a man, dressed as a palmer, lurking and glancing in a very unpalmer-like manner, just about this place, which the outlaws called Black Wood. Will was warmly dressed in a long brown capote, or cloak, which reached almost to his feet, with a hood which covered his head.

The first snows of the winter had already fallen, and most of Robin Hood's band had gone into their winter quarters. While frost and snow lay over the land, there was little travelling done in those days, and therefore a great part of the outlaws had gone to live with kinsmen or poor cottars in out-of-the-way places either in the forest or in villages not far distant. For a time they would dress as peasants, help in the little work that was done, and with this and what animals they trapped or caught, pay for their warmth and shelter until the spring came again.

Robin, with about a dozen of his principal men, lodged either in the secret caves which were to be found in many places through the wide forests, or, sometimes, one or other of the well-to-do forest yeomen, such as Piers the Lucky, Alan-a-Dale's foster brother, would invite Robin and his twelve to stay the winter in his hall. This year Sir Walter de Beauforest had invited him to pass the winter at a grange, or fortified barn, which lay in the forest not far from Sir Walter's manor-house at Cromwell, where Alan-a-Dale and his wife, the fair Alice, now lived in great happiness.

Robin had accepted Sir Walter's invitation, but if the weather was open he never stayed long in one place, and now he was living in a secret bower which he and his men had made at Barrow Down, which lay a few miles east of Mansfield, in a desolate piece of country where were many standing stones, old earthworks and barrows, or graves of the ancient dead. It was in one of these latter that Robin and his men now lived, for they had scooped out the interior of it and made it snug and habitable.

Every morning Will Stuteley and others of the band, having broken their fast in the Barrow, would walk out over a certain distance round their place of hiding, to find whether there were any traces of their enemies having approached during the last few hours. The ground was scanned for strange footmarks, the bushes and trees for broken twigs, and the outlaws were as keen-sighted as Indians, and as experienced in all the sights and sounds which should show them whether strangers had been in the neighbourhood during the hours of the night.

Suddenly Will stopped in the path down which he walked, and looked at the ground. Then, after a keen glance round among the hazels and young oaks which grew near, he knelt and examined a little hollow where in the springtime storm water would run. There was the distinct mark of a slender foot in the yielding earth. He looked further, and found two others of the same marks. They were quite freshly made, for the edges were keenly shown. Indeed, he felt sure that the person who had passed that way could not be far off. But who was it? The marks were those of a young lad or even of a girl. Whoever it was, the person was poor, for he could see marks which showed that the sole of one shoe was broken badly.

Stealthily he crept along picking up the trail here and there. He had proceeded thus some fifty yards, finding that the footsteps led deep among some brambles, when all at once he stopped and listened. He heard a low sobbing somewhere in among the thickest part of the bushes. Very carefully he stole in the direction of the sound, making no noise, until as he turned about a tall hazel tree he saw the figure of a girl a little way before him. She was picking berries from the bramble before her, and placing them in an old worn straw poke or basket which she carried.

As she plucked the berries she wept. Will could see the tears falling down her cheeks, yet it was with restraint that she sobbed, as if she feared to be heard. He saw how her hands were torn and bleeding from the brambles, and that her feet, pushed into her shoes, were uncovered and were blue with the frost.

He made a movement. She turned at the noise, her eyes wide with terror, her face white. Crushing the basket to her breast, she came and threw herself at the feet of Will.

'Oh,' she said in a weak, pitiable voice, 'slay me now, and do not seek my father! Slay me, and look no further! He is nigh to death, and cannot speak!'

Her tears were stayed now, her hands were clasped and raised in appeal, and in the childish face, so thin and wan, was a look that seemed to say that the child had known a terrible sorrow and now looked for nothing but death. She was a Jewess, as Will was quick to note.

The honest woodman smiled, as being the quickest way to cheer the girl. It went to the old outlaw's heart to see such sorrow in the child's eyes and voice.

'My little lass,' he said in his kindly voice, 'I mean thee no harm. Why should I harm thee, clemmed with the cold as thou art? And why art thou culling those berries? Thy poor starved body craves better food than that.'

He took her hands and lifted her up, and the child looked at him bewildered and dazed, as if she did not realise that kind words had been spoken where she had looked for brutal speech and action. She peered into Will's face, and her looks softened.

'You – you are not – you do not know the man – the man Malbête?' she stammered.

'Malbête?' said Will, and frowned. He remembered what Robin had told them of this man, and had heard from wandering men of other crimes and cruelties which this robber and murderer had committed. 'Poor lass,' he said; 'is that wretch thy enemy, too?'

'Yes, sir, of my poor father!' said the girl, and her voice trembled. 'My father fled from the massacre of our people at York – thou knowest of it?'

'Ay,' said Will, and his brow became black and his eyes flashed in anger at the memory of the dreadful deed, when many innocent Jews had been baited by evil knights and the rabble, and having shut themselves up in the castle, had killed their wives and children and afterwards themselves rather than fall into the hands of the 'Christians'.

'What happened to thee and thy father?' asked Will.

'We hid in the castle until all the slaying was over,' replied the girl, 'and then a kindly man did get us forth, and we fled secretly. My father wished to go to Nottingham, where there are some of our race who would aid us if they knew we were in need, but we have starved through these forests, and oh, sir, if you are a good man as you appear, save my father! He lies near here, and I fear – I fear whether – help may not be too late. But, oh, betray us not!'

'Take me to him, poor lass,' said Will, and his kindly tone and look dissipated whatever suspicion still lingered in the heart of the poor little Jewess.

She led the way through the almost impenetrable bushes until they reached a chalky cliff, and here in a large cave, the opening of which was screened by hazel thickets, she showed him her father, an old and white-haired man, dressed in a poor gaberdine torn by brambles and soiled by mire, lying on some bracken. The girl stood trembling as she looked from Will to her father and back again, as if, even now, she dreaded that she may have betrayed her dearest possession into the hands of a cruel enemy.

The old man awakened at their entry, opened his eyes, and in an instant the girl was on her knees beside him, her hands stroking his, and her eyes looking fondly into his face.

'Ah, little Ruth,' said the old man, gazing fondly into her eyes, 'I fear, dear, I cannot rise just yet. I am stiff, but it will pass soon, it will pass. And then we will go on. We shall reach the town in a few hours, and then my little Ruth will have food and fitting raiment. Your cheeks are pale and thin, dear, for you have hungered and suffered. But soon – ah, but whom have we here?

Who is this? O Ruth, Ruth, are we betrayed?'

In the gloom of the cave he had not at first noticed the outlaw, and the despair with which he uttered the last few words showed with what terror his mind was filled for his daughter's sake. Will felt that this was a brave old man who would not reveal the suffering he felt to his daughter, but though he was himself very sick, yet buoyed up her courage.

'Have no fear, master,' said Will, bending down on one knee, so that his eyes looked into the old Jew's face. 'If I can aid thee and thy daughter I will gladly do so.'

'I thank thee, woodman,' said the Jew, and his voice trembled; 'it is not for myself I fear, but for this my little maid, my one ewe lamb. She hath suffered sights and woes such as no child should see or know, and if she were safe I would be content.'

Tears fell down the poor old Jew's face. In his present state of starvation and weakness he felt that he had not long to live; but the greatest anguish was to think that if he died his little daughter would be left desolate and friendless.

'What ye both need,' said Will, his homely mind grasping the situation at once, 'is food and warmth. I can give ye a little food now, but for warmth I must ask the counsel of my master.'

Saying which, Will drew forth from his food-pouch some slices of bread and venison, which he gave to the girl, bidding her eat sparingly. But the girl instantly began to cut up the bread and meat into tiny pieces, and with these she fed her father before she touched the food herself. Though both she and her father had had little food for two days, they ate now with great restraint, and very slowly.

Afterwards Will offered them his pilgrim's leather flask, and when they had drunk some of the good wine which it contained, it was a joy to see how their eyes brightened, and their cheeks began to redden.

'Little Ruth,' said the old man, when they had returned the flask to Will, 'help me to get upon my knees.'

When this had been done, with the aid of the outlaw, the girl also knelt, and to Will's great discomfiture the Jew began to pray very fervently, giving thanks to God for having brought to them him that had delivered them out of death and misery. He called down such blessings on the head of Will the Bowman that the worthy fellow, for all that the light in the cave was but meagre, did not know where to look. When they had finished, Ruth seized the outlaw's hand and kissed it again and again, while the tears poured down her cheeks, but her heart was too full to say a word of all the gratitude she felt.

'Now,' said Will gruffly, 'enough of these thanks and tears. Ye must bide here while I go to take counsel of my master what is best to be done.'

'Who is thy master, brave woodman?' asked the Jew.

'He is Robin Hood,' replied Will.

'I have heard of him as a good man,' said the old man. 'Though an outlaw, he hath more pity and justice, as I hear tell, than many of those who are within the law. Do ye go to him, good outlaw,' he went on, 'with the greeting of Reuben of Stamford, and say that if he will aid me to get to my kinsmen of Nottingham, he shall have the gratitude of me and my people for ever, and our aid wherever he shall desire it.'

The old Jew spoke with dignity, as if used to giving commands, and Will answered:

'I will tell him; but if he aids thee, 'twill be for no hope of thy gratitude or thy gold, but because it is always in his heart to help those in wretchedness.'

'Bravely and proudly spoken, Sir Outlaw,' said Reuben; 'and if thy master is as kindly as thou art, I know he will not leave us to starve and perish miserably.'

Will thereupon set off back to Barrow Down, and arriving at the big mound wherein the outlaws dwelled, he found Robin there and told him of the Jew.

'Thou hast done rightly, Will,' said the outlaw. 'Go thou with two horses, and bring the Jew and his daughter to the Lynchet Lodge hereby, and I will question them concerning this ruffian, Richard Illbeast. I have heard of his evil deeds at York, and I think he is not far from Nottingham.'

It was done as Robin had commanded, and Reuben and Ruth were lodged in a secret hut on the slope of Wearyall Hill, not far from where the outlaws were staying. Both father and daughter were very weak, and the old Jew was much wasted as the result of his sufferings, but with generous food, and the warmth of good clothes and a huge fire, a few days saw them stronger in health

The girl was on her knees beside him

and better in spirits. Their gratitude to Robin was unbounded, but it was expressed more by their shining eyes than by words.

When the old man felt stronger Robin asked him to tell how he had fallen into the wretched state in which Will Stuteley had found him, and Reuben willingly complied.

'Thou hast heard, doubtless, good outlaw,' said the Jew, 'that when the great and brave King Richard was crowned at Westminster last autumn, the rabble of that great city did turn upon the Jews and sack their houses and slay some of my poor people. And your king did punish the ringleaders of the mob who slew and robbed our people, by hanging some and branding others with hot irons. But when, a short month ago, he left the country with his knights and a great army, to go to Palestine upon the Crusade, thou knowest that in many towns the rioting against us began again. Many knights and lords were gathering to depart for the Crusade, and a great mob collected with them. And because many of my kinsmen had lent the knights money, some of the more evil of them excited the mob to burn our homes and to rob us. Such evil deeds took place, as doubtless thou hast heard, in Stamford, Lynn, and Lincoln. I was dwelling at Lincoln, but I travelled to York and so escaped the pillage for a time. Now it chanced that a kinsman of mine, Rabbi Eliezer, a chief man among us, had lent much money to a baron named Alberic de Wisgar, a wasteful and a tyrannous lord. He laid a plot with others against the Jews of York, to plunder them and to destroy the records of the debts which they owed to my kinsmen. They plundered the house of a Rabbi whom they had slain in London, and fearing that the same fate would befall us, for safety we fled with our wives and children into the castle of York. We were there beset by a great mob of Crusaders, apprentices, and country folk, and he that was their leader was an evil man in the company of the Lord of Wisgar. He was named Richard Malbête, or Illbeast, and with much fury he egged on the people to besiege the castle and to endeavour to drag us out. We had no weapons, but with our naked hands we tore the stones from the walls inside and kept back the rabble with these. For three days, without food and without weapons, we beat them away, but when they brought a high engine against us and made it ready for the next morning, then we knew that we could hold out no longer. Never, while mine eyes can weep, nor my mind recall the past, shall I forget the grief, the terror, and the sorrow of that night. Long time we talked, counselling what should be done, though in our hearts most knew that there was but one way for us to take. At length Rabbi Eliezer arose amongst us, and said, "O men of Israel, God – of whom no man asketh, Why dost Thou permit this? – God hath commanded us to lay down our lives for His law, and behold death standeth at the door. Now, therefore, let us freely offer up our lives to God who gave them, as many of our people have done in times past, worthily delivering themselves out of great tribulations." '

For a little while the memory of that night of sadness over-powered the old man; tears rolled down his cheek, and he could not proceed. The little girl Ruth was also weeping softly, but at the same time she strove to comfort her father.

'Do not weep for them, my father,' she said, while she wept bitterly herself. 'God took them, and though they suffered death at the hands of those they loved, they are now in the bosom of Abraham for evermore.'

'Sir,' said the old Jew, 'she says truly. When Rabbi Eliezer had finished speaking we went apart and said no more. I cannot speak of all that then took place. All of us burned or destroyed such goods as we had with us, and those who had no hope slew their dear ones and then slew themselves. But I could not bring myself to do the same. I wished not life for myself, for rather would I have died; but for the sake of this my little daughter I found a place of hiding in the castle, in the hope that when, as would surely happen, the rabble broke in, I might be able at least to find a way for her to escape, though I had no hope of being spared myself. Next morning those who had not been willing to die opened the gates and went forth begging to be baptised, thinking thus to escape the fury of the multitude. From where we lay hidden I saw all that took place. The evil man, Richard Illbeast, came to the first Jew, Ephraim ben Abel, who kneeled before him, pleading for his life. "Where are the treasures of the Jews?" he asked. "Burned and destroyed," said Ephraim. "Where is Rabbi Eliezer?" he then demanded. "He and all but those who are here with me have slain themselves and their families," replied Ephraim. "Then die thou likewise!" said Illbeast, and at the words the rabble slew the kneeling Jews and spared not one. Then the mob poured into the castle, and we lay expecting every moment to be found and dragged forth. After some time they left the castle and rushed away to the cathedral, where, as thou knowest, the king keeps the records of the loans made by my people to the Christians in those parts, and those parchments they burned utterly, so that now Alberic of Wisgar and the other evil knights are free of all their debts.'

'How got you free?' asked Little John, who, with Will the Bowman, Scarlet, and Arthur-a-Bland, were listening with Robin Hood.

'God, in answer to our prayers, softened the heart of a man-at-arms, who discovered us, but would not betray us for pity of our sufferings. He got food for us and soldiers' cloaks to disguise us, and on the second night he took us and let us out of the town by a privy gate, and directed us on our road to Nottingham.'

'Know you what befell those ruffian knights and robbers?' asked Robin.

'The soldier, whom God reward for his noble heart,' said the old man, 'told us that all had fled the town fearing the anger of the king's officers. The knights had quickly gone forward to the Crusade, while of the rabble and the robbers some had fled to Scotland or taken to the forests, and others lay hid in the town. And he said further that the king's justices would visit the ill-doing heavily upon the town, and that already the sheriff and principal merchants were quaking for fear. And now, Sir Out-law,' continued Reuben, 'I have a boon to ask of thee. I have a daughter and a son in Nottingham, to whom we were hastening. They grieve for us as dead, and I would crave that you let one of your men go to their house and tell them that we are safe, and that we will be with them when it shall please you to let us go, and I am strong enough to set forth.'

'Surely,' said Robin, 'that shall be done. Who will go of you and take the message to the Jew's people? What do you say, Will, as 'twas you who found them?'

'I will go with a good will,' said Will Stuteley. 'Give me thy message and tell me where I may find thy kinsfolk, and I will set out forthwith.'

Both Reuben and Ruth were warm in their thanks, and having given Will the necessary directions and messages, Will departed to dress himself in a disguise which would prevent his being recognised by any of the citizens who may have seen him when they had been required to pay toll to outlaws when passing through the forest.

That afternoon, therefore, a pilgrim in his long dark robe, his feet in ragged shoes, a scallop shell on his bonnet and a stout staff in his hand, might have been seen passing through Bridlesmith postern gate an hour before sunset, when the gates would close for the night. He took his way through the streets with a slow stride as befitted a pilgrim who had travelled far and was weary.

Will the Bowman did not think that there was any likelihood of his being recognised in his disguise, but though he seemed to keep his eyes bent humbly to the ground, he looked about keenly now and then to pick up landmarks, so as to know that he was going the right way to the house of Silas ben Reuben, one of the chief men in the Jewry of Nottingham, to whom he was to take the message from the old Jew.

At length Will entered the street of the Jewry, and began counting the number of doors from the corner, as he had been told to do by Reuben, since he was not to excite attention by asking anyone for the house. The outlaw noticed that while several of the house doors were open, through which he could see women at work and children playing, others were fast locked and their shutters closed, as if the dwellers feared that what had happened to the Jews in other towns might happen to them also.

When at length he came to the ninth house, he knocked at the door, which was barred, and waited.

A wicket in the door was opened and a man's dark eyes peered out.

'What is it thou wantest?' he asked.

'I wish to see Silas ben Reuben,' replied Will; 'I have a message for him.'

'What secret words or sign hast thou that thou art not a traitor, who would do to me and mine as has been done to others of our people?' came the stern reply through the wicket.

'I say to thee these words,' went on the outlaw, and said certain

Hebrew words which he had been told by Reuben.

Instantly the face disappeared from the wicket, bolts were drawn, and the door swung open. 'Enter, friend,' said the Jew, a short, sturdily built man. The outlaw entered, and the door was barred behind him. Then the Jew led him into an inner room, and turning said:

'I am he whom thou seekest. Say on.'

'I come to tell thee,' said the outlaw, 'that thy father, Reuben of Stamford, and thy sister Ruth, are safe and well.'

'Now, thanks be to God,' said the man, and clasping his hands, he bowed his head and murmured words of prayer in some foreign tongue.

'Tell me how thou didst learn this,' he said when he had finished his prayer; 'and where they are, and how soon I may see them?'

Thereupon the outlaw told Silas the Jew the whole story of his discovery of little Ruth and her father, and of their sufferings as related by the old man. When he had finished the Jew thanked him for his kindness to Reuben and Ruth, and then went into another room. When he returned he bore in his hand a rich baldrick or belt, of green leather, with a pattern worked upon it of pearls and other precious stones.

'Thy kindness is beyond recompense,' he said; 'but I would have thee accept this from me as a proof of my thanks to thee.'

'I thank thee, Jew,' said Will, 'but 'tis too rich a gift for me. It befits my master more. But if thou wouldst make a gift to me, give me a Spanish knife if thou hast one, for they are accounted of the best temper and make throughout Christendom.'

'I will willingly give thy master this baldrick if he will take it of me,' said the Jew, 'and thou shalt have the best Spanish knife in my store.'

He thereupon fetched such a knife and presented it to the outlaw, who tried the keen blade, and found that it was of the finest make.

It was becoming dark now, and the outlaw wished if possible to leave the town before the gates were shut. Arrangements, however, had to be settled with the Jew as to how and when he would send horses and men to meet Reuben and Ruth at a spot where Robin Hood and his men would take them from their present hiding-place. It was quite dark by the time all things were settled, and the Jew wished Will to stay the night with him, saying there was no one else in the house with him, as he had sent his wife, his sister, and his children into a place of greater safety for fear of the rabble.

'I thank thee, Jew,' said the outlaw, 'but I would liefer sleep at a place I wot of, which is near the gate, so that I may slip out o' the town at the break of day when they first open.'

As the outlaw went along the narrow street of the Jewry after leaving the house of Silas, two men walking together passed him silently, looking at him furtively. They did not seem to have the dress of Jews, and he wondered at the silence of their footsteps. He slowed his own steps to allow them to get farther ahead of him, but they also went more slowly, and kept at the distance of six paces before him. One of them looked swiftly behind from time to time. He knew then that they watched him, and that either because they knew he was of Robin's band, or because he had visited the Jew's house, they meant harm to him.

As he thought thus, he gripped the haft of his Spanish knife and stopped, determined to sell his life dearly if they also stopped and turned round upon him. At the same moment he felt a hand upon his arm, and a voice whispered in his ear:

'Friend of Silas ben Reuben, the spies dog thee. Come with me.'

The outlaw saw a dark form beside him. A door opened noiselessly, and Will was pulled into what seemed to be a narrow winding passage. Along this the hand upon his arm led him for several yards until suddenly he felt the night air blowing upon his face, and he looked up and saw the stars.

'Go to the left,' said the same voice in his ears; ' 'twill lead thee to the Fletcher Gate.'

'I thank thee, friend,' said Will; and strode to the left. A few steps took him into the narrow street which led to the gate named, and Will Stuteley hurried forward, thankful that by the aid of the unknown Jew he had been saved from capture. Without further delay the outlaw went to an inn which overlooked the town wall, and whose landlord asked no questions of his customers. There in the common room Will partook of a frugal supper, and then, ascending to the sleeping-chamber, a large room on the first floor where all the lodgers of the house would sleep when they sought repose, he threw himself in a corner on the straw which covered the floor, and was soon sound asleep.

As time went on, others came up from the room below, found suitable places along the wall, and composed themselves to sleep. Stuteley awoke as each came up, but having glanced at the new-comer by the light of the rushlight which, stuck in a rough tin holder on one wall, gave a dim light about the apartment, he turned and slept again. Very soon the room became almost full, and the later comers had to step over the prostrate forms of snoring men to find places where they could sleep.

After a time, however, the house became quiet; no more men came up into the sleeping-room, and the house seemed sunk in slumber. The wind moaned a little outside the house, and crooned in the slits of the shutter at a window hole, and sometimes a sleeper would murmur or talk in his sleep with thick almost unintelligible words, or fling his arm about as if in a struggle, or groan as if in pain. The street without was dark and silent, cats slunk in the gutter which ran down the middle of the street, or a stray dog, padding through the streets, would come to a corner, sniff the wind and howl.

Before the first glint of dawn had showed itself in the cold street, Stuteley was awake. He loved not houses; their roofs seemed to press upon him, and when in the forest he was wont to issue from the bower or the hut in which he slept, and to walk out from time to time to look at the sky, to smell the odour of the forest, and to listen to the murmur of the wind in the sleeping trees. As he lay there in the dark he longed to be up and away in the cool air of the forest. He cautiously rose, therefore, and feeling his way over the sleeping men, he made his way to the door, where a ladder of rough wooden steps led to the room below.

As he strove to open the door he found that a man's body lay before it. He stirred him gently with his foot, thinking that the man would understand that he wished to open the door and would seek another place.

'A murrain on thee, fellow,' came a voice beside the outlaw. 'Why so early astir? The town gate will not open till I am there. Are ye some thief that seek to flee the city before men are about?'

'No thief am I,' said Stuteley; 'I am but a poor pilgrim who must fare to the holy shrine at Walsingham. And as I have far to go I must needs be early astir.'

By this time the man before the door had risen, and had himself opened the door and stood at the head of the stairs. Stuteley followed him and waited for him to descend, for the stairs were not wide enough for two men to pass. The man who had spoken also came forth, and in the faint dawn they glanced keenly at the outlaw. They were sturdy fellows, and were dressed in sober tunic and hose, as if they were the servants of a well-to-do burgher.

'A pilgrim art thou?' said the one who had spoken already. He laughed in a scornful manner as he looked at Stuteley up and down. 'A pilgrim's robe often covers a rogue's body.'

Saying this, he gestured to the stairs, and Stuteley hastened to descend, feeling that he would better serve his purpose by appearing to be harmless than to answer with a bold speech. The other men followed closely upon his heels, and all three entered the living-room together. Two men sat at a table, and at sight of the two others behind Stuteley they rose and advanced. The foremost, a big man with a villainous cruel look, and the scar of an old wound across his cheek, came forward and said:

'Who have you there?'

'A pilgrim, captain, as he doth declare himself.'

Stuteley saw that he had been caught. His hand leaped to his belt, but at the first movement the two men behind him had gripped his arms.

'Show his left hand,' cried the captain; 'that will show whether this pilgrim knows not another trade! Ah, I thought so!' he went on, as one of them thrust forth Stuteley's left hand, the forefinger of which showed where a corn or hardening had grown by reason of the arrow shot from the bow rubbing against the flesh. 'This is our man – one of that ruffian Robin's band!'

Quick as thought the outlaw wrenched himself free and darted towards the door. He hoped that he might be swift enough to lift up the bar and dash out; but they were too quick for him. Even as he raised the heavy beam which rested in a socket on each side of the door, the four men were upon him. Still holding the bar, he swept round upon them and sent one man crashing to the floor, where he lay senseless. Then, using the beam as a weapon, he beat the others back for a moment. Suddenly, however, the big captain got behind one of his own men, and catching him by the shoulder, he thrust him against Stuteley. Down came the beam on the man's head, stretching him senseless; but before the outlaw could recover himself, the captain and the other man had rushed upon him and overpowered him, holding him down on the floor.

The landlord, roused by the noise, came rushing in, and the captain commanded him to bring ropes. Now the landlord knew Will Stuteley, who had often stayed in his house disguised as a beggar or a palmer, and felt very grieved that one of bold Robin Hood's band should be taken by the sheriff's men. He therefore affected to be very distraught, and ran about from place to place, pretending to look for a rope, hoping that somehow Will might be able to get up if he were given time, and break away from his captors.

But it was all in vain. 'A murrain on thy thick wits!' yelled the captain from where he kneeled holding one of Will's arms. 'If thou findest not ropes in a twinkling, thou rogue, the sheriff shall hear of it.'

'Oh, good captain!' cried the landlord, 'I am all mazed, and know not where anything is. I be not used to these deeds of man-taking, for my house was ever a quiet one.'

Seeing that it was no use to delay longer, the landlord found some rope, and soon Will's arms were strongly bound. While this was being done, the landlord managed to give a big meaning wink to the outlaw, by which he gave Will to know that he would be his friend and would send tidings of his capture to Robin. Then Will was jerked to his feet, and with mocking words was led off to prison.

The landlord sent a man to the forest as soon as the town gates were open. It was late in the day ere he fell in with one of Robin's band, and he told the outlaw, who happened to be Kit the Smith, how Will had been taken, but had slain two men with a door beam before he was overpowered. When Kit the Smith had brought the man to where Robin was seated, deep in the forest, they found that a good burgher, who had been befriended by Robin some time before, had already sent a man who told the

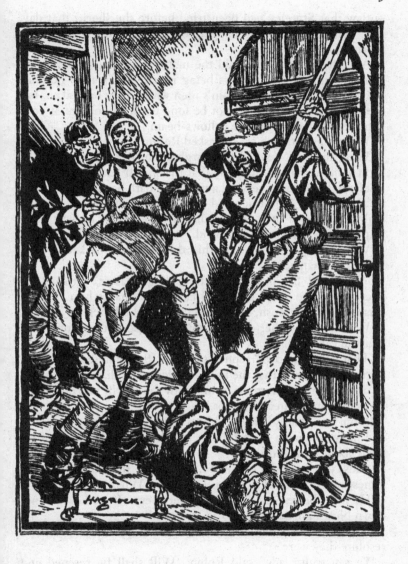

Using the beam as a weapon, he beat the others back

outlaw that Stuteley had been tried before the sheriff that day, and that he would be hanged outside the town gate next morning at dawn.

'Already, as I set out,' said the man, 'I saw the timber being brought and the old gallows being repaired. 'Twas in honour, they said, of the first of Robin's men whom they had taken, but they thought now 'twould not be long ere many others of your band should hang from the gallows-beam.'

'What meant they by that?' asked Robin.

'Well, maister,' replied the burgher's man, an honest, forth-right-looking fellow, 'they say that the sheriff hath took a crafty thief-catcher into his service, a man who hath been in many wars in France and Palestine, and who is wise in stratagems and ambuscades; and they say it will not be long ere he lays some trap which will take all your band.'

'What manner of man is this thief-catcher?' asked Robin. 'How is he named?'

' 'Tis a tall big man, a swashbuckling boaster, with a loud hectoring voice and a great red face. Some name him Captain Bush or Beat the Bush, but others call him the Butcher.'

'Whence comes he?' asked Robin, who did not recognise this boastful captain.

'That no one knows,' replied the man. 'Some do say he is but a rogue himself, and that the king's justice would love to have him in irons. But he is in great favour with the sheriff just now, who takes his counsel in all he does.'

Robin was greatly grieved to hear of poor Will being captured, and his voice had a stern tone in it as he turned to those of his band about him, and said:

'Lads, you hear the evil news. Poor Will the Bowman, good honest old Will, is taken and is like to die. What say you?'

'He must be rescued!' came the fierce cry. 'If we have to pull down Nottingham town we will save him!'

The hard looks on the faces of the outlaws showed how resolute they were.

'Ye say truly, lads,' said Robin. 'Will shall be rescued and brought safely back amongst us, or else many a mother's son of Nottingham shall be slain.'

Robin gave orders for the two townsmen to be entertained and

kept in the camp until the morning, and the men willingly gave
their word not to return to Nottingham. This Robin did so that
no word should leak out of his attempted rescue; for he guessed
that it would be a difficult task in any event to get Will Stuteley
out of the hands of the sheriff and his new 'ancient' or lieutenant,
Captain Beat the Bush.

Meanwhile, in the sheriff's house in Nottingham, the sheriff
was deep in counsel with his thief-taker. They had tried to
question Will, but had naught but defiant answers from the
brave outlaw, who had told them to do their worst with him, but
that they should get no secrets from him.

'Take him away!' the sheriff had cried at last in a rage.
'Prepare the gallows for him, and he shall swing at dawn
tomorrow's morn.'

Without a word Will heard his doom, and walked with proud
look to his dungeon.

'Sir Sheriff,' said Captain Beat the Bush when they were alone,
'I have that to propose which of a surety would enable us to learn
the secret lair of the robber band of Robin Hood.'

'Say on,' replied the sheriff. 'I would give a hundred pounds to
have that rogue and his meinie scotched or slain.'

'It is this,' went on the captain, and his villainous face had a
crafty look upon it. 'Let this man go; he will fly like a bolt from a
bow to his chief in the greenwood. Let two or three sly fellows
follow him and keep him in sight until they know where the
rogues lie hid. Then, when we learn where is their lair, swiftly
thou canst gather thy men, and, led by me, we will surround them
when they look not for attack, and we will take them every one.'

The sheriff frowned gloomily and shook his head.

'Nay,' he said, 'I'll not lose this one that I have. He shall
swing! Once let him go, and the rogue Robin is so full of wiles
and stratagems that, Master Bush, thou mightest find thyself
ambushed and put to scorn.'

'Then,' replied Captain Bush, 'I have another plan, which will
please your worship better. I have told thee how my spies have
kept a watch upon the house of Silas ben Reuben, and how they
saw this rogue enter there and converse some long time with the
Jew. Now I doubt not that there is some evil plot between the
Jew and this rogue Robin o' the Hood. Thou knowest thyself

that the outlaw deals in necromancy and black magic, and I doubt not that he and that evil brood of Jews do plot to work some evil against us Christians.'

'What will ye?' demanded the sheriff in a sudden burst of rage. 'Would you stir up the people to bait and spoil the Jews? Do you plot to have me thrown out of my office, fined to the half of my estate, and every burgher of this town required to pay a third of his goods? That hath been done at York and at Lincoln by the king's justice. Thou rogue!' he ended, fury in his narrow eyes, 'what evil plot hast thou against me? What knowest thou of Silas ben Reuben? Art thou, belike, one of those rogues whom the sheriff and merchants of York would gladly find so as to make thy skin pay for the penalties which the king's justice hath put upon them?'

Captain Bush was not expecting so fierce an outburst, and he looked crestfallen. Indeed, seeing the startled look in his eyes, one would have thought that the sheriff's last question had reached a surer mark than he suspected. The sheriff stalked up and down the room in his rage, and did not see the sudden fear in the other's eyes.

'I tell thee, my brave thief-taker,' he cried in a raging scorn, 'I'll have none of thy plots against the Jews. 'Tis easy enough for a nameless rogue such as thee to stir up a cry to spoil the Jews, and to lead a cut-throat mob of rascals to slay and loot and plunder. But when the king's justice comes to demand penalties it is not thy hide that smarts, nor thy cobwebby pocket that pays. Go, then, get thee from my sight, and see that the gallows is ready by dawn tomorrow, and name no more of thy rascally plots to me.'

'As your worship and lordship pleases,' said the captain in a soft tone. Then with ironical respect he bowed and swept his hat almost to the floor as he retired from the chamber, leaving the sheriff to fume and fret his anger away

'The dolt! the sheep's head!' said Captain Bush to himself as he stood outside and thought for a while. 'When he is not so hot I will make the fool take back his words – for he is an ass that I can fool to the top of his bent. Yet, willy-nilly, I will keep watch on the house of Silas ben Reuben. I doubt not that old Reuben lives, and that Robin is hiding him. Old Reuben knows where his kinsman, Rabbi Eliezer, hath buried his vast treasure, and I will not let that doltish sheriff keep me from trying what a little torture will do to make old Reuben give up his secret. Silas the Jew, I doubt not, will send or go to meet his father and the girl, to take them to some safe place; my men shall follow, and at a fitting spot I will fall upon them, and hale them to some secret place and work my will upon them.'

Thereupon the captain went forth into the market-place and called to him a man who stood chewing a straw, and who looked even more villainous than himself, and said to him:

'Go, tell Cogg the Earless to keep strict watch upon the house of Silas the Jew. Today or tomorrow I think Silas will go forth; let him be followed whithersoever he may go. If, as I think, he will go to some inn to join others of his race with horses, send word to me by one of our fellows. Silas will go to the forest, I doubt not, to meet an old man and a girl. I will come with others, and we must take the old man alive to some secret place.'

The man slunk off across the broad market square and disappeared in one of the narrow crooked lanes that led to the Jewry. Then Captain Bush went to the Northgate, and going forth found that the sheriff's men were busy putting up new beams on the little hill called Gallows Hill, which lay just beyond the town wall.

'Make it strong, lads,' he cried, with a laugh, 'for 'tis to hang the first of that evil band of robbers. And I doubt not that 'twill not be long ere others of his friends will swing from the same beam.'

The sheriff's men said naught, but one or two winked at each other in mock of him. They liked not this upstart braggart who had suddenly been put over them, and they obeyed him unwillingly.

Next morning the dawn broke gloomy and chill. Thick clouds rolled slowly up across the sky, the wind blew bitterly from the east and the smell of snow was in the air. Beside the gate of the town that looked upon the gaunt gallows-tree a poor old palmer sat as if waiting till the gate was opened, so that he could enter the town. He looked towards the gate and then at the gallows, and presently tears came into his eyes.

'Alas,' he said, 'that I should find my poor brother again after all these years, and only to hear that he is to be hanged within this hour.'

This was the elder brother of good Will the Bowman, who, years before, had fled from the village of Birkencar because of having slain a man who cruelly oppressed him. He had made the long and dangerous journey to Rome, there to expiate his crime by prayer and fasting and penance; and then had gone farther still upon the rough and perilous road to Jerusalem, where for two years he had stayed among the pagan Mussulmans. Then he had slowly made his way back to England, craving to see his younger brother again, whom he had greatly loved. Three days before, he had gone to Birkencar, and had heard how Will had fled to the greenwood with Robin Hood. He had come through the forest, and by asking villeins and poor men, he had learned that Robin Hood's band was wintering not far from Nottingham. Pushing on, he had reached Ollerton, and there, at a little inn, a woodman had told him, not knowing who he was, that Will Stuteley was to be hanged at dawn before the north gate of Nottingham. He had come on at once, walking through the forest by night, and had sat and dozed in the bitter wind before the door, so that he could get a sight of his brother, and perhaps a word with him before he died.

As he thus sat, a short, slim, dark man came out of a little clump of bushes at the foot of the hill, and approached the old palmer.

'Tell me, good palmer,' said he, 'dost thou know whether Will the Bowman is to be hanged this morn?'

'Alas and alack!' said the old palmer, and his tears ran forth afresh, 'it is true as ye say, and for ever woe is me. He is my younger brother whom I have longed to see these ten years, and I come but to see him hanged.'

The little man looked keenly at the old man, as if for the moment he doubled his tale; but his grief was too real and his words rang too true to allow of doubt.

'I have heard,' went on the old palmer, 'that he ran to the greenwood with young Robert of Locksley – a brave lad, bold of speech and noble of heart when I knew him. And poor man and villeins have told me as I came through the forest that he hath not changed, but that he fled because he could not brook the oppression of proud priests and evil knights. He was ever a bold lad, and it gladdened my heart to hear their rough mouths say how he had ever befriended the poor and the oppressed. Oh, if he were here now! If he but knew the death poor Will must die, he would quickly send succour. With a few of his bold yeomen he would soon take him from those who have seized him.'

'Ay, that is true,' the dark man said, 'that is true. If they were near unto this place they soon would set him free. But fare thee well, thou good old man, farewell, and thanks to thee.'

So saying, the stranger, who was dressed in the rough and rusty garments of a woodman, strolled away and disappeared into the bushes again.

No sooner had he gone than voices were heard behind the stout wooden gates, iron-plated and rivet-studded, and soon with creaking and jarring the great double doors swung open, and twelve sheriff's men with drawn swords came forth. In their midst was Will Stuteley, bound with stout cords; but his look was bold and his head was held high as he walked, fettered though he was. Behind walked the sheriff in his robe of office, and beside him was Captain Bush, a smile of triumph on his face. At a little distance behind them came a man with a ladder, accompanied by a small group of townspeople, who followed the sheriff's men towards the gallows-tree.

Arrived there, they placed Will Stuteley beneath the arm of the high gallows, and at the word of command the ladder was reared against the post, and a man ran up it holding a rope in his hand.

Will Stuteley, while these preparations were being made, looked around over the bleak country. He had hoped to see the forms of the outlaws issuing from the dark wood which began on the top of the down beyond the hollow at the foot of the gallows hill; but there was no sign of life anywhere, except the figure of a poor old palmer who was running towards them. Will turned to where the sheriff stood, with Captain Bush beside him.

'Now, seeing that I needs must die, grant me one boon,' said Will; 'for my noble master never yet had a man that was hanged on the gallows-tree. Give me a sword all in my hand and let me be unbound, and with thee and thy men I'll fight till I lie dead on the ground.'

The sheriff scornfully turned his back, and would not even condescend to reply to him.

'Thou mayest be the first, thou thieving varlet,' sneered

Captain Bush, stepping up and flicking his glove in the face of the bound outlaw; 'but I caused this gallows to be made fresh and strong, because I think thy death will bring us luck, and that now it will not be long ere most of thy cut-throat comrades shall follow each other up that rope. When I put my wits to work, thy noble master shall smart, look you; for I owe him much for that which nothing shall wipe out between us!'

'I know not of what you charge my good chief,' said Will proudly, 'but if he hath harmed you, 'twas because thou wert a rascal, of that I am sure.'

'Prate not with the robber,' cried the sheriff, who was on tenterhooks until Will should be hanged, so greatly did he go in fear of the wiles and stratagems of Robin Hood. 'Adjust the rope and end him!'

'Sir Sheriff,' cried Will, 'let me not be hanged. Do but unbind my hands and I will die fighting with them alone. I crave no weapon, but let thy men's swords slay me!'

'I tell thee, rogue, thou shalt die by the rope,' cried the sheriff in a rage; 'ay, and thy master too, if it ever lie in my power.'

At that moment, into the circle of sheriff's men pressed the poor old palmer, tears streaming down his cheeks. He came to Will and put both hands upon his shoulders.

'Dear Will,' he said, 'thou rememberest me? Heavy is my heart to find thee in this plight. Far have I wandered, but ever have I longed for the day when I should see thy face again, and now – '

The rough hand of Captain Bush was thrust between them, and next moment the palmer lay on the ground, half senseless. The captain kicked him as he lay.

'Here,' he said, 'take this rubbish away and cast it in the ditch there!'

But the old palmer got up slowly, and with a last look at Will turned away and limped towards the sheriff.

'He is my younger brother, Sir Sheriff,' said the old man. 'I have come from the Holy City, and my heart yearned to see him.'

'Put the rope about the rascal's neck, and up with him!' shouted the sheriff, ignoring the trembling palmer before him.

'Farewell, dear brother,' said Will. 'Sorry I am that thou hast returned only to see me hung from the shameful tree. But my noble master will avenge me!'

Captain Bush turned and smote his fist heavily upon Will's mouth.

'Take that, thou thieving rascal and cut-throat,' he cried, 'for thy vain boasting. 'Twill not be long ere thy worthy master himself will need avenging.'

The coiling rope descended from above upon the ground beside Will, and Captain Bush picked it up and placed the noose over Will's head. The outlaw looked with terrible eyes into the face of the other and said:

'I said thou wert a rascal, and if thou canst beat me thus when I am bound, I know thou art less than the lowest thief.'

For answer the captain tightened the noose savagely about Will's neck, and, turning, he shouted to the sheriff's men to haul on the rope which was passed over the gallows-beam, so that Will should be dragged off his feet and pulled up until he slowly strangled.

'To the rope, fellows,' he cried hoarsely; 'altogether! . . . one . . . two . . . '

The word that would have jerked Will into the air was never uttered. A stone came flying straight and swiftly, and hit the captain full on the left temple. With a low groan he fell like a log at the feet of the outlaw. At the same time Little John leaped from a bush below the hill, and accompanied by Ket the Trow, from whose hand had come the stone that had laid Captain Bush low, he ran towards Will. Swiftly he cut the bonds about Will's hands, and then, dashing at a sheriff's man who was running towards him with uplifted sword, he caught the fellow full in the breast with one fist, while with the other hand he tore the sword from his grasp.

'Here, Will,' he said with a joyful laugh, 'take thou this sword, and let us defend ourselves as best we may, for aid will come quickly if all goes well.'

Back to back stood Will and Little John, while the sheriff, recovered from the stupefaction caused by the sudden events of the last few moments, found his voice and furiously bade his men seize the villain who had cut the prisoner loose.

The men advanced in a body against the two outlaws, urged by the angry cries of the sheriff, and their swords clanged against those of the two outlaws. For a few moments the attack was furious; then suddenly, like the boom of angry bees, three great arrows dashed among them. One quivered in the body of a man next to the sheriff, and the latter turned and saw fast coming over the down a troop of men in green with taut bows. At their head was a man dressed all in red, with a bow taller than himself, and as he ran he fitted a great arrow to it, that looked as long as a lance.

'Haste, haste,' cried the sheriff. 'Away! away!'

So fearful was he lest next moment he should feel that long arrow pierce his side that, without more ado, he picked up his robe and ran towards the city gate for dear life, followed swiftly by his men, except two. One lay still, having been slain by the first arrow; and over the body of the other Ket the Trow was kneeling. With the rope that was to have hung Will Stuteley, he was deftly binding the arms of the still unconscious Captain Bush.

Robin and his men ran up, and there was much shaking of hands with Will Stuteley, and patting on the back and rough jests and cheering words between them all.

'I little thought,' said Will, his honest eyes lit up with thankfulness as he looked from Robin's face to the faces of his fellows, 'that I should get free of that rope. It was tight about my throat, and I was praying, when – whang! – came the stone. Who threw it?'

He looked about him for a reply.

' 'Twas I, master,' came a voice from about their feet, whence they had not expected it to come. Looking down they saw Ket the Trow just finishing his task. 'Master,' he said as he rose from his knees, 'I would not slay this fellow, for I thought thou wouldst sooner have him alive. He hath done thee much evil, and had it in his mind to do much more.'

Robin stepped up and looked at the face of the unconscious man.

' 'Tis Richard Illbeast!' he said. 'Ket, clever lad, I thank thee! Now justice shall be done to him at long last.'

For fear that the sheriff should get aid from the knights in the castle, Robin gave instant orders. A horse was quickly brought up from where it had been left in hiding by Little John, for use in case Will had been in need of it, and the body of the Jew-baiter was thrown across it. Then with quick strides the outlaws left the spot, and the gate-guard, looking from his chamber over the great doors, which he had closed by command of the sheriff as he hurried through, saw the outlaws disappear into the dark leafless forest on the farther down.

When the band had threaded many secret ways until they had reached the depths of the forest, thus making pursuit almost impossible, Will Stuteley left the side of his brother the palmer, with whom he had been having much joyful talk, and went to Robin and told him that he had arranged that Silas should go that day two hours after noon, with men and horses, to meet his father Reuben and his little sister Ruth, and that he had appointed a spot called the Hexgrove or Witchgrove, on the highroad by Papplewick, where they should meet. As time pressed, therefore, Robin called Ket the Trow and told him to push forward quickly to Barrow Down, where he was to prepare the old man and the girl for the journey, and then he was to lead them to the Hexgrove, where Robin and his band would be waiting.

Having arranged this, Robin turned in the direction of the place indicated, and pursued his way with less haste. By this time Richard Illbeast had revived, and his evil eyes, as he realised where he was, told more than words the hatred in his heart against Robin and his men. His sullen looks glanced from face to face of the men walking beside the horse on which he lay bound, and in their stern looks as they met his he knew there was as little mercy for him as there would have been in his own heart if they had fallen into his hands.

Trained woodman as he was, Robin never travelled through the forest without having scouts thrown out on all sides of him, and to this habit of perpetual watching he had owed many a rich capture, and avoided many an ambush. When they were already half a mile from the Hexgrove, a scout came running up to Robin and said:

'Master, Dick the Reid (Red) saith there is a man in rich dress with six archers riding down the road at great speed. He will reach the Witch trees about the time thou reachest them.'

Having given his message, at which Robin merely nodded, the scout disappeared again to take up his place ahead. Robin quickened the pace of the party and gave a quick eye at the figure of Richard Illbeast to see no bonds were loosened.

In a little while the band of outlaws were hiding in the dense leafless thickets on both sides of the grove. Very soon they heard the rapid beat of horses' hooves, and round the turn of the track came a horseman, short and sturdy of build. He wore a rich black cloak, edged with fur, fastened on the right shoulder by a gold buckle in which shone a rich ruby. A white feather jutted from his black beaver hat, also fastened by a jewel. The horse he bestrode was a fine animal, richly caparisoned. If his dress had not bespoken the rider to be a man of authority and power, the masterful look on his heavy red face, with beetling eyebrows, thick jaw, and stern eyes would have said plainly enough that this man was accustomed to wield wide powers of life and death. Yet there was also a dignity in his look and bearing which showed that he had good breeding.

Behind him were six archers, dressed in stiff jerkins, their legs also thrust in long leather boots reaching halfway up their thighs. Stout men and stalwart they were, with quick looks and an air of mastery. Robin's heart warmed to them. Such doughty fellows ever made him long to have them of his company.

At sight of the richly dressed man in front Robin had smiled to himself, for he knew him, and then, seeing how rapid was the pace at which they were riding towards where he and his fellows were hidden, he chuckled. When the horsemen were some six yards away Robin led the horse from out of the thickets into the road right in the path of the pounding horsemen.

Richard Illbeast, turning his face towards them, went a sickly pale. At the same time the leading horseman, reining his steed with a strong hand, came to a halt some few feet from Robin, and having shot one keen glance at the bound man he turned round and cried in a curt voice:

'There is our man! Seize him!' at the same time pointing to Richard Illbeast, who writhed in his bonds at the words.

Three of the archers spurred forward as if to lay hands on the bound man, when Robin drew back his horse and, holding up his hand, said:

'Softly, good fellows, not so fast. What I have I hold, and when I let it go, no man living shall have it.'

'How now, fellow!' cried the man in the rich cloak. 'I am marshal of the king's justice. I know not how thou hast captured this robber and cut-throat. Doubtless he has injured thee, and by good hap thou hast trussed him on thy horse. But now thou must give him up to me, and short shrift shall he have. He hath been adjudged worthy of death a many times, and I will waste no more words over him or you. Want you any more than justice of him?'

Robin laughed as he looked in the face of the justice's marshal. The six archers gaped at such hardihood, nay, recklessness, in a man who looked to be no better than a poor woodman. Men usually doffed the hat to Sir Laurence of Raby, the marshal of the king's justice, and bent the knee humbly, yet this saucy rogue did naught but laugh.

'Justice!' cried Robin scornfully. 'I like thy words and thy ways but little. All the justice I have ever seen hath halted as if it were blind, and I like thy hasty even less than thy slow justice, Sir Marshal. I tell thee thou shalt not touch this man.'

'Seize the prisoner, and beat down the peasant if he resists,' cried the marshal angrily.

The three archers leapt from their horses and came swiftly forward. When they were within the reach of an arm, Robin put his fingers to his mouth and whistled shrilly. There was the noise of snapping twigs, and next moment the three archers recoiled, for twenty stalwart outlaws, with taut bows and gleaming arrow points, stood on both sides of the road.

The marshal went almost purple with rage. 'What!' he cried, 'thou wouldst threaten the king's justice! On thy head be it, thou knave, thou robber!'

'Softly, good marshal,' replied Robin with a laugh. 'Ye know who I am, and ye know that I reckon the king's justice or his marshal at no more than the worth of a roasted pippin. Thy justice!' He laughed scornfully. 'What is it? A thing ye sell to the rich lords and the evil-living prelates, while ye give naught of it to the poor whom they grind in the mire. Think ye if there were equal justice for rich and poor in this fair England of ours that I and my fellows would be here? Justice! by the rood! I tell thee this, Sir Marshal, I know thee for a fair man and an honest one – hasty and hot perhaps, yet straight in deed except your will be crossed. But I tell thee, if thou wert as evil as others of thy fellows, thou shouldst hang now as high as this rogue here shall shortly hang, and on the same stout tree!'

The outlaw's voice rang out with a stern stark ring in it, and his dark eyes looked harshly in the face of the marshal. For a moment the latter's eyes were fierce; then his face cleared suddenly, and he laughed:

'Thou rascal, I know thou wouldst! I know thee, Robin, and pity 'tis so stout a fellow is driven to the woods.'

'Stay thou there, Sir Marshal,' said Robin sternly, 'and thou shalt see justice done as well and more cleanly by men who ye say are outside the law as thou canst do it, who sell the king's justice.' Then, turning to Little John, he bade him release Richard Illbeast from the horse, and set him beneath a bough.

Just as this was done, out of the woods came riding the old Jew Reuben and his daughter, accompanied by Ket the Trow and four outlaws. The little girl, Ruth, cast her keen glance round the strange assembly, and suddenly caught sight of the evil face of Richard Illbeast. With a shriek she leapt from her horse, and running to Robin, fell on her knees before him, crying out in a passion of words:

'That is he who slew our poor people! Oh, save my father! Save my father! Let him not hurt us!'

Then she rushed away and stood by the side of her father, clutching him with both hands, while with flashing eyes and trembling form she turned and defied the scowling looks of Richard Illbeast.

'Reuben of Stamford,' Robin cried, 'is this the man whom ye saw slaying thy people at York?'

'Ay,' replied the old Jew, 'it is indeed he. With his own hand I saw him slay not only the hale and strong, but old men and women, and even – may conscience rack him for the deed – little children.'

'And thou, Sir Marshal, what crimes hath thy justice to charge against this knave?'

'Oh, a many!' said the marshal. 'But one will hang him as high as Haman. He slew Ingelram, the king's messenger, at Seaford, and robbed him of a purse of gold; he filched a pair of spurs from the house where the king slept at Gisors, in France; he slew an old and simple citizen of Pontefract, and when he swore to pass beyond the sea as an outlaw, and was followed by the sons of the citizen, he by a trick escaped them after slaying two and wounding a third. But for the evil deeds done at York he hath been proclaimed far and wide, and my master the king's justice hath been much angered to learn that the miscreant had fled, who led the murdering and robbing of his majesty's loyal Jewish subjects. But enough, Robin! Up with him, and let us begone!'

Not a word spake Richard Illbeast, but he glared about with wild and evil eyes, and knew that the bitterness of death, which he had meted out to others so often, was his at last. And thus he died, with no appeal for mercy or pity, for he knew too well that he had never given either the one or the other to those who had craved it of him ere he slew them.

When all was done, the marshal bade goodbye to Robin with hearty words, saying quietly in his ear as he walked with him:

'Robin, 'tis not only the poor folk that have thought well of many of thy deeds, believe me. Thy justice is a wild justice, but like thy bolts, it hits the mark. I forgive thee much for that.'

'Fare thee well, Sir Marshal,' replied Robin. 'I have had little to do with thy justice, but that little hath driven me into the forest as thou seest. Yet I would have thee remember to deal gently with poor men, for thou must bear this in mind, that many of them are pushed to do violent deeds because they cannot get justice from them whom God hath placed over them.'

'I will not forget thy words, good Robin,' said the marshal; 'and may I live to see thee live in the king's peace ere long.'

When, a little later, Silas and his men came up, the old Jew and Ruth were given into their charge, and Robin sent twelve of his men as a guard to convey them to the town of Godmanchester, where the Jews would take up their abode for the future.

The noise of Robin's deed was carried broadcast through the countryside. Men and women breathed again to think that so evil a man as Richard Illbeast was slain at last, and Robin's fame for brave and just deeds went far and wide.

CHAPTER EIGHT

How Robin Hood Slew the Sheriff

It was a year and a day since Robin had lent the four hundred pounds to Sir Herbrand de Tranmire, and again he sat in his bower, and the rich odours of cooking pasties, broiling and roasting capons and venison cutlets blew to and fro under the trees. Anon Robin called John to him.

'It is already long past dinner-time,' said Robin, 'and the knight hath not come to repay me. I fear Our Lady is wroth with me, for she hath not sent me my pay on the day it is due.'

'Doubt not, master,' replied Little John; 'the day is not yet over, and I dare swear that the knight is faithful and will come ere the sun sinks to rest.'

'Take thy bow in thy hand,' said Robin, 'and let Arthur-a-Bland, Much, Will of Stuteley, with ten others, wend with thee to the Roman way where thou didst meet the knight last year, and see what Our Lady shall send us. I know not why she should be wroth with me.'

So Little John took his bow and sword, and calling up the others, he disappeared with them into the deeps of the forest which lay close about the outlaws' camp. For an hour Robin sat making arrows, while the cooks cast anxious glances in their pots now and then, and shook their heads over the capons and steaks that were getting hard and overdone. At length a scout ran in from the greenwood, and coming up to Robin said that Little John and his party were coming with four monks and seven sumpter or baggage horses, and six archers. In a little while, into the clearing before Robin's bower came marching the tall forms of Little John and his comrades, and in their midst were four monks on horseback, with their disarmed guard behind them.

At the first glance at the face of the foremost monk Robin

laughed grimly. It was Abbot Robert of St Mary's Abbey! And the fat monk beside him was the cellarer.

'Now, by the black rood of York!' said Robin, 'ye be more welcome, my Lord Abbot, than ever I had thought thou wouldst be. Lads,' he said, turning to those of his fellows who had run away from Birkencar, 'here is the very cause of all thy griefs and pains whilst thou wert villeins, swinking in the weather, or getting thy back scored by the scourge; it was he who forced thee to flee and to gain the happy life ye have led these several years in the greenwood. Now we will feast him for that great kindness, and when he hath paid me what the Holy Mother oweth me – for I doubt not she hath sent him to pay me her debt – he shall say mass to us, and we will part the greatest friends.'

But the abbot looked on with black looks, while the cellarer, fat and frightened, looked this way and that with such glances of dread that the foresters laughed with glee, and jokingly threatened him with all manner of ill-usage.

'Come, Little John,' said Robin, 'bring me that fat saddle-bag that hangs beside the cellarer, and count me the gold and silver which it holds.'

Little John did so, and having poured out the money on his mantle before his master, counted it and told out the sum. It was eight hundred pounds!

'Ha!' said Robin, 'I told thee so, Lord Abbot. Our Lady is the truest woman that ever yet I knew, or heard tell of. For she not only pays me that which I lent her, but she doubles it. A full gentle act indeed, and one that merits that her humble messengers shall be gently entreated.'

'What meanest thou, robber and varlet?' cried the abbot, purple in the face and beside himself with rage to see such wealth refted from his keeping. 'Thou outlaw and wolf's-head, thou vermin for any good man to slay – what meanest thou by thy tale of loan to Our Lady? Thou art a runaway rogue from her lands, and hast forfeited all thou ever hadst and thy life also by thy evil deeds!'

'Gently, good abbot,' said Robin; 'not on my own account did Our Lady lend me this money, but she was my pledge for the sum of four hundred pounds which I lent a year ago to a certain poor knight who came this way and told a pitiful tale of how a certain evil abbot and other enemies did oppress him. His name, abbot, was Sir Herbrand de Tranmire.'

The abbot started and went pale. Then he turned his face away, and bit his lip in shame and rage to think that it was Robin Hood who had helped Sir Herbrand, and so robbed him and the lords of Wrangby of their revenge.

'I see in all this, Sir Abbot,' said Robin sternly, 'the workings of a justice such as never was within thy ken before. Thou didst set out to ruin and disgrace Sir Herbrand. He fell in with me – was that by chance, I wonder? – and by my aid he escaped thy plots. On his way home three evil knights set on him from that nest of robber lords at Wrangby. Two were slain, and Sir Herbrand and his squire went on their way unharmed.'

The abbot glared with shame and rage at Robin, but would say no word.

'Hadst thou not better forsake evil and oppressive ways, Lord Abbot,' went on Robin, 'and do acts and deeds more in the spirit of Him who died upon the tree for the sake of the sinfulness of the world? But now, lads,' he went on, turning abruptly to his men, 'we will dine our guests in our generous greenwood way, and send them off lined well with venison and wine, though their mail bags be empty.'

And right royally did the outlaws feast the abbot and the cellarer and their guard. The abbot indeed made sorry cheer and would not be roused, and ate and drank sparingly, almost grudgingly, for he felt the shame of his position. To think that he, the Lord Abbot of St Mary's, one of the richest and proudest prelates in Yorkshire, should have been outwitted, flouted, and thwarted by a runaway yeoman and his band of villeins, who now sat around him casting their jokes at him, urging him to make merry and to be a good trencherman! Shame, oh, shame!

When dinner was ended, Robin said: 'Now, Lord Abbot, thou must do me a priestly office this day. I have not heard mass since yesterday forenoon. Do thou perform mass, and then thou mayest go.'

But the abbot sullenly refused, and all Robin's persuasions were in vain.

'So be it,' said Robin, and ordered ropes to be brought. 'Then tie me this unpriestly priest to that tree,' he commanded. 'He

The abbot stood tied to the tree like a felon

shall stay there till he is willing to do his office, and if it be a week, no food shall pass his lips till he do as I desire.'

Not all the prayers and entreaties of the high cellarer or of the other monks availed to move the stubborn heart of the abbot at first, who stood tied to the tree like a felon, looking with anger on all about him. The high cellarer and the other monks appealed to him to do what the outlaw required, so that he should get quickly out of their hands, but it was only after long persuasion that the abbot consented.

Reverently Robin and his men listened to the sacred words, and just as they had risen from their knees a scout came running in to say that a knight and a party of twenty men-at-arms were approaching. Robin guessed who this might be, and therefore he commanded the abbot to wait awhile. When Sir Herbrand, for he was the knight, rode into the camp, and after dismounting came towards Robin, he was astonished to see the angry face of the abbot beside the smiling outlaw.

'God save thee, good Robin,' said Sir Herbrand, 'and you also, Lord Abbot.'

'Welcome be thou, gentle knight,' replied Robin. 'Thou hast come doubtless to repay me what I lent thee.'

'I have indeed,' answered the knight, 'with a poor present of a hundred good yew-bows and two thousand steel-tipped arrows for your kindness.'

'Thou art too late, Sir Herbrand,' said Robin, with a laugh; 'Our Lady, who was thy warrant for the sum, hath sent her messenger with twice the sum to repay me. The good abbot hath come with eight hundred pounds in his saddle-bags which he hath yielded up to me.'

'Let me go, thou mocker,' cried the abbot, his face red with shame. 'I can bear no more. Thou hast put greater shame upon me than ever I can forget.'

'Go then,' said Robin sternly, 'and remember that if I have put upon thee so grievous a shame, thou and thy evil servants have put burdens upon poor folks that many times have weighed them down in misery and death.'

Without another word the abbot was helped on his horse, and with his monks and guards rode out of the camp back along the road to their abbey.

Then Robin related to Sir Herbrand how the abbot had fallen into his hands, and Sir Herbrand said:

'I doubt that for so proud and arrogant a prelate as Abbot Robert of St Mary's such a shame as thou hast put upon him will eat out his life. But, by Our Lady, for his high-handed deeds he deserves such a shame. He hath been a tyrant all his life, and his underlings have but copied him.'

Robin would not take back the four hundred pounds which the knight had brought with him, but he gladly accepted the hundred good bows and the store of bolts which he had brought for a present. That night Sir Herbrand and his company spent in the greenwood with Robin, and next morning, with many courteous and kindly words, they parted, the knight to go back to his manor, and Robin to go deeper into the greenwood.

Now it befell with the abbot as Sir Herbrand had thought. Such great distress of mind did he suffer from the shame and disgrace, that his proud mind broke down under the thought, and never again was he so full of pride and arrogance. In a month, indeed, he fell sick, and was ill and weak for all the rest of that year until, when the next spring came, he died of grief and vexation, as the brothers of the abbey declared. And they buried him richly and with great pomp.

Then the monks gathered together and elected one of their order to be abbot in his stead, and sent him they had elected to London, so that he might be formally accepted by the High Chancellor of England, William de Longchamp, who ruled the land while King Richard was in Palestine fighting with Saladin for the possession of the Holy Sepulchre. But the Chancellor, urged by his own wishes and the wishes of his cousin, Sir Isenbart de Belame, did reject the man chosen by the monks, and in his stead appointed a nephew, Robert de Longchamp, to be abbot.

This Robert, as might be expected, was of a fierce and wily character, and he determined that in some way he would capture Robin Hood and destroy him and his band. Therefore he entered into plots with his kinsmen at Wrangby, with Sir Guy of Gisborne, and with the sheriff of Nottingham. Many ambuscades, sudden onfalls, and stratagems did they prepare either in the forest of Sherwood or in that of Barnisdale; but so wary was Robin, so many and watchful were his scouts, and so zealously did the villeins in the forest villages aid him by giving timely warning, that never did Robin lose a man in all these attempts. Often, indeed, his enemies, who were lying in ambush for him, fell themselves into an ambush which he had made for them, and escaped only with the loss of many men.

At length there was peace for some months, and some of Robin's men believed that the sheriff and the Wrangby lords were tired of their continual defeats and would not attempt to attack them any more. Then, one day, as Robin and Much were walking disguised as merchants through the town of Doncaster, they saw a man ride into the market-place, and checking his horse he cried out:

'Oyez, oyez, oyez! Hear, all good people, archers, serjeants and men-at-arms, woodmen, foresters, and all good men who bear bows. Know ye that my master, the noble sheriff of Nottingham, doth make a great cry. And doth invite all the best archers of the north to come to the butts at Nottingham on the feast of Saint Peter, to try their shooting one against the other. The prize is a right good arrow, the shaft thereof made of pure silver, and the head and feathers of rich red gold. No arrow is like it in all England, and he that beareth off that prize shall for ever be known as the greatest and best archer in all the northern parts of England beyond Trent. God save King Richard and the Holy Sepulchre!'

Then, turning his horse, the crier rode out of the town to carry his tidings throughout the countries even up to the Roman Wall which ran from Carlisle to Newcastle.

'What think you of that, master?' asked Much. 'Is it not some sly plot of the sheriff's to attract thee into his power, since he knoweth that thou wilt never let this shooting go without thou try thy bow upon it?'

'I doubt not, indeed, that such may be their plot,' said Robin, with a laugh; 'nevertheless, we will go to Nottingham, however it fall out, and we will see if the sheriff can do any more in the open than he hath done in the greenwood.'

When they got back to the camp at the Stane Lea, where the outlaws were then staying, they found that all the talk was of the trial at the butts of which many had heard the cry made by the sheriff's messengers. Robin took counsel of his chief men, and it was decided that the most part of the outlaws should go to Nottingham on the day appointed, entering into the town by various gates as if they came from many different parts. All should bear bows and arrows, but be disguised, some as poor yeomen or villeins, others as woodmen or village hunters.

'As for me,' said Robin, 'I will go with a smudgy face and a tattered jerkin as if I am some wastrel, and six others of ye shall shoot with me. The rest shall mingle with the crowd, and should it be that the sheriff means ill, then there will be bows bent and arrows buzzing when he shows his treachery.'

On the day appointed, which was fair and bright, great was the multitude of people which gathered by the butts. These were pitched on a level piece of green sward outside the northern gate, and not far from where the gallows stood, from which Little John had rescued Will Stuteley. Away to the north, beyond the gently rising downs, lay the green and waving forest, and down the roads from Mansfield and Ollerton the wayfarers still thronged, anxious to see the great feats of archery which should give fame through all the North Country.

A scaffolding of seats was set up near the shooting-place, and in this sat the sheriff, some of the knights of the castle of Nottingham and others of their friends. Near by stood the officers of the sheriff, who were to keep the course and regulate the trials.

First came the shooting at a broad target. It was placed at two hundred and twenty yards, and a hundred archers shot at it.

Each man was allowed three shots, and he that did not hit within a certain ring twice out of thrice was not allowed to shoot again. Then the mark was placed at greater distances, and by the time it was set up at three hundred yards the hundred archers had dwindled down to twenty.

The excitement among the crowd now began to grow, and when the butt was removed and the 'pricke' or wand was set up, the names of favourites amongst the competing archers were being shouted. Of the seven outlaws, one had fallen out, and there remained Robin, Little John, Scadlock, who had become an excellent bowman, Much the Miller's son, an outlaw named Reynold, and Gilbert of the White Hand, who by constant practice had become very skilful.

At the first contest of shooting against the wand, seven of the twenty failed, among them being Scadlock and Reynold. Then the wand was set farther back at every shooting until, when it stood at four hundred yards, there were not more than seven archers remaining. Among these were Robin and Gilbert; three others were bowmen in the service of the sheriff, the sixth was a man of Sir Gosbert de Lambley, and the remaining one was an old grey man of great frame and fierce aspect, who had said he was a yeoman, and called himself Rafe of the Billhook.

Now came the hardest contest of all – 'shooting at roavers' as it was called, where a man was set to shoot at a wand of which he had to guess the distance, so that he had to use his own wit in the choice of his arrow, and as to the strength of the breeze.

'Now, bully boys of Nottingham, show thy mettle!' cried a stout man with a thick neck and a red face, who stood near the sheriff's seat. He was Watkin, the chief officer or bailiff of Sheriff Murdach. He had taken the place of Richard Illbeast, and like him had got the worst in several attempts to capture Robin Hood, whom, however, he had never seen.

'Forward, sheriff's men,' cried a citizen in the crowd, 'show these scurvy strangers that Sherwood men are not to be overborne.'

'Scurvy thyself,' said a voice somewhere in the rear. 'Yorkshire tykes be a breed that mak' Sherwood dogs put their tails atween their legs.'

The horn sounded its note to show that the contest had begun, and all eyes were bent upon the rival archers. The Nottingham men went first, and of these two failed to hit the wand, the arrow of one going wide and the other's falling short. The third man struck the top of the wand with his bolt, and the roar of triumph which went up showed how keenly the defeat of the other two Nottingham men had been felt.

Then Robin stepped up to the shooting-line. He had put aside the huge six-foot bow which he had used for shooting at the butt, and now bore one which was but a yard in length, but so thick that a laugh went up here and there, and a young squire cried out mockingly:

'Does this ragged wastrel think he can shoot with that hedge pole?'

'Stand at twelve score paces and see!' said a quiet voice somewhere near at hand.

'He'll drill a bolt through thy ribs at fifteen score paces,' said another, 'and through thy mail shirt as well.'

Robin, in a ragged and frayed brown tunic and hose, with a hood of similar hue, raised his bow, notched his arrow, and looked for one long moment at the mark. He had let his hair and beard grow longer than usual, and both were unkempt and untidy. With the aid of some red dye he had coloured his face, so that he looked to be but a dissipated haunter of ale-houses and town taverns, and men wondered how he had shot so well as to keep up so far.

'Dry work, toper, is't not?' cried a waggish citizen. A great laughter rose from the crowd at the joke. The archer seemed not to notice it, and shot his bolt. All craned their necks to see how it had sped, and a gasp of wonder came and then a hearty shout. The wand had been split in two!

'Well done, yeoman!' cried a well-dressed citizen, going up and clapping Robin on the back. 'Thy hand and eye must be steadier than it seems by thy face they ought to be.' He looked keenly in Robin's face, and Robin recognised him as a burgher whom he had once befriended in the forest. The man knew him and muttered as he turned away, 'I thought 'twas thee. 'Ware the sheriff! Treachery is about!'

Then he strolled back to his place in the crowd. The other three now shot at the mark. Rafe of the Billhook missed the wand by the width of three fingers' span, and the bolt of Sir Gosbert's man flew wide. Young Gilbert of the White Hand now shot his arrow. Very carefully he measured with his eye the distance of the wand, chose an arrow with a straight-cut feather, and then discharged it. The bolt made a beautiful curve towards the wand, and for a moment it seemed that it must strike the mark. But a wandering breeze caught it and turned it, so that it flew about a hand's space to the left. The crowd cheered, however, for the youth and courteous bearing of the lad made them feel kindly towards him.

The contest now lay between the sheriff's man, by name Luke the Reid or Red, and Robin. In the next shooting there was no difference between them, for the bolt of each fairly struck the wand. Then the sheriff spoke:

'Ye are fairly matched, but you cannot both have the golden arrow. Devise some play that shall show which of you is the keener bowman.'

'By your leave, my Lord Sheriff,' said Robin, 'I would propose that we look not on the wand while it is shifted to some distance you may choose, and that then we turn and shoot while one may count three. He that splits the wand shall then be judged the winner.'

There were murmurs of wonder and some mocking at this proposal. It meant that a man must measure the distance, choose his bolt, and shoot it in a space of time that allowed little judgement, if any.

'Are you content to accept that, Luke the Reid?' asked the sheriff of his man. The latter stroked his grey beard for a moment, and said:

' 'Tis such a shoot I have seen but thrice made, and only once have I seen the wand struck, and that was when I was a boy. Old Bat the Bandy, who was the chief archer to Stephen of Gamwell, was he who split the wand, and men reckoned that no one north of Trent could match him in his day. If thou canst split the wand, yeoman,' he said, turning to Robin, 'then for all thou lookest like a worthless fellow, thou art such an archer as hath not been seen in the North Country for the last fifty years.'

'Oh,' said Robin, with a careless laugh, 'I served a good master who taught me the bow, but such a shoot as I propose is not so hard as thou deemest. Wilt thou try it?'

'Ay, I am willing,' returned Luke, puzzled at Robin's careless air; 'but I tell thee beforehand I cannot hit the wand.'

The two archers were then commanded to turn their backs, while an officer of the sheriff's ran to the wand and moved it ten paces farther off. Then at the word of the sheriff, Luke turned, and while Watkin the chief officer counted slowly 'One – two – three!' he shot his arrow. The great crowd held its breath as the arrow sped, and a groan of disappointment broke from them when they saw it curve to earth and stick in the ground, some six paces short of the wand.

'Now, boaster!' cried the bull-necked officer angrily to Robin. Then, speaking quickly, he shouted, 'Turn! one – two – three!'

Robin's arrow sped forth as the word 'three' was uttered, and men craned their necks to mark the flight. Swiftly and true it sped, and sliced the wand in two. Men gasped, and then a great shout rose, for though Robin, being a stranger and looking to be but a mean fellow, had turned most of the crowd against him, the sense of fair play made them all recognise that he had fairly won the prize.

Luke the Reid came up to Robin and held out his hand to him. 'Thou'rt a worthier man than thou lookest, bowman,' he said, and his honest eyes looked keenly into Robin's. 'So steady a hand and clear an eye go not with such a reckless air as thou wearest, and I think thou must be a better man than thou lookest.'

Robin shook his hand and returned his keen look, but said no word in reply.

The note of the sheriff's horn rose as a signal that the prizes were to be given. There were ten of these for those who had shot the best according to certain rules, and one by one the men were called up to the sheriff's seat and his wife presented the gift to the successful archer. When it was Robin's turn he went boldly to the place and bent his knee courteously to the lady. Then the sheriff began to speak, and said:

'Yeoman, thou hast shown thyself to have the greatest skill of all who have shot this day. If thou wouldst wish to change thy present condition and will get leave of thy lord, I would willingly take thee into my service. Come, archer, and take from my lady the golden arrow which thou hast fairly won.'

Robin approached Dame Margaret, and she held out the golden arrow to him, smiling kindly upon him as she did so. He reached out his hand to take the gift and met the lady's eyes. She went pale, her mouth opened as if she was about to speak; then she bit her lips, returned Robin's final courtesy, and immediately burst out laughing. Robin knew that she had recognised him, but that she would not betray him. The knowledge that the sheriff was inviting the outlaw who had once put him to such shame to become his man tickled her sense of humour, so that she could not keep from bursting into a long fit of laughter.

The sheriff looked keenly at his wife and then suspiciously at Robin, as the latter turned away and tried to get among the crowd. Men and women pressed about the outlaw, however, congratulating him with rough good humour, and Robin could not hide himself from the sheriff's eyes. Suddenly, something familiar in the look of Robin struck the sheriff. He rose quickly and whispered in the ear of the bull-necked man, who, turning, saw Robin in the midst of a crowd of men bearing bows, who seemed to be talking to him as they all walked away. Watkin the bailiff plunged forward and thrust this way and that among the archers, bidding them in a thick fierce voice make way in the name of the sheriff.

Suddenly men turned upon him and shouldered him off. 'Let me come, varlets,' he cried. 'I will have thee whipped and branded. I am Watkin the sheriff's bailiff!'

'Let him go, lads,' rang out a clear voice. It was Robin who thus commanded his men who had rallied about him.

'I arrest thee, Robin Hood, outlaw! in the name of the king!' shouted Watkin, though he was still some paces away.

'Enough of thy bellowing, thou town bull!' said Little John, who was beside Watkin, and picking up the sheriff's man, the giant ran with him to the outskirts of the crowd and dumped him heavily on the ground, where he lay dazed for a few moments.

A bugle note rang clear and shrill. It was the call of the greenwood men, and from all parts of the wide grounds the outlaws gathered. Another horn sounded, and the sheriff's men formed in ranks, with bows strung. Men and women in the crowd between the two parties fled this way and that shrieking with fear, and at a word from the sheriff his men shot a flight of arrows against the men of the greenwood. Next moment, however, the great clothyard arrows of the outlaws snored back in reply so thick and strong, that the sheriff's men, or such as could run, darted this way and that into shelter.

Slowly and in good order the outlaws retreated, sending their arrows into the sheriff's men, who now, under the furious leadership of Watkin, were following them closely from cover to cover. Once they saw a man ride swiftly away from where the sheriff stood, and enter the town.

'That means, lads, that they go to beg help from the castle,' said Little John. 'Once we reach the greenwood, however, little avail will that help be.'

The forest, however, was still nearly a mile away, and the

outlaws would not run. From time to time they turned and shot their arrows at their pursuers, while keeping a good distance from them and taking care that none got round their flanks.

Suddenly with a groan Little John fell, an arrow sticking from his knee.

'I can go no farther, lads, I fear,' he cried. Robin came up to him and examined the wound, while the sheriff's men, seeing the outlaws check, came on more swiftly.

'Master,' said Little John, 'for the love thou bearest me, let not the sheriff and his men find and take me alive. Take out thy brown sword instead and smite my head off, I beseech thee.'

'Nay, by the sweet Virgin!' cried Robin, and his eyes were pitiful, 'I would not have thee slain for all the gold in England. We will take thee with us.'

'Ay, that we will,' said Much; 'never shall I and thee part company, thou old rascal,' he went on. Saying this, he lifted John upon his broad back, and the outlaws went on again. Sometimes Much put John down for a moment, and notching an arrow to his string, took a shot at the sheriff's men.

Then they saw a large company of archers on horseback issue from the town gate, and Robin's face went stern and grim at the sight. He could not hope to win the shelter of the forest before this troop came upon him, and fight as they would, they must in the end be overwhelmed. Robin looked around for some means of escape, but saw none. Already the mounted men were gaining upon them, and the sheriff's men were holding to the stirrup leather of their allies and leaping and running beside them over the down. Three knights were at the head of the troop, and the sheriff rode in front of all.

Rapidly the outlaws retreated, and at Robin's command they fled along a hollow or combe in the downs which would lead them to a knoll of trees, where he thought they could make a last desperate stand. Suddenly he remembered with some bitterness that they were near the castle of Sir Richard at Lee. He knew that Sir Richard loved him, and would help him if he begged aid of him, but seeing that by helping an outlaw Sir Richard would lose lands and life, Robin knew that he would have to make his last flight alone, although within an arrow flight of his friend's castle.

They gained the knoll of trees, and Robin arranged his men and gave them short sharp orders. Behind them rose the castle of Sir Richard, but Robin looked not that way, all his attention being given to their enemies, who were now rapidly coming up. Suddenly a small figure ran up the knoll and came to Robin. It was Ket the Trow.

'Master,' he said breathlessly, 'a troop hath been sent round by the Levin Oak to take thee in the rear. Look, where they ride!'

Robin looked, and grim despair entered his heart. He saw that it was impossible to make a stand. At that moment a knight in armour came riding furiously from the direction of the castle of Sir Richard at Lee. It was Sir Richard himself.

'Robin! Robin!' he cried, 'thou canst not hope to save thyself. Withdraw to my castle. Come at once, man, or all is lost'

'But thou losest life and land if thou dost shelter me!' cried Robin.

'So be it!' said the knight. 'I lose them any way, for if ye stay here I stay with thee, Robin, and end with thee.'

'Come then,' replied the outlaw. 'Friend indeed as thou art, I will accept thy aid and requite thee to the full for thy nobility.'

Not a moment too soon did the outlaws reach the drawbridge. In good order they retreated, and barely did they avoid being caught in the rear by the horsemen who had ridden to cut them off; but a strong flight of arrows dealt destruction among them on the very verge of the ditch, and when they had recovered, they saw Robin was the last to step across the drawbridge, which then rattled and groaned its swift way up, putting the yawning water of the ditch between them and their prey. For a moment the troop, headed by Watkin, the sheriff's officer, stood shouting threats at the walls, until a flight of bolts among them caused them quickly to draw off, taking their dead and wounded with them. They rode to join the main body of the sheriff's forces, who now came up and halted at a respectful distance from the castle walls, on whose battlements steel caps now gleamed amid the bonnets of the outlaws.

The sheriff sent a herald under a flag of truce, charging Sir Richard with harbouring and aiding an outlaw against the king's rights and laws, to which Sir Richard made a valiant answer, in legal form, saying that he was willing 'to maintain the deeds

'*I can go no farther, lads, I fear*'

which he had done upon all the lands which he held from the
king, as he was a true knight'. Thereupon the sheriff went his
way, since he had no authority to besiege Sir Richard, who
would have to be judged by the king or his chancellor.

'Sir Richard,' said Robin, when the knight came from the wall
after giving his reply to the sheriff, 'this is a brave deed thou hast
done, and here I swear that whatever befall me, I do avow that I
and my men shall aid thee to the last, and whatsoever help thou
needest at any time, I will eagerly give it thee.'

'Robin,' said Sir Richard, 'I love no man in the world more
than I do thee, for a just man and a brave, and rather than see
thee fall into the hands of the sheriff, I would lose all. But I have
ill news for thee. Walter, the steward of Sir Richard FitzWalter,
sent a message to me this morning, saying that his master is dead,
and that Fair Marian is in danger of being seized by the strongest
lord amongst her neighbours, so that she may be wedded to one
of them and her lands meanwhile held and enjoyed by them.'

'Now, by the black rood!' said Robin, 'the time hath come
when I said I would take sweet Marian into my keeping. Sir
Richard, I will instantly set forth to Malaset and bring Fair
Marian back to the greenwood. Father Tuck will wed us, and she
shall live in peace with me and my merry men.'

Quickly, therefore, Robin selected twenty of his best men, and
as soon as harness, arms, and horses had been obtained for them
all from their secret stores in the forest caves, the band set off
towards the western marches, where, in the fair valleys of
Lancashire, the castle of Malaset stood in the midst of its broad
lands.

On the evening of the second day they approached the castle
and found it shut up, dark and silent. A clear call on a bugle
brought a man to the guardroom over the gate. This was Walter
the Steward, and quickly, with the aid of the menservants, the
bridge was lowered, the portcullis raised, and Robin and his men
were welcomed by the brave steward into the great hall.

'Where is the Lady Marian, Walter?' asked Robin.

'Alas, Master Robin, I know not!' replied Walter, wringing his
hands and the tears starting from his eyes. 'If thou dost not
know, then I am indeed forlorn, for I had thought she had fled to
thee. She slept here last night, but this morning no signs could

be found of her anywhere about the castle!'

'This is hard to hear,' said Robin, and his face was full of grief. 'Hath any robber lord or thieving kinsman seized her, think you?'

'Several have been here since when, three days ago, my lord was laid in his tomb in the church,' replied Walter, 'but ever with her wit and ready tongue my lady spoke them fair and sent them all away, each satisfied that he was the kinsman to whom she would come when her grief was past. Yesterday there came the sacrist of St Mary's Abbey, and did bring with him the order of the king's chancellor, William de Longchamp himself, the Lord Bishop of Ely, commanding her to hold herself and all she possessed as the ward of the king, and telling her that tomorrow would come Sir Scrivel of Catsty, to be the king's steward and to guard her from ill.'

'Scrivel of Catsty!' cried Robin angrily, 'Scrivel the catspaw rather, for he's naught but a reiving mountain cat, close kin to Isenbart de Belame! I see it all! The new abbot of St Mary's hath got his uncle the chancellor to do this, and under cover of being but the steward of the king's rights, he will let that evil crew of Wrangby take possession. But, by the black rood, I must find what hath befallen Marian, and that speedily!'

Next day and for several days thereafter Robin and his men scoured the marches of Lancashire for many miles, asking of the poor folk, the villeins, beggars and wandering people of the road, whether they had seen a tall maid, brown of hair, straight and queenly of figure, pass either alone, or in the power of a band of knights or men-at-arms. But all was in vain. No one had seen such a maid, and at the end of a week Robin was in despair.

Meanwhile word was sent to him by Walter that Scrivel of Catsty with a hundred men had taken possession of the castle, and was furious to learn that the Lady Marian had disappeared. He also was sending everywhere to learn where she had fled. So earnest did he seem in this that Walter thought that he and the Wrangby lords had not had any hand in kidnapping Marian, and that either she must have fled herself or been taken by some party of her kinsmen.

Full of sorrow, Robin at length turned his horse's head towards Barnisdale, and he and his band rode with heavy hearts into their camp by the Stane Lea one morning when the sun shone warmly, when the birds sang in the boughs and all seemed bright and fair. Hardly had Robin alighted, when there came the beat of horses' feet rapidly approaching from the south, and through the trees they saw the figure of a lady riding swiftly towards them, followed by another. Robin quickly rose, and for the moment joy ran through his heart to think that this was Marian! But next instant he recognised the lady as the wife of Sir Richard at Lee.

When she rode up to Robin, he knelt courteously on his knee for a moment. She was greatly agitated, and was breathless.

'God save you, Robin Hood,' she said, 'and all thy company. I crave a boon of thee.'

'It shall be granted, lady,' replied Robin, 'for thine own and thy dear lord's sake.'

'It is for his behalf I crave it. He hath been seized by the sheriff – he was hawking but an hour agone by the stream which runs by a hunting-bower of his at Woodsett, when the sheriff and his men rushed from the wood and seized him. They have tied him on a horse and he is now on his way to Nottingham, and if ye go not quickly I doubt not he will soon be slain or in foul prison.'

'Now by the Virgin,' said Robin, and he was wondrous wroth, 'the sheriff shall pay for this. Lady,' he said, 'wait here with thy woman until we return. If we have not Sir Richard with us, I shall not return alive.'

Then he sounded his horn with curious notes which resounded far and wide through the forest, so that scouts and watchers a mile off heard the clear call through the trees. Quickly they ran to the Stane Lea, and when all had assembled, there were seven score men in all. Standing with bows in hand, they waited for their master to speak. He stood by the lady where she sat on her palfrey, and they could see by his flashing eyes that he was greatly moved.

'Lads,' he cried, 'those that were with me when we shot at the butts in Nottingham know how courteously this lady's brave lord befriended us, and saved us from death. Now he hath himself been seized by the sheriff, who, learning that I was far from Barnisdale, hath dared to venture into our forest roads and hath seized Sir Richard at Woodsett, where the knight hath a hunting-seat. Now, lads. I go to rescue the knight and to fight the sheriff. Who comes with me?'

Every outlaw of all that throng held up his bow in sign that he would volunteer, and a great shout went up. Robin smiled proudly at their eagerness.

'I thank thee, but you cannot all go, lads,' he cried. 'As the sheriff hath a stout force with him, eighty of you shall go with me. The others must stay to guard the camp and the knight's lady.'

Soon all was ready, and silently the band, with Robin at their head, sank into the forest, and quickly yet stealthily made their way to the south-east, towards the road which the sheriff must take on his way back to Nottingham. The sheriff's spies had learned that Robin had disappeared from Barnisdale, and that Little John, still unable to move because of the wound in his knee, had been left in command. Therefore, hearing that Sir Richard had left his castle at Linden Lea and had gone to a hunting-lodge on the outskirts of Barnisdale, the sheriff had thought this would be a good opportunity of capturing the knight, and thus gain the commendation of the Bishop of Ely, the king's chancellor, who had been furious when he had heard how the knight had rescued Robin and defied the law.

Now that the sheriff had captured the knight, he was very anxious to leave the dangerous neighbourhood, for he feared that Robin might return at any time. He therefore pushed his men to do their utmost, and while he himself rode beside Sir Richard, who was bound securely on a horse, the company of fifty men-at-arms had to walk, and in the hot noonday sun of the summer they moiled and sweated woefully at the pace set by the sheriff.

When they reached the town of Worksop, which lay upon their route, the sheriff would only stay long enough before the chief inn to allow each man to have a stoup from a black jack, and would allow no one to rest beneath the wide chestnut tree that threw its dark and pleasant shade in the scorching road. Then onward they had to go, their own feet kicking up the dust which in less than a mile caked their throats again.

At length they got among the deep woods and hills of Clumber Forest, and the sheriff felt more at ease in his mind, though he did not abate the pace at which he went. Under the shade of the great oaks and chestnuts, however, the men felt less exhausted and pushed on with a will.

There was a long steep hill upon their road called Hagger Scar, and up this they were toiling manfully, when suddenly a stern voice rang out.

'Halt!' it cried, and at the same moment, as the men-at-arms looked about them, they saw that on each side of the forest-way stood archers with bent bows, the gleaming arrows pointing at each of their breasts. The whole company stood still, and men angrily murmured beneath their breath.

Out of the wood some ten paces from the sheriff stepped Robin, his bow strung and a fierce look on his face.

'So, sheriff,' he cried, 'you learned that I was away, and therefore stole up to seize my friend. By the Virgin but thou hadst better have stayed within thy town walls. I tell thee I will spare thee no more. Not since seven years have I had to go so fast on foot as I have had to do this morn, and it bodes no good to thee. Say thy last prayer, for thy end hath come.'

Now that he knew that his last hour had really come, the sheriff was brave.

'Thou lawless wolf's-head,' he cried, 'the chancellor will harry every thicket in these woods to catch thee for this deed. I – '

He spoke no more. Robin's arrow pierced the chain-mail coat he wore, and he swayed and fell from the saddle to the ground, dead. Then Robin went to the knight and cut his bonds and helped him from the horse.

'Now,' said he to the sheriff's men, 'throw down thy weapons!'

When they had done this he told them to march forward, take up the body of their master, and proceed on their way. They did as he had commanded them, and soon the fifty men-at-arms, weaponless and sore at heart for having been so completely conquered by the bold outlaw, disappeared over the crest of the hill.

Turning to the knight, Robin said: 'Sir Richard, welcome to the greenwood! thou must stay with me and my fellows now, and learn to go on foot through mire, moss, and fen. Sorry I am that a knight should have to leave his castle to his enemies without a blow and to take to the woods, but needs must when naught else can be done!'

'I thank thee, Robin, from my heart,' said the knight, 'for taking me thus from prison and death. As for living with thee and thy fellows in the greenwood, I wish no better life, since I could not live with braver men.'

Thereupon they set off through the leafy wilderness, and before evening had rejoined the lady of the knight, and great was her joy and gratitude to Robin and his men for having restored her husband to her. A feast was prepared, and Sir Richard at Lee and his dame were entertained right royally, and they said that though they had lost castle and lands, they had never been happier than on this the first night of their lives as outlaws in the greenwood.

When the camp was hushed in slumber, and there was no sound but the crackle of the dying embers of the fires and the rustle of the wind in the trees overhead, or the murmur of the little stream beside the camp, Robin took his way into the dark forest. He was very unhappy and much distressed by reason of the disappearance of Fair Marian. He pictured her a captive in some castle, pining for liberty, oppressed by the demands of some tyrant kinsman or other robber knight, who had captured her for the rich dowry which would go to him she wedded.

Filled with these fears, therefore, Robin determined to walk through the forest to the green mounds where Ket the Trow and Hob o' the Hill lived, to hear whether either of those little men had learned any news of Marian. As soon as he had learned of his lady's danger when he had reached Sir Richard's castle, he had sent off Ket the Trow to Malaset to watch over Marian, but had since heard nothing from the troll, and this silence was very disquieting.

Though the woodland paths were sunk in the deepest darkness, Robin found his way unerringly through the forest, and when he had greeted and left the last scout, watchful at his post, be passed through the dark ways as stealthily as a wild animal. Thus for some miles he went, until he knew that he was approaching Twinbarrow Lea, as the glade was called where the green homes of the little men lay. Cautiously he neared the edge of the clearing and looked out between the leaves of the tree beside him.

From where he stood, his eyes being now quite used to the darkness, he could plainly see the two green mounds, for he was on that side of them which was nearer to the forest. Everything seemed to be held in the silence and quiet of the night. Only the wind rustled in the long grass or whispered among the leaves. From far away on the other side of the glade came faint cries of a hunting owl, like a ceaseless question – 'Hoo-hoo-hoo!' Near by, he heard a stealthy footfall, and turning his head he could see the gaunt form of a wolf standing just on the edge of the forest, its head thrown up to sniff the breeze from the mounds. Suddenly there came a scurry away in the thickets to the rear, a quick shriek, and then stillness. A wild cat had struck down a hare. The wolf disappeared in the direction of the sound to see if he could rob the cat of its prey. A long fiendish snarl greeted his approach, and Robin expected to hear the fury of battle rise next moment as the wolf and wild cat closed in mortal combat. But the snarl died down. The wolf had declined the contest.

Looking intently towards the mound, Robin was now aware of a dark space on the flank of the farther one which looked like the outstretched figure of a man. He knew that this mound was the one in which the brothers dwelt, and he wondered whether Ket or Hob was lying out there sleeping. He thought to give the call of the night-jar, which was their signal by night; but suddenly he saw the figure move stealthily. He watched intently. He knew this could not be either of the brothers, for the man's form was too large, and it wriggled with infinite slowness upwards towards the top of the mound.

Robin knew then that this was some enemy trying to spy out the place where the two little men lived. He wandered if it was one of his own outlaws, and he grew angry at the thought. He had always commanded that no one should approach the mounds or seek to force his company on the little people. If it was indeed one of his men, he should smart for it.

By this time the figure had almost reached the top of the mound, and Robin stepped quietly forth with the intention of going to the man to bid him be gone. Suddenly, against the sky-line there leaped from the top of the mound the small figure of a man, which precipitated itself upon the form which Robin had first seen. For a moment the latter was taken by surprise; it half rose, but was pushed back, and instantly the two forms were closed in a deadly grapple. Robin rushed up the mound towards them, catching the glint of knives as he approached. He heard the fierce panting of the two fighters as they struggled on the steep, slippery side of the mound. They pressed this way and that, losing their footing one moment, but regaining it the next. Just as Robin reached them and could see that it was Ket the Trow and one of his own outlaws, Ket thrust the other from him, and the man fell, rolling like a log down the side of the mound, and lay at the bottom still and inert.

'What is this, Ket?' asked Robin. 'Hath one of my own men tried to break into thy house?'

'He's not one of the band, master,' said the panting man, stanching a wound on his shoulder with one hand. 'He is a spy who hath followed me these three days, but he'll spy no more.'

Together they descended the mound, and Ket turned over the dead man. Though the body was dressed like one of Robin's men, he knew by the face that it was not one of his outlaws.

'How is it he wears the Lincoln green?' asked Robin.

'He slew a poor lad of thine, Dring by name, by Brambury Burn,' said Ket, 'and took his clothes to cover his spying.'

'Poor lad,' said Robin; 'Dring was ever faithful. But what hast thou been doing by Brambury Burn? 'Tis far north for thee to roam on the quest I gave thee. How ran the search so far?' asked Robin eagerly, wondering if Ket had aught to tell.

'Thereby hangs my tale, master,' said Ket. 'But do thou come into the mound and listen while I bind my wound.'

Robin followed Ket up the flank of the great barrow. He had only once been inside Ket's home, and he knew that the method of entry was not by the door on the side, which indeed was too small for a man of ordinary girth to enter, but by the chimney, which could be made wide enough to admit him. On the top of the mound was a dark hole, down which Ket disappeared, after telling Robin to wait until he showed a light.

Soon Ket's face appeared in the light of the torch at the bottom of a slanting hole, the sides of which were made of stones. Taking out one here and there Ket made the aperture wider, and then Robin, by alternately sliding and stepping, climbed down the slanting chimney. There was still another similar passage to descend, but at length he stood on the floor of the apartment which was the home of Ket and Hob and of their mother and two sisters. By the light of Ket's torch, which he stuck between two stones, Robin saw that the walls of the cave were made of stones, deftly arranged, without mortar, one above the other, so that the whole chamber was arched in the form of a beehive, the height being some eight feet.

When Robin had helped Ket to bind up a deep wound on his left shoulder, and a cut or two on his arm, the little man looked up into his master's face with a bright, merry air, and said:

'If thou'lt promise to make no sound I'll show thee a treasure I ha' found but lately.'

'Ket!' said Robin in eager tones, 'hast thou really found my dear lady? Oh, good little man!'

For answer Ket beckoned Robin to follow him to a part of a chamber which was curtained off by a piece of arras that must at one time have adorned a lord's hall. Peering behind this, Robin saw reclining on a horse-cloth thrown over a couch of sweet-smelling ferns the form of Marian, sleeping as softly as if she was in her own bed of linen at Malaset. Beside her was the small, slight form of one of Ket's sisters, her dark hair and pale skin showing vividly against the auburn locks and brown skin of Marian. A long time he gazed happily on her face, until at length Ket roused him by whispering:

'Look not on her with such intentness, or her eyes will surely open and seek thine!'

Silently Robin and Ket crept away to the farthest corner of the chamber, and Ket then told his tale.

'When you sent me away to watch over the Lady Marian until you came,' said Ket the Trow, 'I reached the castle by Malaset Wood at evening, and I crept into the castle when no one saw me. I found the Lady Marian in her chamber, and already she had resolved to fly to you, leaving no word behind, so that steward Walter and her people should not be judged guilty of aiding her escape. I bade her wait for you, but she yearned for the open moors and would not stay. By a secret way we issued from the castle at dawn, and took to the moors. Master Robin, thy lady is a wood-wise lass, though over quick to act. She feared that there were those of her enemies who watched the castle, and therefore she would not have us walk together lest, as she said, if both were taken or I was slain, there would be no one to tell you. We started out on the way which should lead us to meet you; but

not two miles had we wended ere from the thickets on Catrail
Ring twenty men sprang out and seized her. I barely 'scaped
them by creeping back, for they would not believe she was alone,
and they sought for me. They were men of the Thurlstan lord,
whom ye know to be close sib to him of Wrangby. Fierce and
evil-looking were they, and not over gentle with my lady, so that
more than once I had it in mind to loose a bolt in the throat of
Grame Gaptooth their leader. They put her on a spare horse
which, with others, lay in the covered way to the Ring, where
they had lain and watched the castle in the valley below. All
through the livelong day I followed them, and grievous was that
journey. Fast they travelled, keeping to the moors and the lone
lands, so that hard was I put to it to hold to them on my two feet.
That night they reached Grame's Black Tower on the Wall, and
when I heard the gate clang down, well, my heart dropped with
it, for, as thou know'st, that peel tower is a fearsome place, and
not to be broken into like a cheese. Next day they sent two riders
south, and I knew that they went to tell the evil man Isenbart
that they held thy dear lady and could strike at thee through thy
tenderest part. Two days I wandered round that evil and black
tower, conning how I could win into it and out again with my
dear lady unscathed. On the evening of the third day the riders
returned with others, and these were from Sir Isenbart, and at
their head was Baldwin the Killer, come to take my lady to the
dungeons of Wrangby. Thou know'st, master, that we little
people have many secrets and strange lore, and some unkent
powers, and how we can break and overcome hard things. It was
so now, and by the aid of that knowledge I was able to see the
weak part of that strong peel. I think, master, there is no castle
that I cannot break into, however high and strong it be, so I put
my thinking to it. I entered that peel tower in the dark, and I let
down my brave lady from the wall, but ere I left I put so heavy a
mark on some that slept that never will they rise to do evil more.
Far did we go that night, and ever was she bold and brave. She
lay hid by day while I fared abroad to get us food; but by
Brambury Burn I met young Dring, and he was hot to go and
find thee and tell thee the good news. That rogue that lies dead
on the mound outside saw me and Dring as we spoke, and knew
me for thy friend, and thinking to win the favour of the

Wrangby lords, he slew Dring, and putting on his clothes followed me. I reached here but four hours agone, and ever since my lady hath slept.'

'Let her sleep long, brave lass,' said Robin, 'for she must have sore need of it. I cannot thank thee enough, good Ket,' he went on, 'for having brought her safe and sound out of such peril. What reward shall I make thee that is fitting?'

'Master,' said Ket, 'there is no need to talk of rewards between thee and me. I and mine owe our lives to thee, and whatsoever we do, you or I, is for the love we bear each other. Is it not so?'

'It is so,' replied Robin, and they gripped hands in a silent oath of renewed loyalty to each other.

Robin slept in the trolls' mound that night on a bed of fern with Ket beside him, and in the morning great was the joy of Marian when she awoke to find Robin himself was near by. Much loving talk passed between them, and both said that never more would they part from each other while life should last. That very day, indeed, Robin went to Father Tuck to prepare him for their marriage.

CHAPTER NINE

King Richard Meets Robin

When it became known throughout the countryside that Robin the outlaw had wedded Marian FitzWalter, heiress to the wide lands of Malaset and ward of the king, some men wondered that he could be so daring as to fly thus in the face of the king's rights, while others were glad that Robin had been so bold, and had shown how he set at naught the powers of prelates and proud lords.

For some time there were rumours that William de Longchamp, the king's chancellor, was going to send a great army into the forests of Clipstone, Sherwood, and Barnisdale, to stamp out and utterly destroy this bold and insolent outlaw. It was said that armies were to go from the strong castles of Nottingham in the south, Tickhill and Lincoln in the east, the Peak in the west, and York in the north, and they were to sweep through the forest, leaving the dead bodies of all the outlaws bristling with arrows or swinging from high trees.

But nothing came of this. Very soon, indeed, William de Longchamp had been chased from the kingdom for his pride and oppression, and the castles of Nottingham and Tickhill had fallen into the hands of Earl John, the king's brother; and for nearly three years after that the nobles and prelates were so full of their own bickerings and quarrels, that they had little memory of the saucy deeds of an outlaw.

Then all good men sorrowed to learn that their gallant King Richard had been captured and lay imprisoned in a castle in Germany, and that a vast sum was demanded for his ransom. To raise the money every man was taxed, be he a layman or a monk; citizens and yeomen, knights and squires had to pay the value of a quarter of their year's income, and the abbots were required to give the value of a year's wool from the vast flocks of sheep which they possessed.

Many men paid these taxes very grudgingly, and the money was long being collected. Meantime the king whiled away the long hours in his prison, feeling that, as he wrote in a poem which he composed at that time and which men may still read:

True is the saying, as I have proved herein,
Dead men and prisoners have no friends, no kin.

During all this time Robin and Marian had lived very happily in the greenwood. She had lost her wide lands, it was true, and instead of living in a castle with thick walls, and being dressed in rich clothes, she dwelt in a wooden hut, and had the skins of animals or plain homespun Lincoln green wherewith to clothe herself. But never before had she been so happy, for she was with him she loved best, and ever about her was the free life of the fresh woods and the wild wind in the trees.

So much did Robin desire that his king should speedily be freed that, when he learned what taxes were imposed in order to raise the king's ransom, he collected the half of all his store of gold and silver, and having sold many fine garments and rich clothes, he sent the whole of the money under a strong guard to London, and delivered it into the hands of the mayor himself, who, having opened the parcel when his visitors had gone, found therein a piece of doeskin on which was written:

'From Robin Hood and the freemen of Sherwood Forest, for the behoof of their beloved king, whom God save speedily from his evil enemies at home and in foreign parts.'

Thereafter, also, Robin set aside the half of all he took from travellers and placed it in a special secret place, to go towards the king's ransom. When, also, he heard that any rich franklin well-to-do burgess or yeoman or miserly knight, abbot or canon, had not yet paid his due tax, Robin would go with a chosen party of his men and visit the house of the man who begrudged liberty to his king; and if the yeoman or knight did not resist him he would take from the man's house what was due for the tax, but if, as sometimes happened, the man fought and resisted, then Robin would take all he could find, and leave the curmudgeon and his men with their wounds and their empty purses.

For fear, therefore, that they should lose much more, many hastened to pay at once the tax which otherwise they would never have paid; and some from whom Robin had taken what was due were forced to pay again by the king's tax-gatherers. The tales of Robin's dealings spread abroad far and wide, until they got to the ears of Hamelin, the stout Earl of Warenne himself, who was one of the king's treasurers, and he declared heartily that it was a pity the king had not such a tax-gatherer as Robin in every county, for then the king would have been freed in a few weeks. He learned all he could concerning Robin, and said in the hearing of many noble and puissant lords, that he would like to see that stout yeoman, for he seemed to be a man much after his own heart.

When King Richard was at length released from prison, most of his enemies who were holding castles on behalf of his brother John, who had plotted to win the crown for himself, gave them up and fled for fear of the king's vengeance. Others were besieged by the friends of King Richard and surrendered after a little while. There were certain knights who held the castle of Nottingham for Earl John, and they resisted the besiegers very fiercely, and would not give up the castle to them. When King Richard landed at Sandwich after coming from Germany, he heard how the castle of Nottingham still refused to submit to his councillors, and being greatly angry, he marched to that city and sat down before the castle with a vast army. He made an assault upon it, and so fiercely did he fight, that he captured part of the outer works and laid them in ruins, and slew many of the defenders. Then he ordered gibbets to be erected in sight of the besieged, and upon them he hung the men-at-arms whom he had captured, as an example to the rebels within the castle.

Two days afterwards the wardens of the castle, among whom was Ralph Murdach, brother of the sheriff whom Robin had slain, came forth and surrendered the castle, and threw themselves upon the mercy of the king. He received them sternly, and ordered them to be kept under a strict guard.

Now when the king and his lords sat at dinner one day, it was told King Richard how there was a bold and insolent outlaw who harboured with many lawless men in the forests of Clipstone, Sherwood, and Barnisdale, which lay north of Nottingham.

More especially did his chancellor, William de Longchamp, wax wroth at the recital of Robin's crimes.

'Such a man, my lord,' he said, 'thy father King Henry, of blessed memory, would not have suffered to commit his crimes for all these years, but most surely he would have sent an army of archers into the forests where he hideth, and would have hunted out every rogue and hung him forthwith.'

'It was thy office, my Lord Bishop, to do this,' retorted Richard sternly. 'I left thee to rule my land justly, and to keep down robberies and murders and brawls, but thou seemest to have added to the confusion and disorder.'

Many of the nobles who hated the bishop smiled to see the look of chagrin on William de Longchamp's face. They had chased him from England because of his pride and oppression, and the king's reply pleased them mightily.

'Moreover, sir,' said Hamelin, Earl de Warenne, 'had my Lord Bishop been able to hang this stout outlaw, it is likely your highness would have been longer in prison.'

Men looked in surprise at de Warenne as he said this, and saw the smile on his face.

'How is that, de Warenne?' asked King Richard. 'What had this rascal to do with my release?'

'This, sire,' was the reply, 'that though he loves his king's deer overmuch, wherein he sins with many others, both rich and poor, it seems that he loves his king also, and in that he doth exceed the love that many of thy knights and lords bear thee. He lives by taking toll from travellers through thy forests, and, as I have been informed, he had gathered much wealthy gear and a store of money. Half of that wealth he did send to my Lord Mayor of London, and the amount of it was an earl's ransom. With it he sent a message which ran: "From Robin Hood and the freemen of Sherwood, for the behoof of their beloved king, whom God save speedily from his evil enemies at home and in foreign parts." Further, sire,' de Warenne went on, while men looked at each other in wonder, 'he took upon himself the office of tax-gatherer for these parts, and many a fat canon, abbot, or prior who would not have paid the tax which was to set thee free, and many a miserly burgess, knight, or yeoman, hath had a visit by night from this outlaw and been forced to pay the tax. By my head, but as men have told me, they have had to pay their tax twice over – once to Robin Hood, and again to the treasurer's sergeants – and much they grieved thereat!'

The king laughed heartily, and his nobles joined in his merriment.

'And the toll and tax which he thus gathered,' went on de Warenne, 'this outlaw sent again to the Lord Mayor with this message, as I am told: "For to release my lord the king, from unwilling knights, monks, and other surly knaves who love him not a groat's worth, by the hands of Robin Hood and his men of the greenwood." '

'By my faith,' said Richard, and his look and tones were earnest, 'this is a man in whom much sense of right and justice must dwell. 'Tis clear he knoweth and loveth freedom greatly, and hath much pity for those who have to sit in duress and see the sunlight crawl across the floor of their cells. By the soul of my blessed father, if other of my liege subjects had been as loving and as busy in my behalf as this outlaw, I should not have pined in the castle of Hagenau by many a month!'

He looked darkly around the table, and many a face went a little pale, for some knew that they had not been over zealous in raising the great sum which would release their lord. Many, also, had been beguiled a little by the promises of that traitorous brother of the king, Earl John of Mortaigne.

'By my faith, but I will see this outlaw,' said the king, 'and know what sort of man he is. How did he break the law?'

'By the slaying of my brother, sire,' said William de Longchamp. 'He slew Sir Roger on the highway, and afterwards he slew five men-at-arms of the abbot of St Mary's at York. Since then his murders and robberies have been numberless.'

'I think he slew your brother, Lord Bishop, because Sir Roger would have seized FitzWalter's daughter, the Lady Marian,' said de Warenne in a quiet voice. 'Is it not so? Your brother, with a party of varlets, set upon her and her villeins in the forest, and would have borne her off to his castle, which some men call Evil Hold, as I learn, but that this outlaw was in hiding near, and slew Roger with an arrow through his visor.'

'And, by my halidom,' said King Richard, who ever praised brave deeds that had to do with the saving of ladies from

ill-usage or oppression, ' 'twas a righteous deed if, as I remember, 'twas not the first lady thy brother Roger had oppressed, my
Lord Bishop!'

William de Longchamp looked fiercely at Earl de Warenne,
who smiled carelessly at his enemy's wrathful glances.

'I will have you to know, sire,' said William the Chancellor,
turning to the king, 'that if you may not deem the slaying of my
own poor kinsman of much worth, yet this thief and murderer,
Robin Hood, hath done deeds of late that shall surely not gain
him thy favour. He hath slain the sheriff of Nottingham, Robert
Murdach; he hath wed the Lady Marian, one of thy wards; and
moreover hath caused a knight whose lands lie near this castle to
go with him and thieve and rob in thy forests.'

'What is the knight's name?' asked the king, and his look was
stern, for though he might be willing to overlook many things in
a mere yeoman, he would have little mercy for a knight who
forgot his honour and turned outlaw.

'It is Sir Richard at Lee, and his lands lie by Linden Lea, near
by Nottingham,' said William de Longchamp.

'I will seize his lands,' said the king angrily, 'and his head shall
be cut off – the recreant! Make proclamation,' he went on,
turning to one of the clerks of the treasury who stood behind his
seat, 'that whosoever taketh that knight and brings his head to
me shall have his lands.'

'If it please you, sire,' said an old knight, who stepped forth
from a group of richly dressed lords waiting behind the king, 'I
would say that there is no man living who could hold the
knight's lands while his friend Robin and his men can range
through the forest and draw a bow.'

'Who are you?' asked the king, 'and how know you this?'

'I am John de Birkin, sire,' said the old knight, 'and Sir
Richard at Lee was my friend. Since Sir Richard fled, the new
sheriff of Nottingham hath striven to hold his castle and lands in
thy name, but no man will bide there. As they walk to and fro
upon the fields they are pierced by arrows from the woods, their
servants are beaten or have run away, and all the villeins that
dwell upon the land have joined their master in the greenwood.'

'By the soul of my father,' said the king, starting from his seat,
'if ye speak true, then the best men dwell in the forests, and the

caitiffs are law-abiding fools that pretend to rule for me while they let me pine in my prison. I will see this outlaw – look you, de Birkin, send word to this rascal outlaw that he shall have my protection while he cometh and goeth, for I would willingly speak to him who loves me, yet who slays my sheriff and knights.'

When the castle of Nottingham had been surrendered into the hands of the king he went hunting in the forest of Sherwood, which he had never before seen, and he was much pleased with the giant trees he found therein, the beautiful smooth glades, the cliffy hills, and the rolling downlands. On that day the king's party started a hart by Rufford Brakes, which was so fleet and strong that it led horsemen and hounds for many miles north-wards into Barnisdale forest, where, it being late, and the twilight falling, it was lost. That night the king slept at the house of the Black Monks of Gildingcote, and next day he sent his huntsmen through the forests, making proclamation at various villages, castles, and towns that the hart which the king had hunted and lost the day before should henceforth be called a 'hart royal proclaimed', and that no person should kill, hurt, or chase the said hart, which was described by certain distinguishing marks by which any good woodman would instantly recognise it.

King Richard went hunting through the forest every day, and did not stay in one place; but never could he get to learn where Robin Hood was hiding. At last he called to him the chief forester of Sherwood, by name Sir Ralph Fitz-Stephen.

'Knowest thou not, Sir Forester,' asked the king, 'where my messenger may get word with this outlaw? Thou keepest this forest ill, since thou permittest seven score outlaws to live in it unmolested, and to slay my deer at their will. Find me this Robin Hood, or thou shalt lose thy office.'

Ralph Fitz-Stephen was a bold man, and he made reply:

'My lord king, it is not whether I or your Majesty may find Robin Hood, but rather whether Robin Hood will permit himself to be found. I make bold to say, sire, that these several years past have I striven to capture him and his band, and I have aided the sheriffs of every county which march on the forest shaws, but this outlaw is a very fox for hiding, and hath as many holes. Nevertheless, I will do all I may to bring him to thee.'

Fitz-Stephen thereupon gathered together all his foresters, told them what the king had said, and took counsel with them what had best be done to give the king his desire. Some advised one thing and some another, until the chief forester lost patience with them all.

'Out on ye, ye chuckleheaded loons!' he cried. 'If this rascal outlaw were only half as wary as he is, he would still play with such louts as ye be. Little wonder ye have never been within a mile of catching him. Away with thee to thy "walks", and I will rely upon my own wits.'

Very crestfallen, the foresters went about their duty. Most of them bore the marks of wounds given in many a scuffle with Robin and his men, and they felt that unless their master hit upon some means of finding the outlaw and bringing him to the king, they would soon lose their posts as foresters, which though on occasion brought them wounds or blows, yet gave them opportunities of gaining much pelf and of oppressing poor folks and gaining money or goods from them.

Two days later, Ralph Fitz-Stephen came to where the king was staying at the castle of Drakenhole, and craved audience of him. When he saw the king he bent on one knee, and when King Richard had commanded him to speak, he said:

'Sire, I have learned that since you have kept in these northern parts, the outlaw Robin has been haunting the roads by Ollerton, stopping rich travellers and taking of their wealth. Now I give thee counsel in what way thou mayest get word with this rascal. Take five of thy lords – those who are not hasty or quick of temper, I would advise, lest they betray who ye be before thou hast word with the outlaw – and borrow monks' weeds [garments] from the abbot of Maddersey across the river here. Then I will be your guide, and I will lead you to the road where Robin and his comrades do haunt, and I lay my head on it that ye shall see that rascal ere you reach Nottingham.'

'By my faith,' said Richard with a hearty laugh, 'but I like thy counsel, forester. Do thou get the monkish garb from my Lord Abbot for myself and thee and my five lords, and we will go with thee.'

Though the day was already far gone, Richard would set out at once, and as soon as the monks' garments were brought he put

the great black gown over his rich surcoat, which blazed with the
leopards of Anjou and the lilies of France, and then upon his
head he put a hood and a wide-brimmed hat, such as ecclesiastics
wore when they travelled. He was very elated at the prospect of
so strange an adventure, and joked and laughed with the five
knights whom he had chosen to go with him. These were
Hamelin, Earl de Warenne, Ranulf, Earl of Chester, Roger
Bigot, William, Earl of Ferrers, and Sir Osbert de Scofton.

In an hour they were on the road, the party having the
appearance of five rich monks or chief officers of some great
abbey, travelling on the business of their house. Two horses
heaped with their baggage followed after, and behind them were
three more larger horses, piled with provisions, table ware and
other rich gear. The horses were in charge of two foresters, who
were disguised as monkish servants.

For an hour they rode until it was dark, Richard joking with
his knights or at times carolling in his glee. When night
compelled them to call a halt, Ralph Fitz-Stephen suggested that
they should turn a little from their way to the house of the
canons of Clumber, where they would be sure of a lodging for
the night. This was agreed to by the king, and after a short ride
through the forest, they were received in the canons' guest
chamber. Except for a merchant and his three men who were
already eating their meal, and a man who, by his careless air and
dress, and his possession of a citole or little harp, seemed to be a
minstrel or jongleur, the great hall was empty. The king's party
did not tell anyone who they were, or they would have been
invited into the private hall to sup with the canons; but King
Richard preferred to remain unknown.

Food was therefore brought forth from the store carried on
the sumpter horses, and the king and his lords and Ralph Fitz-
Stephen ate at one of the tables in the hall, which was dimly
lighted by three or four torches which spluttered and flared and
smoked in their sockets on the pillars.

'I tell thee thou art a fool!' came suddenly the angry voice of
the merchant. He seemed to be in altercation with the jongleur,
who laughed and twanged his citole as he made some mocking
reply. 'Such a wastrel as thou art knoweth not the value of
money, and its loss, therefore, is nothing to thee.'

'What a moil and a coil thy money causes thee, good merchant!' replied the minstrel. 'Thou art condemned from thy own mouth. He that hath money seems ever in fear of losing it. Tell me, canst thou ever sleep soundly at night? Doth thou ever trust wholly one of these thy men? Art thou not ever in fear of some footpad dashing upon thee and cutting thy throat for thy pelf? No, he that hath money taketh unto himself a familiar fiend, which for ever tortures and torments. As for me, why, I have no money, and therefore I care not.'

He twanged his citole, and broke out gaily into the snatch of a gay song.

'Look you, merchant,' he went on, while the other glared sullenly at him, 'I never had more than two rose nobles at a time, and so fearful was I that some wretched fool would say I had stolen them, or would try to steal them from me, that I made haste to spend them, and when the last had gone I felt happy again. Give me a corner away from the wind at night, a little meat and bread and a drink of wine each hour, my citole and the open road before me, and thou, Sir Merchant, may keep thy books of account, thy bales of rich gear, and thy peevish laments over losing a few poor pounds to a bold outlaw.'

'The rogue! He should have his eyes burnt out and his ears cropped!' cried the merchant. 'If I had told him truly all I had, I should not now be robbed of every groat I made at Nottingham Fair!'

'Ha! ha! ha!' laughed the jongleur loud and long. 'There sits the wind, does it? The outlaw played his old trick upon thee, did he? and thou didst fall – thy miserly soul could not tell the truth, and therefore when he found that thou hadst more money than thou didst confess, he took it all! Ha! ha! ha! Sir Merchant, if thou hadst wanted thy money less thou wouldst at least have had some of it now.'

'What sayest thou?' cried the king from where he sat, turning towards the merchant. 'Who hath robbed thee?'

'Who hath robbed me, Sir Priest?' replied the merchant with a jeering voice, for the monks were not beloved by merchants, because of the high tolls and dues they demanded for leave to sell goods in their markets, 'who else but that limb of Satan – that landloping rogue Robin Hood! And if thou travellest that road tomorrow, Sir Priest, I hope he may do as much to thee as he hath done to me.'

'Lord, man, thou art as sore as a bear whose ears the dogs have scored!' said the minstrel, laughing. 'Speak with more reverence to the Church and their servants. Think ye, old sore head, 'twas such as they did baptise thee a Christian – if indeed thou art a Christian and not an unbelieving dog of a Moslem – and with their aid alone thou shalt die and be buried – if ye be not thrown on the roadside at the end as I have seen many a richer man and a finer spoken one!'

The merchant glared and snarled at the minstrel, then turned away and, wrapping himself in his cloak, seemed wishful to forget his loss in sleep.

'Count not his words against him, Lord Abbot,' said the minstrel. ' 'Tis not the man who speaks, but the merchant robbed of his profits. Hallo, here's someone that's as blithe as the merchant is gloomy.'

The door of the hall had opened to the knocking of another wayfarer, and across the straw and rushes on the floor came a poor-looking old man and woman. They were raggedly dressed, and each bore a small bundle, which probably contained all they possessed.

'God bless ye all, gentles,' said the old man, and his face was wreathed in smiles as he doffed his ragged cap, first to the dark-robed monks and then to the minstrel, who grinned in reply, and getting up, swept his own hat with its ragged feather in an elaborate bow before the old man.

'Greeting to thee, old merry heart!' he said. 'Did I not know that the nearest alehouse is twelve long miles away, I would charge thee with having in thee the blessed liquor of the ruddy grape. What cheer, nunks?'

'Sir,' said the old man gleefully, as he put his bag down on the bench, 'I ha' met the finest adventure and the gentlest nobleman that ere I ha' known or heard on. 'Twas but four short miles out of Ollerton, and oh, but I had a dread of the woods! Thick they were with trees, and every moment I was afraid that out of the dark some fearsome robber would dart and cut our throats for the few poor pennies we have.'

'We be only poor folk, sir,' interjected the old woman, who

had a gentle face, though her hands were knotted and lined with a lifetime's toil, 'and we be not used to travelling. We be going to get our poor son from prison at Tickhill.'

'How got thy son in prison, dame?' came a kindly voice from among the black-robed monks. It was the king who spoke.

The old woman was almost overwhelmed at being addressed by one who spoke with an air of nobility, for she was only a poor wife of Nottingham. She curtsied low and replied:

'Oh, Sir Priest, he was tired of the hard toil for Master Peter Greatrex the armourer, and he wandered away to do better, though I begged him to stay with us. And after many months we ha' learned that he ha' been took up for wanderin' and ha' been chained so long in prison at Tickhill till one foot is perished from him. And so we be going to claim him and take him home again.'

'But, good soul,' said the king, 'they will not deliver thy son out of prison to thee.'

'Oh, but we be his parents, Sir Priest,' said the old woman, and tears came to her eyes, 'and we be sure our Dickon hath done no wrong. Surely they will give him to us.'

'Ay, old lass,' said her husband, 'dry thy tears and let be to me. Ha' I not Robin Hood's own words that he will see to it that when we get there they will give Dickon up to us?'

'And is Robin the gentle nobleman ye have met today, old man?' asked the king.

'Ay, Sir Priest, saving your presence, he is that. For 'twas he sent one of his men to us – they spied us through the leaves as we passed along the fearsome road – and when I thought 'twas a thievish rogue come to spoil us, why, 'twas a messenger from Robin himself, who would have us speak with him.'

'I would ha' run e'en then, sirs,' said the old woman, 'so feared was I of this Robin Hood, for he's a great outlaw as I've heard tell. But my old man said – '

'I bade her have no fear, sir,' went on the old man, impatient of his wife's interruption, 'for I told her Robin was too good a man, as I heard tell, to rob poor folks, and belike he would but learn from us whether any rich merchants or priests – saving your presence – were coming behind us. But he asked us naught of that. Nay, sirs, 'twas the gentlest nobleman he was' – the old fellow became quite excited as he went on; his face flushed, his eyes shone, and his hands gestured this way and that. 'He asked us all about ourselves, who we were, whence we came, whither we were wending, and why. Then he ordered them to bring food and wine – he fed us as if we were lord and lady, waiting upon us with his own hands – sirs, 'tis the truth I'm telling ye, as heaven is my witness. Then he crammed bread and meat into my bundle here, and a bottle of wine, and led us to the road again. And he gave me this,' he held up a coin which flashed dully in the torch-light: it was a silver penny; 'and his last words were, "Old lad, I'll see to it that thy son is given to thee when thou gettest to Tickhill. And if any saucy rogue stops thee on the road and would harm or rob thee, say to him that Robin gives thee peace through the forest land, and charge the rogue to let thee go, lest the fate of Richard Illbeast befall him." '

'Saw one ever such a cross-grained rascal as this Robin,' came the shrill voice of the merchant, who had heard all. 'From me he taketh all I possess, and to this old churl, who knoweth not the value of a groat, he giveth a silver penny, and belike it is one the rogue stole from me!'

'Oh, cease thy noise, old huckster!' cried the minstrel sternly. 'I tell thee when the great trump sounds, 'twill be Robin will pass before thee up to St Peter's knee, or I know not what is a good man and a noble doer. I will make a poem of this that thou tellest me, old man, for indeed 'tis a deed worthy of a poet's praise, and of the fame a poet's song can give to it.'

The old man and his wife sat down to their meal; the minstrel became silent and absorbed, his eyes half closed as he murmured broken words over to himself, and began composing his poem; and the merchant and his men again wrapped themselves in their cloaks and turned to slumber on the truckle-beds ranged along the room.

Meanwhile the king had beckoned to de Warenne, and in a low voice asked what Robin had meant by 'the fate of Richard Illbeast', on which the Earl and Ralph Fitz-Stephen told the king all that had happened at York, of the flight of the leader of the mob who massacred the Jews, and of the capture of Richard Illbeast by Robin, who had executed him for his many crimes in the very presence of Sir Laurence de Raby, marshal of the king's justice. When they had finished speaking the king was silent for some time, and was sunk in deep thought. At length he said:

'Methinks this is no common man, this Robin Hood. Almost it seems that he doth right in spite of the laws, and that they be wrong indeed if they have forced him to flee to the greenwood and become outside the law. He robs the rich and the proud who themselves have robbed to glut their greed and their pride; but he giveth aid and comfort to the poor, and that seemeth to be no man's desire to do. I will gladly see this man, and by the favour of heaven I will make him my friend.'

Then the king gave orders that beds should be set up, and all retired to rest.

Next morning the party of the king had not proceeded more than five miles along the leafy highway leading to Ollerton, when suddenly out of the wood came a tall man, dressed in an old green tunic and trunk hose of the same colour. In his hand he bore a great bow taller than himself, at his side was a good sword, and in his belt a dagger of Spanish steel. On his head was a velvet hat, and stuck therein was a long feather from a cock pheasant's tail.

Manly of form and keen of look was he; his face and neck were browned by the summer sun, and his dark curls hung to his shoulders. He lifted his sharp eyes to the foremost rider and said, holding up one big brown hand as he did so:

'Stay, Sir Abbot. By your leave ye must bide awhile with me.'

He placed two fingers in his mouth and whistled shrilly. Almost immediately, out of the shadow of the trees came forth some twenty archers on each side of the road. Each was dressed in green tunic and hose, torn and worn in places; but each was a stout man of his hands, well knit and bold of look, and each bore a bow.

'We be yeomen of this forest, Sir Abbot,' said Robin, for the first man had been the outlaw himself, 'and we live on the king's deer in this forest, and on what rich lords and knights and priests will give us of their wealth. Give us, then, some of thy money ere thou wouldst wend farther, Sir Abbot.'

'Good yeomen,' replied the king, 'I have with me no more than forty pounds, for I have stayed with our king at Blythe, and I have spent much on lordings there. Nevertheless I willingly give thee what I have.'

The king commanded one of the cloaked figures behind him to produce his purse, which being done was handed to Robin, who took it and said:

'Lord Abbot, thou speakest like an honest and a noble man. I will therefore not search thy saddlebags to know whether thou speakest truth. Here,' he said, 'are twenty pounds which I render to thee again, since I would not have thee fare away without money to spend. The other twenty shall be toll for thy safe journey. Fare thee well, Lord Abbot.'

Robin stood away to let the horses pass, taking off his hat in a dignified salute as he did so. But the abbot placed his hand in his breast and produced a piece of parchment, which he opened with much crackling of the stiff skin. There was writing upon it, and below hung a big red ball of wax, bearing a seal upon it.

'Gramercy, good yeomen,' said the king, 'but I bear with me the greetings of our good King Richard. He hath sent thee his seal and his bidding that ye should meet him in Nottingham in three days' time, and this shall be thy safe conduct to and fro.'

Robin looked keenly into the shadowed face within the cowl of the abbot as he approached and took the parchment. He bent on his knee to show his respect for the king's letter, and said:

'Sir Abbot, I love no man in all the world so well as I do my comely king. His letter is welcome, and for thy tidings, Sir Abbot, do thou stay and dine with us in greenwood fashion.'

'Gramercy,' said the king, 'that will I do willingly.'

Forthwith the king and his knights were led on foot into a deeper part of the forest, where, under the trysting tree of the outlaws, dinner was being cooked. Robin placed a horn to his lips and blew a curious blast. Hardly had the last notes died away ere from all parts of the forest which surrounded the glade in which they sat came men in green, with bows in hand and swords at their side. Each had the quick, brave look of men used to the open air and a free life, and each, as he approached where Robin stood, doffed his hat to his leader.

'By the soul of my father,' muttered Richard into the ear of de Warenne, 'this is a seemly sight, yet a sad one. These be fine men, and they be more at this outlaw's bidding than my own knights be at mine.'

The king and his knights did full justice to the good dinner set before them, and when it was over Robin said:

'Now, Lord Abbot, thou shalt see what manner of life we lead, so that when thou dost return to our king thou mayst tell him.'

Thereupon targets were set up at which a chosen number of the outlaws began to shoot, and so distant and small was the mark that the king marvelled that any should hit it. But he marvelled more when Robin ordered a wand to be set up, from the top of which hung a garland of roses.

'He that doth not shoot through the garland,' cried Robin, 'shall lose his bow and arrows, and shall bear a buffet from him that was the better archer.'

' 'Tis most marvellous shooting,' said Richard, as he sat apart with his knights. 'Oh, that I could get five hundred as good archers to come with me across the sea! I would riddle the coat of the King of France, and make him bow to me.'

Twice Robin shot at the mark, and each time he cleft the wand. But others missed, and those who fell before Robin's buffet were many. Even Scarlet and Little John had to bear the weight of his arm, but Gilbert of the White Hand was by now almost as good an archer as Robin. Then Robin shot for the third time, and he was unlucky, for his bolt missed the garland by the space of three fingers. There was a great burst of laughter from the archers, and a cry of, 'A miss! a miss!'

'I avow it,' cried Robin, laughing, and just then he saw through the trees at the other end of the glade a party riding towards them. They were Fair Marian his wife, clad in green, with her bow and arrows beside her, and with her were Sir Richard at Lee and Alan-a-Dale and Dame Alice his wife.

Robin turned to the abbot and said:

'I yield my bow and arrow to thee, Lord Abbot, for thou art my master. Do thou give me such a buffet as thou mayst.'

'It is not fitting to my order,' said the abbot, and drew his cowl closer about his face to hide it from Robin's keen glance and from the eyes of the party riding towards them.

'Smite boldly, Sir Abbot,' urged Robin; 'I give thee full leave.'

The king smiled, bared his arm, and gave so stout a blow full on Robin's breast that the outlaw was hurled some feet away and almost fell to the ground. He kept his feet, however, and coming to the king, from whose face the cowl had dropped away by reason of the violence of his blow, he said:

'By the sweet Virgin, but there is pith in thy arm, Lord Abbot – if abbot thou art or monk – and a stalwart man art thou.'

At this very moment Sir Richard at Lee leaped from his saddle and, doffing his hat, ran forward, crying, ' 'Tis the king! Kneel, Robin!' The knight knelt on his knees before the king, who now thrust the cowl from off his head of brown hair, and revealed the handsome face and blue eyes, in which a proud but genial light shone, of Richard Cœur-de-Lion. Then he tore aside the black robes he wore, showing beneath the rich silk surtout blazoned with the leopards of Anjou and the fleur-de-lys of France.

Robin and his outlaws and Alan-a-Dale kneeled at the sight, and Fair Marian and Dame Alice, getting from their horses, curtsied humbly.

'By the soul of my father,' said Richard with a gay laugh, 'but this is a right fair adventure. Why do ye kneel, good Robin? Art thou not king of the greenwood?'

'My lord, the King of England,' said Robin, 'I love thee and fear thee, and would crave thy mercy for myself and my men for all the deeds which we have done against thy laws. Of thy goodness and grace give us mercy!'

'Rise, Robin, for, by the Trinity, I have never met in the greenwood a man so much after my heart as thou art,' said the king. He caught Robin by the hand and lifted him to his feet. 'But, by the Virgin, thou must leave this life and be my liege servant and rule thyself as a lawful man.'

'This will I do willingly, my lord the king,' said Robin, 'for I would liefer keep thy law and do what good I may openly than live outside the law.'

'So let it be,' replied the king; 'I have heard all that thou hast done. Thou hast wedded a rich ward of mine against all my right and due! Is this fair lady she who hath left wealth and honours and lands for love of thee?'

Fair Marian cast herself upon her knees before the king, who gave her his hand to kiss, after which he raised her to her feet.

'Come,' said the king, 'thou hast given up much to come to thy good archer, fair lady. I can only agree that thou hast chosen a bold man and a brave one. Thou wert ward of mine, and I give thee willingly where thou hast already given thyself.'

So saying, the king joined the hands of Robin and Marian, both of whom felt very happy in having the king himself pardon them for so wilfully acting against his rights.

'But,' went on the king, smiling, 'thou hast committed so many bold deeds, Robin, that I must doom thee to some punishment for them. Go thou and lead a quiet life after these years of strife and hiding. Take thy fair dame and dwell with her on her lands at Malaset, at peace with my deer and all thy fellow-subjects. Uphold the laws which my wise councillors make for the peace and prosperity of this realm. By so doing thou shalt win my pardon.'

'My lord king,' said Robin, deeply moved at the king's generosity, 'for this thy great mercy and favour I will ever be thy faithful and loyal servant.'

'See to it, de Warenne,' said Richard, 'that Robin, by virtue of his dame Marian, be put in possession of all her lands and dues.'

'I will see to it, sire,' said the stout Earl Hamelin, 'the more eagerly because I look forward to having Robin's good help in collecting thy taxes with due promptitude in the manors and boroughs on the Lancashire marches.'

The king laughed and turned to Robin. 'For thy aid in gathering my ransom I give thee thanks,' he said.

Then Robin brought Sir Richard at Lee to the king, who heard Sir Richard's prayer and was pleased to give him his lands again, and to grant him full pardon for having offended against the laws in giving aid to Robin.

Finally, Alan-a-Dale and Dame Alice kneeled before the king, who heard how they, with Sir Walter de Beauforest, the lady's father, had incurred the enmity of Sir Isenbart de Belame, and ever lived in fear of that knight's sudden attack upon their manors and lands. The king inquired narrowly of the deeds of the lords of Wrangby, and his brow went dark with anger when he heard of their manifold and wicked oppressions.

'They are an evil brood!' he said at length sadly. 'But I and my dear father's other undutiful sons did bring them to life, for we plunged the realm in wicked wars and confusion. And my brother John would do the same while I am fighting for the Holy Sepulchre, and these evil lords thrive in his company. De Warenne, I will speak further as to these lords of the Evil Hold! Let me but

Robin receives a buffet from King Richard

settle with that traitor, Philip of France, and thrust him from my lands in Normandy and Aquitaine, and I will come back and sweep these evil castles from the land, and stamp out the nests of vipers and serpents that shelter behind their strong walls.'

Two days later the king's messenger handed a parchment to the gate-guard at the castle of Wrangby, and would not stay for food or lodging, as a sign of the king's displeasure. When Isenbart de Belame read the writing on the parchment his mouth went wry with a bitter sneer.

'So!' he said mockingly, 'the king takes outlaws to his bosom because he wants good archers for his wars in Normandy. And he will have me to know that any harm done upon Sir Walter de Beauforest, Alan de Tranmire or Dame Alice, or any of their lands, manors, villeins, or other estate, will be crimes against the king, to be punished as acts of treason.'

He dashed the parchment to the floor, and his eyes flashed with evil fire.

'I must bide my time a little longer,' he muttered to himself. 'Who knows? The king will play at castle-taking with Philip of France. He may be slain any day, and then when Earl John shall take the throne, I shall have licence to do all I wish with that insolent outlaw and all his friends. I will bide my time.'

As the king had bidden him, Robin went with Fair Marian to the lands of Malaset, and received them back from the guardian-ship of Scrivel of Catsty, who yielded up the castle, the manor, and the fair broad lands with an evil grace. There Robin dwelled in peace and comfort, tending the estates of his wife with good husbandry and careful rule, guarding the lands from encroach-ment by neighbouring lords, and knitting all his villeins and freeholders to himself by his kindliness and frankness.

With him went Hob o' the Hill and Ket the Trow, together with their two sisters. Their mother had died in the 'howe', or green mound, a little while before, and they had therefore wished to leave the place. Little John also went with Robin, and Gilbert of the White Hand, who married Sibbie, one of the fairy sisters, and lived in a cottage which Robin gave to them. The other sister, Fenella, wedded Wat Graham of Car Peel, a brave fighter from the borderlands, and their children were long said to have the fairy gifts of second sight, invisibility, and supernatural strength.

The other outlaws all yielded to King Richard's offer of high wages and great loot, and went with him to Normandy, there to fight the French king and the rebellious 'weathercocks' of Poitou. Most of them left their bones there; a score or two came back, after King Richard was slain, some rich with plunder, others as poor as they went forth, and all these gradually drifted to Malaset, where 'Squire Robin,' as he was called, settled them on lands.

With those who came back from France were Will the Bowman, Scarlet, and Much, the Miller's son. Arthur-a-Bland was slain at the taking of the castle of Chaluz, where the king also met his death, and Scadlock was drowned in a storm at sea, just outside Rye. With the old outlaws who remained, Robin formed as fine a body of fighting men as ever marched south under the banners of the barons when, in the year 1215, they at length set their hands to the struggle with their king to wrest from him freedom from tyranny and oppression.

Sixteen years thus passed over the heads of Robin and his fair spouse Marian; and in spite of the trouble and confusion which agitated the minds of men and brought disorder into the kingdom when King John defied the pope, these were happy years at Malaset.

But in his castle of Wrangby Sir Isenbart de Belame still brooded on the vengeance he would wreak upon Robin Hood, and bided his time in patience. And to him often came Sir Guy of Gisborne, and with them spoke Sir Baldwin the Killer, Sir Roger of Doncaster, and Sir Scrivel of Catsty, and all took secret counsel together how they should best take and slay Robin when the time came.

CHAPTER TEN

The Burning of Evil Hold

It was an early winter day in the year 1215. A band of men were marching across the high moorlands east of the wild waste lands of the Peak. At their head rode Robin Hood, clothed in chain mail, the helm upon his head sparkling in the westering sun. Behind him came sixty of his men, bronzed, honest-faced yeomen, each with his bow and quiver, and a sword strapped to his side. A score of them were his old outlaws, and head and shoulders above them stalked Little John, his brown, keen eyes looking sharply this way and that over the wide moors which stretched away to the purple distance on every side. Immediately behind Robin walked Ket the Trow, sturdy though small, a fighter, yet a man of craft in every look and gesture of him. Not far off were Scarlet, Will Stuteley, and Much, the Miller's son.

The face of Robin wore a thoughtful, even a moody air. He had gone with the barons when they had wrested the charter of liberty from the tyrannous hands of John; and had stayed south with them, believing that the fight for freedom had been gained. Then suddenly they had learned that foreign mercenaries were landing to aid the king against his rebel barons; the foreign hordes, thirsting for blood and plunder, had been seen in such strength that the barons had almost lost heart and had retreated. Many had gone to defend their own castles and lands when they learned that the king's mercenaries had stolen north, harrying, burning, and slaying, and Robin Hood had done likewise, fearing lest evil should befall his gentle wife in the peaceful vale of Malaset upon the marches of Lancaster.

Robin wondered, indeed, whether he had started too late. At every step of the way northwards they saw the marks of rapine and massacre where the king had passed with his foreign hordes. Every house and village they passed was destroyed by fire, corpses lay stiff on the snow, or weltered on the hearthstone which had known the laughter and the joy in life of those who now lay dead. Smoke rose over the wintry horizon, showing where the burning and slaying of the ruffianly army of the shameless king still went on. One castle which they passed was a smoking ruin, and in its blackened and smouldering hall they found two young ladies, one dumb with grief, the other half mad in her sorrow, leaning over the body of their father, an old knight, whom his king had tortured to death in an attempt to wring from him the place where he had hidden his store of money.

Now and then, as he rode, Robin raised his head and glanced quickly before him. He dreaded lest he should see a cloud of smoke which should show that some band of the evil army of the king had come so far westwards to Malaset. But against the violet clouds of the wintry sky where the sun was sinking there was no blur of rolling reek.

At length the road descended from the moors and wound round crags and limestone cliffs down towards the valley of Malaset. Almost unconsciously Robin pushed on faster, so eager was he to reach a point where, at a bend in the road, he could see the castle. At length he reached the place, stopped for a moment, and his men, hurrying behind him, heard him give a dreadful cry. Next moment he had struck spurs into his horse's flanks and thundered down the sloping track.

They reached the bend and looked upon the low keep of the castle. A light grey smoke, as if from smouldering timber, rose from the pile, and a dreadful silence brooded over all. The men groaned, and then began to run, uttering fearful cries of vengeance and despair as they rushed towards ruined homes and slain loved ones.

With a strange, cold calmness on him, Robin leaped from his horse in the courtyard, in which bodies of men lay here and there, still and contorted. He strode into the hall; a thin reek of smoke filled the apartment. The place had been fired, but the fire had not caught. Only some broken benches smouldered in a heap, amidst which the bodies of defenders and their assailants were mingled together in the close fierce embrace in which they had given each other death. Up the winding stair in the wall he strode, to the solar or lady's bower.

The door was shut, and he opened it gently. There in the light of the westering sun lay a figure on the bed, its face very white and set. It was Marian. Her body was draped in black, and was very still, and he knew that she was dead. On her breast her long fair hands were folded, and her dark hair framed her face and breast in a soft beauty. A short black arrow lay beside the corpse.

A sudden movement came from behind the arras, and the slight figure of a woman darted towards him and threw herself on her knees before him. It was Sibbie, wife to Gilbert of the White Hand, the fairy maid who had been tirewoman to Fair Marian. She did not weep, but her face looked up into his with grief in the great brown, faithful eyes.

'Who has done this, Sibbie?' asked Robin in a quiet, low voice.

'Who but that fiend Isenbart de Belame!' said the woman in a fierce restrained voice. 'He slew her while she spoke with him from the gate-guard room. With this arrow – the selfsame arrow which my brother Hob shot in his table at Evil Hold – he let out her dear life. She fell into my arms, smiled at me, but could not speak, and so died. On the second day – 'twas but yesterday they left – they stormed the castle, but bitter and hard was the fighting in the courtyard and the hall, and then, for fear you should return, they plundered far and wide through the manor, and so left, with Hob my brother wounded and a prisoner, and ten others, whom they promised to torture when they reached Evil Hold again.'

Ket the Trow had crept into the room immediately behind Robin and heard all. His sister turned to him and silently they clasped hands. Then, loosing them, they each raised the right forefinger in the air, and swiftly made a strange gesture as if they wrote a letter or marked a device. It was the sign of undying vengeance by which the people of the Underworld vowed to go through flood and fire, pains and pangs, and never to slacken in their quest, never to rest, until they had avenged the death of their lady.

Robin bent and kissed the cold forehead of his wife. Then, uncovering, he knelt beside her and prayed. He spoke no word, but he craved the aid of the Virgin in his vow to stamp out utterly the life and power of the lord of the Evil Hold and all his mates in wickedness.

That night, by the light of torches, the body of Marian was

lowered to the grave beside her father and her kinsfolk in the little church of Malaset, while in the castle those of the villeins and freemen who had fled from their farms and holdings at the approach of de Belame and his evil horde were busily engaged in furbishing up arms and harness. All were filled with a hard resolution, and each had made up his mind to die in the attempt to pull down the Evil Hold and its power.

At dawn, in silence, Robin and his band set forth. They did not look back once, but stubbornly they mounted the moorside road and kept their faces fixed towards the east. At the same time Robin sent a messenger to Sir Herbrand de Tranmire, now an old man, reminding him of his promise to aid him in breaking down the castle of Wrangby, and asking, if he could not come himself, to send all the men he could spare, well armed, to meet Robin at the Mark Oak by Wrangby Mere. Similar messages were sent by Robin to other knights and freemen who had suffered from the oppression of de Belame. Many had promised 'Squire Robin' aid if ever he needed it, for all had recognised in him a brave man and a generous one; and all had known that someday they would have to join their forces with him to end the villainies and wicked customs of the Evil Hold.

On his way to Wrangby, Robin called at the castles and manor-houses of other knights to ask their aid. Some places he found were gutted and in ruins, with their brave defenders lying dead, the prey of their king's malignant cruelty. Many men, however, quickly responded to his appeal, so that when at evening, as the twilight was creeping over the misty moor, Robin rode in sight of Wrangby Castle, he had three hundred men at his back, sufficient at least to prevent the garrison from breaking forth.

He stopped a bowshot from the great gate and sounded his horn. On the tower above the portal appeared two men in complete mail, one wearing a bronze helmet which shone dully in the faint light.

'I would speak to Isenbart de Belame!' cried Robin.

'Wolf's-head!' came the reply, like the snarl of a wolf, 'you are speaking to Sir Isenbart de Belame, lord of Wrangby and the Fells. What do you and your rabble want?'

'I will tell ye,' cried Robin. 'Deliver yourself up to me with the prisoners you have taken! You shall have the judgement of your peers upon your evil deeds, and for the murder of my wife, the Lady Marian. If you do not do this, then we will take your evil castle by storm, and the death of you and your men shall be on your head!'

'If ye do not leave my lands by dawn,' was the fierce reply, 'you and your tail of whipped curs and villeins, I will come out and beat you to death with my dogwhips. Go, wolf's-head and rascal! I will speak no more with thee!'

With a gesture, as if he had no more attention to bestow on creatures so mean, he turned aside and spoke to the other knight who was with him. Both had their visors down, and in the gathering twilight their figures were becoming dimmer every moment. Suddenly a little figure sped forward in the gloom before Robin's horse, then stood still, and the twang of a bowstring was heard. Next moment the knight beside de Belame was seen to put his hands to his visor and then stagger. He recovered himself instantly, however, and drew an arrow from between the bars of his helmet. With a gesture of rage he dashed it over the battlements and yelled something in derision which could not be heard.

It was Ket the Trow who had made this marvellous shot in the twilight, so that men wondered that it could have reached the mark so unerringly. Yet by reason of the fact that the bolt had been shot at so great an angle, the arrow had only torn the flesh on the forehead of the knight.

That night Robin and his men hemmed the castle closely, so that no one could come out or go in unseen. Under the Mark Oak he took counsel with the knights who had brought aid.

'Squire Robin,' said one, Sir Fulk of the Dykewall, 'I cannot see how we can hope to beat down that strong keep. We have no siege engines, we cannot break down the wall in any place, the ditch is full of water, and I doubt not that such a man as de Belame is well provisioned for a long siege.'

'I see no reason why we should not take the castle,' said young Squire Denvil of Toomlands, as eager and brave as a hawk. 'We can get the Wrangby peasants, who hate their lords, to cut down trees and make rafts for us. With these, and under cover of our shields we can pole across the ditch and cut the chains of the drawbridge. Then we can prise up the portcullis, and once within can hack down the gate.'

After long council, this seemed the only way by which they could hope to take the castle. It would mean the loss of many lives, no doubt, but the walls of the castle were thick and high, and there was no other way out or in but by the great gate. Ket the Trow was called and bidden to go to the villeins of Wrangby in the hovels a mile from the castle, and ask them to come to aid Robin in rooting out their evil lords. In an hour he returned.

'I went to Cole the Reeve,' he said, 'and gave him the bidding. He called the homagers [chief men] and told them what you wanted. Their eyes said they would quickly come, but long they thought in silence. Then one said, "Six times hath the Evil Hold been set about by strong lords, and never hath it been taken. Satan loves his own, and 'tis vain to fight against the evil lords. They have ever had power, and will ever keep it." And they were silent to all I urged upon them, and shook their heads and went away.'

Robin thereupon commanded parties of his own men to take it in turn during the night to cut down young trees to make rafts with them, and short scaling-ladders to get at the chains of the drawbridge, and by the light of torches, in amongst the trees, the work went on all night, while Robin went from place to place seeing that strict guard was kept. Just before daybreak he took some sleep, but was awakened by the arrival of a band of peasants from Wrangby, the very men who, the night before, had refused to aid him against their lords. At their head was an old man, grey, of great frame and fierce aspect. In his hands he bore a tall billhook, with a long wide blade as keen and bright as a razor. When Robin saw him he knew him for one of the men who had shot with him at the contest at Nottingham before the sheriff.

'Master,' said the old man, going to Robin, 'I bring you these men. They denied you last night. They were but half men then, but I have spoken with them, and now they will help you to pull down this nest of bandit lords and slayers of women and children and maimers of men.'

'I thank thee, Rafe of the Billhook,' replied Robin, and turned to the peasants. one of them stepped forth and spoke for his fellows.

'We have taken the oath,' he said, 'and we will go with thee to the end. Rather we will be destroyed now than live longer in our misery under our evil oppressors.'

The poor men seemed depressed and subdued, as if all the manliness had been beaten out of them by years of ill-usage at the hands of their lords.

'Ye will not fail, brothers,' said Rafe, and his look was fierce as he shook his huge billhook. 'I swore, when they thrust me from my cot in Barnisdale Wood and slew my wife and my boy, that I would come back and help to root these fiends out of their nest of stone. The time has come, brothers, and God and the Virgin are fighting for us.'

'You are Thurstan of Stone Cot, whom de Belame thrust from your holding thirty winters ago?' asked Robin.

'You speak truly,' replied Thurstan; 'I have returned at my appointed time.'

Under the guidance of this man, and with the eager help of Little John and Gilbert of the White Hand, preparations were soon ready, and after a good meal had been taken and mass had been heard, the rafts were carried down to the ditch before the great gate. Showers of arrows greeted them, but the raft-bearers were supported by archers who were commanded by Scarlet and Will Stuteley, and who scanned with keen eyes every slit in the walls. Their bolts searched out and struck everything that moved behind the arrow slits, and anyone who came to the battlements of the castle was hit by several arrows. Quickly the rafts were launched and poled across the ditch, and ladders were reared on the sills beside the huge drawbridge which blocked up the portcullis and the gates beyond. Soon the blows of iron upon iron told how mightily the smiths were striving to cut the chains on either side which held the drawbridge up. For a time it looked as if they would have an easy task, for Robin's archers made it impossible for anyone to lean from the battlements to shoot them. Suddenly, however, the inside gates were thrown open and a crowd of bowmen began to shoot at the smiths through the bars of the portcullis. One smith fell from his ladder into the ditch, a great arrow sticking in his breast; the other had his hand transfixed.

Others took their places at once, however, and Scarlet, Will the Bowman, and two other archers stood on the ladders with the smiths, and returned the shooting as best they could, though the space was so confined that hardly could they draw their bows. At length a shout went up – one chain was cut through and the drawbridge shook and trembled. A few more blows with the hammer on the other side, and with a mighty crash the draw-bridge fell across the moat, being smashed in half by reason of its weight. Robin and a select band of archers swarmed over the ruined drawbridge, which held together sufficiently to allow of this, and shooting between the bars of the portcullis, poured in such flights of arrows that the garrison, which was indifferently provided with bowmen, was compelled to retreat behind the gates, which finally they had to close.

Then a great tree trunk was run forward by forty willing hands, and the bridge having been covered with rafting to support the weight of extra men, the battering-ram was dashed against the portcullis. Again and again this was done, the archers on the bank picking off those on the castle wall or at the arrow slits who tried to shoot down the besiegers. Many of Robin's men were killed, however, for the defence was as bitter as the attack, and everywhere in the castle could be heard the voices of Sir Isenbart and his fellow-knights, Sir Baldwin, Sir Scrivel, or Sir Roger of Doncaster, angrily urging the archers and stone-throwers to continue their efforts. Several of Robin's archers and those of the ramming-party, though these had shields over their heads, were either killed or disabled by bolts or crushed by huge stones, but still the great tree trunk hammered at the portcullis, making it to shake and crack here and there.

At last the castle gate was thrown open again, and a deadly flight of arrows flew out, dealing death from between the bars of the portcullis. But Robin led up his archers, and again compelled the garrison to retreat, while other men-at-arms took the vacant places beside the ram, the head of which was now so split and torn that it seemed like a mop. Still it thudded and crashed against the bars of the portcullis, two of which were so bent and cracked that soon the great grille would be broken through sufficiently to allow men to enter.

Robin, Sir Fulk, and another knight, Sir Robert of Staithes, were standing beside the ramming-party urging them on, Robin

with a watchful eye on the inner gate, lest it should open again to
let forth a shower of bolts.

'Three more good blows from master oak, lads,' cried Robin,
'and in we go. The wooden gate will not keep us long!'

Just then there came quick shouts from Will the Bowman,
who stood with his archers on the bank.

'Back! back!' he cried; 'they throw fire down!'

'Into the moat!' shouted Robin, hearing the warning cries.
Most heard him and jumped at once. But other poor fellows
were too late.

Down from the battlements poured a deluge of boiling tar,
and quickly after came burning brands and red-hot stones. Some
half-dozen men who had not heard the cries were whelmed in
the deathly rain and killed. The lighted brands and red-hot
stones instantly set fire to the rafting, the drawbridge and the
ram, which were covered with tar, and soon a furnace fire raged,
cutting off the besiegers from what a few moments before had
seemed almost certain victory.

Robin and those who had escaped swam to the bank, while
Will and his archers searched the walls with their arrows. But
they had not been able to prevent the tar from being heaved
over, for the men who had dragged the cauldron to the battlements had been protected by shields held before them by others.

Robin looked at the gulf of fire before him, and at the angry
and gloomy faces of his men.

'Never mind, lads,' he cried. 'They can't get out themselves,
and when the fire has burned itself out we will cross by fresh
rafts. A few more blows and the bars will be broken enough to
let us in. Will and you, Scarlet,' he cried, turning to Stuteley and
the other old outlaw, 'see that you let no one of the evil crew
mend those broken bars.'

'He will have to mend the hole in his own carcass first,' said
Scarlet, with a laugh. He cocked his eye quickly over arrow slit
and battlement as he held his bow in readiness to shoot.

It was now past noon, and while a party watched the portcullis,
and others took a hasty meal, a third party were sent with the
peasants to cut fresh rafts.

As Robin was directing the work of the woodcutters, he saw,
coming over the moor, a great party of footmen, preceded by

two knights on horseback. His keen eyes gazed at the blazons on their shields, and at sight of the three white swallows of the one, and the five green trees of the other, he waved his hand in welcome. They were Sir Walter de Beauforest and young Alan-a-Dale, and in a little while they were shaking hands with Robin.

'We received thy message yesterday,' said Sir Walter, 'and we have come as quickly as we could. I trust we have not arrived too late'

'Nay, the castle hath not yet fallen into my hands,' said Robin, 'and your forces will be welcome.'

He then related what had been done and the plans he had made for taking the place, which they found were good, and promised to aid him all they could. Alan told him that Sir Herbrand was sending a party to help Robin, but being old and feeble he could not come himself, much as he would like to have struck a blow against his enemies of Wrangby.

Now all this while Ket the Trow wandered through the camp with a gloomy look. Sometimes he took his place with the archers by the moat, and his was the keenest eye to see a movement at an arrow slit or on the battlements, and his was the swiftest arrow to fly at the mark. But things were going too slowly for Ket. He yearned for a speedy and complete revenge for the murder of his beloved mistress. Moreover, he knew that inside that castle his loved brother Hob lay in some noisome dungeon wounded, perhaps suffering already some cruel torture.

Round and round the castle Ket went, creeping from cover to cover, his dark eyes searching the smooth stone of the walls for some loophole whereby he could enter. He had been inside once, when he had shot the message on the table before Sir Isenbart de Belame, when Ranulf of the Waste had been slain. That night he had followed some of the knights when they had returned from a foray, bringing rich gear as spoil and captives for ransom. He had been close on their backs, and in the confusion he had marched in through the gate and had secreted himself in the darkness. Then at night he had crept down a drain which opened out some twelve feet above the ditch, and, under cover of a storm of wind and rain, had dropped into the water and so got safely away.

But now, try as he might, the great high walls baffled him, for he could see no way by which he could win into the strong keep. Once in, he doubted not that he could worm his way to his brother, release him, and then slay the guards and open the gates to Robin and his men.

He lay in a thick bush of hazel at the rear of the castle and scanned the walls narrowly. Now and then he cast his eyes warily round the moorland to where the forest and the fells hemmed in the Wrangby lands.

What was that? At one and the same moment two strange things had happened. He had seen a sword flash twice from the battlements of the castle, as if it was a signal, and instantly there had been a momentary glint as of a weapon from between the leafless trees of a wood on the edge of the forest some half a mile away. He looked long and earnestly at the point, but nothing stirred or showed again.

'Strange,' thought Ket; 'was that a signal? If so, who was he to whom the man in the castle was making signs?'

Ket's decision was soon taken, and like a ferret, creeping from bush to bush, he made his way towards the wood. He reached the verge and looked between the trees. There, with the muzzles of their horses tied up to prevent their making a noise, lay some thirty fierce moss-riders. He knew them at once. They were the men of Thurlstan, from whom he had rescued Fair Marian several years before. A man raised his great shock head of white hair and looked over the moor towards the camp of the besiegers. Then his teeth showed in a mocking sneer, and Ket knew that this was old Grame Gaptooth himself, lord of Thurlstan.

' 'Twill be dark in an hour, and then we will make that rabble fly!' said the old raider.

Ket guessed at once, and rightly, that these marauders, kinsmen to Sir Isenbart, had ridden to join him in the plundering foray of King John, lured by the hope of slaughter and booty. They had discovered that the castle was besieged, had made their presence known to their friends in the castle, and now lay waiting for the short winter day to end. Then they would ride down fiercely among Robin's band, and by their cries they would give Sir Isenbart the signal to issue forth. Then, surprised, and taken between two forces, who knows? perhaps Robin Hood and his men would be cut to pieces.

With the stealth of a wild cat, Ket began to back away and to creep deeper into the wood behind where the moss-riders lay. With infinite care he proceeded, since the cracking of a twig might reveal his presence to the fierce raiders. When he had covered some fifty yards he carefully rose to his feet and then, like a shadow, flitted from tree to tree through the forest towards the camp of Robin.

The Thurlstan men heard from where they lay the shouts of men as they yelled defiance at the garrison; and the short, sharp words of command of Robin and the knights as they supervised the placing of the rafts of timber in the ditch before the gate. Then, in a little while, the twilight and the mist deepened over the land, the forest seemed to creep nearer, and darkness descended rapidly.

'Now, lads,' said Grame Gaptooth, getting to his feet and grasping his horse's bridle, 'mount and make ready. Walk your horses till ye are a hundred yards from where thou seest their fires burning, then use the spur and shout my cry, "Gaptooth o' the Wall." Then with spur and sword mow me those dogs down, and when Belame hears us he will come forth, and the killing will be a merry one between us. Now, up and away!'

Quietly over the long coarse grass the raiders passed, and then, with a sudden fierce shout, they dashed upon the groups about the fires. But, strangely enough, the men-at-arms they rode among turned as if they expected them; three knights rode out of the gloom against the raiders, and amidst the shouts of 'Gaptooth o' the Wall, Gaptooth o' the Wall,' the fierce fighting began.

Counselled by Ket the Trow, Robin had ordered his men to retreat a little towards the castle, so that the garrison should hear clearly when the border men attacked them; and this was done. Eagerly the moss-men followed, and their enemies seemed to fly before them. They pressed on more quickly, still shouting their war cry. Suddenly they heard answering cries. 'Belame! Belame!' came like a fierce bellow from the castle gate, which was dashed open, the portcullis slowly mounted, and out from its yawning jaws swept knights and men-at-arms. Robin had placed the rafts over the blackened timbers of the drawbridge, so that the garrison could come out without delay, and over these they came in a mad rush, causing the timbers to heave and rock, and soon the cries of 'Gaptooth' and 'Belame' mingled in fierce delight.

Suddenly, above the din, came the dear call of a bugle from somewhere in the rear. At the same time three short, sharp notes rose from beneath the castle walls. Out of the forest of the Mark Oak swept ten knights and a hundred men-at-arms, the force which Sir Herbrand had sent, and which had arrived as darkness fell, in time to form part of the plan which Robin and the knights, with the counsel of Ket the Trow, had formed for the destruction of their enemy.

The men who had seemed to be caught between those who shouted 'Belame' and those who cried 'Gaptooth' now suddenly came back in greater numbers. The troop of de Belame heard the rush of men behind them where, as they thought, they had left none but their own garrison; and the moss-riders turned, as avenging cries of 'Marian! Marian!' answered by other shouts of 'Tranmire and St George' sounded fiercely all about them.

Then indeed came the fierce crash of battle. Caught between the two wings of Robin's party, which now outnumbered de Belame and his friends, the Wrangby lords fought for dear life. No quarter was asked or given. Peasant with bill or axe fought men-at-arms on foot, or hacked at the knight of coat-armour on horseback; and everywhere Rafe of the Bill fought in fierce delight, his glittering bill in his hand, looking out meanwhile for Sir Isenbart himself. Robin also sought everywhere in the gloom for the slayer of his wife. Distinguishable by the bronze of his helmet, Sir Isenbart raged like a boar to and fro, dealing death or wounds with every blow, chanting the while his own fierce name. Robin saw him and strove to follow him, but the press of battle kept them asunder. Close behind Robin stalked Little John, a huge double-headed axe in his hand, making wider the path cleared by his master through their foes.

'John, for the love of the Virgin, go strike down that bronze helm,' cried Robin at length. 'It is de Belame! Man, for love of me, let him not escape!'

Little chance there seemed of that now, even if the brave, fierce tyrant wished to run. He was checked in his path of slaughter now, for Rafe of the Bill and twenty Wrangby villeins had surrounded him, tearing at his limbs, wrenching at his armour to drag him down among their feet. Long years of

hatred and misery thrilled in every nerve, but more skilful with
the humble weapons of the soil than with arms, they went down
before his keen sword like stalks of wheat before the sickle.
Swiftly he struck here and there, shaking off his assailants as a
bear tosses off the dogs. Rafe strove to reach him with his great
bill, thrusting and hacking at him, but de Belame's stout shield
received all the fierce blows, and for the moment it seemed that
he would win through.

Robin and John broke through the weakening ranks of their
foes at last, and leaping over the dead that lay in heaps they
rushed towards Sir Isenbart. But too late they reached him.
With a great shearing blow, the bill in the vengeful hands of old
Thurstan had lighted upon the right shoulder of the knight,
cutting deep into the bone. Another moment and the bill would
have swept de Belame's head from his shoulders, but Robin
caught the stroke on his shield, crying:

'Kill him not; the rope shall have him!'

Rafe dropped his bill. 'Ay, you are right,' he growled. 'He
deserves not to die by honest steel – let the hangman have the
felon.'

De Belame, his right arm paralysed, yet kept his seat and cried:

'Kill me, wolf's-head! Kill me with thy sword! I am a gentleman of coat-armour! I yield not to such carrion!' He thrust spurs
into his horse, and strove to dash away from among them.

But the great arms of Rafe were about him, and they dragged
him from his seat.

'Coat-armour,' snarled the fierce man. 'Had I my way I would
blazon thy skin with as evil a pattern as thou and thy fiends have
cut on poor folks' bodies. Coat-armour and a good hempen rope
will go well together this night!'

'John and you, Rafe, bind up his wound, then bring the
prisoner to the castle, which I doubt not is ours,' said Robin, and
he would not leave them until he saw the wound bound up.
Then, securely tied, de Belame, silent now and sullen, was
carried towards the castle.

The battle had ceased everywhere by now. Few of the Wrangby
men were left alive; so fierce had been the hatred of them that no
more than a dozen had staggered away in the darkness, and
among these was only one knight, Sir Roger of Doncaster, a sly

man who preferred plotting to fighting. Of the moss-riders not one was alive, and Gaptooth himself had ridden his last cruel foray.

As to the castle, following the plan which Ket the Trow had made, this had been quickly seized. With young Squire Denvil and a chosen party of forty men, Ket had silently hidden in the water beside the rafts which lay before the great gate. When de Belame and his men had dashed from the castle in exultant answer to Gaptooth's call, and the gate-guard were standing under the portcullis, certain of victory and grumbling at being left behind and out of the killing, dripping men had risen as if from their very feet, and hardly had they realised what it meant before death had found them. Then, silently, Ket and the Squire of Toomlands, followed closely by their men, had swept into the castle, cutting down all who opposed them. They had gained the place without the loss of a single man, and as all but a dozen of the garrison had sallied out to what all had thought was certain victory, the struggle had been brief.

A little later, into the hall where Sir Isenbart and his fellow-knights had often sat carousing over their cups or torturing some poor captive, came Robin and such of the knights who had aided him as had come unharmed through the battle. Taking his seat in de Belame's chair at the high table, the knights in other seats beside him, Robin bade the prisoners be brought in. Torches gleamed from the pillars of the hall on the scarred, hacked armour of the conquerors, and the face of every man-at-arms, peasant, and knight was hard and stern as he looked at the group which entered.

There were but two prisoners, Sir Isenbart de Belame and Sir Baldwin the Killer, who had received his name for the cruelty and number of the deaths he had inflicted in years of rapine and foray throughout the lands of Wrangby and the Peak. As the door of the hall opened men heard the sound of distant knocking of axes on wood: the gallows were already being reared before the gate of the Evil Hold.

'Isenbart de Belame,' began Robin in a stern voice, 'here in thy castle, in thy hall where often thy miserable captives, men and women, rich and poor, gentle and simple, craved thy mercy and got naught but brutal jests or evil injury – here thou comest at last to find thy judgement. All who have anything to charge against this man de Belame, or his comrade in cruelty and oppression, Baldwin, stand forth, and as God hears and sees all, tell the truth on peril of their souls!'

It seemed as if the whole body of yeomen, peasants, and franklins standing by would come forward to charge upon the two scowling knights deeds of wrong and cruelty. 'He put out my father's eyes!' cried one. 'The harvest failed one year,' cried another, 'and because I could not pay him my yearly load of wheat, he pressed my son to death,' said another. Others stepped quickly up, and each gave in a few harsh words his tale of cruel deeds. When all had ended, Ket the Trow stood forth.

'With his own evil hand that man slew the kindest lady between Barnisdale and the Coombes o' the Moors,' he cried, and pointed his finger at de Belame. 'He slew her while she spoke to him from her castle gate, and he laughed when he saw her fall.'

'He stood by and jested when Ranulf of the Waste tortured by fire our father, Colman Grey!' cried Hob o' the Hill, limping forth with bandaged leg and arm, and shaking his fist at de Belame, whose face was white as he saw the hatred burn on every face about him.

'It is enough – and more than enough!' said Robin at last. 'What say you, Sir Knights? These men are of knightly blood and wear coat-armour, and so should die by the sword. But they have proved themselves no better than tavern knifers and robbers, and I adjudge them a shameful death by the rope!'

A great shout of assent rang through the lofty hall, 'To the rope! to the rope with them!'

'We agree with thee, Squire Robin,' said Sir Fulk of the Dykewall when silence was restored. 'Both these men have lost all claim to their rank. Their spurs should be hacked from their heels, and their bodies swung from the gallows.'

It was done. Amid the shouts of triumph of the fierce men standing about, Little John hacked off the spurs from the heels of the two Wrangby lords, and then with a great roar of rageful glee they were hurried out amid the surging crowd, torches tossing their lurid light upon hard faces and gleaming eyes, whose usual good nature was turned to savagery for the moment.

When the act of wild justice had been done, pitch and tar and oil were poured into every chamber of the castle, and torches were thrust in, and lighted straw heaped up. Then all fled forth and stood before the black walls, through whose slits the black and oily smoke began to curl. Leaping tongues of fire darted through the ropy reek and coiling wreaths, and soon, gathering power, the fire burst up through the floors of the great hall and the chambers above, and roared like a furious torrent to the dark sky. Great noises issued as the thick beams split, and as balk and timber, rafter and buttress fell, the flames and sparks leaped higher until the light shone far and wide over the country. Shepherds minding their sheep far away on the distant fells looked and looked, and would not believe their eyes; then crossed themselves and muttered a prayer of thankfulness that somehow the Evil Hold of Wrangby was at length ruining in fire. Bands of plunderers from the king's evil army, as they streamed across the highlands of the Peak, or on the hills of Yorkshire, saw the distant glare, and did not know then that one of the blackest strongholds of their callous king and his evil lords was going up in fire at the hands of those who, long and cruelly oppressed, had risen at last and gained their freedom.

Next morning a smoking shell of shattered and blackened stones was all that was left of the strong castle that had been the sign of wrong for at least two generations. A white smoke rose from the red-hot furnace within the walls which still stood; but so rent and torn and seamed with fire were the stones, that never again could they be made fit for habitation.

Robin rode forth from the shadow of the Mark Oak, where he and his army had passed the night, and looked at the smoking ruins and the two stiff gallows which stood before, on each of which hung, turning round and round, the bodies of the evil Baldwin and de Belame.

Doffing his steel cap, Robin bent his head and in silence gave up a prayer to the Virgin, thanking her for the help she had so amply granted him. His men gathered round him, and taking off their helms prayed likewise.

From over the plain came a crowd of peasants – some running, some walking slowly, half disbelieving their own eyes. Some among them came up to Robin, and old men and women, their faces and hands worn and lined with toil, seized his hands and kissed them, or touched his feet or the hem of his coat of mail with their lips. A young mother lifted up the baby she held in her arms, and with tears in her eyes told the child to look at Robin Hood, 'the man who had slain the evil lords and burned their den!'

'Master,' said Rafe of the Bill, 'go not far from us, lest someone as evil as those lords that now swing there shall come and possess again these lands, and build another hold of fiends to torture this land and its poor folk.'

'By the sweet Mother of Heaven,' said Robin Hood, and held up his right hand in the oath gesture, 'while I live no one shall possess these lands who ruleth them not in justice and mercy as I would have him rule them!'

'Amen!' came in deep response from all about him.

CHAPTER ELEVEN

Of the Death of Robin Hood

Never again, after the death of his wife Marian, did Robin Hood leave the greenwood. The lands at Malaset were taken by a distant kinsman of the Earl FitzWalter, who ruled them well and treated his villeins and yeomen kindly, with due regard to the customs of the manor.

Many of those who had been outlaws with Robin and had become his tenants at Malaset refused to go back there, but once having tasted again the wild free life of the greenwood, kept with Robin; and the numbers of his band swelling by reason of the cruelties and slaying, sacking, and plundering by the tyrannical king, they eagerly fell in with Robin's proposal to harass the royal army. Therefore, when Wrangby Castle had been levelled with the ground, so that not one stone stood upon another, Robin fared north and, taking to the woods and waste places, hung upon the flanks of the marauding Flemings, Brabanters, Saxons, and Poitevins who composed the king's army. Many a raiding party, engaged in some dreadful deed of plunder and torture of knights or yeomen, did Robin and his brave men fall upon, and with their great war arrows destroy or rout them utterly, thus earning the gratitude of many a knight and dame, villein and franklin, who ever after held the name of Robin Hood in special reverence.

When at last King John died at Newark by poison, and his son Henry was crowned and acknowledged king by all the great barons and lords of the realm, Robin took possession of his old quarters in Barnisdale and Sherwood. The land was still full of oppression and wrongdoing, for the king was but a boy; some of the evil lords refused to give up the castles they had seized during the war between John and his barons, and having long lived by pillaging their neighbours, would not now cease their habits of living by plundering and spoiling those weaker than themselves. Whenever, therefore, Robin had word, by a breathless villein or weeping woman, who came begging for his aid, that some evil deed was on foot, he issued with his chosen band from his forest lairs, and so stealthily he passed through the land, and so suddenly his arrows flew among the wrongdoers, that it was seldom he failed to beat back the rascally lords and their companies of thieves, besides giving them fear of his name and of his clothyard arrows which never missed their mark, and that could pierce the thickest chain-mail.

By good hap the councillors of the young king gave the lands of Wrangby into the keeping of a just lord, a kinsman of Earl de Warenne, who treated his villeins and tenants with mercy, so that soon the memory of the evil days of oppression and cruelty under Sir Isenbart de Belame became so faint that it seemed almost as if they never could have been.

But in other parts of the kingdom oppression and misery still stalked through the land. Insolent barons sent parties of armed men to seize the young king's lands in various places, and either put his tenants to death or chased them away into poverty; weaker neighbours were ever in fear of being attacked and slain, or their lands wrested from them, and under cover of this disorder robbery and extortion were committed daily. Indeed, bands of highway robbers wearing the livery of great lords infested the forest roads and lonely ways in many parts of the country, ready to fall upon merchants travelling with their wares, or even upon poor villeins or franklins carrying their goods to market.

One day Robin was with Little John and Scarlet on the borders of Sherwood and Barnisdale. They were waiting for news of a party of evil men who had begun to haunt that part of the country, and who were in the pay of Sir Roger of Doncaster. This was the knight who, with some ten men-at-arms, had managed to escape from the fight before Evil Hold. Robin knew that Sir Roger's aim was to lie in ambush for him one day and to kill him, but until now the outlaws had not actually come into touch with the marauders.

They sat in a small glade which was screened all round by

thick bushes of holly, but from their place of vantage they could see through the leaves up and down the two main tracks or roads through the forest. By-and-by there came the sound of a scolding squirrel, and Robin responded, for this was a sign between the scouts. In a few moments Ket the Trow came into the glade and went up to Robin.

'Master,' he said, 'I and Hob have watched the manor-house, at Syke, of Roger of Doncaster. He and his men left at dawn this morning, and have gone towards the Stone Houses by Barnisdale Four Wents. I think they lie in wait there to fall upon the bishop's convoy of food and gear which goes today from Wakefield Abbey to Lincoln.'

'Up, John,' said Robin, 'and thou, Scarlet, and do thou go quickly to the Stane Lea and take all the men thou canst find and try thy wits against that robber knight and his hedge-knifers. As for me, I will follow thee anon.'

With instant obedience Little John and Scarlet started off, and soon were lost in the winding paths of the forest. Ket stood still and waited for further instructions.

'Ket,' said Robin at length, 'do thou go to Will the Bowman, and bid him bring the score of men he hath watching with him, and scatter them across the road and forest tracks from Doncaster hitherwards. If thou seest thy brother Hob, send him to me.'

With a gesture of his hand that showed he understood, Ket turned and vanished into the forest, wondering a little at his orders. If, thought he, Sir Roger's men were going north-west to Barnisdale, and Robin had sent his men to waylay them, why did he wish to have the southern road from Doncaster watched? Ket was quick of wit, however, and he thought: was it because Robin believed that Sir Roger's journey towards Barnisdale was a feint, and that another party would be sent south in the attempt to seize or slay Robin? He remembered that very often his master's keen brains knew more than any of his scouts could tell him.

When Ket left him, Robin went out of the glade into the road and began to walk under the leafy boughs. When he had gone about half a mile towards the south he came to a small path which ran through the trees at the side, and looking down this he saw a low-browed man, with a cruel look, dressed like a yeoman, standing looking furtively up and down the narrow path. In his hand he bore a bow, and a quiver of arrows hung beside him.

'Good-morrow, good fellow,' said Robin. 'Whither away?'

'Good-morrow to you, good woodman,' replied the yeoman, who was taken somewhat by surprise at Robin's quiet approach, and his eyes glanced here and there, and did not look straight at Robin. 'I ha' lost my way through the forest. Canst thou tell me my way to Roche Abbey?'

Robin seemed to look at him carelessly as he replied: 'Ay, I can lead thee into thy road. Thou hast come far out of thy way.'

'Ay, 'tis easy in this pesky forest to go astray,' said the yeoman grumblingly.

'When didst thou find thou wast wandering out of thy road?' asked Robin.

'Oh, but an hour or two,' was the reply. 'I was told at Balby that my road lay through the hamlet of Scatby, but hours have I walked as it seemeth, and never a roof do I see in these wild woods.'

Robin laughed. He could have told the man that he must have been wandering since the previous midday, when he had seen him through the leaves skulking like a wild cat through the forest-ways, as if wishful to spy on someone, but desiring not to be seen himself.

' 'Tis but a mile or two more thou must go,' replied Robin, 'and thou wilt strike the right road. But by the bow thou bearest it would seem that thou shouldst be a good archer.'

'Ay,' said the man with a crafty look, 'I am as good a bowman – and better – than many a braggart thief who ranges these woods and shoots the king's deer.'

'Then let us have some pastime,' said Robin, 'and see who is the better archer of us two.'

'I am with thee,' said the man, and drew an arrow from the quiver beside him. His eyes looked narrowly at Robin, and there was an evil glint in them.

Robin went to a hazel bush and cut down two straight hazel wands, which he peeled in their upper parts, so as to show up more plainly. One of these he stuck in the ground where they stood, and from the top he hung a rough garland of dogwood leaves, which were now turning red in the autumn, and therefore stood out against the white of the hazel.

'Now,' said Robin, 'let us measure off fifty paces. I will set this other wand at the place from whence we shoot.'

While doing all this Robin did not turn his face from the other man, who all the time had had his arrow half notched upon his string, as if eager to begin the shooting. He laughed as they walked side by side measuring off the distance.

' 'Tis a plaguy hard shoot thou wouldst have us try,' he said with a growl; 'I am used to bigger marks than these new-fangled rods and wreaths.'

Robin took no notice, but went on counting until he had completed the fifty paces, and the man, almost as if against his will, sullenly walked with him. Robin bade the man shoot first at the mark, but he said he would rather Robin had the first try. Robin took two arrows from his quiver and shot one at the mark. The arrow went through the garland, about two fingers' span from the wand.

'I like not this way of shooting,' growled the low-bred man. ' 'Tis such shooting as thou seest silly squires and village fools use.'

Robin made no reply, and the man shot at the mark. As was to be expected, he missed the garland altogether and his arrow went wide.

'Thou needest more practice, good friend,' said Robin. 'Trust me, 'tis well worth thy while to test thy skill at a fine mark such as this. 'Tis no credit to creep up and shoot on top of thy game from behind a tree – often a long shot is the most honest. I will try again.'

So saying, Robin took careful aim, and this time his arrow went true to the mark, for it struck the thin wand and split it in twain.

' 'Twas not fair shooting!' cried the other in a rage. 'A flaw of wind did carry thy bolt against the wand!'

'Nay, good fellow,' said Robin in a quiet voice, 'thou art a fool to talk so. 'Twas a clean shot, as thou knowest well. Do thou go now and take this wand here and set it up in place of that which I have split. I will cut a new one, and we will set it up at thirty paces, so that thou mayest have a little practice ere I lead thee on thy way.'

With muttered words and dark looks the rascal took the wand which stood where they had been shooting, and went away with slow steps towards the split mark fifty paces away. When he had got some twenty paces he turned his head quickly and saw that Robin was apparently busy at a hazel thicket, searching for a straight stick. Swiftly the rogue put an arrow to his string, and shouted as the bolt left his bow:

'Thou art the mark I seek, thou wolf's-head!'

Robin seemed to fall into the bush as if struck, and with a cruel laugh the man stepped nearer as if to make sure that he had really slain the outlaw for whom he had been spying so long. He could see the legs sticking out stiffly from among the hazels, and he grinned with delight. Then, putting his fingers to his lips, he whistled long and shrill, and came forward at a run to gloat over his victim.

But suddenly with a jerk the dead man arose, and in one hand was the arrow which the would-be murderer had shot. It had missed Robin, who, however, had pretended to be struck; and the bolt had caught in the thicket before him. Already it was notched to the bow which Robin bore in his other hand. The man came to a sudden standstill, a cry on his white lips.

'Thou bungling hedge-knifer!' said Robin with a scornful laugh. 'Even the mark at which thou hast been loosing thy arrow these two days thou canst not strike, and that at twenty paces! Ay, thou canst run, but thy own arrow shall slay thee!'

The man had turned, and with swift steps was running this way and that from side to side of the path, so as to confuse Robin's aim.

Robin drew his bow to its utmost, and paused for one moment; then the string twanged with a great sound, and the arrow sped. The man gave a yell, jumped three feet clear up into the air, then fell flat upon the ground, the arrow sticking from his back.

At the same moment, Robin heard the sound of breaking branches beside him, and hardly had he thrown down his bow when out of the hazel bush beside him leaped a strange figure. For a moment, as Robin took a step back to give him time to draw his sword, he was startled, so weird was the figure. It seemed as if it was a brown horse on its hind legs which dashed towards him. The great white teeth were bared as if to tear him, and the mane rolled behind, tossing in the fury of attack.

Then Robin laughed. The horse's skin contained a man; in

one hand was a naked sword, in the other a buckler. It was Sir Guy of Gisborne who, with the fire of hatred in his eyes, now dashed upon the outlaw.

'Ha, ha! Guy of Gisborne, thou false knight!' cried Robin mockingly. 'Thou hast come thyself at last, hast thou? For years thou hast sent thy spies, thy ambushers, thy secret murderers to slay me, and now thou hast come to do the deed thyself – if thou canst!'

Guy of Gisborne said no word in reply. Fierce hatred glared from his eyes, and he rushed with the fury of a wolf upon his foe. Robin had no buckler, but he had that which was almost as great a guard; for while the other beat full of rage upon Robin's blade, the outlaw was cool of brain and keen of eye.

For some time naught was heard but the clang of sword upon sword as stroke met guard. Round and round they trod in this fierce dance that should end in death for one of them, each with his eyes bent upon the keen looks of the other. Suddenly Robin's sword leaped over the guard of the other's sword, and his point pierced and ripped the horse's hide and cut into the shoulder of Sir Guy.

'Thy luck hath fled, Guy of Gisborne!' said Robin in triumph. 'Thou didst 'scape with thy life once from thy burning house in that horse's hide, and thou didst think it would bring thee luck against my sword point.'

'Thou wolf's-head! Thou hedge-robber!' cried Guy of Gisborne. ' 'Twas but a scratch, but my good sword shall yet let thy life out!'

With a double feint, swift and fierce, Guy thrust under Robin's sword arm. His point cut through Robin's tunic of Lincoln green, and a hot spark seemed to burn the outlaw's side. Guy's point had wounded him slightly. It did not check Robin for an instant. Swiftly as a lightning stroke the outlaw lunged forward, and ere Guy could recover Robin's sword had pierced his breast. The cruel knight dropped his sword, staggered back, spun round once, and then fell heavily to the ground, where he lay still as a stone.

Robin, breathless, leaned upon his sword as he looked down upon his slain enemy.

'Thus,' he said, 'my sword hath avenged, by the aid of the pitiful sweet Virgin, all the cruelties and oppressions which thy

Robin meets Guy of Gisburne

evil will and cruel mind hath caused – the torture of poor men by hunger, scourging, and forced labours, the aching hearts of women and children, whom thy evil will did not spare from blows and tears. Would that my sword could slay as easily the tyranny and wrongdoing of all those in high places today who make poor men weep and suffer!'

Turning, he saw Hob o' the Hill approaching him, who now ran up and said:

'Master, I saw the good fight and the shrewd stroke thou gavest him. There is only one now of all thy enemies who yet liveth, and he is Sir Roger of Doncaster.'

'Nay, Hob,' replied Robin; 'there are a many of the enemies of poor men who yet live in their strong castles and carved abbeys whom I shall never slay.'

'Ay, ay, master, thou speakest truth,' said Hob. 'While the poor villein hath to sweat at his labours and suffer blows, and is kept for ever at his chores, unfree, possessing naught, not even the wife and child he kisseth when he leaves for his work in the dawn, so long shall we have enemies. But now, master, I come to tell thee that Roger of Doncaster's men have doubled south, and even now are at Hunger Wood. I guess that they do but follow the orders of this slain steward here, and will to ambush thee.'

'Where are Will the Bowman and his men?' asked Robin.

'They are scattered upon the southward road, and do spy upon Roger's rascals.'

'Go thou and hasten to Little John. Bid him turn back if he hath not already learned that Roger's men are coming south. Let him get behind them, but not so that they know he is nigh them. When he is north of Hunger Wood, bid him make two horns through the woods so as to encompass the rogues. Then with Will's men I will drive them back, and John should see to it that not one escapes alive. 'Twill be a lesson to my enemies not to put their heads into the wolf's mouth again.'

Swiftly Hob darted away, while Robin hastened towards the Doncaster road, where he soon found Will the Bowman waiting in a glade.

'How now, master,' said old Will, grizzled and grey, but as hale and sturdy as ever; 'my scouts tell me that these rascals are many and do come through the woods as if they feared naught.

'Tis said that a wily rogue, a Brabanter cut-throat named Fulco the Red, doth lead them, and he has warred through France and Allemain and Palestine, and knoweth all the arts of war. We are but a score here, and Little John and his party are three miles to the north-west.'

'I have sent Hob to tell Little John to return,' replied Robin. 'He will be here in an hour. Till then we must hold these rascals in check. John will smite them in the rear, and I think for all their rascally knowledge of burning and plundering which they have gained under our tyrant king, these Flemings and Brabanters will yet find death at our English hands.'

In a little while a scout came in to say that the enemy was marching towards Beverley Glade, and Robin instantly ordered the score of archers under Will to hide themselves in the thickets on the edge of the glade. Soon, issuing from the trees on the other side of the clearing, could be seen the headpieces of the foreigners. Fierce and cruel were the faces of these men, for they warred for any hand that paid them well, because of the loot and the wealth which they obtained in the lands where they fought. The English peasant hated these foreign marauders bitterly, for they spared neither women nor children, and were most tyrannical and cruel.

There were some fourscore of them, twenty of them with crossbows, and at their head was a man with a red face of fierce aspect, clothed in complete mail from head to foot. They advanced warily, with scouts on their flanks amidst the trees, and they looked to and fro keenly as they advanced. Each of the men-at-arms bore a buckler in his left hand, and his naked sword flashed in the other. Not until they were within twenty paces of the thickets where the outlaws lay hid did Robin give the signal agreed upon. Then, at the shrill whistle, twenty great arrows boomed through the air, and so true was the aim of each that as many of the enemy staggered and fell, each with the great shaft sticking deep in the thick jerkin or in the throat. Among those that fell were fifteen of the crossbowmen.

At another call, and before most of the marauders had recovered, another flight of arrows was launched against them, and twelve more fell dead or wounded.

Then with a fierce yell of command the leader, Fulco the Red,

dashed forward into the thickets, followed by his surviving men,
who still outnumbered the outlaws. As quick as ferrets and as
stealthily, Robin's men retreated, running from tree to tree, but
whenever opportunity offered, a great arrow buzzed out from
some innocent-looking bush, and another rascal fell writhing in
his death-throes. The others ran here and there fiercely searching for their hidden enemies. Three of the outlaws were slain in
the first rush, but as the foreigners dashed from bush to bush
and looked behind this tree and that, they were marked by the
wily woodmen, and again and again the grim song of an arrow
suddenly ended in a death-cry as it reached home in some cruel
heart.

Nevertheless, the band of mercenaries pressed forward and
the outlaws had to retreat, for they could not dare to meet the
others in the open. So fiercely did Fulco follow upon the
retiring woodmen that several more fell to the sword, and
Robin saw with anger and despair that already he had lost eight
men. He wondered what he should do to check the enemy, but
was at a loss.

Suddenly he saw Fulco dash forward at a bush where he had
seen a lurking outlaw. It was Gilbert of the White Hand, who,
finding himself discovered, and not having time to draw his bow,
sought safety in flight. He rushed close beside the tree behind
which Robin stood, Fulco following with uplifted sword. As the
Brabanter passed, Robin dashed forth with sword in hand and
beat at the foreigner. The latter quickly parried the blow with
his buckler, and next moment had swung round and had fiercely
engaged Robin. Round and round in a wild fight the two
wheeled, their swords clanging, as stroke on stroke was guarded.
Suddenly one of the other men crept up, resolved to slay Robin
from behind. Will the Bowman saw what he intended and
dashed forward, sword in hand, only to be hewed down as
another Fleming leaped from behind a tree. The old man cried
out with his dying breath, 'Robin, guard thee!'

An arrow flew from a bush, and the man who was creeping
upon Robin leaped up, then fell heavily and lay still. A second
arrow slew the man who had slain Will Stuteley, and then for
the time both parties in their hiding-places seemed to stand and
watch the combat between the two leaders.

The Brabanter, famed for his sword play as he was, had found his match. Such strength of wrist, such force of stroke as was in Robin, he had never met before, and it was in vain that he tried his wiles upon the slim man who seemed to be surrounded by a cage of steel, while yet it was only the one sword that leaped so swiftly to guard. Fulco, rageful at the long resistance, was wearing out his strength in vain though fierce attacks. Suddenly he saw Robin's eyes gleam with a strange look which almost fascinated him with its fierce intentness. Then he saw the outlaw make a pass which laid his left breast open. Quickly the Brabanter, parrying the pass, dashed his point at Robin's breast. The outlaw leaped aside, Fulco's sword lunged into the empty air, and next moment, with a great sweep of his arm, Robin's sword had hewed deeply into the neck of the marauder, who fell dead at his feet.

A great cheer rose from the throats of the outlaws, and heartened by the victory, the bowmen pressed into the open and sought their enemies. These, losing courage at the loss of their leader, began to retreat, running backwards from tree to tree. But in vain they sought shelter. The deadly arrows, like great bees, searched their hiding-places narrowly. Sometimes they would gather heart and dash back at the venturesome outlaws, but only for a time. They would be compelled to retire before the hail of arrows which converged upon them, bringing wounds and death from enemies who had instantly disappeared.

Suddenly, from three directions behind them and beside them, came the challenging call of the blackcock. So saucily it sounded, that from hidden outlaws here and there chuckles of laughter rose, while others wondered whether it could indeed be Little John, whose warning cry this was. An answering call from Robin reassured them on that point, and soon through the trees could be seen coats of Lincoln green darting from tree to tree.

At the knowledge that this meant that they were taken in rear and flank, the Brabanters and Flemings, knowing that from the hands of Englishmen they could expect no mercy, rushed together, resolved to sell their lives dearly.

It is needless to dwell upon the last fight. It could but end in one way. The Englishmen hated these foreign invaders with a hatred too deadly for mercy, and as they shot them down they knew that their arrows were loaded with vengeance for

unutterable deeds of murder and cruelty committed upon de-
fenceless women, little children, and unweaponed men, when
these marauding wretches had spread like a plague through the
land under the banner of King John, bringing ruin, fire, death,
and starvation to hundreds of humble homes and peaceful
villages.

Roger of Doncaster, waiting with his half-dozen men-at-arms
on the edge of the forest, wondered why Guy of Gisborne and
Fulco lingered so long. There were no cries of triumph heard
coming through the dim aisles of giant trees, no flash of arms
could be seen, however often he sent twos and threes of his men
into the forest to meet the victors.

Then at last they saw a charcoal-burner coming with his sack
of coal through the trees. Two men-at-arms caught him and
brought him up to where the knight sat on his horse. Sir Roger
asked him whether he had not seen a troop of men-at-arms
coming through the wood.

'Na, na,' said he in his rough speech; 'no living man ha' I seen,
but I ha' seen a pile o' foreign-looking men lying dead in
Beverley Glade, and each had a clothyard stickin' in un. There
mun be threescore of un!'

Sir Roger dragged his horse round, a savage oath on his lips.
'That wolf's-head is the fiend himself!' he said. 'No one can
fight against him in his woods.'

Quickly he and his men hurried off, leaving the charcoal-burner
looking after them. 'Ay, ay,' said he under his breath, 'no one of
thy cruel rascals can hope to get aught but death while Robin is
king o' these forests. Three or four score there were of the
murdering Easterlings, and each had Robin's sign upon him.'

For many years afterwards the place where Robin had wreaked
such vengeance upon the foreign mercenaries was called Slaughter Lea instead of Beverley Glade, and for a long time villeins
and others who passed near the mound which marked the pit
where Robin had buried the slain told the tale to each other.

After this, for many years Robin was left undisturbed in the
forests of Barnisdale and Sherwood, and, outlaw though he was,
most good men came to respect his name, while those that were
oppressors feared him. Never was there a cruel deed done by
some lord on his vassal but Robin exacted some recompense

from the haughty knight; and when a poor man's land was invaded by a stronger, it was Robin's hidden archers who made the place too hot for any but the rightful owner to dwell upon it.

Indeed, I should want a book of the same length as this one to relate all the famous deeds which Robin did while he was in the greenwood at this time. For fifteen years he dwelled there, and every year his fame increased by reason of the deeds he did.

Thus, one great deed was that long fight which he waged on behalf of young Sir Drogo of Dallas Tower in Westmorland. The border men, robbers and reivers all, had thrust Sir Drogo from his lands because he had punished one of their clansmen, and the young knight was in sore straits. With the aid of Robin and his archers he beat back the mossmen, and such terror did the clothyard arrows inspire that never again did a Jordan, Armstrong, Douglas, or Graham venture to injure the man who was a friend of Robin's.

Then there was that deed, one not of warfare but of peace, when Robin compelled the young squire of Thurgoland to do justice and kindness to his mother. She had been a neif, or female villein, on the lands of Sir Jocelyn of Thurgoland, doing the chores and labours of the field. But she was beautiful and modest, and Sir Jocelyn had loved and married her. While her lord and husband was alive she was a freewoman, and she lived happily with Sir Jocelyn. They had a son, named Stephen, who was of so crabbed and harsh a nature that men said he could be no son of the noble Jocelyn and the kindly Avis. When Sir Jocelyn died, Stephen was lord, but the wicked law of that day said that Avis was now again a serf on the land of her son, having lost her freedom with the death of her husband.

For withstanding her son's unjust wrath against a poor villein of the manor, Stephen swore he would be revenged upon his mother. Therefore he had her thrust from the manor-house in ragged attire, and compelled her to house with her villein kin (which of course were also his kin) in a hovel in the village. With spirited words Avis reproached her unnatural son, but in all meekness yet dignity she went about the hard tasks again which for thirty years her hands had not known; while her son took to himself the evil companions which he knew his mother had detested, and which she had ever advised him to avoid.

The story of his thrusting his mother into villeinage spread far
and wide, shocking all good men and women. They wondered as
the weeks went by that some judgement from heaven did not fall
upon so unnatural and harsh a son; but he still rioted in his hall,
and nothing seemed to trouble him.

Then, one winter's night, as Squire Stephen held high revel
among his boon companions, into the hall strode threescore
men in dark robes, and amid the terror of the assembled guests
the squire was seized and taken away, in spite of all his furious
rage. For a time no one knew whither he had gone. Then the
tale went round the country that the squire was working as a
villein on the lands of a manor in the forest, and that Robin
Hood had willed that thus he should live until he had learned
how to act as a man of gentle rank.

For long months Squire Stephen was held a captive, compelled
to work like any poor villein of his own kindred, until at length
he was shamed and penitent, and confessed that he had been a
boor and was not worthy to hold the rank which mere birth had
given him. Then, in his villein weeds [garments], he had
returned to Thurgoland, and seeking out his mother where she
worked in the village he had begged her forgiveness, and when
with tears she had kissed him, he had taken her by the hand and
made her mistress of the manor-house, and ever afterwards lived
nobly as had his father before him.

Men reckoned this was a great deed, and praised the names of
Robin Hood and Father Tuck, who by precept and manly
counsel had shown Squire Stephen the errors of his life.

There were other deeds which Robin did; such as his fight
with the sea-pirate, Damon the Monk, who had harried the coast
of Yorkshire so long and cruelly, but whom Robin at length
slew, in a great sea-fight off the bay which is now called Robin
Hood's Bay, where the pirate ship was brought ashore, after
Robin had hanged all her men on their own yard-arm.

One day when Robin had thus passed some ten years in this
second period of his outlawry, a lady rode into his camp at the
Stane Lea, and getting down from her horse went up to where
he stood, and greeted him. For a moment Robin did not
recognise her.

'I am thy cousin,' she said at length with a smile, 'Dame Alice

of Havelond. Dost thou not remember how thou didst aid me
and my husband more than a score years ago when two evil
neighbours oppressed us?'

'By my faith,' said Robin, and kissed his cousin on her cheek,
' 'tis so long since I have seen thee that I knew thee not.'

He made Dame Alice very welcome, and she and her two
women and three serving-men spent the night in a little bower
which Robin caused to be made for them. She and Robin spoke
long together about their kinsfolk, and how this one and that
one had fared, and what had befallen some through the troubled
times. Her own husband, Bennett, had died three years before.

'Now,' said she at length, 'I am an old woman, Robin, and
thou art old also. Thy hair is grey, and though thy eyes are keen
and I doubt not thy strength is great, dost thou not often long
for a place where thou canst live in peace and rest, away from the
alarms which thy life here must bring to thee? Couldst thou not
disband thy men, steal away, and live in my house with me at
Havelond? None would trouble thee there, and thou couldst live
out in peace and quiet the rest of thy life.'

Robin did not delay in his answer.

'Nay, dear cousin,' he said, 'I have lived too long in the
greenwood ever to crave any other living place. I will die in it,
and when my last day comes, I pray I be buried in some glade
under the whispering trees, where in life I and my dear fellows
have roamed at will.'

'Then,' replied the dame, 'if thou wilt not seek this asylum with
me, which I offer to thee in memory of that great kindness which
thou didst for my dead husband, then I shall betake myself to
Kirklees and live out my last years in the nunnery of which, as
thou knowest, our aunt, Dame Ursula, is abbess. I would have
thee come to me whenever thou wishest, Robin, for old age
makes us fond of our kin, and I would see thee often. And I doubt
not that Dame Ursula, though she speaketh harshly of thy violent
deeds, would give thee welcome as befitted the son of her sister.'

Robin promised that he would not forget to visit Kirklees to
see Dame Alice, and this he did once in every six months, as
much for the purpose of seeing his cousin as to have at her hands
the medical treatment which his ageing years seemed to demand
more and more. In those days women had much lore of

medicinal herbs, and instead of going to doctors when they felt sick, people would go to a woman who was famed to have this knowledge, and she would give them medicine. Men also believed that if a vein in the arm was cut and a certain amount of blood was allowed to escape, this was a cure for certain diseases. It was for this purpose, also, that Robin Hood visited Kirklees Nunnery, and he stayed there for two or three days at a time, in order that the wound in his arm might thoroughly heal.

On these visits he often saw his aunt, Dame Ursula, the abbess. She was a dark, lean woman with crafty eyes, but she always spoke fair to him. She often asked him when he was going to buy a pardon and to leave his homeless life, so as to endow some religious house with his wealth for the purpose of getting salvation for his soul.

'Little wealth have I,' Robin would reply, 'nor shall I ever spend it to feed fat monks or lazy nuns. While my forest freres stay with me, and I can still use the limbs God hath given me, I will bide in the greenwood.'

'Nevertheless,' she often said, 'forget not thy aunt and cousin here at Kirklees, and come when thou mayst desire.'

Now it happened one day, late in the summer, that Robin felt giddy and ill, and resolved to go to Kirklees to be tended by his cousin.

'Go with me, Little John,' said Robin, 'for I feel I am an old man this day, and my mind is mazed.'

'Ay, dear Robin, I will go with thee,' said Little John, 'but thy sickness will pass, I doubt not. I would that ye did not go into that nunnery, for ever when ye have gone I ha' wondered as I waited under the trees without whether I should see thy face again, or whether some evil trick would be played on thee.'

'Nay, John,' said Robin, 'they will play me no tricks. The women are my kinsfolk, and what enemies have we now?'

'I know not,' replied John doubtfully, scratching his grizzled head; 'but Hob o' the Hill hath heard that Sir Roger of Doncaster is friend to the nuns of Kirklees.'

'An old man he is, as we are all,' said Robin, 'and I doubt not he thinketh little evil of me after all these years.'

'I know not,' said John; 'but an adder will bite though his poison be dry.'

They prepared to go to Kirklees, Robin and John on horses and the rest of their band on foot. When they arrived at the edge of the forest which overlooked the nunnery, Little John and Robin dismounted, leaving the horses with the men, who were to hide in the woods until Robin returned. Then, supported by John's arm, Robin walked to the gate of Kirklees, where John left him.

'God preserve thee, dear Robin,' he said, 'and let thee come again soon to me. I have a fear upon me this day that something shall befall thee to our sorrow.'

'Nay, nay, John,' said Robin, 'fear not. Sit thou in the shaw, and if I want thee I will blow my horn. I have my bow and my sword with me, and naught can harm me among these women.'

So the two old comrades in arms parted with warm handclasps, and Robin knocked at the great iron ring upon the door. Very soon the door was opened by his aunt, who indeed had been watching his approach from a window.

'Come thou in, Robin,' said she with wheedling tones, while her crafty eyes looked in his face with a sidelong furtive glance. She saw that he was ill, and a smile played over her thin lips. 'Come in and have a jack of ale, for thou must be wearied after thy journey.'

'I thank thee, dame,' said Robin, and wearily he stepped in. 'But I will neither eat nor drink until I have been blooded. Tell my cousin Alice I have come, I pray thee.'

'Ah, Robin,' said his aunt, 'thou hast been long away from us, and thou hast not heard, I ween. Thy cousin died in her sleep in the spring, and now she lies under the churchyard mould.'

'Sorry I am to hear that,' replied Robin, and in the shock of the news he staggered and would have fallen, but that his aunt put her arm about him. 'I – I – repent me,' he went on, 'that I came not oftener. Poor Alice! But I am ill, dame; do thou nick my arm and blood me, and soon I shall be well, and will trouble thee no more.'

'Of a surety, 'tis no trouble, good Robin,' said the abbess, and she guided him into a room remote from the living-rooms of the nunnery. She led him to a truckle bed which stood in one corner, and he lay down with a great sigh of relief. Then he bared his arm slowly, and the abbess took a little knife from a satchel which hung from her girdle. She held the brown arm now much thinner than of yore, and with the point of her knife she cut deep into a thick blue vein. Then, having tied the arm so that he should not move it, she set a jar beneath the cut in the arm as it hung outside the bed.

Then she went from the room and quickly returned with some drink in a cup. 'Drink this, good Robin,' she said. ' 'Twill clear thee of the heaviness which is upon thee.'

She raised Robin's head and he drank the liquor to the lees. With a sigh Robin sank back on his pillow and smiled as he said:

'Thanks, best thanks, good aunt. Thou art kind to a lawless man.'

He spoke drowsily; his head fell back upon the pillow and he began to breathe heavily. The drug which the abbess had placed in the cup was already working. The dame smiled wickedly, and she went to the door of the room and beckoned to someone outside. A man crept into the chamber – an old, thin man, with white hair, sly, shifty eyes, and a weak, hanging lower lip. She pointed with one lean finger to the form of Robin Hood, and the old man's eyes shone at the sight. His gaze followed the drops of blood as they oozed from the cut vein and dripped into the jar beneath.

'If you were even a little like a man,' she said scornfully, 'you would draw your dagger and give him his death yourself – not leave it to my lancet to let his life out drop by drop.'

Robin stirred at the sound of her voice, and the thin old man turned and skipped from the room in terror. The abbess followed him, her beady black eyes bent upon his shifty looks. She drew a long key from her satchel and locked the door of the room where Robin lay.

'When will he be dead?' asked the old man in a whisper.

'If the blood floweth freely, he will be dead by night!' said the abbess.

'But if it do not, and he dieth not?' said the old man.

'Then I and Kirklees Nunnery are richer by thirty acres of good meadow land,' replied the abbess mockingly, 'the gift of the good Sir Roger of Doncaster; and you, Sir Roger, will have to find some other way of killing this fox. Why dost thou not go in thyself and do it now?'

She held out the key to him, but he shrank away, his teeth gnawing at his finger nails, his baleful eyes gleaming angrily at the mocking face of the abbess.

Sir Roger of Doncaster, coward and poltroon, had not the courage to slay a sick man, but turned and slunk away. He left the house and rode away, his chin sunk on his breast, enraged to think how the abbess despised him, and how she might yet outwit him in the wicked conspiracy they had made together for the slaying of Robin Hood.

Little John sat patiently in the shade of the forest trees all the afternoon. When the long shadows began to creep across the wolds he wondered why Robin had not appeared at the door as was his wont. In his anxiety Little John arose and walked impatiently up and down.

What was that? Faintly, from the direction of the nunnery, he heard three bugle blasts – Robin's call!

With a roar like that of an enraged bull, Little John shouted to the men hiding in the thickets:

'Up, lads! Heard ye those weary notes? Treachery is being done our poor master!'

Snatching up weapons, the whole band rushed after Little John, who ran at top speed to the nunnery gate. With blows from a hedge-pole they battered this in, and with the same weapon they beat down the door, and then amid the shrieks and prayers of the affrighted nuns they poured into the place.

Very cold and stern was Little John as he stood before the bevy of white-faced women.

'Ha' done with thy shrieking!' he said. 'Find me the abbess!'

But the abbess was nowhere to be found.

'Quick, then, lead me to where my master, Robin Hood, is lying.'

But none knew of his having come to the nunnery. Full of wrath and sorrow and dread, John was about to order that the whole place be searched, when Hob o' the Hill pushed through the outlaws and said:

'I ha' found where our master lies.'

They stormed up the stairs after Hob, and having reached the door they broke the lock and rushed in. What a sight met their eyes! There was their master, white and haggard, with glazed eyes, half reclining upon the bed, so weak that hardly could he raise his head to them.

Little John threw himself on his knees beside Robin, tears

streaming from his eyes.

'Master, master!' he cried. 'A boon, a boon!'

'What is it, John?' asked Robin, smiling wanly upon him, and raising his hand he placed it fondly on the grizzled head of his old comrade.

'That thou let us burn this house and slay those that have slain thee!'

Robin shook his head wearily.

'Nay, nay,' he said, 'that boon I'll not grant thee. I never hurt woman in all my life, and I'll not do it now at my end. She hath let my blood flow from me, and hath taken my life, but I bid thee hurt her not. Now, John, I have not long to live. Open that casement there and give me my bow and an arrow.'

They opened the casement wide, and Robin looked forth with dim, dying sight upon the quiet evening fields, with the great rolling forest in the distance.

'Hold me while I shoot, John,' said Robin, 'and where my arrow falls there dig me a grave and let me lie.'

Men wept as they stood and watched him hold the great bow in his feeble hand, and saw him draw the string while he held the feather of the arrow. Once he alone of all men could bend that bow, but now so spent was his life that his strength barely sufficed to draw it half-way. With a sigh he let go, the arrow boomed through the casement, and men watched with dim sight its flight over the fields until it came to ground beside a little path that led from the meadows up to the forest trees.

Robin fell back exhausted, and Little John laid him gently down.

'Lay me there, John,' he said, 'with my bow beside me, for that was my sweetest music while I lived, and I would have it lie with me when I am dead. Put a green sod under my head, and another at my feet, for I loved best to sleep on the greensward of the forest whiles I was alive, and I would lie upon them in my last sleep. Ye will do this all for me, John?'

'Ay, ay, master,' said John, choking for sheer sorrow.

'Now kiss me, John – and – and – goodbye!'

The breath fluttered on his lips as John with uncovered head bent and kissed him. All sank to their knees and prayed for the passing soul, and with many tears they pleaded for mercy for

Robin shoots his last shaft

their bold and generous leader.

They would not suffer his body to stay within the nunnery walls that night, but carried it to the greenwood, and watched beside it all through the dark. Then at dawn they prepared his grave, and when Father Tuck, white-haired and bent now, came at noon, all bore the body of their dear master to his last resting-place.

Afterwards, the outlaws learned of Sir Roger of Doncaster's visit to the nunnery while Robin lay dying, and they sought for him far and wide. To escape the close search which Hob o' the Hill and Ket his brother made for him, Sir Roger fled to Grimsby, and barely escaped on board a ship with a whole skin, so close was Hob behind him. The knight sought refuge in France, and there he died shortly afterwards, lonely and uncared for.

When Robin died, the band of outlaws speedily broke up. Some fled overseas, some hid in large towns and gradually became settled and respectable citizens, and others again hired themselves on distant manors and became law-abiding men, if their lords treated them not unkindly.

As for Little John and Scarlet, they were given lands at Cromwell, where Alan-a-Dale now was lord over the lands of the Lady Alice; while Much was made bailiff at Werrisdale, which also belonged to Alan-a-Dale, his father, Sir Herbrand, being now dead.

Gilbert of the White Hand would not settle down. He became a great fighter in Scotland with the bow and the sword, and his deeds were sung for many years by many a fireside in the border lands.

What became of Hob o' the Hill and his brother, Ket the Trow, nobody ever knew for certain. The little men hated the ways of settled life, and though Alan-a-Dale offered them lands to live on, they preferred to wander in the dim forest and over the wild moors. The grave of Robin Hood was ever kept neat and verdant, though for a long time no one knew whose were the hands that did this. Then tales got abroad that at night two little men came out of the forest from time to time and put fresh plants on the grave and cut the edging turf clean. That these were Ket and Hob no one doubted, for they had loved Robin dearly while he lived, and now that he was dead they could never stray far from his grave.

ALL
THESE
BODIES

OTHER BOOKS BY KENDARE BLAKE

Three Dark Crowns

One Dark Throne

Two Dark Reigns

Five Dark Fates

Queens of Fennbirn

ALL THESE BODIES

KENDARE BLAKE

MACMILLAN

First published in the US 2021 by Quill Tree Books
an imprint of HarperCollins Publishers.

First published in the UK 2021 by Macmillan Children's Books
an imprint of Pan Macmillan
The Smithson, 6 Briset Street, London EC1M 5NR
EU representative: Macmillan Publishers Ireland Ltd, 1st Floor,
The Liffey Trust Centre, 117–126 Sheriff Street Upper
Dublin 1, D01 YC43
Associated companies throughout the world
www.panmacmillan.com

ISBN 978-1-5290-5289-3

1 3 5 7 9 8 6 4 2

A CIP catalogue record for this book is available from the British Library.

Printed and bound by CPI Group (UK) Ltd, Croydon CR0 4YY

KNOWN MURDERS AT THE TIME OF
MARIE CATHERINE HALE'S ARREST,
September 18, 1958

MINNESOTA

St. Paul

Minneapolis

SEPTEMBER 18, 1958
The Carlson Family;
Infant survived.
Black Deer Falls, MN

AUGUST 29,
1958
Stacy Lee Brand-
berg and Richard
Covey
Madison, WI

AUGUST 8, 1958
(Discovered on the 16th)
Walter and Evangeline Taylor
Sioux City, IA

AUGUST 13, 1958
Merrill "Monty" LeTourneau
and an unidentified drifter
Highway 30, East of Dunlap, IA

AUGUST 24, 1958
Cheryl Warrens
Mason City, IA

IOWA

Ames

AUGUST 18, 1958
Jeff Booker and
Stephen Hill
*Mobil Service Station
Clarion, IA*

AUGUST 6, 1958
Angela Hawk and
Beverly Nordahl
Norfolk, NE

Omaha

Des Moines

AUGUST 3, 1958
Peter Knupp
Loup City, NE

ncoln

Spri

CHAPTER ONE

May 1, 1959

IN THE SUMMER of 1958, the murders that would come to be known as the "Bloodless Murders" or the "Dracula Murders" swept through the Midwest, beginning in Nebraska and sawing through Iowa and Wisconsin before turning back to my hometown of Black Deer Falls, Minnesota. Before it was over, the murders would claim the lives of seventeen people of different ages and backgrounds. All would be discovered with similar wounds: their throats slit or their wrists cut. A few sustained deep cuts to the inner thigh. Each of the victims died from blood loss, yet each of the crime scenes was suspiciously clean of blood.

Bloodless.

By the end of August, the murders had tracked eastward, closer and closer to the Minnesota border. We'd been following the trail in the papers, marking each new victim on the map. When those two college kids were found killed in an abandoned house outside of Madison, Wisconsin, it was like a sigh of relief. It was terrible, what'd happened to those kids. Richard Covey and Stacy Lee Brandberg had been their names. They'd been graduate students and engaged to be married. We were sorry that it had happened to them. That it had happened at all. But at least they'd been all the way over in Madison. The murders had passed us by, Minnesota had been spared, and whoever had done it—and *how*ever they had done it—they were probably most of the way up to Canada.

Black Deer Falls is only one hundred seventy miles from the Canadian border, back in the other direction. There was no reason for the killers to turn around, to cross another state line. We thought we were safe.

And then, on the night of September 18, the murder spree that had held the country in its thrall for the entire month of August ended here when it claimed the lives of Bob and Sarah Carlson, and their son, Steven.

The only perpetrator in the murder spree to be found would be apprehended that night: a fifteen-year-old girl named Marie Catherine Hale. She was found standing in the middle of the Carlsons' bodies, which, like all of the others, had been drained of blood. But unlike all of the others, we knew where the blood had gone: Marie Hale was covered in it from head to toe.

It was the story of a century. The story of a lifetime. It should have happened in Chicago or New York and been handled by cops and reporters who had seen it all before: the guys in movies ducking past speeding cars, hats pulled down and collars up against the rain. A short, silver pistol tucked up his sleeve and a cigarette burned down to his knuckles. It should have happened there, and been handled by them. Not in rural Minnesota, where nothing ever happened but more of the same, and not handled by my dad and our nearing-retirement public defender. Not handled, unbelievably, by me.

Michael Jensen. Seventeen-year-old nobody from nowhere, who wanted to be a journalist someday but hadn't gotten further than delivering papers. Unqualified. Untested. Take your pick of descriptors that mean a kid in over his head.

But sometimes the story chooses the writer, not the other way around. Or so says my mentor, Matt McBride—he's the editor of our local Black Deer Falls *Star*—and in this case it's especially true. Marie Catherine Hale chose me to tell her story. Me to hear it, when she could have had anyone—and I do mean anyone: Edward R. Murrow himself would have made the flight out.

So this is that story. Her story, taken down in the pages that follow. When we found her that night, in the middle of all those bodies, I didn't know who she was. I thought she was a victim. Then I thought she was a monster. I thought her innocent. I thought her guilty. By the time she was finished, what she told me would change the way I thought, not just about her but about the truth.

Tell the truth and shame the devil. I always thought that would be easy. But what do you do when the truth that you're faced with also happens to be impossible?

CHAPTER TWO

The Night of the Murders

THE NIGHT THAT the Carlsons were killed I was over at my best friend Percy's place. It was a warmish night for September and we'd gone out to their falling-down barn so Percy could grab a smoke without catching a glare from his stepmom, Jeannie.

"So, what do you want to do?" Percy asked. Then he answered his own question as he stamped out his ashes to make sure he wouldn't start a fire in the old hay. "Not much to do."

"Never much to do," I said. I turned around in the barn and picked through one of his dad's piles of junk.

"Beats doing homework."

"I guess." I held up what looked to be a very old and half-empty can of motor oil. "Where does your dad get this stuff?"

"Wherever he can," Percy replied. Most of the barn was full of junk that Percy's dad, Mo, had picked up at auctions or off the side of the road or taken off the hands of neighbors. Everyone in town knew that if you had garbage you took it to Mo Valentine before you took it to the dump.

The Valentine house was a farmhouse, like most others that sat outside town. But it wasn't a farm. It hadn't been a farm in a long time, though they did have one cornfield rented out for someone else to till. The rest had been sold off or turned to swamp or let go back to forest that made for good deer and squirrel hunting.

"I swear he's got some kind of disease," Percy said. "That makes him see worth where there isn't any."

"Like, a fool's gold disease?"

"Yeah, exactly. My old man has fool's gold disease. Did you just make that up?"

I shrugged. Maybe I hadn't; it seemed like something that might really exist. I stuck my head out through the door and looked at the house. Jeannie was still up—I could see her sitting in the living room, paging through a magazine. I wanted to go back inside. Jeannie was nice, and even pretty, but Percy hadn't warmed up. She was Mo's third wife (which meant he'd had two more wives than most any man in town) and Percy's heart was rough now when it came to mothers, after his own ran off and another had divorced Mo and moved across town to pretend like the Valentines had never existed.

"You asked anybody to Homecoming yet?" Percy asked. "I heard Joy Davis say she wouldn't mind going with a certain sheriff's son."

"How'd you hear that? Or did you just ask her for me?"

He grinned.

"Thanks, Perce. But I can get my own dates."

"It hasn't looked like it lately. And now that Carol's stepping out with John Murphy—"

"What does that matter?"

"John Murphy is a senior. He's the football captain. Now that he's got your old girl you've got to—"

"Why do I have to?" I asked. "It's not like I can do any better than Carol anyway." Carol Lillegraf and I dated for almost three months last spring. She was the dream girl: long blond hair, red lips, long-legged, and tall, and dating me was a calculated move. Going out with the respectable sheriff's son was a good way to ease her Reverend father into the idea of dating altogether. I wasn't surprised when she ended things just before summer.

"She's a cheerleader now," I said. "So who am I supposed to date to compete? The head cheerleader?"

Percy came out of the pile red-faced. Rebecca Knox had just made head cheerleader, and Percy had been in love with Rebecca Knox since the fourth grade.

"We'd better get you home," he said, "before you say something you'll regret about the future Mrs. Valentine."

I chuckled. But as he snuffed out his smoke, Mo showed up at the door of the barn with their two black Labradors.

"You boys come on out to the truck." He looked at me. "Your mother just called and said your dad and the boys need help out at the Carlson farm."

"My dad?" I asked as we followed him out into the dark. We got into his pickup and he whistled for the dogs to jump into the back.

"What's happening?" Percy asked. "Why are we bringing Petunia and LuluBelle?"

"She said to bring the dogs. She said they were asking everyone to."

Percy and I looked at each other. The last of the Bloodless Murders had been three weeks ago to the day, long enough for people to start to relax, for the curfews to ease, for the gin-fueled posses sitting around armed on front porches to disband. It was over. That's what we thought. But Mo was spooked. He pulled out of the driveway so fast that the dogs banged against the side of the truck bed and Percy had to remind him to be careful.

It was a ten-minute drive from the Valentine place to the Carlsons' out on County 23, and by the time we got there, we could see it was something bad. Two cruisers were parked in the driveway with their lights on and my dad's old pickup was parked behind those. Other guys had gotten there before us and parked along the sides of the dirt road. They'd all brought their dogs, too, if they had them; I saw Paul Buell and his dad jogging up the driveway leading their friendly spotted mutt.

"Shit," Mo cursed. "I should've brought leashes. Percy, find something to use."

"Find what to use?" he asked, but we got out and looked. All we found was some old, half-rotten bailing twine in the bed of the truck. So we doubled it up and looped it through the girls' collars. Then we got them down and followed Mo toward the lights. I could make out the shape of his shotgun, pointed at the sky.

"Did you notice he had the gun with him?" I asked.

"He must've had it down by our feet," said Percy. "What the hell's going on out here?"

We got up to the house. All the lights were on inside. Across the driveway and yard, they were all on at the neighbor's as well: the war widow, Fern Thompson, lived in a tiny place so close to the Carlsons' that it might have been part of the same property. There were almost a dozen of us gathered in the driveway between the two houses. Besides me and Percy, Paul Buell was the only kid. The rest were fathers and I knew them all. It looked like my mom had called them off a list from church. They were all carrying shotguns.

"What's going on?" Percy asked again.

I looked at Paul and shrugged, but he only shrugged in reply.

I didn't know what it could be that would make my dad drag us out here, but he must have needed us in a hurry, or he would have called in help from the state patrol. It was chaos in the driveway: the dogs were barking, and the men half shouting questions over the top of the noise. Petunia and LuluBelle were excited to see the other dogs, and I kept one hand on LuluBelle's collar, afraid that the rotten twine would snap.

Someone crossed the driveway, headed toward Widow Thompson's place, and the Labrador lunged. It was Bert, one of my dad's deputies, and he was carrying a striped cat.

"Bert!" I called. "What are you doing?"

He ignored me and went on, and Widow Thompson met him at her door. He placed the cat in her arms. Bert was white as a sheet and looked unsteady on his legs, like any minute all two hundred eighty-five pounds of him was going to collapse onto Widow Thompson's front stoop.

"Rick!" one of the men shouted when he saw my dad. "Rick, what's happened?"

I looked back toward the Carlson house. My dad had just walked out of it and came toward us. I scanned his face, but it was no use. He looked like a cop that night. The only trace of my dad was a flicker in his eyes when he saw me, like he was surprised and kind of sorry.

"Thank you for coming out," he said. "We've got a real bad situation in there."

"What do you mean?" Mr. Buell asked. "Are Bob and Sarah okay? The kids?"

"They've been murdered," my dad said. There was a long beat of quiet. A few dogs barked. Especially one near the house, a black-and-brown-speckled hound that belonged to the Carlsons, and after a minute, Bert went over and got him and shushed him up. Those of us gathered in the driveway started to fire off questions again, and I looked at Paul Buell. He was crying. My mom shouldn't have called him. He was too close to Steve Carlson. But she didn't know.

"Listen, this is what I need," my dad said loudly. "Teams of two and three. Armed, no exceptions. Dogs if you have them. I've called in State Patrol and there are roadblocks going up, but if the killer fled on foot, they won't have men here in time. We're the best chance." He counted us off into teams and finished with me, Percy, and Mo Valentine. He gave Mo a longer look to make sure he hadn't been drinking too much.

"I want you out in all directions. When you get to a neighbor, knock on the door but only to let them know you're out there. We don't need the whole county stumbling around in the dark. Check the creek and west toward the tree line." He pointed to Mr. Hawkins and Mr. Dawson. Mr. Hawkins had been in the army. "You two check the outbuildings."

"Who are we looking for?" Mr. Dawson asked.

"It looks like a Bloodless," my dad said grimly.

My hand slipped off LuluBelle's collar and Percy grabbed for her as the rest of the search party mobbed in on my father.

It was impossible to imagine that what my dad said was true. That the Carlson family—Bob and Sarah, Steve, who I knew—was lying in there dead. And not only dead but murdered by the most famous killer in the country.

I stared at the windows, numb. As a hopeful future journalist, I followed the Bloodless Murders in the papers that summer even more closely than everyone else. But the articles didn't satisfy me. It was the same facts, the same victims' names, the same lack of conclusions. Sometimes they used the same word three times in a paragraph or the same phrasing in two different articles, as if the reporters were as terrified as we were, right there at their typewriters.

The curtains of the Carlsons' living room were drawn, and from where we were in the driveway I couldn't see much of anything. My feet slid right, and right another step. I drifted closer to the house until I could peer through the space between the fabric panels. I didn't see anything at first but part of the ceiling and some photographs hanging on the walls. And then I saw someone standing in the middle of the room. She had her back to me, and she looked wet. Like she'd been swimming in her clothes through red water.

I moved a little closer and saw Charlie, my dad's other deputy. He was pacing, farther into the room, and he was holding a baby. He was bouncing her and kissing the top of her head, and he had one hand out like a stop sign toward the girl covered in blood, which is what I realized she was coated in. But except for that hand, he ignored her like she wasn't there at all.

"The baby," I said. Everyone in the driveway looked at me and then toward the windows. "The baby's all right?"

"The baby is all right," my dad said, and held back a few of the men who tried to go past him. "You're not going in there. No one's going in there that doesn't have a star on his chest."

Who is that? I wanted to ask. Who is that girl? But my dad set his jaw. I wasn't supposed to be by the window. And I was supposed to clam up.

I looked back and the girl was staring at me.

It's impossible to describe what I saw in her face, even though I'll never forget what she looked like. She was drenched in blood. Slicked with it. Her hair was saturated, and the blood looked wet in places: on her neck and where it leaked from her hair to run down her cheeks. That was the first time I saw Marie Catherine Hale. We did not actually speak that first night. But I still count that as our first meeting. Sometimes a look is all it takes, and the look that she fixed on me wasn't the look of someone silently ticking off the new faces of strangers. She saw me like she already knew me. I could almost hear her say my name, "Michael. Hello, Michael," in her low, surprising voice. Looking back now, sometimes I think I really did.

My dad ordered us to start the search and I snapped back to attention. Percy and Mo called for me, and the teams went off in their designated directions. I looked toward my dad, but he didn't see me. He called to Bert, who was still minding the Carlsons' dog, and they went back into the house together.

"Can you believe this?" Percy asked when Mo ran back to the truck for a flashlight. "Steve. The whole family. I don't believe it."

"Not the whole family," I said. "The baby's okay."

"And thank god for that. Not even the Bloodless could kill a baby."

"Perce, go help Mo with the flashlight. I'll meet you down at the truck."

He looked at me a minute, holding on to both dogs. Then he dragged them away, grumbling that he didn't know what use a pair of duck dogs were going to be, anyway, when it came to tracking.

I lingered in the driveway a while longer. Just long enough to see Marie be escorted out to Bert's police cruiser. He'd put his jacket over her shoulders, and later he would tell me that he put a blanket down to cover the back seat, but the blood still leaked through. I remember wondering where it was that she was hurt. She was covered in red from head to toe, and I knew that not all of it could be hers. I thought perhaps she'd been cut somewhere on her head, where the blood seemed thickest. But I was wrong.

After they cleaned her up at the station, they found not a scratch on her. Not a single drop of it had been hers.

CHAPTER THREE

A Girl Soaked in Blood

MO LED PERCY and me across the road from the Carlson place, south, toward town. It was the least likely direction that the killer would have gone, and I knew my dad had sent us that way on purpose because of me, or maybe because of the beer on Mo's breath. Petunia and LuluBelle jogged happily beside us through the dead fall grass and underbrush, but I kept looking back at the house. I'd been working at the jail since I was a kid, sweeping floors and washing windows mostly, but I'd been a sheriff's son most of my life. I could've helped, if they'd have let me.

But as the lights from the cruisers and the Carlson house disappeared and the sounds of the other men and dogs faded, I started to pay attention. I realized that we were looking for a killer. Actually hoping to find him, and not just any killer but the most famous killer in the country, who carved up his victims and left no blood behind. Except there'd been plenty of blood on the girl standing in the Carlsons' living room. Maybe that was the secret, and we would find the killer crouched by the creek and covered in it, too.

"You're making too much noise," Percy said to me.

I slowed. Percy and Mo were hunters, with practiced hunter's walks. Even the Labradors knew how to tread softly.

"I should have stayed back," I said.

"I'm glad you didn't. I feel about ready to jump out of my skin."

"Percy," Mo hissed. "Quiet."

But I could hear it in his voice. And I could see it in the way the shotgun shook in his grip. Mo didn't want to go either. There was a lot of nothing south of the Carlson house, just the creek where it crossed back and a lot of trees between there and town for someone to hide in. We'd been braver together in the driveway, when we were angry about our neighbors lying dead in their house. Now we went slow, and then slower, listening for the barks and shouts that meant someone else had found him first.

We got to the tree line, close enough to hear the water gurgling in the creek. And then the dogs refused to go on.

Percy tugged on Petunia's makeshift leash.

I patted LuluBelle. "Come on, girl."

But she only whined and dug her paws into the ground.

"Petunia! Lulu! Get on!" Mo ordered. "It's just water. You're duck dogs you two stupid—" He reached for their scruffs and tried to pull them along. The Labradors whined and barked. Eventually one of them snapped at his hand.

"What's gotten into them?" Percy asked.

I grabbed LuluBelle's collar again and buried my fingers in her fur. "Maybe we should listen."

Mo cussed and stood taller in the dark. The beam of his flashlight cast back and forth, and I held my breath looking into it, afraid that at any moment it would show a face in the trees.

"I guess I'll go myself," said Mo. "You boys stay with the dogs." He hadn't taken more than a couple of steps before something got up and moved, something big that snapped twigs and crashed through the underbrush. The dogs went crazy barking. Neither Percy nor I could hang on. I think the twine broke in the middle but Lulu might have just pulled it out of my hands.

"Petunia! Lulu!" Percy shouted as they ran.

"Goddamn it!" Mo shouted.

We stood frozen. The dogs weren't running toward the sound. They were running away from it. Mo pushed us behind him and pointed his gun at the creek.

"Backtrack to the Carlsons'," he said. "Find the girls and get them into the truck. I'm right behind you."

We found the Labradors back at the road, circling nervously and whining. We caught them and loaded them up, and Mo joined us not long after, breathing hard from running. Then we stood by the truck and let our hearts slow. In the safety of the light cast from the house and the red and blue flashing from the cruisers, it was easy to recover our nerve.

"Percy," said Mo, "drive Michael home and then take the dogs back and stay with Jeannie."

"What about you?" Percy asked.

"I'll go to the house and join up with another search party. You boys shouldn't be out here anyway."

"At least take one of the dogs."

"So I can chase her around again? They're no use without proper leashes."

"But Pop—"

"Just go home and I'll see you in the morning."

Percy and I drove to our house in town with the black Labs between us on the bench seat. When we pulled into my driveway, I said, "You okay? You want to stay over?"

He thought about it, petting the dogs.

"I'd better go home. I don't think Mo wants Jeannie to be by herself."

"Okay." I looked at my house. All the downstairs lights were on, and it looked safe. I knew my mom would probably be heading in to the jail a few blocks away, and I would need to stay home and look after my little sister, Dawn, even though she would already be sleeping.

Before I got out of the truck, I gave LuluBelle a good scratching. Even then when none of us wanted to admit it, I couldn't help thinking that those dogs turning tail had saved us from something.

I went inside and found my mom with her coat already on, ready to go to the jail like I'd figured.

"Are you going to stay the night?" I asked.

"I imagine so," she said. "They're going to book the girl in to stay."

"Book her? Why?"

"I don't know, Michael. Look after your sister." And then she left. She went to the jail to help the doctor clean Marie up. They wiped her down from head to foot, examined her, and found no injuries. Then my mom put her into a bath, and later she told me that even after all the wiping, the water in the bath turned as red as beet soup.

My mom didn't stay the night. The women's cell sat alone, connected to the rest of the jail on the western end of the second floor above the sheriff's office. It was built into the kitchen of our former family home, from back in the days when the sheriff used to live on the premises, and is separated from the men's cells by a few layers of brick and plaster and a good forty feet. We didn't live there anymore; my father, the sheriff, Richard Jensen, built us a new house, in town. Not so far from the jail that he couldn't still walk to work on a nice day, but far enough to keep my little sister from hearing any questionable language from rowdy prisoners sobering up in the cells downstairs. On the rare occasions when the women's cell had an occupant—Mrs. Wilson after being caught a few too many times for intoxicated driving, for example—my mother still stayed there. She didn't like to leave them alone in that drafty place, surrounded by bars and walls, even though most of the female prisoners stayed only one night. Marie Catherine Hale would remain there for one hundred and forty-four, alone for all but three.

After my mom left, I went up to my room. I tried to finish up my homework. I read a little. Mostly, I lay on my back and thought about the Carlsons and the Bloodless Murders.

At the time of Marie's arrest we thought that the murders had begun in early August, that Peter Knupp in Loup City, Nebraska, had been the first. From there, the killings seemed to escalate: a pair of student nurses with their throats cut on August 6, a trucker and a hitchhiker on the thirteenth, an elderly couple in Iowa on the sixteenth. And so it went on, with new victims found every few days until the students in Madison when everything stopped. A week went by. Then another. Lights still burned late into the night and doors that had never before been locked found themselves with new dead bolts, but that would just be the way of things now. Twelve people were dead. Twelve people bled out in their own homes or in their cars, or at their jobs, like that poor gas station worker Jeff Booker, murdered in the service office.

The papers increased their circulation by transfixing us with details: so little blood had been found at the crime scenes and no one knew how or why. The wounds were very clean. Very neat. No one was stabbed. They were cut at the throat or at the wrists, sometimes deep in the leg. "Could it have been the work of an ordinary kitchen knife?" the papers asked. Maybe. But so far, none had turned up missing at any of the victim's homes.

I don't know how much time passed with me lying there thinking. But I was still awake when my parents came home a while later, and I heard them talking softly downstairs.

"The baby," my mother said. "What's going to happen to the baby?"

I thought of that little baby, a two-year-old girl named Patricia.

She had been inside the house, in the very same room when it happened.

"The neighbor said Sarah had a sister," my father said. "I imagine she'll go with her."

My mother is a tall tough woman. An equal to my dad in both heart and height, or so he liked to tease. But when he said that, she started to cry.

I imagined them there in the kitchen: his arms around her back, turning her gently back and forth, his chin resting on the top of her head. She had cried before, when terrible things had happened. When the Ernst family's station wagon had rolled during the blizzard of '54 and killed everyone inside, including their five-year-old boy, Todd, she'd cried for days. But that night her crying sounded different. What happened to the Ernst family was a tragedy. What happened to the Carlsons was maddening. It was terrifying. It was inexplicable.

They came upstairs a few minutes later, and my dad came down the hall after he saw my light was still on.

"Michael, you awake?"

"Yes, sir."

He poked his head in. "You all right? Dawn all right?"

"Yes, sir."

My father looked over his shoulder and stepped inside. He closed the door behind him so my mother and sister couldn't hear.

Before he spoke, he sat down on the foot of my bed like he hadn't done since I started high school.

"I'm sorry about their boy. About your friend Steven."

"Me, too," I said, and I started to cry. My dad put his hand on my back. I was surprised I had cried. Even though it was terrible, we hadn't known the Carlsons well, and my father was wrong when he said Steve and I were friends. I knew him and we'd palled around some at school. He played football. I preferred baseball and even during baseball season I was more interested in books. But in the months following their murders I would come to learn more about Steve and the Carlsons than I ever imagined. The whole town would, so that by the end of the investigation we would think of them almost as our own family, and mourn them in a way we never would have had they simply died in some accident.

My father gave a big sigh and got up off my bed.

"You should get some sleep now," he said. "Everything is all right tonight, and tomorrow won't be easy."

He put his hat back on.

"You're going back out?"

"Someone's got to stay at the jail, and we need men at the Carlsons'. State's coming in to give us a hand with the extra patrols and the roadblocks. No one's getting to their beds tonight."

"Dad," I said as he turned to go. "What about the girl?" I hadn't stopped thinking of her, of her face and her eyes. Her body soaked with blood.

"Marie Hale. Her name is Marie Catherine Hale."

"Who is she? How did she manage to escape?"

He stopped with his hand on the doorknob.

"I don't think that she did."

CHAPTER FOUR

The Loss of the Carlsons

BEFORE THE MURDERS came to Black Deer Falls there had been twelve known victims.

Peter Knupp, 26, from Loup City, Nebraska. He'd been found on August 3, lying on his front porch with his throat slit.

The student nurses, Angela Hawk and Beverly Nordahl, both aged 22, found sitting upright in their car in Norfolk, Nebraska, on August 6, not far from a roadhouse bar.

The elderly couple were Walter and Evangeline Taylor, found on August 16 but killed on August 8. They were discovered in bed with their wrists cut on the outskirts of Sioux City, Iowa. Some thought their deaths had been a mutual suicide caught up in the sensationalism of the moment.

On August 13, truck driver Merrill "Monty" LeTourneau, 40, along with an unidentified drifter, were found a mile apart on Highway 30 near Grand Junction.

August 18: Jeff Booker, 24, and Stephen Hill, 25, gas station attendants killed in the same attack, their bodies found a day apart, as Stephen Hill's was located across the road in an open field, his pants around his ankles and a deep cut in his inner thigh.

August 24: Cheryl Warrens, 34, a waitress at a truck stop in Mason City, where Monty's rig had been abandoned.

And then the graduate students in Wisconsin on August 29: Richard Covey, 24, and Stacy Lee Brandberg, 23.

No doubt their names are familiar. But perhaps none is more familiar than Marie Catherine Hale. The way it was splashed across the headlines and her photo posted on the nightly news, it would be impossible not to know her or to have formed an opinion one way or the other. Murderess. Accomplice. Hostage. Seductress. Victim. Over the course of the investigation she would be characterized in every one of those ways. But those were only headlines. They were only guesses. Easy labels to fit her into easy boxes.

Marie Hale was a pretty girl, not quite sixteen, more than a full year younger than me, though she often seemed much older. She was pretty but not the beauty the papers said she was beneath the flattering photos they printed. Most days of her incarceration she spent standing beside the window of her cell, wearing borrowed clothing—pants that were too long and had to be rolled to the ankle, a white buttoned shirt—and her brunette hair tied back with a short piece of black ribbon. She wore no makeup and never asked for any, except for a tube of red lipstick my mother gave her, to cheer her up, my mother said, though later she would remark that it looked somehow much darker on Marie than it had on her.

She was quiet, and her cell was kept very clean, though I never saw her clean it. She spent most of her time looking out across the parking lot and into the long stretch of trees that separated the jail from the county highway. When she moved, it was to pace, slowly, but with a patient sort of purpose. She reminded me of the large cats I once saw stalking me through their enclosure at the Como Zoo on a family trip to the state capital. Harmless but only for the bars.

It might seem strange that I would think so. I was a young man and an athlete, fit from a summer spent racing after balls in center field and delivering papers. But any man twice my size would have felt the same. She was unsettling. When she paced, and when she sat, very still and so calm, her eyes just like they were the night I saw her slicked and covered in the Carlsons' blood. I tell myself I never really feared her, but at first I would only dare to reach through the bars when she was standing by the window. Only then did she seem as small as she was, only then did she seem as lost—like a girl awaiting a thunderstorm or a strike of lightning.

I told Percy about her the morning after the murders when he picked me up for school. I told him how I'd seen her inside the Carlsons' living room. I guess I shouldn't have, just like I shouldn't have looked. But I'd known Percy since the day he saw me in first grade and decided he would be my best friend. I could trust him.

"How's your dad doing?" I asked as we sat in the school parking lot.

"How's *your* dad doing?" Percy asked back. Then he sighed. "I wonder if anyone else's dogs turned chicken like ours did. You don't really think it's a Bloodless killing, do you? I mean, that'd be too awful."

"Would it be better if it wasn't?" I asked. "Would it have been kinder to Steve and his mom if it had been Bob who had done it? If he'd just snapped and taken a hatchet to everybody?"

"No," Percy said. "Christ, the things you think of."

But I was wondering, too, whether it was really a Bloodless Murder. It hadn't been exactly the same. There had never been anyone found alive at any of the other crime scenes, for a start. And there'd never been any blood. Or at least not as much as had covered Marie Catherine Hale.

"I don't want to go in there," Percy said, staring at the school. "I feel like as long as I don't go in there, none of it actually happened."

But it had happened. Search parties were still out looking for the killer. The state patrol had come in to set up roadblocks and do door-to-door house checks. There at the school it could have been any other day. But if we looked farther out, we'd have seen cops and men and dogs, combing through the fields. Socking us in. I tapped Percy twice on the arm with my fist, and we got out and went inside.

The Carlsons were a successful family. Not well-to-do but respected. The farm had been in the family for two generations, and people in town knew Mr. Carlson as a good farmer, with either a real knowledge for crop rotation or the inside track on obtaining federal subsidies, depending on who you asked.

Their son, my classmate Steve, was universally liked. Not the best player on the football team but he made first string. He wasn't funny, but he was quick to laugh, which is often just as important.

And the night before, someone went into the Carlson farmhouse and slit each of their throats. It was already being whispered that they were killed close enough together that, had they reached out, they could have held hands.

Percy and I walked through the halls riding the news of the Carlsons' deaths like a strange sort of ripple—it was easy to see the difference between those who knew and those who didn't, and stranger still to watch the news hit: to see Joanie Burke's face go slack and watch her reach out and grab for the arms of the person who told her. I saw Carol coming down the hall and knew that she knew; her eyes were blank and red-rimmed.

"Michael," she said, and then she just stood there hugging her books. A cry rang out from somewhere, and it woke her up, and she shook her head and walked away.

Our class at Black Deer Falls High School is made up of 212 students. The entire school, from freshmen to seniors, amounts to 1,169. Steve's sudden and permanent absence ran through us like a crack through ice. It was something we treaded around lightly until we were sure it would hold. All day long we waited for one of our teachers to receive a slip of paper at the door and announce that it was all a mistake, that Steve was fine, just out with flu. Even I was waiting for that.

By the time the day was over, I was exhausted. People figured I knew what had happened, since Sheriff Jensen was my dad, and I didn't mind them asking. But there were only so many times I could say that I didn't know.

"You've got to go by the jail," Percy said when we met at my locker.

"I just want to go home."

"No you don't. You've had your nose stuck in the papers all summer and now that the Bloodless Murders are here and the witness is sitting in your dad's jail, you're going to tell me you want to go home?"

I glanced at him. Practically since the moment it happened I'd been thinking of what a story it was. What a headline, dropped so suddenly into middle-of-nowhere Black Deer Falls. I wondered how Matt McBride would write it up for the *Star*. I wished I'd been around at the Carlson house when he'd showed up on the scene. I started to think about asking him if I could help him out. And every time I thought that, I hated myself for it.

"Look," said Percy. "I know it's real now. I know it's Steve. But that makes it more important, doesn't it? For you to find out. For us."

"Don't you think I'll seem like a—" A busybody, a grubbing opportunist. "Like a snoop?" I asked.

"Well, yeah, but," he said, and shrugged. "Come on, I'll drive you."

By the time Percy dropped me off in the parking lot of the sheriff's station, my curiosity had won out. I had to know if the murders of Steve and his parents had really been a Bloodless killing. Part of me even hoped that they were. And it wasn't just me. The whole town was torn between grief and wanting that mark for Black Deer Falls on the map. We didn't know then what it would mean; we were caught up in the story like everyone else.

I went inside, figuring I'd ask around and see if Bert or Charlie needed any help or ask Nancy if she wanted me to run any errands. I half expected it to be empty, for my father and the deputies to be working the scene out at the farm. But when I got there, my dad was standing in the door to his office, surrounded by both of his deputies. Of the three of them, only Charlie looked fresh, but then he always did, with his thick dark eyebrows and slicked-back hair. My dad looked like he might fall asleep standing up with a cup of coffee in his hand.

"Michael," my dad said, and the deputies turned.

"Hi, Michael," said Charlie.

"Hey, Mikey," said Bert, before looking back at my dad and stepping out of his way.

"You shouldn't be here today, son."

"I'm sorry, sir," I said. "I just thought you could use the extra help."

"I don't know that there's much to do." He rubbed his eyes. "I should be getting home myself soon to try and get some sleep. I guess you can clean up around here a little. Give me a half an hour. Then we'll go home together."

I nodded, and my presence was soon forgotten as I busied myself emptying trash bins and pushing in chairs. My dad and the deputies moved into the relative privacy of his office, and I went on down the halls, putting things back in storage closets that had been left out, and noting the peculiar quiet from the holding cells. They could have been empty. They often were on a weekday afternoon. But I had the distinct impression that they were not and the jailed men were simply silent, as if they, too, were intently listening for anything that could explain what had happened.

When I reached the door to our old kitchen and the women's cell, it was almost by accident. It was my old house, after all, and I often wound up there. My feet just carried me in that direction if I wasn't paying much attention. I'd look up, and there would be the door. Brown wood, painted white on the jail-facing side, as if the change of color provided another layer of separation between the two adjoining structures.

I stopped and stared at the white paint. All of a sudden I felt like I was a kid again, that my mother would be inside, standing at the stove or seated at the table. But there was only a girl on the other side, in the cell, and she must have heard me come up the steps. She must have been waiting. Wondering what I was doing there. So I opened the door.

They had cleaned her up. Gone was the blood, soaked and streaked from head to foot, down the bathtub drain. Gone were the blood-drenched clothes, stained so dark that I could barely remember what they were.

Marie Catherine Hale wasn't facing me when I came in, and her hair was dry now, and soft-looking, a deep brown that lightened at the edges. She didn't turn when she heard the door, just kept looking through the window at the parking lot and a sliver of street below, and beyond that the heavy, wide lines of trees that stand between the jail and the highway.

"It will be dark soon," she said. "I was wondering if I would see you. Michael."

"You know my name," I said.

"They talk about you a lot."

She turned. Her eyes were large and hazel, flecked with brown and not the reddish-brown I'd imagined after seeing her so drenched in blood. Her voice was low and calm. Businesslike.

"You shouldn't be here," she said, and then, before I could agree: "Or maybe you're thinking that I shouldn't be here. But you'd be wrong." She smiled a little, just with the corner of her mouth. "I'm—"

"Marie Catherine Hale," I said. "I know."

"I know you know. But that's all you know. All they know." She had her hair down that day. Out of the ribbons she favored later, for court. "You can just call me Marie, you know. You don't need to say the whole thing."

"But that's what they'll call you in the papers, if you make the papers," I said.

"I've already made the papers. The reporters got here this morning. You missed them, I guess, but you won't. I'm about to make your little town briefly, uncomfortably, famous."

Briefly, uncomfortably, famous. I liked her choice of words. "How old are you?" I asked.

"I'll be sixteen in December. You got a smoke?"

I patted my pockets even though I didn't smoke myself. "Sorry."

She turned away from the window in a fast spin and paced the short length of the cell before plunking down on the bed, which was better than what the men's cells provided but still not much more than a cot. "Figures. They wouldn't give me one downstairs either. Said I was too young."

"You seem older."

She frowned slightly. "Yeah. People always think I'm older than I am."

She tapped her fingernails against the bars. When she looked at me again, a thrill went through my whole body—she'd been there; she'd been in that house when it happened—but it was more than that. Marie Hale was not the kind of girl I was used to talking to. She was a fast girl, with her smokes and the way she moved, that direct look in her eyes. She was the kind of girl the sheriff's son is supposed to ignore.

"What happened to you?" I asked. "What were you doing at the Carlsons'?"

"That's a long story."

"I love stories," I said. "Long, short, and in-between."

Her eyes sharpened, focusing in on me like they had through the Carlsons' window. It had been nearly impossible to piece those two images together, the girl covered in blood with this one, until that moment.

"Is that why you're here?" she asked. "To get the story?"

"No," I said. I gestured quickly to the rest of the room, the attached kitchen, the bare dining table with only one chair. "I used to live here. I wasn't even sure that you would be in the cell. There's got to be someplace more comfortable you could stay until your family can come and get you."

"My family," she said, and laughed.

The words seem foolish to me now, but at the time I didn't know what was so funny. No matter what my dad seemed to think, I couldn't imagine that she was anything other than a lucky girl who had survived a horrible attack.

"No one's coming to get me," she said. "They're charging me downstairs."

"Charging you?"

"As an accomplice."

"But that's crazy."

"Why is it crazy?" she asked.

"Because you're just a girl," I said. And even though I knew she wasn't, she could have been from Black Deer Falls. She was no big-city sophisticate or a tanned blond from California. She talked the same way we did. Walked the same way. Went to our same churches.

"But did you?" I asked. "Are you?"

She shrugged. "Better not say any more." She held up her right hand, as if she were taking an oath. "Anything I say can be held against me in a court of law. And you'd better get out of here. Go back where you came from before you're missed."

I turned to go without another word, thinking she must be lying about her age to be able to order me around like that.

"Michael," she called out. "When you come back: bring some smokes."

CHAPTER FIVE

The Funerals

OVER FIVE HUNDRED people attended the funerals of Robert, Sarah, and Steven Carlson. They spilled out onto the lawn of First United Baptist, which wasn't even the Carlsons' church (they were Methodists) but the only one in town large enough to be up to the task. Folks came from all over the county and even into the Dakotas, people who had never so much as met a one of them. The viewing line before the three ivory caskets stretched far beyond the parking lot and took more than two hours.

It was a hell of a thing, seeing those three caskets draped with roses and daisies and closed so tightly. One of them with Steve inside—Steve, who a week ago had run into me accidentally in the hallway, and those were our last words, our last interaction, an inane cluster of laughter and fake punches.

It didn't make sense that he could be dead. That he could be killed, and be killed in his own house, just lying there without fighting. None of the victims ever seemed to put up a fight.

"I don't understand how it could've happened," I whispered, and my dad squeezed my shoulder.

"I don't either. But we shouldn't talk about it here." My family was already singled out because my father was the sheriff. All eyes were upon us when we approached the caskets.

Except for little Patricia's. The surviving toddler squirmed in her aunt's arms in the front row, chubby fingers reaching for the wide brim of her aunt's black mourning hat. She looked so unknowing. So happy. I wondered what she'd seen in her house that night, what she would remember. If when she grew up she would have her own story to tell.

I looked away to see Matt McBride. He was there covering the funerals, and he'd been watching me as I watched Patricia, so I slipped away from my family and made my way over to him.

"Hello, Mr. McBride."

"Hello, Michael." He shook my hand. "How are you?"

"I'm all right, sir. How are you? Is your wife—?"

"Over there, talking to Bob Carlson's brother, Neil." He smiled. "I think she just doesn't want to be seen with me when I have this camera around my neck." He held it up when he said so. I'd seen him before the service started, taking photos of the caskets draped in flowers. And then again, photographing mourners in the viewing line. Other, out-of-town reporters had been stopped at the door. But Mr. McBride had known the Carlsons, and we were used to seeing him around photographing us at events and at the county fair.

I remember thinking how at ease he looked. How professional. He knew I wanted to be a journalist someday. I'd blurted it out one afternoon that summer when I was delivering papers for him, and he talked with me about it for a long time even though he'd been on his way out the door. We stood in front of the offices of the *Star*, in front of the windows with the title emblazoned across them in flaking gold paint, and he let me ask him about everything I could think of.

"I heard you were at the house that night, in one of the search parties," he said. "I'm sorry; that must have been hard."

I nodded, and he looked at me sympathetically.

"Well, Michael," he said. "I won't keep you. But if you need anything, I'll be around."

After the funerals, Percy and I went to the boat landing on the south end of Eyeglass Lake, a hard-to-find hideaway for upperclassmen and the occasional bunch of kids hunting frogs or turtles. It's not used much anymore for boating or fishing—the water teems with weeds and lily pads. Eyeglass Lake may have been clear as a pair of eyeglasses once, but that was a long time ago, and my dad and his deputies generally consider it too much of a pain to check up on.

Percy backed his car up so that it faced the road and set the parking brake so we wouldn't wind up in the drink. Then we got out and I leaned up against the taillight while he got two beers from the trunk.

"Watch the rust," he said as I popped the top, and I slid over a few inches to keep it from staining my good trousers.

After a few swallows, Percy said, "I've never seen that many people crammed into a church before. Or that many unfamiliar faces."

"Me neither."

"Did you talk to her?" he asked.

"Who?"

"Don't play dumb."

"Marie Catherine Hale," I said. "Yeah, I saw her."

"So what's she like?"

"I don't know. A girl."

He threw something into the water, a rock maybe or the tab of his beer. "I heard they're charging her with the murders, but that can't be right."

"It isn't right. Not exactly. They want her to give up her accomplice. The real killer. But she hasn't yet." The real killer. The man who had done it. No one believed that it could have been her. She was a girl, and girls didn't kill. She was small, when Monty LeTourneau had been big. She was weak, when Steve and his father had been strong. But no one had any problem believing that she had helped.

"Your dad must be going apeshit," said Percy. "He talked to Judge Vernon yet?"

"No one knows what to do," I said. The truth was, my dad, our prosecutor, even our judge were out of their depth. The Bloodless Murders had crossed state lines and had multiple seemingly random victims. They'd never encountered anything like it.

"What does that mean for the girl?" Percy asked. "They won't put her in the chair?"

36

"Minnesota doesn't have the chair," I said. I knew that because I'd asked my dad the same question. When we had capital punishment, we had preferred hanging. "But Nebraska has the electric chair, and that's where it all started."

Percy stared out at the dark water. "Seems stupid of her not to give him up. Seems worse than stupid, to let him go free, keep on killing."

"They'll get him eventually." There had never been more than one Bloodless Murder in the same town. But just the same, we kept our eyes on the trees. Then Percy took his beer and threw it into the lake.

"What'd you do that for?"

"I don't know." He stuffed his hand into his pocket. "This day makes me not want to drink. Those caskets. And all those people . . ."

All those people. On one hand, it was touching that strangers would come and give our community's loss more significance. On the other, it robbed us of our intimacy. But everyone in attendance had been properly somber and restrained. And if a few had stared a little too long, well, that was to be expected, wasn't it? When something was as horrible as that?

I took a last drink and threw my beer into the lake beside Percy's. The funerals were an event not because so many strangers had come. It was a spectacle because it was a spectacle. The Carlsons' deaths had been a spectacle.

"And that baby," I whispered.

I thought of her cherubic, reaching arms. I imagined her sitting on the floor of the living room in the Carlson farmhouse within a few steps of her dead parents and her dead brother. I imagined Marie Hale standing in the same room, red from head to toe.

Widow Fern Thompson had been the one to telephone Charlie at the sheriff's office. None of us had known her husband; she had moved to Black Deer Falls after he died and bought a small house with their savings and his service pension. She was well into her sixties, with no children, and was a bit of a shut-in, and every now and then the ladies at our church would get together and go to her house to bring her a luncheon.

When she called the sheriff's office, she told Nancy that something was wrong at the Carlson place. The lights were still on and the cat had been meowing to be let in. And she could hear the baby crying. Charlie had been hanging around the station that night, as he liked to do when Nancy was working—everyone knew he was sweet on her, and with her bright blond curls and rose-lipped smile, most of the rest of us were sweet on her, too—so he said he'd go out to the farmhouse and take a look. It was Nancy who urged him to get my dad on the radio and bring him along. Charlie'd tried to refuse; there was no reason to bother my dad with something like that, but Nancy'd insisted. There was a note in Fern Thompson's voice, she said, that she didn't like.

Fern kept a rather constant eye on the Carlsons. She alerted them when the family dog ran out into the marshes or when John P. delivered the mail and failed to close the box properly like he did sometimes at our place and the letters spilled out onto the grass. The investigators latched on to that: that the

Widow Thompson's habits weren't something that any murderer just passing through could have known. It was further evidence, they said, that the killer was not from Black Deer Falls, as if we had had any doubt.

"Let's get out of here," Percy said.

"Where are we going?"

"The park. Everyone's going down there to have a drink for Steve."

"I thought you weren't in the mood to drink," I said. "Who's 'everyone'?"

"Everyone who can slip their parents and make it. And they want you there, Sheriff's kid." He opened his door and leaned through to pop the passenger side open.

"So the girl," he said as we pulled out of the landing, "is she pretty?"

"What?"

"They say she's pretty. Black hair, blue eyes, red, red lips . . ."

"Her hair is brown," I said. "And her eyes are hazel. And she's all of fifteen years old."

"Near sixteen. It's not like she's a freshman."

"Is that all you think about? Typical Valentine."

I laughed, and when he tried to punch me in the ribs the car jerked back toward the reed-filled lake. The things that came out of his mouth sometimes. Percy was a regular in detention and by now was an expert at washing chalkboards and classroom windows. He was always goofing about his romantic future and his many wives. Sometimes it was four. Sometimes it was six, like

Henry VIII. It definitely had to be more than three, so he could best his old man.

It was a short drive to the park, and when we got there the sun had just gone down.

"Michael Jensen," someone said, and tossed me a beer. It happened fast, and I couldn't see who it was. The voice sounded maybe like it was Joe Conley or Morgan Todd, both football players like Steve and to me almost indistinguishable aside from the different numbers on their backs.

I cracked it open. "Thanks for the invite." They'd started a fire but kept it burning low in case one of the deputies rolled through. In the orange glow I could make out faces: everyone gathered around was from the football team. I figured they'd extended my invitation for insurance—if they did get caught, at least they had the sheriff's kid there as a shield. As for Percy, he was an always-welcome addition for his clowning, and since he could usually score the most beer.

We stood around and drank to Steve. One beer disappeared and then two, and three, and Percy played his usual trick of lighting his shoes on fire. Those closest to Steve, the ones he would have called his best friends, weren't there that night and I was glad. It was too soon.

"So have you seen it?" Joe Conley asked. "The house, I mean."

"Why would he have seen it?" Percy asked back. His usually affable voice was sharp with warning, and I realized he'd had less to drink than he'd been putting on.

"I just thought he might. His dad's the sheriff, and he works at the jail. I'm just asking is all. I mean, who are they sending to clean it up?"

"Nobody," I said. "Charlie and Bert have already been through it taking photographs, but my dad says the FBI is sure to want a turn."

"The FBI," Morgan said, and whistled. "In Black Deer Falls. Who'd have thought the biggest murder spree of the century would end up here?"

"Who says it's over?" said someone else. "You think the girl did it by herself?"

"None of this makes sense," Joe said, and wiped his face. "I half don't believe it. I half think those coffins were empty. I wish they were." He looked at me. "If we went to Steve's, who'd be there to stop us?"

"There's a state police car parked there from dawn to dark."

But it was after dark.

CHAPTER SIX

The Carlson Farmhouse

WE KNEW IT was a bad idea. But something had come over us, standing there together with the fire going—the grief and beer had combined with blurry feelings of shock and the pent-up frustration of a long summer of light sleep and locked doors. Not a one of us said we shouldn't go. We just piled into our cars and drove north on the long stretch of County 23.

The drive wasn't more than fifteen minutes, the last stretch of it out on back roads, unpaved. We spotted a line of pheasants crossing in our headlights just before we got to it: a few hens and a rooster, his dark green head feathers flashing—and Percy pulled over well shy of the start of the Carlsons' long gravel driveway. Joe was with us in Percy's car, and the rest of the guys followed in two cars behind.

"No sign of a cruiser," Percy said. "Maybe we should still drive past and take a look?"

Joe exhaled and twisted in his seat to look around. Up the road stood a red mailbox with the Carlsons' name on it printed in white paint. It was a pretty place, I'd always thought, a white gabled house with gray shutters nestled in a copse of maple trees.

"They could've stayed late, parked behind the barns," Percy said, and nodded toward them, two large barns, red with white trim in the daylight but only hulking shadows in the dark.

"Don't be chicken," Joe said, and when I didn't say anything, Percy threw the car into drive.

We pulled right up beside the front porch, like we would have if we were stopping by to see Steve or picking him up to go to the drive-in over in Pelican Rapids, two things we had never actually done. We stared up at the house. Already it seemed haunted, though not by ghosts; I had no notion that we would go inside and discover the specter of Steve and his murdered parents. The house was haunted by the experience. It had been stained by the horror that took place within its walls, and even though it stood empty, it would never quite feel empty again.

"Aw, hell," Percy said suddenly.

"What?"

"Widow Thompson is sure to have seen us. She's probably on the phone to your dad's office right now."

"Maybe not," Joe said. "Maybe she's still out with the rest of them at one of the repasts."

I looked closely at Fern Thompson's place. Someone would have picked her up and taken her to the funeral. But they might have also dropped her off again, tired and with a small casserole to put into her refrigerator. If she was home, of course she had seen us. She was watchful before and would be even more so now, and it made me sad to think how afraid she must be living so close to something like that and how much lonelier she would be without the Carlsons' lives to look in on. I opened the car door and stepped out.

"What are you doing?" Percy exclaimed, and got out after me.

Mrs. Thompson knew who I was. I hoped she would understand that we were there not to gawk but because we needed to see; that she would understand when we didn't quite understand ourselves. "Fern Thompson is a nice lady," I said to Percy. "She took in Steve's cat when none of the relatives seemed to want it. My dad told me."

"Oh," Percy said. "That was good of her. And it's good to think . . . that they both have company still." He turned toward Mrs. Thompson's house and gave a little wave in the headlights, turning on that Valentine charm that I had to admit let him get away with more than he ought.

I turned back to the Carlson house. I wondered how long it would remain the Carlson house. In the memory of Black Deer Falls, probably forever. But it was a nice place, on a nice plat of land. It would be a shame for it to stay vacant, to fall apart slowly, its beams sagging, dust and cobwebs taking over the shelves and corners. They didn't deserve this, I thought, and I meant every one of them: Steve and his family, the house, his cat, and his old hound dog.

"Are you sure you want to do this?" Percy asked as Joe got out and the other cars rolled in and shut off their lights. But nobody answered. We were there already.

We went in through the back door.

"Christ," Percy said, examining it. "It doesn't even have a lock."

"Lots of doors don't have locks," said Joe.

"Maybe they didn't used to," he corrected him. "But after this summer . . ." He trailed off. Lots of locks had been added once the murders started. But no one really imagined we would need them.

We stepped farther into the house and Percy and some of the other guys flicked on their lighters. We let Joe lead the way through the mudroom and then the kitchen, with the pantry off to the right. It was freshly clean—the cupboards shut and the dishes put away, a pair of salt and pepper shakers shaped like little milk bottles rested beside the stove—and I got the sense that someone had tidied it up. Maybe even Bert, after the photos were taken and the room was processed. It was something I could see him doing, going through the kitchen and setting things right that had been knocked over.

"This feels weird," Percy said, "like breaking into somebody's house." He winced. "Well, I know we are, but you know what I mean."

"Yeah. I know what you mean." We were breaking into somebody's house. Except those somebodies were dead. That the house remained filled with so much of their lives—family photos, a stack of clean folded clothes on the bottom step of the staircase—shouldn't have surprised us, I guess, but it did. We were walking through the last echoes of the Carlsons and each new personal thing that rose out of the darkness into the light from our lighters made us jump.

"We shouldn't be in here," one of the others whispered. "It feels wrong."

"Then you shouldn't have come," said Joe.

"No, I mean the house feels wrong," he hissed back.

It was true. The house was beginning to lose its lived-in feel. It had been mostly shut up since the bodies had been moved out and the homey smells of cooking and fresh fabrics and Steve's mother's perfume had begun to settle into the carpets. It was starting to smell like the old farmhouse that it was. I tried not to breathe too deeply, afraid to catch the scent of dried blood or rot. I imagined I could smell it even though I knew the blood at the scene had mostly been on Marie Hale. And even though I knew that Steve's and his parents' bodies hadn't lingered for more than a few hours.

Percy walked into the hallway, footsteps light as a cat's. He reached out and touched a bit of lace beneath a painted vase full of dried flowers, careful to keep the flame of his lighter at safe distance.

"This could be any of our houses," he said.

We looked at each other uncomfortably. Even though the lace and painted vase were nothing like what was inside Mo and Jeannie's place, it really could have been any of our homes. It could have been any of us lying dead that night.

We walked through the hall, and Percy put his hand on the banister, his foot rising to rest on the bottom step beside the pile of folded laundry.

"Well," Percy said as the stair creaked, "no need to go up there, right?"

I looked over his shoulder, through the wide open square that led to the living room. Joe was already there, his lighter tilted toward the floor. It was bare except for chalk marking lines.

I stepped past Percy and went into the room where the Carlsons had died.

Their living room was only a little bigger than the one in our house. A fireplace was set at the south end, and above it was a dark wooden mantel clock. It was no longer running and had stopped at 10:22. The electricity to the house had been shut off but I didn't know when, so there was no way of knowing whether the clock had been stopped intentionally after the murders.

Joe pointed at the floor and asked, "What do you make of that?"

I shrugged. I couldn't make any more sense than anyone else of the marks and numbers the investigators had made in chalk. But staring at it, there was something disturbing about the impermanence—as if the whole of the murders could be blown away by a good wind or rubbed away with our hands.

"There's not much here," Joe said, sounding disappointed. He turned to the couch. It was untouched. Unstained and not the slightest bit askew.

"Hang on," said Percy. "Didn't you say that girl came in covered in blood? Like, covered in it?"

"Yeah."

"So where is it? Where's the rest?"

We looked around. It infuriated me suddenly, to think that Steve and his family had died in this sterile, preserved room. That they had died without a fight, without screaming, with Mrs. Thompson settled into her rocking chair just across the driveway.

"And it's weird that this floor is bare," said Percy. "Was there carpet? Maybe Bert and Charlie tore it up?"

"No, there used to be a rug here," said Morgan. He pushed through us and bent down.

"Under the couch. There's something under the couch."

We dropped to our knees and tugged on it, a large rolled-up rug. Bert, Charlie, or my dad must have rolled it out of the way to mark up the floor. We looked each other in the eye and then unrolled it across the wood.

There was blood on the rug all right, though not three bodies' worth. Instead there were several small pools, close enough together that we could imagine it all: which came from the first body and which from the second and third. We could imagine how they lay, each close enough to the other to touch.

"Christ," Percy said. "We should get out of here."

"Don't get sick," I cautioned. I'd seen him get sick over a deer before. As recently as last season, when he shot one younger than he thought she'd been. A big fawn essentially, barely out of her spots.

"I won't," he said, but he was breathing hard like he was about to. "What the hell's that in the middle?"

I bent to peer at the center of the carpet, where spots of red dotted the rug in an uneven circle. Blood had been smeared and tracked from there in small footprints. And there were smudges near where the bodies bled as well. I swallowed.

"That's the girl."

It was where Marie had stood as all the blood on her hair and clothes dripped down.

"Something's not right," said Joe. "How did she get covered in their blood? It's too clean—" He gestured to the carpet as his voice grew louder, indecently loud in the quiet.

"Take it easy—"

"There must be more! Where is it?"

She had been coated in all of their blood; I'd seen it with my own eyes. I stared at the small sterile spots where Steve and his parents had died—where they fell, where they lay. How did it get from their wounds onto her? Thick and wet and smeared across her face. Soaked into the roots of her hair, red running down to the ends. Enough to saturate her clothes from her shirt to the socks in her shoes. Like it had been poured over her from a bucket.

Walking around on the unrolled carpet, trying to imagine Steve and his parents' final moments, I'd nearly forgotten that anyone else was there, until Percy yelped, "Jesus!"—and grabbed me by the elbow.

"What?" I half shouted.

His arm was stretched out. His lighter was shaking.

"There was a face in the window."

We looked, but whatever he had seen was gone. Nothing there but darkness and the shadows of Mrs. Carlson's lilac bushes.

"I don't see anything," Joe said.

"It was there," Percy said. He said "it" and not "they," and for some reason that made the back of my neck prickle.

"Where there?" I asked.

"Just . . . there!"

"Standing or crouching? A man? A woman? Maybe Fern Thompson?"

"It wasn't Fern Thompson," he said, and gave me a look. But he couldn't explain who it was. The face had simply been there, he was sure of it. Pale and up close and staring. And then it was not. We didn't have much time to ponder it because that's when we heard the distinct sound of tires crunching up the gravel driveway.

"Oh shit," Morgan said.

"Quick, help me roll this up." Joe bent down over the rug. Lighters went out and we hurried to the sides of the carpet, holding our breaths against the faint scent of blood.

"I guess old Widow Thompson wasn't as understanding as you hoped."

We got to our feet in time to hear the back door open, and for Charlie to yell:

"Percy Valentine. Michael Jensen." I couldn't help but notice the way his tone changed between our names—unsurprised for Percy and disappointed for me. We hurried back through the hallway and into the kitchen, and when he saw us, he shook his head, his hands on his hips, feet spread wide like a gunfighter about to draw. "And the rest of you. Let's go, boys."

"Yes, sir," we said, and walked quickly past.

"What the hell were you doing in there? You didn't mess with anything, did you?"

"No, sir."

As we got into Percy's car to follow Charlie to the station, Percy asked, "So how long did Widow Thompson give us before she called you in?"

"Widow Thompson?" Charlie squinted quizzically. "I just saw the backs of your cars when I passed by on the road."

I looked across the yard to Mrs. Thompson's house. She may not have called us in, maybe hadn't seen us drive up at all, but she was watching now. I could see her plainly against the yellowed lace of her curtains. She had Steve's tomcat, who I later learned was called Mr. Stripes, nestled in her arms.

"Is it just you, Charlie?" I asked, even though I saw only the one patrol car. "Bert didn't come?"

"Just me."

"Then who was in the window?" Percy whispered.

CHAPTER SEVEN

At the Station

THE BUNCH OF us being marched into the station was as embarrassing as anything I'd ever experienced. Charlie made me go in first, and I must've been a sorry sight: head hanging, shoes scuffing the floor. He hadn't put cuffs on us or anything, but it felt like he had. I'd never been so ashamed, and I'd never resented anyone so much as I resented Joe Conley and the other guys, though I guess that was kind of unfair.

My dad was standing there; he knew what we'd done. I expected his face to be red to bursting. But he just pulled me aside and whispered, "I expect you know why those boys asked you and Percy along for this." It wasn't a whupping, I suppose. But it was almost worse. He knew we'd been used. And that we should have known better.

"Your parents are coming to get you," my dad said as we stood lined up against the wall and window of his office.

"So, we're not in trouble?" Morgan asked.

"I would guess you'll be in plenty. But not from the law. This was stupid, boys. Stupid and disrespectful. The Federal Bureau is sending out their investigators in the morning, and after that, I'm sending Charlie and Bert out to get rid of everything out there: the rug, the chalk." My dad frowned at me. "Anything that would be worth gawking at."

Down the line, a few of the guys teared up again, and I almost spoke. It hadn't been about that, for them. It had been about Steve.

"Sheriff Jensen, sir," said Joe Conley, "my dad's on shift at the seed factory—"

"Don't worry; we already put a call in. He's on his way."

"He's leaving his shift?"

Percy and I looked at each other. At school we all knew that Joe's father was mean as a snake. That despite Joe's height and athletic build he would sometimes show up in the locker room with bruised ribs and strange marks on his back.

"Can you call and stop him?" Percy asked. "My old man has to come from there, too, and he won't mind. We could bring Joe home, and then I could drive my car and he wouldn't make me leave it—"

"Percy," my dad said. "Shut up."

After that he left us, to stew, I guess, all of us standing there and waiting for the ax to fall. One by one we were taken away, wincing at the storm clouds on our fathers' brows and envious of the ones who were picked up by their mothers, even if Jake Clapper's mom did thump him with her handbag something fierce.

Pretty soon, it was only Joe, Morgan, Percy, and me.

"Hey," Percy hissed to me.

"What?"

"You should tell your dad. About the face."

The face he'd seen in the window out at the Carlson farm-house.

"You're sure it wasn't Charlie?" I asked.

He shook his head. "Couldn't have been. It was already gone when we heard Charlie pull up. And it didn't look like him. No hat."

"Well, who did it look like?"

But he couldn't say. I asked him about it often over the coming weeks, but in the end he couldn't even be sure if what he saw was a person.

I took a deep breath and went over to my dad.

"What is it, Michael?"

"I don't think we were the only ones at the Carlsons' tonight. Percy says he saw someone else. Standing outside looking in through the living room window."

He reached up and rubbed his eyes and forehead. He was still exhausted, and I felt guiltier than ever.

"But no one else in the house?" he asked.

"Not that we saw."

"All right. I'll send Charlie back out to take a look around, and Nancy," he called across the room to her, "will you call out to State Patrol and see if they'll give us a hand with a twenty-four-hour watch on the Carlson house?"

"Will do."

He turned back to me. "Anything else?"

"No, sir," I said, and returned to my place against the wall.

"I'm sorry we got you into this, Jensen," Joe said.

"You didn't get me into anything," I said. And it was going to be worse for him anyway.

It was another hour before Joe's dad showed up. He walked in looking irritated, but as soon as he saw my father, he shook his hand and apologized for the whole mess. Even thanked him for being so understanding about it since Joe was so broken up about Steve. They made small talk for a few minutes, chuckling about their delinquent sons, Joe's father shaking his head amiably, his big broad shoulders still built like he played football. That niceness was what made him dangerous. If he'd have been a drunk and a screwup like Mo, none of us would have been afraid to talk. But to say Joe's father was cruel? Who would have believed us?

As he and my dad were talking, the door to the interrogation room across the station opened and Marie Hale stepped out with Edwin Porter, our public defender. We all stared, and Mr. Porter tried to hurry her along, but she put her hand on his arm. I didn't know what was going to happen as she stood there, facing us. I was afraid that Joe and Morgan and maybe even Mr. Conley would start shouting at her, demanding to know what she knew. Maybe that's what would have happened, if there hadn't been so few of us left by then. Instead, Mr. Conley broke the stillness by walking to his son and taking him by the collar.

Marie's eyes narrowed as the Conleys left the station, like she sensed that something wasn't right. I wondered what else she'd heard, how much she knew about why we were there and what we'd done. We hadn't heard any sound from inside the interrogation room, but I'd been in there and I knew it wasn't soundproof.

Mr. Porter tried to guide Marie back toward the stairs that led to her cell, but she tugged a little against him and stared through the windows that faced the parking lot. Then her eyes narrowed again, and she looked at me and motioned with her chin. I knew immediately what she meant. Joe's dad hadn't bothered to wait until they got home. He'd pulled him into a dark spot beside the building.

I pushed off the wall and went to the window. I could see them. Just the shapes of them pressed against the wall.

"Dad!"

I called him over and he looked. Then he pushed through the door with Charlie not far behind.

"Stay inside, the rest of you," Charlie ordered. He pointed to Mr. Porter and Marie. "And get her back up to her cell!"

Nancy got to her feet behind the receptionist desk and hurried to help, a set of keys jangling in her hands.

"Come on, dear," she said, and I couldn't tell whether she was speaking to Marie or Mr. Porter, a small man with a bald pate and wisps of dark hair. She ushered them through the station toward the stairs, and Marie looked over her shoulder at me.

"What do you think's happening out there?" Percy asked. It had gone quiet after my dad's initial shouts. Then it started again, and we heard a new voice join in.

"Oh Christ, it's Mo," Percy groaned. "He's bound to make things worse."

But he didn't. Though Mo can sometimes complicate things, he also has a knack for speeding things up, and within two minutes he and my dad came back inside the station with Joe walking between them. Joe was crying, and his nose and lips were bloody. In the parking lot, Mr. Conley started his car and drove away.

"Should have dragged him in here and thrown him in a cell," Mo said angrily.

"Next time," my dad said. "If there is a next time. For now . . ."

"He can stay with us," Morgan said. "We're used to it."

"Is that all right with you, son?" my dad asked, and Joe nodded.

"I don't know what's keeping my mom," said Morgan. "My dad has the car, but she can usually ask our neighbor. . . ."

"Percy and I'll take them," Mo said. "You boys ride with me in the truck and Percy can follow behind in that rust-bucket car of his."

"All right," my dad said. "I'll call Mrs. Todd and tell her to expect you."

It wasn't long after they left that my dad gave up his silent treatment and led me out to the cruiser to go home.

"Thanks for doing that, Dad," I said as we drove. "It was . . ." I searched for the right word. Brave. Heroic. Good.

"It was nothing," he said softly. Then he shook his head and patted my knee. "I didn't mean that. It wasn't nothing. It was just another bad, bad thing."

"But Dad—"

"It's all right. I know we can't fix all of it. But it would be nice, right now, to fix just one."

That night, long after the rest of my family was asleep, I sat awake in my bedroom thinking about the Carlson place. The empty rooms like time had stopped. The dark pools of blood soaked into the carpet. And that strange red circle the size of a girl. Every Bloodless Murder had more questions than answers. But these were questions about people we knew. I imagined Steve, lying with his throat cut across from his mother and his expression of disbelief as they both died. I imagined his father, trying to protect everyone. Except that it didn't seem he had. He had lain down right beside them, and his blood had formed a similar, quiet stain.

When I finally slept, in my dreams I was inside that house. Only Steve's father was my father. And my mother and Dawn were standing in the Carlson living room on top of that stained carpet. In the dream I couldn't save them. In the dream, they were standing there but they were already dead.

CHAPTER EIGHT

Monsters

AS PENANCE FOR what I'd done and not at all to eavesdrop, I spent a lot of time that weekend sweeping up and doing chores around the jail. And after a little while, Bert and Charlie stopped treating me like I was in trouble and things went back to normal. Normal enough that Nancy, our receptionist, didn't think it strange to ask me to go upstairs and see Marie.

"What for?" I asked.

Nancy shrugged. "She heard you were here and asked for you. I don't see much harm in it as long as you don't stay too long." She glanced out the windows. It would be growing dark soon. Everyone's mother wanted them home before dark those days.

I made my way through the building, past the empty offices and the corridor that led to the men's cells—also empty, as if even the drunks were respectfully restraining themselves on account of the murders. I mounted the steps to the women's cell and my old house with its white-painted door. It occurred to me that Marie and I were nearly the only two people inside the whole place.

It was irresponsible of Nancy to let me go. She hadn't even asked Charlie for the okay. But Nancy was beautiful enough to be famous and, as such, she pretty much had her run of things. Not to mention, after her personal tragedy—Nancy had lost her little girl in a house fire some years back, along with her husband—not even my dad had the heart to scold her.

I knocked on the door to the women's cell. When I got no reply, I opened it a fraction and said, "Marie?"

"Yes?"

"May I come in?" I pushed the door a little farther, wide enough to see a sliver of her back. She was seated on her bed in another pair of blue jeans and possibly the same white shirt.

"This isn't my room, Michael," she said. "It's a jail. You don't need to ask permission."

I hesitated. When it became clear that I was unable to move without say-so, she said, "And I did ask you to come. So come in."

She had her hair down again, brushed back from her face. One knee was drawn up, hands folded in front of it with her fingers intertwined. She was staring out the window, though from that angle she wouldn't have been able to see much but a few treetops and some sky. I stepped into the room and awkwardly shuffled about, trying to decide whether to stand or to pull a chair over from the kitchen.

"You don't smell like beer anymore," she said. "Like you did the other night."

"Oh," I said, and wiped at my chest like the scent was still there and would come off. "I'm sorry."

She shrugged. "I'm used to it. Maybe it even reminds me of home."

"Where is home?"

"Nebraska," she said. "You know that."

But by then Nebraska was only a guess. No one had been able to locate a girl by the name of Marie Catherine Hale and there were no girls reported missing who matched her description, aside from a few runaways whose families would later shake their heads when they were shown Marie's picture, disappointed and also relieved.

She turned on her bed, and the movement barely caused a shift in the thin mattress, the edges of which were carefully made with what my mother called "hospital corners." She looked me up and down.

"Though none of the fellas I knew walked around smelling like beer in a necktie."

I remembered what we were wearing that night—our church clothes from attending the funerals.

"The funerals were that day."

"Oh," she said.

She didn't ask about the Carlsons' funerals, not the whole time she was with us. It might have seemed macabre if she had. Perverse. At times during our conversations I wondered whether she realized that and the omission was deliberate.

She did, however, ask if I knew them.

"You must have," she said. "In a small, kind town like this."

"I did. Steve was in my year at school."

"What was he like?"

"Steve? He was nice. He played football . . . tight end, I think."

"And you knew him a long time?"

"Since first grade at least."

"What else?"

"What do you mean?"

"What else can you tell me about him?"

"I don't know if I should." And at that point there wasn't much more to tell. It was still too soon for the folks of Black Deer Falls to have mined each other's memories, to revisit our every interaction with the Carlsons and go through their belongings until we all felt like better friends. And being there with Marie felt wrong. Talking about his life with the girl who had been found slicked with his and his parents' blood. Even though it was hard to believe that she had anything to do with it. Every time I looked at her my brain wrestled with the sight of her the same way any jury would have: she couldn't have done it. She wouldn't. She was too small. Too young. Too pretty. And she was a girl. Only her accomplice could make it make sense. After we had him, then we could look on her as we pleased, casting her as the frightened hostage or the present-day Bonnie Parker who seduced him into it and egged him on.

Marie sighed. She stretched her arms up over her shoulders and something in the stretch made me look away, as if it was too intimate. I thought again that we were alone and I had rarely been alone with a girl except on dates to the drive-in or the café.

"You didn't bring any smokes, did you?"

"I forgot. Next time, I promise."

"Next time," she said quietly. "Well then, what did I ask you here for?"

I watched her as she tucked her knees up under her chin and hugged her legs. How many times had I seen my little sister, Dawn, sitting on the porch swing just the same way, her little brow furrowed, eyes narrowed to slits and hard as marbles, thinking unknowable young girls' thoughts? But Marie Hale had far more secrets than Dawn. There were so many things I wanted to ask. How did the murders happen? Why were there no signs of a struggle? Why were they chosen? *Where was the blood?*

Always, always, where was the blood.

It seemed impossible that she could know.

"Do you believe in monsters, Michael?"

"Monsters? Not since I was seven."

"Seven. That's pretty old to, I guess. But it's not right either. Deep down we all believe in monsters."

Her gaze drifted back to the window.

"Before this is over, you won't believe the kinds of things you'll hear about me. Maybe even about your friend Steven. He'll be the one they focus on, you know. Not his old father or his adult mother. Just him. So young and handsome. And that little baby, so tragically left behind." She snorted. "Like it'd been better if . . ." Marie stopped. She didn't like talking about that baby. She never wanted to hear about Patricia, except for once weeks later when she asked if the aunt who took her in had really wanted her.

"Did your friend Steven date a lot? Did he get around?"

I thought it was an odd way to phrase it; boys didn't "get around."

"He dated some. Nice girls, mostly."

"Mostly?" she asked. "Isn't that the only kind you have here?" She slid her hands down her legs and fiddled with the rolled cuffs of the jeans she wore. She looked nervous—no, not nervous. Restless. Like it was taking all of her restraint to stay on that cot. I wished I smoked; I'd have given her one just to calm her down.

"It won't matter anyway," she said. "Who he dated. They'll find everything out. Where they went. What they did in the backs of cars, because even the nice girls do *something*. Maybe they'll keep the details out of the papers. But they'll hint. Like they did with those two nurses. Just a small note that they were regulars at the roadhouse and had many acquaintances there. *Acquaintances.* Damn reporters." Shockingly, she spit on the floor.

"You've been following the papers."

"Of course we were. But it isn't just the reporters. It's everyone. If the victim is young or beautiful, such a tragedy, they say. Such a loss. That's how it starts." She cocked her head, coquettish. "Then they change their tune. Not enough to be . . . defamatory. Just enough to make folks wonder: What could something so beautiful have done to deserve it?"

"No one could deserve that," I said quietly.

"I know." She sighed and put her feet down. "But it doesn't stop them from wondering. Have you ever heard of Mercy Lena Brown?"

I shook my head.

"She was a girl from Exeter, Rhode Island, who lived in the 1800s. She died when she was nineteen, and shortly after, her neighbors became convinced that she was returning from the grave and draining the life from her brother. So they dug her back up and cut her apart—they cut off her head so she wouldn't rise again; they burned her heart in the town square and fed her poor brother the ashes."

"That's—" I said as my mind struggled to recall what little I knew of New England. Hadn't the Salem witch trials been not long before that? Wasn't the whole region prone to fits of hysteria, with each citizen granted a torch and pitchfork upon reaching majority age? "That's ghoulish. And ridiculous."

"I suppose it was," said Marie. "But it wasn't to them." At the time, I had never heard of Mercy Brown. It sounded made-up. A folk-legend. But it wasn't. It was one of many fear-induced exhumations peppered throughout New England and even stretching into the Midwest. When I was researching it, I actually found some references to exhumations in Minnesota.

"Tuberculosis is what she died of," Marie said. "A doctor said that when they cut her open, but no one cared. They fed her tubercular heart to her brother anyway, and they did it with their father's permission."

She smiled a little at those final words.

"Did it save him?" I asked. "The brother?"

"No, it didn't save him! Michael." She shook her head at me. "He joined her in the cemetery, not six months later. Of course, they left *him* whole." We both laughed a little. I was embarrassed to have asked.

"You know," I said, "Steve wasn't really my friend."

"I figured. You two . . . didn't seem a matched type." She leaned back and stretched her neck. "The prosecutor from Nebraska's on his way," she said, and raised her nose like she could catch his scent. "I guess they're going to charge me there, too. They must be finding my footprints and fingerprints everywhere. Putting it all together."

"Why don't you just tell them who was with you?" I asked. "Why don't you just give him up?"

"Because," she said simply, "it wouldn't do any good."

After that I went back downstairs. Nobody saw me coming back from the women's cell, or if they did they didn't say anything, maybe to save themselves the headache of telling my dad.

I walked over to Charlie as he sat at his desk doing paperwork and pretending not to steal glances at Nancy.

"Charlie?"

"Yeah, Michael?"

"Did you go back out to the Carlson farm last night to have a look around?"

"Right after you and your dad left for home. Didn't find anything—no other tire tracks, no evidence that anyone had been messing with the doors."

"No footprints in the flower beds?"

"Not a one. And I checked all around the house, not just where you said by the living room window. I even woke poor Fern

Thompson to ask if she'd heard anything, so she won't thank you for that."

"Okay. Thanks anyway," I said softly.

I went home that night, and didn't think anything more of Percy's "face in the window." At the time, it was easy enough to believe it had all been in his imagination.

CHAPTER NINE

The Prosecutor from Nebraska

DISTRICT ATTORNEY BENJAMIN Pilson arrived in Black Deer Falls on September 24, six days after the killings of Steve and his parents. He was six-foot-two, with a straight back and a fine haircut, and he blew into town with a mind to take charge of an investigation he viewed as having been poorly handled by the small-town local authorities. He wasn't wrong about that exactly—my dad and the deputies had made no headway with Marie, and evidence from the Carlson house hadn't yielded any new clues about the killer or his methods, but you would have thought Pilson was the lead federal investigator from the way he burst into my dad's station, all necktie and stiff handshakes. He didn't pay much attention to Bert, but he was downright charming to Nancy, leaning over her desk and complimenting the big gold brooch she wore every Wednesday. As for me, sweeping quietly in the back, I might as well have been invisible. Until later, when he had a use for me, which told me everything I needed to know about the kind of man Benjamin Pilson really was.

My dad took Pilson into his office, but he didn't close the door. It wasn't hard to slide up with my broom and overhear what they were saying.

Turns out, he had come to try and take Marie.

"We'd like to get her down to trial in Nebraska," he said.

"I'm sure you would," my dad replied. "And I'm sure you will, eventually. But from what I understand we have the best shot right here: a suspect found at the scene of the crime, covered in blood, and a room full of finger- and shoe prints."

"That is true. You and your deputies are owed more than a cold beer. I hope you'll let me buy you one on behalf of the citizens of Nebraska."

"Thank you," my dad said. "I'm sure Charlie and Bert won't say no to that."

"Were they the first on the scene?" Pilson asked.

"Charlie and myself. We secured Miss Hale and the surviving minor child and conducted an initial search of the premises."

"That must have been harrowing. I've heard you were acquainted with the victims?"

"I was. And I don't mind telling you it was the hardest thing I've ever had to do."

Pilson paused. "So it was just you and . . ."

"Deputy Charles Morris," my dad supplied. "Joined shortly by Minnesota State Police."

There was a beat of silence. My dad's tone was losing its ease.

"I wish you'd found a murder weapon," Pilson said finally.

"So do I," my dad said. "But no one has that I've heard of."

"I heard you had some trouble out there the other night. Some local boys, compromising the scene."

My broom froze in my hands.

"I don't know how you heard that, Mr. Pilson, but the scene had already been processed. And I don't know what your hurry is. Nebraska will have its turn, just like Wisconsin and Iowa."

"Wisconsin can't place her at the scene. Not so much as a footprint. And I spoke to the Iowa prosecutor this morning and he's happy to continue their investigation while I take a run at it first. I'm not trying to take anything away from you; I want to work in conjunction with you—"

"From Lincoln."

"Yes, from Lincoln."

I heard the creak of my dad's chair as he leaned back. "I think we'd like to keep her here."

There was a pause, and Pilson asked, "What have you gotten out of her? A name? A motive?"

"As for a name, only her own."

"Marie Catherine Hale," said Pilson. "We had no luck tracking down anyone with that name either. But we're working on it. She's probably from Nebraska, after all, since Nebraska is where this all started."

He'd been right about that, even if he didn't truly know it then. He was thinking of the first known victim at that time: Peter Knupp from Loup City.

"I'd like to meet with the prisoner," Pilson said.

"Of course."

I quickly moved away as my dad got up to show Mr. Pilson to the interrogation room. This time Pilson noticed me, and after an appraising glance he shot me a fast hard wink.

"Bert," my dad said, "will you please bring Miss Hale to speak with the Nebraska District Attorney?"

Bert went up and got her, and on her way through the station she looked at me. Then he escorted her inside.

"Kind of a pretty thing, isn't she?" Pilson said.

"Barely more than a child," said my dad.

"Has she seemed traumatized? Frightened? Has she given any explanation for her involvement?"

"She hasn't said much of anything."

Pilson walked in and closed the door.

I wish I could have listened, but every eye in the station was on the interrogation room. And anyway, it wasn't long before Marie started to shout.

"You can't do that, you dirty bastard! I didn't do anything! I didn't do it!"

Nancy and I looked at each other; Nancy had her hand to her mouth. Marie had been so calm and quiet since the night of the murders. After another minute, Pilson came out and straightened his tie while Marie continued to wail and curse.

"What on earth did you do?" my dad asked.

"She'll calm down," Pilson replied. He held out his hand, and my dad, ever polite, shook it. "I'll see you in St. Paul in a few days, Sheriff Jensen. I've arranged a special hearing with the district court." He glanced back at the interrogation room, and the screaming girl inside. "You'll get some peace and quiet again after I take her with me to Lincoln." And then he strode out of the building, leaving my dad to clean up the mess.

"She won't quit," Bert called as he tried to calm Marie. "Sheriff!"

My dad reached for his handcuffs.

"Not the cuffs, Rick," Nancy objected.

"It's only for a minute. We can't have her injuring herself."

He went in and we listened to them wrestle—to Marie screeching and to my dad's voice, always steady, telling her he wasn't going to hurt her. Pretty soon it was quiet except for her breathing (and Bert's).

"What did he say to you," my dad asked, "that upset you so?"

I crept closer until I could see her, hands cuffed to the table, half standing and arms taut against the bonds like a horse trying to pull free. She looked right at me.

"He wants to try me for felony murder!"

"But you didn't kill anyone," I said. "Did you?"

"No!"

At the time we didn't know that in Nebraska, a person could be convicted of felony murder even if they were not the one with their hand on the knife or their finger on the trigger. Nor did we know that such a conviction could result in a penalty of death. We thought that Pilson was just blowing smoke.

"If you're innocent, it would go easier if you'd tell us what happened," my dad said. "Just explain it to us, piece by piece. Even if you can't give us his name."

Marie closed her eyes and shook her head fiercely. "He wants to kill me," she kept saying. "He wants to kill me."

"You have to defend yourself, Miss Hale. Or we can't help you."

She opened her eyes.

"I'll tell *him*," she said, and nodded to me.

"What, you mean Michael?"

"Yes. Michael. I'll tell him everything. But only Michael."

CHAPTER TEN

The District Courthouse

I THOUGHT I'D misheard. Marie Catherine Hale, the only witness and presumed accomplice to the killing spree that had frozen the entire country, chose me to hear her story.

"Absolutely not," my dad said to me when we got home.

"But why not?" my mom asked.

My dad and I turned. We hadn't seen her standing in the kitchen, the glasses that usually hung around her neck perched on the end of her nose, using her thumb to hold her place in a novel.

"What?" my dad asked. "And how do you know about it already?"

"Nancy called me from the station. She said that Michael is the only one the girl's been willing to talk to."

"Nancy." My dad put his hands on his hips and shook his head like he was going to give her an earful, but we knew he would do no such thing. He looked at my mom. "You can't want him to do this."

"Didn't you tell me last night that you weren't getting anywhere?"

"That's not the point." He glanced at me and spoke in a low whisper. "The things he would have to hear—he's just a boy."

"I'm seventeen," I said. Then they looked at me and I looked at the floor.

"You weren't inside that house," my dad said. "You didn't see those bodies."

"He won't have to see, though, will he? Just to hear."

"If we agree to this, it'll amount to a confession, and he'll be privy to the entire investigation. Blood evidence. Autopsy reports. The photographs of the Carlsons and the rest of the murders, too."

My mom paled. She hadn't thought of that. Honestly I hadn't either. But I would be lying if I said I didn't want to do it. I wanted to see and I wanted to hear and I wanted to be the first to know. Even then I knew that Marie's confession was the story of a lifetime, the interview any reporter in the country would have killed for.

"Linda," my dad said. "You don't want him to see all that, do you?"

I didn't dare move a muscle while she thought about it, afraid to look too young and make her say no. Afraid to seem too eager and make her say no for a different reason.

"If that's what she wants," my mom said, "and the judge says it's all right, then who are we to say he can't? She deserves to confess, doesn't she, if she played a part in it? And Bob and Sarah and Steven . . . don't they deserve it, too?"

My dad's shoulders slumped.

After that, getting the other officials to sign on was easy. Mr. Porter reviewed the request, and after determining that it didn't violate any of Marie's rights, he agreed to advocate for her at the district court hearing that Nebraska DA Pilson had set up. Our prosecutor also gave the okay, and—a little surprisingly—so did the DAs from Wisconsin and Iowa. I didn't know them and have never seen their pictures, but in my imagination they look a lot like Mr. Porter: balding and tired around the eyes, long past dreams of courtroom glory.

But what it really was, was that none of them really wanted Marie. They wanted him. The one who the search teams and state patrol were still looking for. The one who might kill still more.

When Mr. Pilson heard about the confession, he dismissed it as a joke, though it was later heard from a woman who worked at the St. Paul hotel where he was staying that he smashed the telephone down so hard he cracked it.

Benjamin Pilson was not about to let a girl's whims derail his plans. He was of the fire-and-brimstone sort, firmly on the punishment side of the punishment versus rehabilitation argument. He was not swayed by Marie's youth nor by her sex nor by the incredulity that she would be capable of committing such heinous murders. He wanted her brought to Nebraska in chains. He wanted her dragged before a jury. He may have also been coming up for reelection.

The day of Marie's hearing, I rode with my dad in his cruiser while Marie rode in a separate transport driven by Charlie and accompanied by Mr. Porter and my mom. The drive to St. Paul took several hours, and by the time we arrived I was already sweating through my good church shirt. One hearing would decide whether Marie would stay in Minnesota or be transported back to Nebraska. It would decide whether my part in the story was just beginning or whether Marie and the Bloodless Murders would vanish from Black Deer Falls as abruptly as they came.

My dad found a parking space down the street, and I got out and looked up at the Ramsey County Courthouse, a tower of golden limestone with rows of windows running down it like silver ribbons. There was a flurry of black cars and reporters between us and the entrance.

"What am I doing here, Dad?" I asked. I had no experience in interrogation; I had never taken a confession. I was a would-be journalist who had delivered papers and chatted with a local editor.

"You don't have to do this, Michael," my dad said. "Not any of it."

But I did, didn't I? For Steve and his family, and for the other victims we hadn't known. Marie Catherine Hale had to talk. Whoever had cut that bloody trail through four states was still out there, and she was the only person alive who knew who he was.

I took a breath and walked toward the crowd of people that stretched down the street and even across it, flooding the sidewalk that looked across the Mississippi River to Harriet Island. The city smelled like exhaust and, from farther away, of something fried in butter and the meaty whiff of a hamburger. My stomach rumbled, but I couldn't have eaten a bite. There were so many reporters. When we reached them their car doors cracked open and they spilled out around us like eager insects. Pilson had said it would be a quiet hearing. But I would come to learn that Benjamin Pilson loved the press.

"Is it true she was found alone and covered in blood?"

"Were the bodies bled like those kids in Wisconsin?"

"Had they been bound? What about the baby?"

Cameras flashed right after the questions, as if the questions weren't important and were only meant to rattle us, to coax out the perfect expressions of horror. Then, just as quickly as they'd come, they disappeared, pushing and shoving back toward the street.

Marie had arrived.

The papers hadn't published any photos of her yet—they couldn't, as no one had been able to verify her identity—so the country hadn't been able to paint any kind of picture. Was she pretty? Ugly? Poor? No one could say. But that would change. The photo that everyone came to associate with Marie Catherine Hale was taken as she walked into the courthouse.

She looked different in her court clothes: a mid-length black skirt belted at the waist, a white blouse with long sleeves, and a dark green sweater draped over her shoulders. Her hair was tied back with what would become her signature black ribbon, and she was helped along by an escort of Edwin Porter on one side and my mother on the other. My mom was well-prepared for the task; she used one hand to fend off reporters and kept the other clamped onto Marie's thin elbow. Marie flinched and pulled a little in her grip as she shied away from the flashbulbs. Later, the photos would show a very pretty, somewhat reluctant girl with a fashionable hairstyle and carefully done makeup. A few caught her gazing wistfully away, toward the river. Toward better days, thought some. Toward escape, thought others. But the photograph that stuck was one of her smiling—just with one side of her mouth. It had only been a moment—a reporter had called out some silly thing, and she had smiled. But that instant would damn her in so many minds as the murderess who smiled while people lay dead. In the photos her lips appeared dark. They were often called crimson.

"Where'd she get the lipstick?" I asked.

"Your mother gave it to her," my father said, a bit dazedly. "She got her ready before the trip. I didn't know your mother owned a lipstick like that."

Inside the courthouse, the frenzy of reporters was worse. A regular circus, my dad said.

"They're only doing their jobs," I replied. But the looks in their eyes were as quick and blank as a bird's hunting for bugs in the grass.

Inside the courtroom we took seats behind our prosecutor, Mr. Norquist, who had come to represent the interests of the people of Minnesota—a formality since he had already agreed to Marie's request. Marie's lawyer, Mr. Porter, was beside him. And Marie would have the final chair.

"You doing all right, Michael?" Mr. Norquist asked me.

"Yes, sir."

"Good. You shouldn't need to say anything more than, 'yes, your honor,' should the judge ask you anything." He nodded to Benjamin Pilson when he came in and took his seat on the opposite side. Pilson just smiled, lines going deep into the sides of his mouth.

It was a closed hearing—cobbled together and as informal as could be wrangled. But it felt plenty formal to me. And after the buzzing crush of the street and the interior of Memorial Hall, my fingers twitched to loosen my tie.

"So," the judge said, and folded his hands together. "All of you are here to fight over who gets to prosecute this little girl first."

"That's . . . a bit of a mischaracterization, your honor," Mr. Norquist said. "We all of us in every state wish to get to the bottom of this."

"All right." The judge studied some papers. "And Wisconsin and Iowa agree that Minnesota can take the first crack at it. But not you, Mr. Pilson?"

"That's correct, your honor," Pilson said.

"And why is that? Nebraska isn't even the state where the most murders occurred"—that dubious honor went to Iowa—"so why take her back there? Simply because it's where it all began?"

"Yes, your honor. And because, since Nebraska is where it all began, we feel certain that Marie Catherine Hale is from our state. That she is a daughter of Nebraska."

"A Nebraska daughter," the judge mused, "subject first to Nebraska discipline."

Pilson handed a sheaf of photographs to the bailiff. The judge looked through them as Pilson described them at length.

"Peter Knupp. A lifelong resident of Loup City, Nebraska. Only twenty-six years old. He worked night shifts as a machinist and had recently purchased his first home. On the morning of August third he was found on the front porch of that home, laid out and bled like a hog. Cuts at his throat, and the interior of the thigh. Angela Hawk. Twenty-two. Found beside her good friend Beverly Nordahl, also aged twenty-two. They were discovered sitting upright in the driver's and passenger seats of Miss Hawk's car with their throats slit."

The judge pursed his lips and set down the photos. "We've all heard these facts before. We've read about these heinous and vicious acts and agree that they were heinous and vicious. Is that the only point you're trying to make?"

Our prosecutor, Mr. Norquist, stood.

"Your honor. The fact is Marie Catherine Hale was apprehended in Minnesota. Covered in the victims' blood. And it is in Minnesota that she has agreed to confess her level of involvement. To give these families the comfort of the truth and provide the country with answers regarding the—impossible nature—of these crimes!"

The judge paused. Mr. Norquist had said the magic word. *Answers.* Answers were what we craved, even more than justice. Why hadn't they struggled? How had he done it? And where, where was all the blood?

"I've been informed there is ample evidence tying these new

killings to the others," the judge said. "We do know they're connected? More blood was found on this young lady, after all, than at all of the other crime scenes combined."

"Her fingerprints and some footprints have now been identified at other scenes," Pilson affirmed.

"But no evidence of anyone else? A larger, stronger perpetrator?"

"No, your honor."

"And now she wishes to recount the events of the killings to one young"—he looked down at his papers—"Michael Jensen?"

"Which is a ridiculous notion," Pilson began. But the judge silenced him.

"I think it's time to hear from the girl in question. Miss Hale?"

Marie looked up. "Yes, sir?"

"Why would you want to give your statement in this way?"

She looked at Mr. Pilson. "He wants to say I killed them when I didn't."

"And do you understand that anything you say during the investigation can be used against you in a court of law?"

"Yes, sir."

"And do you understand that under this agreement you have been offered no protections against further prosecution—no deals—and may become subject to punishment depending upon what is discovered through your statements?"

Marie hesitated again, this time for much longer. "I just want to tell my story. And for him not to be able to kill me for something I didn't do!"

"Kill you?" the judge asked, and looked to Pilson.

"Your honor, in the State of Nebraska one does not need to be the perpetrator of a murder in order to be convicted of felony murder," Mr. Pilson said. "And the conviction may constitute a sentence of capital punishment."

The judge blinked. "The death penalty?"

We were all silent. Marie was so young. And a girl.

"Yes, your honor," said Pilson. "And just so there is no future confusion on the part of Miss Hale, I want it known that I believe the State of Nebraska has a right to justice on behalf of these young people whose lives have been cruelly taken."

Marie's attorney, Mr. Porter, stood quickly, skidding his chair slightly across the marble floor.

"Your honor, are we discussing execution for a girl who is willing to fully cooperate—?"

"As she sees fit," Pilson said. "She's only cooperating as she sees fit."

"She is fifteen years old," Mr. Porter said.

"Nearly sixteen. Based on the birth date she has provided. Not that we've been able to verify it or to find record in any state of a person by the name of Marie Catherine Hale. . . ." He leafed through his papers as if he might suddenly find some. "Yet the State of Minnesota is ready to accept whatever tale this alleged murderess wants to tell, when she stands accused of participating in the willful slaughter of fifteen individuals, including a father, mother, and son killed with their youngest daughter watching.

"I had heard that Minnesota was a kind part of the country,

but perhaps 'kind' was the wrong word. Perhaps the word is 'fool-hardy.'"

My dad gave a soft, annoyed snort. I expected that the judge would remind Mr. Pilson that he was standing before a Minnesota court. But he turned his attention to Marie.

"Miss Hale."

"Yes, your honor?"

"Do you understand that you are entitled to a defense and are in no way obligated to admit to any involvement or wrongdoing prior to your trial?"

"I don't want there to be a trial."

"Do you mean then to enter a plea of guilty and waive your right to a trial by a jury of your peers?"

"No, sir. I only want to tell Michael what happened."

"Miss Hale, how exactly are you acquainted with Michael Jensen?"

"He's the sheriff's son. He was there when I was brought in. And he's visited me a couple of times."

"Has he made you any promises? Coerced you in any way?"

"No, sir."

"And you," he said to me, "Mr. Jensen. Are you willing to undertake the recording of Miss Hale's accounting, knowing the grievous responsibility it entails?"

"I am, your honor."

"Your honor," said Marie, "all I ask is to stay at the jail in Black Deer Falls and tell my story to who I choose. I don't want anything else."

The judge looked at Marie, sadly, like he thought she was making a mistake.

"Why not tell an adult?" he asked. "Mr. Porter, or even that nice lady behind you?" He gestured to my mother.

"Because, sir," she replied, "I know I'm young but I've been around long enough to know that you can't really trust adults."

"Sweetheart, that's not true."

"I only want to tell Michael."

"But why?"

"Because he's the only one who'll believe me."

The judge waited a long time, until he was sure she wouldn't be moved.

"Counselors, approach."

Pilson and Mr. Norquist went, with poor Mr. Porter hurrying behind. Mr. Porter would tell me later that he had bargained for all he was worth. That nothing swayed the Nebraska DA except the dangling of the bigger fish: if Marie gave up her accomplice and he was subsequently convicted, Mr. Pilson would lobby his governor to spare Marie's life.

"Marie Catherine Hale," the judge said. "It is the decision of this court that you be granted your request. In Minnesota you were arrested and in Minnesota you will stay."

Pilson scowled. "The State of Nebraska would ask that it be allowed to appoint its own investigators to verify whatever claims are made by the accused."

"You spend your taxpayers' money however you see fit, Mr. Pilson."

Mr. Porter cleared his throat. "And should Miss Hale's confession lead to the capture or arrest of the primary perpetrator, we would argue for leniency in sentencing."

"Mr. Porter, that is an argument for another day." The judge banged his gavel, and Mr. Porter shrank. Over the years that he had been our prosecutor, I'd seen him go before Judge Vernon lots of times. But that day he seemed rattled, like he had never pled a case.

As we walked out of the building, well behind Marie and the throng of reporters, I heard Pilson call my name.

"Young Michael Jensen," he said, and shook my hand.

"Yes, sir."

"Thank you for coming here today, son." He smiled. It was all ease and no hard feelings. "I guess I'll see you back in Black Deer Falls." He walked away. We'd pass him again in front of the courthouse, surrounded by reporters.

"He's coming back to Black Deer Falls?" I asked.

"By the time all this is over, I expect he'll nearly be a legal resident," quipped Mr. Porter, and my dad chuckled. Mr. Porter looked at me regretfully. "Kidding aside," he said, "you know this is only just beginning. It isn't just justice that hangs in the balance. It's Marie Hale's life. None of this is going to be easy. Or fast."

He was right about that. Marie Catherine Hale would be with us into the winter, until she was transferred to Lincoln for her trial, and execution.

"Something else on your mind, Ed?" my dad asked. "You seem uneasy."

"I suppose I am. There's something about Marie. Something that hasn't sat quite right."

"What's that?" my dad asked.

"She has never once indicated that she's sorry."

CHAPTER ELEVEN

An Unqualified Interviewer

BY THE TIME I returned to school the next day, word about the confession had already spread throughout Black Deer Falls. Ever since the funerals and our ill-advised break-in of the Carlsons' home, my name had been passed around in frantic whispers, and I kept thinking of what Marie had said, how she figured that Steve and I hadn't been friends. How we weren't a matched type: Steve the all-American athlete and me the by-the-book sheriff's kid who read too much and didn't care if his baseball team made the playoffs.

Before Marie, people had known who I was, but I'd still been invisible. After the court decided I could interview her, it was like I'd been painted red. My English teacher, Mr. Janek, watched me from behind his desk for the first five minutes of class as if he expected me to present a note asking to be excused. When I didn't, he got up and stumbled through his lesson, making the chalk cry against the board and looking at me every time he did it, like it was my fault.

In the halls between classes, I existed in a bubble of quiet. Except for Percy.

"So," he said, and leaned against my locker. "When do you start?"

"I'm going to see her after school. But I don't know if she'll say anything important, or if I'm supposed to—" I stopped. It occurred to me for the millionth time that I had no idea what I was doing.

"You nervous?"

"Yeah. Really nervous."

My dad had coached me a little, running me through the facts of the case, cautioning me against leading her in one direction or another. "Don't put any ideas into her head," he'd said. "Just let her talk." He'd brought out a map of the United States and marked the locations of the murders with a red pen, writing the dates beside them and tracing the likely trail of the killers along the highways through Nebraska to Iowa, to Wisconsin and back to us. "If there are any inconsistencies, don't call her out. Don't be confrontational. We can go through it all together, after you're finished."

"What have you heard," I asked Percy, "around town?"

Percy shrugged. "Jeannie says there's a women's coalition forming at church, but they can't decide whether it's a coalition to run her out of town or to protest her being locked up in the first place."

"Is Jeannie still keeping that shotgun by the door?"

He nodded. My parents were still locking the extra locks, too, and keeping Dawn's curfew well before dark. It wasn't over for us. The eyes on me weren't just curious; they wanted me to do something. I was used to them looking at my dad that way. I never realized how heavy it would feel.

"The Nebraska DA wants to kill her, Percy."

He blinked.

"But he won't," he said. "I mean, lock her up forever, sure. But she's a girl. Nobody's going to execute a girl, no matter what she did."

"Maybe." I looked at the clock on the wall above our lockers. "I don't know how to talk to her. I don't know what to say."

"What do you mean?" he asked.

"I mean she's gone through something." But I couldn't figure out how to tell him what I meant. That something had happened to Marie Hale in a way that nothing had ever happened to us. Guilty or innocent, she'd traveled through something terrible. That made her different, and it made her intimidating, no matter whether she was younger than I was or if she was a girl.

"Maybe I should talk to Mr. McBride," I said. "Do you think he would mind?"

"Do I think he would mind," Percy said, and made a face. "I think he'll jump all over it. Go over at lunch and I'll cover for you in history."

By covering for me, he meant clowning so hard that Miss Murray couldn't think of anything besides rapping him across the knuckles. Good old Percy.

So at lunch, I made my way across town to the *Star*, where Mr. McBride welcomed me despite it being during school hours.

"Michael," he said when I poked my head into his office. He stood up and came over to shake my hand. He never treated me like a kid—not since I had told him I wanted to become a journalist. He treated me like I already was one, even though I was really just another of his delivery boys. "What brings you by?" I stood there for a moment, dumbfounded, but he just smiled, a thin man with dark brown hair that my mother judged as "a little too long but becoming for his profession." He wore a gray button-up shirt and a tie, like he did most days. He almost never wore a jacket. He had glasses with black frames over blue eyes, and they made him look sharp. Clever. I used to wish my own eyes were no good so I would need a pair.

"You don't need to tell me why you're here," he said. "I heard about the Hale confession." He walked back around his desk and sat down, an invitation to sit across from him.

"It's really more of an interview," I said. And what an interview it was. After it was over I could attend any journalism program that I wanted, and the college would probably pay for it. Not bad for a kid from Nowhere, Minnesota.

Mr. McBride knew that, too, but he just smiled, happy to wait in the silence. He was a good interviewer.

"It shouldn't be me," I blurted finally. "It should be you. Or Walter Cronkite."

"My name in the same breath as Walter Cronkite's." He grinned. "I appreciate that. But there's really no way of knowing whether

I, or Walter, would fare any better than you. She requested you, Michael. And she could have requested anyone."

I managed a laugh. "I guess I would just . . . I could use some advice. My dad's coached me on procedure, but that's not the same."

"I suppose you try to find common ground."

I looked at him and thought of Marie the night of the murders. Her eyes, staring out from behind a mask of blood.

"I don't know if I want to find common ground."

Mr. McBride sighed. "I knew the Carlsons, too, Michael. But Marie Catherine Hale is still a person. Still a human being. Any commonalities you come across are normal, and nothing to feel guilty about."

"Maybe I'm worried that I won't remain . . . objective."

He watched me for a long time. He probably figured that I was going to make a mess of things for everyone involved. I'd always thought of him as a sort of outsider in his small neatly kept house on the west end of Main Street. Friendly, but distant, as if as our designated recorder, he needed to reserve room for judgment. Some thought of him as strange or snobbish. Some pitied him for his wife, Maggie, who was also a bit of an oddity: she wore her hair in pretty braided buns and mumbled my name every time we met so I wondered if she actually knew it. They had no children, which some would say was another mark against them, and my mother noted that the couple did not speak to each other much at parties.

But there was a photograph of them on his desk, taken on their wedding day. In it, they looked happy, but I couldn't really say.

They kept to themselves, and it was that more than anything that separated them from us, in this town that seeks to know everything for the good of all.

"What do you want, Michael?" he asked. "What are you after? And think very hard before you answer."

"I'm after the truth," I said finally.

"That's what all good journalists are after. That's all you're looking for."

CHAPTER TWELVE

Interview Begins, September 1958

BEFORE I LEFT Mr. McBride's office to go to the jail and see Marie, he'd said one more thing: "Michael, know your stuff.

"It isn't for you to judge her guilt or innocence. It's only for you to uncover the facts. And being armed with all the information will only help with that."

Maybe I should have taken that advice. My dad had already given me the file on the Carlsons, and letters had been sent to the Wisconsin and Iowa DAs requesting their case files. But I hadn't had the nerve to look. I'd tried—I must've opened it ten times. But I wasn't ready to see those photographs. I wasn't ready to see Steve like that. I knew that once I had, that would be the only way I could ever think of him: dead, and with his throat cut.

And besides, if I'm honest, I already felt like an expert in the Bloodless Murders, just from reading the papers.

When I got to the station, Bert went to fetch Marie down to the interrogation room. While I waited, I poked my head into my dad's office.

"Hi, Dad."

"Hi, son. Shouldn't you be in school?"

"Maybe?" I suggested.

"Well. I'm sure Principal Wilkens will understand. But if he wants to set you to washing blackboards beside Percy for a week, I'm not going to argue."

"Wouldn't that cut into my time with Miss Hale?" I asked, and he narrowed his eyes like I was too smart for my own good. But before he could say anything more, Bert walked Marie through the station. She seemed listless; her arms hung at her sides and her shoes scuffed against the floor.

"Go on," my dad said.

I went into the interrogation room.

"You let me know if you need anything, Mikey," Bert said. Then he tipped his hat to Marie and hurried out. He stood right outside for the duration of the interview.

Marie turned her head toward me. She had her hair held back like she had at the courthouse, tied with a long black ribbon.

"Mikey? Is that what you like to be called?"

"No. Definitely not Mikey." I hate when Bert calls me that. But he'd been doing it since I was eight and I can't break him of it now.

"Shouldn't you be in school?"

"I guess so."

She gave a sort of smirk. "Special privileges. You're welcome."

"When's the last time you were in school, Marie?"

"I never did any high school. Had to stop. Get a job."

I knew lots of kids who stopped coming to school, but only after their sophomore year—farm kids who were needed at home. And they were mostly boys.

"How . . . how have you been in here?"

"I'd be better if you brought me those smokes," she said. "Why?"

"When I was younger and we lived upstairs, I used to have a hard time sleeping. I could hear the echoes from the jail downstairs or the cars starting in the parking lot."

Marie shrugged. "I like it fine. It's nice, actually, to know that there's always someone awake and paying attention." She stretched her shoulders and rolled her head a little on her neck. She said she slept fine but she seemed tired. "When *I* was younger, I used to have a hard time sleeping, too. But only because of the kind of kid I was."

"What kind of kid was that?"

"The kind who knew even back then that the dark was a whole other world. That it soaked up the daylight one like a biscuit dipped in coffee."

I sat down across from her. Her large hazel eyes were too old for her face. It might seem like I'm lying about that—inserting it after the fact. But I always thought that about Marie. That the trauma had aged her. Took the life out and left something else behind.

On the table between us, I laid out sheets of paper. Clutched in my fingers was my most reliable ink pen.

"Well," she said. "Aren't you eager."

I started to put them away but she shook her head. I'd imagined things going differently. I'd imagined myself shouting questions and her breaking down and confessing in tears. But confess to what? Anyone looking could see she wasn't a killer. Anyone except for Pilson, and he only wanted someone to pay—not for justice, but for the headlines and his picture in the papers.

"How did you get mixed up in all this, Marie?"

She shrugged and looked past me. "Same way every girl gets into this much trouble." She looked back. "A boy."

"A boy? What boy?"

My pen hovered in midair.

"What happened to that one you came in here with the other night?" she asked. "The one who got beat up in the parking lot."

"Joe? He's staying with friends. He's safe."

Marie snorted.

"He's not safe."

"Maybe his dad will finally straighten up, now that my dad's involved." But even when I said it, I knew it wasn't true. Marie sighed.

"Well, where do you want to start?" she asked.

"How about with the boy's name?"

She shook her head.

"Then how about some confirmation? That the person who killed the Carlsons and those graduate students, Stacy Lee Brandberg and Richard Covey, Cheryl Warrens"—I threw in the name of the

murdered truck stop waitress, a victim who was rarely mentioned—
"was the same person."

Marie sat quietly, fingernails scratching at the top of the table.
She seemed almost annoyed.

"Was he the same person?"

"Yes," she said finally.

"And who was it?"

"A man."

"A man? You said it was a boy earlier."

She shrugged like there wasn't any difference.

"Will you tell me his name?"

"Nope."

"Why not?"

"Because it wouldn't matter. It was just something he went by."

"So you didn't know his real name?" No one was going to
be happy about that. It was the piece of information they most
wanted. But she could still tell us enough to find him.

"What else can you tell me about him?"

"Not much. He was handsome."

"Handsome how?"

"Like a film star."

"Was he tall?" I asked. "Dark- or fair-haired?"

"Not tall," she said. "But he could be seen when he wanted to
be. You know that kind of person? Presence." She snapped her
fingers. "Just like that. And gone just as fast."

"You knew him well?"

"I came to."

"Had you known him all your life?"

Marie sighed again, and I started to panic. Maybe it wasn't going the way she'd imagined either. Maybe she'd change her mind about the whole thing.

"What about the blood?" I asked. "How did the blood get onto you like that?"

Marie frowned. "I don't want to start like this."

"Okay. That's okay. We can start wherever you want."

"I don't know where I want to start."

But we had to start somewhere. I tried to be patient. After all, what were only words to me were much more to her—they were images and sounds, screams and bright red splashes. They were memories.

Then I thought of the Carlson farmhouse. The pile of folded laundry. The rolled-up rug stained by dripped and pooled blood. I thought about the strange red circle that she had left on it. I really hadn't stopped thinking about that, or about her, sticky and soaked from head to toe. She'd looked like she'd walked through a fountain, like the blood had sprayed everywhere. But I'd been inside that house. I'd seen the spotless walls.

"I'll have to know about the blood eventually," I said.

"Just not yet."

"Why? I'm not here to judge you, Marie."

"Maybe not, but you will."

Despite her tough-cookie routine and the scowl on her face, she was scared. I was scared, too. She had seen things that I couldn't imagine. She had done things. Horrible things, yes, but I had never done anything. I'd never even ventured outside of Minnesota except for family vacations.

I reached across the table and laid my hand over hers. It wasn't something I would normally do; it had taken me three dates with Carol to do as much last winter. Marie looked at me curiously. She was a pretty girl, and she knew that. She turned her palm over and curled her fingers around mine. They were small and cold.

"The weapon," she said. "Everyone's wondering about that, aren't they? It was a straight razor."

I took my hand back and wrote. The surety of my penmanship was a comfort. I'd taken shorthand courses at school for the last two years. So had Percy, actually, though he only enrolled to be nearer to all the girls learning for secretarial work.

"The same straight razor every time?" I asked. I've always thought of a straight razor as dangerous, less a tool than a wild animal—something to handle with constant care, same as a scalpel or a hunting rifle. Things like that have a will of their own; they're designed to cut, to injure, and they carry that purpose inside them like a frequency on the radio. Having read about the state of the victims in the papers that summer—deep cuts to the neck, the wrists, the inner thighs—I had already figured that the weapon was something of that sort. But when Marie confirmed it, the image of the straight razor loomed in my mind: real and dangerously light. I could practically hear the sound of it sliding open.

"Almost always the same," Marie replied quietly.

"But what happened to the blood?" I'd seen my dad cut once at the barber, just a nick. It took a moment to start bleeding, like the cut was so fast that it surprised the skin. But these went straight to the vein. There must have been so much. There should have been a mess.

"He drank it."

I stopped writing.

"What do you mean, 'He drank it'?"

But before she could respond, all hell broke loose. Mr. Pilson burst into the station and started to complain loudly about some kind of writ or motion. Both his and my father's voices raised; he actually tried to get into the interrogation room but Bert's big body blocked the door.

"What's he doing here?" Marie cried.

"It's all right, Marie." I stood up. I don't know who I was trying to comfort. Then the voices softened, and Bert let Pilson in.

He stalked in angrily and my dad came in and put his arm across Pilson's chest, as near as he could manage without touching. I'd seen him employ that move before when he was trying to corral Fred Meeks, the farmer, when he was on one of his more belligerent benders.

"Why is he in here alone, without counsel?"

"That's what she requested," my dad said, and Pilson cast him a rude look.

"I want to be here for every interview."

"Then I don't want to talk," said Marie.

"Mr. Pilson, let's step into my office. I'm sure Michael's been making good progress."

"Good progress," he sneered. Truthfully I thought I was until she said the part about the killer drinking the blood.

"What's our killer's name, then, Michael?" he asked.

I thought of a tongue cleaning the edge of a blade. Cleaning it like a cat, over and over, until every drop was gone. But it couldn't have been that way. It would have had to be collected and drunk as from a bowl or a glass, like red milk, and the idea of that made my stomach flip.

"Well?"

"She hasn't told me."

"And I won't," Marie added, and I wished she'd be quiet. If she mentioned the blood drinking we were as good as through. Pilson would go back to the judge and they'd laugh us out of the room.

"Then what good is this?" Pilson asked.

"What good is a name?" Marie responded.

"So we can find him. So we can catch him."

"You haven't even found me, and I'm sitting right in front of you."

"That's because I suspect you've given us a fake name. Miss Hale."

Marie swallowed, and her eyes narrowed angrily. For how much of a liar they took her for, she didn't seem to be very good at it. She had no poker face.

"Bert," my dad said, "please escort Miss Hale back up to her cell."

"Yes, sure, Rick." He slid through us and got her up. The look Marie gave Pilson as she left—I wouldn't have been surprised if she had stuck out her tongue.

"You know she can't be trusted, don't you, son?" Pilson said after she was gone. "You know she's just buying time."

"I don't know that," I said. "Not yet."

He turned to me and his face transformed, all the anger gone. "I know she might not look like much more than a girl, but Marie Catherine Hale is a young woman. A conniver. She'll say anything to gain your sympathy. She'll cry. She'll bat her eyes. A girl like that is prone to lies by her very nature. She's not to be believed."

"Yes, sir," I said. And quick as that, he walked right out of the station.

Bert came down the stairs.

"Well?" he asked. "What'd he want? How'd you get him to leave?"

"We haven't seen the last of him," my dad said. And we hadn't. Benjamin Pilson took a room at Mrs. B.'s boardinghouse over on the corner of 9th and Pine. It's nicer than the motel out by the highway, where visiting patrolmen often stay over. Mrs. B.'s serves a fine breakfast every morning and brunch on Saturdays, open to the public. The other four rooms are most often uninhabited, and several of the ladies' church groups use the parlor to host events and socials. I like to think of Mr. Pilson hunched over the desk in his lace-furnished room, poring over his notes and case files while the Lutheran knitting circle laughs and gossips on the floor below. He stayed with us for weeks on end—God knows what was happening in Nebraska while he was away. I heard my parents talking about him a few times, saying how the case had become an obsession, how he'd hung his whole career on it.

"Michael."

I pushed away from the wall and turned to my dad. "Yes, sir?"

"Take Mr. Pilson with a grain of salt."

"Yes, sir."

"He's had his career but I've also had mine. I've interrogated a lot of people. Only a few have been true liars. The others . . ." He rubbed his eyes. It had been another long day for him, in a long line of long days. "I just mean that lots of people think they know what they know, or know what they saw. They're not liars. They're just wrong."

CHAPTER THIRTEEN

An Impossible Story

I GAVE MARIE a few days to cool off after that initial interview. And so I could, too. My dad's words ran through my head beside Pilson's warning. *She's not to be trusted. She's a liar by nature. She's not a liar. She's just wrong.*

But how wrong could she have gotten it? How could she be mistaken when she said he drank the blood?

I couldn't tell my dad about that part. If I had told him so soon, he would have called the whole thing off. But I did tell him about the razor. He passed that detail on to Pilson, but neither of them seemed impressed. What good was a murder weapon without the actual weapon? It was just another phantom, and one we could have guessed.

I replayed that first interview in my head so many times. Too many times, and now the real memory is lost. I can't remember how she looked when she told me what the murder weapon was, if her lips curled around the words *straight razor* or if she spat them like a bad taste. I don't remember the tone of her voice when she said, "He drank it," or if there was any hesitation before she replied. I don't remember if it sounded like she was making it up as she went.

Of course, I knew she had to be. Because what she was saying—what she was saying it was that had killed all those people and that had killed Steve and his family . . . was a vampire.

A vampire. Like capes and bats and Bela Lugosi.

When I finally went back to the station, I managed to get in without anyone seeing me. My dad was out, Charlie was nowhere to be seen, and the reception desk was empty. I didn't feel like waiting, so I went up to Marie's cell, hoping with every step that she'd take that one part back. Recant it or even ignore it completely. Had I opened the door and found her sitting there smiling, seemingly without any memory of what she'd said, I would've gone along with it.

"Where you been?" she asked when I opened the door. She seemed excitable, and relieved to see me.

"My dad wanted me to stay away until everything got sorted with Mr. Pilson."

"And now it has?"

"Not exactly. This is just a visit, not an interview."

She glanced at my hands, which were empty. I'd brought no paper, no pen. And we were upstairs, alone except for the bars. All of a sudden the cell felt less like a cell and more like a girl's bedroom where I wasn't allowed.

"Why did you say what you did?" I asked.

"Which part?"

I scowled, and she started to laugh.

"I'm sorry," she said. "I didn't mean to just tell you like that. I didn't know I was even *going* to tell you. But the look on your face!"

"So it was a joke? It was supposed to be funny?"

"No." Her laughter died off and she cocked her head, pouting like I was kind of a drag. "This isn't funny. But some things *are* funny no matter how not funny something is."

What about those student nurses? I wanted to say. What about those kids in Wisconsin, lying dead on the ground? Were they funny, too?

But that would've stopped Marie cold.

"I didn't expect you to believe it right away," she said, and shrugged. "I know how it sounds."

Like you've been watching too many movies, I wanted to say. Like you're crazy. But instead I asked, "Can you prove it?"

"Seeing is believing." She sighed. "And I can't exactly show you. But yes, I think I can. After I tell you everything. I mean, the truth is the truth."

The truth is the truth. But what's the truth about vampires? What are the facts about fiction? There didn't seem to be much point in going on if this was the story she was set on telling. But just the same, I didn't want to stop. So I thought about what Mr. McBride had told me, about what my job was. There was still a killer on the loose, and Marie's story was the only one we had.

"Okay," I said.

"Okay," she said, and smiled.

"They're going to lock you in a hospital somewhere, you know. Maybe they'll lock me in, too."

"You'll be fine," she said. "Sheriff's son."

"Is that why you picked me? That's why lots of people pick me."

"For your clean ironed shirt and your handsome face? Sure. And because of how you helped your friend that night when his father got out of line. And because you just happened to be there." She shrugged. "It's like you said: they'd have thrown me in a loony bin. Anyone else wouldn't have given me a chance."

We watched each other for a long time, her seated on her bed and me standing near the door. I didn't know what we would be when the interview was over: enemies or allies. I didn't know if Marie would be alive. If she would be in prison or free. I turned to go.

"You'll come back, though?" she asked.

"Yeah. I'll come back."

By the following Monday, my dad and the attorneys reached a compromise with Pilson, so the interviews could continue. When I found out I was relieved, but mostly excited. It was becoming nearly impossible to pay attention in class, but none of my teachers expressed concern, as if the importance of the investigation outweighed the importance of my education. Only one teacher spoke up: Miss Murray. People noted that of all the faculty she was the least affected by the Bloodless Murders and had been heard more than once criticizing folks for gossiping about the Carlsons' deaths. People around town started calling her "high and mighty" and said she had a lot of nerve looking down on us in the wake of a tragedy.

The other teachers let me go. I was never penalized for late work. No one called on me in class. Even Coach Harvey, my baseball coach and the tenth-grade physical education teacher, had only good things to say when the interviews started. Of course, that's before he knew I would be quitting the team. When I finally did, he got so mad he almost punched a wall, though I don't know why. I'd never been a standout player, and he must've known that I only joined because Percy was on the team already.

I think he sensed that Marie would pull me away. From the start, folks in Black Deer Falls resented her for the brutal change she had brought, and they were unwilling to give anything else up to her, least of all the steady son of their admired sheriff.

I went back to the jail to continue the interviews on Monday afternoon and Marie was already there, hands folded in her lap uncuffed while my father bent over a tape recorder, boxy and gray. It took up most of the space on one end of the table.

"What's that?" I asked.

"Mr. Pilson's compromise," he replied. "If he can't be in the room, he wants everything on tape. This contraption will record your conversations, and I'll deliver the tape to him every night."

"Every night?"

"Or every week. Whatever I can reasonably fit into my schedule," my dad said, and smirked. He punched a button with his index finger, bent over the tape recorder and said, "October sixth, 1958, four oh seven p.m. Interview of Marie Catherine Hale. Recording taken by Sheriff Richard Jensen, now leaving the room. Interview conducted by Michael Jensen." He straightened, and nodded to me before exiting and closing the door behind him.

"You agreed to this?" I asked Marie. She had her hair tied back with the black ribbon again, and the white blouse was tied at her waist and rolled to her elbows over the sleeves of a dark green sweater.

"He'll hear it anyway," Marie said. "Sooner or later, everyone will hear it." Then her expression turned impish, and she reached up and hit a button to stop the tape.

I jumped. "I don't think you can do that."

"Will they know? Is it wrong that part of me wants to tell you lies and boring things just so Mr. Pilson will have to listen to them for hours and hours?"

I smiled. "Maybe he'll fall asleep and have to start all over again when he wakes up."

Marie laughed. Then she reached back to the tape recorder and switched it on again.

"Should we continue where we left off?" I cleared my throat. The recording bothered me more than it seemed to bother Marie. It made me self-conscious, and a little suspicious—tape recordings were a tactic used by insidious foreign governments. But, I supposed, it was only insidious if you didn't know that you were being taped.

"I guess."

I set out my paper and pen. Even though the conversations were being recorded I wanted my own notes, and the recorder couldn't capture everything: Marie's demeanor, her nervous tics and gestures, whether she seemed sad or bored or conflicted.

"Where we left off," I muttered. But I didn't even know where that was. Or rather, I knew, but the phrase, "Tell me more about this vampire fellow" wouldn't come out of my mouth.

"Does your mother iron your shirts so neatly?" Marie asked. "Or do you do it?"

"My mother does."

"I like your mother. She found me those clothes for court and gave me her lipstick. You have a little sister?"

"I do," I said. "Her name is Dawn."

"That's a nice name."

"Do you have any sisters, Marie? Any brothers?"

She shook her head. "It was just my mother and me. Until he came along."

"He? You mean the killer?"

"No," Marie said, and rolled her eyes. "I mean, him. My step-father." That word she did say like a bad taste.

"You didn't like him?"

"No."

"Why not?"

"Because he was terrible."

"How was he terrible?"

She shifted around in her seat. "You know it'd be nice if we could do these in my cell instead of this little room."

"Maybe," I said. "We could move the tape recorder onto the kitchen table. I'd have to stay outside the bars."

"But you could sit close, if you wanted."

She was toying with me, flirting. Batting her eyelashes, like Pilson warned me she would.

"How was your stepfather terrible?" I asked again. "In what way?"

She exhaled sharply.

"In the same way that lots of men are terrible."

"Like in the way that my friend Joe's father is?" I asked, but Marie looked into the corner and refused to answer.

"All right, then, what can you tell me about the first murder? The murder of Peter Knupp." When I said his name, she glanced at me and then away as if he was of no interest. "Did you know him before the murder?" No response. "Was he chosen at random? A robbery, maybe? He was alone in his home—"

Marie sighed but otherwise remained silent.

"He was cut at the neck, and the inner thigh. Bled out."

"Yes, Michael," she said finally. "We were just reminded of this by Mr. Pilson at the hearing."

"Well, do you have any feelings about it? Did you see it happen? He was the first victim; it can't have been easy—"

"He wasn't the first victim."

I stared into her steady hazel eyes.

"The first victim hasn't been found."

My pulse pounded. Another body, another Bloodless Murder. One that no one had discovered or simply not connected to the case? A dozen questions hurtled through my head, crowding it so I couldn't think straight. "Who?"

"I don't want to talk about this."

"But this is what we're here to talk about."

"Not like this."

"Marie, they want to execute you."

"Well, they can't, all right? Because I didn't know! I didn't know what he was and what he was going to do. I thought he was just going to take me away. I didn't know he was going to kill her!"

"Kill who?"

"My mother."

My eyes flickered to the tape recorder. "He killed your mother," I said. Killed her, perhaps right before Marie's eyes.

"And my stepfather. The first murders were my mother and my stepfather. There were two."

"When did the murders occur?" I reached for my pen.

"June," she said, her voice toneless. "Early June. The second, maybe. Or the third."

Early June. Peter Knupp hadn't been discovered until August 3. It had been supposed that he had been dead for several days, but that was still a long time between killings.

"What were their names?" I asked.

"I'm not giving you their names," she said. "I gave you mine."

I wanted to press for more, but I didn't have the heart. Marie's eyes were shiny. She was trying not to cry.

"Do you want to stop for now?"

"Yes," she said. "I'd like to stop."

The minute I offered I wondered if maybe I should have pushed harder. I wondered what Matt McBride would do. He would never shy away from the hard questions.

"All right," I said. "But next time we'll talk more, about the blood drinker."

Marie chuckled a little as she wiped her face. "The blood drinker. That's a good name. He'd like that."

CHAPTER FOURTEEN

A Surprising Discovery

AS MY DAD and the investigators reeled at the news of the murders of Marie's mother and stepfather, my mind kept returning to Marie's story. As they searched for the murdered couple—running down lead after lead of bodies found alone or separately, whether they had died from blood loss or not—I walked around in a haze, trying to think of what could make Marie tell me the things she had. A vampire. The pale, waxy-skinned, walking undead. She was pulling my leg. Except she didn't seem to think it was a joke.

I considered that she could have been fooled. That the killer had pulled off that much of a trick through sleight of hand and props. People had been fooled into things before. All those people in Exeter, Rhode Island, who dug up and cut apart Mercy Brown. In the early 1700s, in Southeastern Europe, a rural town had been so convinced of a vampire in their midst that the government had to install official investigators, and all talk of blood drinking was grounds for imprisonment. That was a long time ago—but not so long ago, people were convinced that a glug of snake oil could cure whatever ailed you.

I'd always thought of those people as gullible.

Marie did not seem gullible.

The Nebraska authorities couldn't find the bodies of Marie's mother and stepfather. Not for all their searching. After a while they figured she'd just been lying again, another lie piled on top of the rest.

"Let them think so," Marie said as the days ticked by. "Let them keep looking."

"You don't want them found," I said one afternoon in the interrogation room. "Your parents?"

"My stepfather wasn't my parent," she said.

"Then why tell us about them at all?"

She shrugged and gestured to the space around and behind her. "Gives them something to do." And by *them* I took her to mean the investigators.

"You never ask me if we've caught him," I said.

"Well, I figure I'd have heard if you did," she said. "And besides. I know that you won't."

"We will," I said, "if you help us."

She shook her head.

"What can I tell you anyway, stuck in here? Any plans he had could have changed. All those men out combing through fields should go home and go to bed. Give their poor dogs a rest." Then she cocked her head at me and asked about Percy's Labradors.

About how the other dogs were that she'd seen through the crack in the drapes at the Carlson farm. She seemed more interested in talking about them, and we talked about dogs for the rest of the session, and how she'd never had one of her own.

That's how it went with Marie sometimes. If I kept at her, there were days I was able to turn the conversation back around, but usually not.

"Don't be rattled," Mr. McBride said when I stopped by his office in early October. "But don't be deterred. Right now she has the luxury of the court's patience. When they catch him, that will all change."

"When we catch him, they'll force her to talk?" I asked.

"Just the opposite," he said. "After he's caught, what she has to say will hardly matter at all."

"Want to come to my place this weekend?" Percy asked me as we walked through the parking lot to his car one day after school. I hadn't seen him much. I'd been at the jail with Marie almost every day after class.

"Huh?" I said.

"Mo got new hunting gear. We can try it on, scout the places for the stand." Percy had been going on about a new hunting stand for weeks. He'd had his eye on a good-looking buck. He'd seen it close to a dozen times that summer, and knowing Percy, that meant he'd become far too attached to the animal to ever be able to shoot it.

"Sounds good," I said.

"You planning on asking Carol to Sadie Hawkins?" he asked.

"Isn't the point of a Sadie Hawkins for the girls to ask us?" Percy knew this perfectly well; he'd spent the better part of the week avoiding speaking with Sandy Millpoint just to give Rebecca Knox a chance to work up the nerve.

"I've seen Carol looking your way, that's all." We got to Percy's car and I set my books on top while he lit a quick smoke. Carol was across the parking lot, standing with some friends around her green four-door Ford. She had the sides of her bright blond hair pinned back with little pearl clips and she looked fantastic: peach lipstick and blue eyes—she was nearly as tall as I was when she wore high heels. But looking at her that day, I found myself comparing her to Marie—her light hair to Marie's dark; her tall, long-legged grace with Marie's smaller, sharper quickness. I knew it was wrong to think of Marie in the same way that I thought about Carol. I knew that from the start.

"I guess I'll go if she asks me."

We got into Percy's car and he tapped the dash, then the steering wheel, and pumped the brakes twice, a ritual that he insisted had kept the car going all these years. I shoved my books against a burlap sack in the middle of the bench seat and rested my arm atop them.

Percy glanced at me as he backed the car out. Normally this kind of news about Carol would have dominated the conversation for the rest of the night. We were both a little surprised to find that I didn't care. I looked at her again and still felt a small familiar tug inside when she smiled. They'd be going to the café after school for fries and shakes. But not me. I would be going to the jail. I wondered how Percy fared, going without me. Being a clown, he could fit in anywhere, with anyone. I envied him that sometimes.

"It's strange to think about dances after all this," I said. "After Steve and his parents." I looked out the window and thought I felt Percy give me a nudge through the burlap sack, almost like a caress.

"Life," Percy said. "It goes on."

That it did. Unfair as it was, we couldn't huddle around Steve's grave forever. I looked across the sports fields, where the school grounds abutted the Lutheran cemetery—pretty, groomed hills lined with headstones and small granite monuments, a few angel statuettes that I'd heard some folks call very nice but a tad grandiose. It wasn't the same cemetery where the Carlsons were buried, but I felt like they were there all the same.

Again Percy nudged my arm through the sack. Only both of Percy's hands were on the wheel.

"Percy, what do you have in this sack?"

"I thought that was your sack," he said as I lifted it up and a fat three-foot-long snake fell out across the bench seat.

Percy screamed. He jerked the wheel and sent the car onto the curb, nearly taking out the tailgate of a parked brown pickup truck. Then he threw the car into park and we both leaped out.

"What in the jumping hells is that?"

The snake's gray-and-black body—if you could call it a body—writhed sluggishly across the worn leather into the space where I'd just been sitting. I darted forward and shut the door. So did Percy, on the other side.

"Shoot! We should have waited until it tried to crawl out and then slammed it in between! How did it get in there?"

By then, our shouting had attracted a small crowd, and someone went running back into the school. It wasn't five minutes later that Bert arrived in a police car and found us all standing around looking useless. He got out with his hand on his service pistol, his eyes wild like he would need to fire at someone at any moment.

"What's going on here?"

Percy and I pointed into the car. The snake was still sprawled inside. Bert approached the window. Then he dropped his hand from his revolver and opened the door.

"What are you doing?" Percy shouted.

Bert leaned into the front seat just as Principal Wilkens arrived, jogging through the parking lot with a shotgun.

Bert pointed at him, as stern as I'd ever seen. "You put that away." Then he bent back into the car and took hold of the snake, crooning to it as sweetly as if it were a baby. "She's only a python," he said when he emerged with the snake curling eagerly around his hands and forearms. "She's not going to hurt anybody. How'd she get into your car, Percy?"

"Hell if I know," Percy exclaimed. "It was rolling around in a burlap sack. Someone must have thrown it in there."

"Who?" I asked.

He shrugged. "Everybody knows that my doors don't lock."

Bert was barely listening. He held the snake up in front of his face and looked into its eyes. "Lucky she didn't die. She was moving closer to you because she was cold. Not enough sun today to heat the car up, and reptiles are cold-blooded. They can't produce their own heat."

"How do you know so much about herpetology?" Principal Wilkens asked, and I was impressed that he knew the word; I had to look it up later in my dad's encyclopedias. Herpetology: the study of reptiles and amphibians.

Bert shrugged. "I've liked them since I was a kid. If she doesn't belong to anybody, I'll take her home. I have an empty fish tank that should do just right."

Percy glanced at me. I'd never actually been inside Bert's house, and just then I didn't particularly regret that. Bert reached into the car for the burlap sack and placed the snake tenderly inside. Then he got into his car and drove away with his new pet.

All of us kids sort of turned to Principal Wilkens, still standing there with his shotgun.

"These kinds of pranks are dangerous," he said loudly. "If anyone knows who did this to Mr. Valentine's automobile, I encourage you to speak with me in my office."

CHAPTER FIFTEEN

Good Cops

THE INCIDENT WITH the snake. I hardly gave it a thought at first. There were so many other things on my mind and nothing had come of it: we hadn't been hurt—even the snake was safe as Bert's new pet. It was a strange prank to pull but that's all I thought it was. I'd even considered it hadn't been left for me at all but for Percy. There was no reason yet to think otherwise.

The fruitless search for the bodies of Marie's mother and stepfather had distracted Pilson for a short time, but it wasn't long before he listened to the interview tapes and heard me say the words *blood drinker*. I had to come clean after that. I expected to be pulled off the case immediately. But when I told my dad he just nodded quietly, like he'd expected she would say something like that.

Pilson, on the other hand, came down like a thunderstorm— I was there when he questioned her and I've never heard such shouting from inside the interrogation room, from him and Marie alike.

"If you don't stop with these wild stories, I'll drag you back in front of a judge!"

"Go ahead and do it, then! Because this is the only story I have to tell!"

I felt for Pilson at first. I really did. Even if he went about it poorly and even if his motivation wasn't exactly pure, he was still after the truth just like the rest of us. If only there'd been an easier way to get it. In the old days, people used to believe that the corpses of murder victims would bleed if brought into the presence of their killers. But not even that would have worked in the case of Marie Hale, as those bodies had not a drop left.

I hung back with my dad near his office while Pilson had his go at Marie, and I remember how intently he listened to what was going on inside the interrogation room. How he seemed poised on the balls of his feet, ready to intervene if it went too far.

I told him that maybe the interviews were a mistake. "Maybe she really is just stalling. Maybe the only reason she chose me was because she thought she could get one over on someone her own age."

"Does Marie strike you as a liar?" he asked, and I thought about it hard, for the hundredth time.

"No, sir."

"She doesn't strike me as one either. We don't know what she went through. If she's hiding something, she's not hiding it from you so much as herself."

He stared at the interrogation room door.

"Keep going for as long as she wants to," he said. "For as long as they'll let us."

When Pilson came out, he snapped his fingers at my dad and directed us into his office. That raised my eyebrows, but my dad took a deep breath and patted me on the shoulder, his way of saying it was fine, that Mr. Pilson was upset, and we should let that one pass. We joined him in my dad's office and shut the door; he had his hands on his hips and was staring at the wall, brow creased deep.

"Look at this." He pointed to my father's calendar, a monthly of paintings of white-tailed deer. The month of October was blank except for a few scribbled appointments, and large black X's crossing off the days.

"You've had her in your custody for weeks. Weeks. And all you have is a made-up story about a dead mother and a lot of rambling about a movie monster in a cape and fake teeth. No new leads. Nothing. Nothing! Look at these—" He slapped his palm against the marked dates. "Wasted days."

My dad crossed his arms. He had a cup of coffee in his hand and raised it toward the calendar.

"You know what I see, when I look at that, Mr. Pilson? All those X's?"

"What's that?"

"Relief."

Pilson turned.

"I see days when no one died," my dad went on. "No bodies found."

"Well, you know what I see?" Pilson asked. He tore the calendar off its nail and tossed it at my dad's feet. "I see a murderer getting away."

He walked past us and left the station without another word to anyone, leaving my dad to pick up the calendar and poke a new hole for the nail. I asked Marie once why she insisted on antagonizing Pilson so badly, but she only shrugged and said that with a man like him there was no winning anyway. That even if every victim had turned up alive again she would always be guilty. Guilty of wasting his time. Guilty of being poor. Of being a girl. She said from the moment she met him she could tell that all he wanted was to find a way to strap her into Nebraska's electric chair. But the joke was on him. Because she requested hanging.

CHAPTER SIXTEEN

Pilson

I CAN'T RECALL if I disliked Benjamin Pilson on sight. He had a clean-cut, good-looking face and carried himself with confidence. He looked like you would expect a DA to look: maybe he styled himself after the ones in the movies, or maybe they styled themselves after him. I do know that almost every single thing I learned about him subsequent to that first impression made me like him less. Now, maybe I hate him. So I guess I could have hated him from the start.

I was picking up cough syrup for Dawn at Anderson's Drug Store one day when he approached me in the street.

"Michael," he said. "I've been meaning to buy you lunch. Where in town can we get a good cheeseburger?"

I took him a few blocks over to the Sportsman's Café. It didn't have the best cheeseburgers, but they were decent and it was close, and I didn't want to spend any more time in his company than

I had to. We slid into one of the cream-colored booths and he ordered two cheeseburgers with fries, a soda for him, and a vanilla milkshake for me. I resented the milkshake—it seemed like he was trying to point out my youth. But maybe that was unfair. Either way, my mother raised me to be polite so I drank every drop and ate the cherry, too.

For a while we talked about innocuous things: he asked me about school and what position I played on the baseball team; I asked him how long he'd been the DA in Lincoln. His easy way felt genuine even though I knew it was practiced—putting people at ease one minute only to knock them off balance the next is something even our DA knew how to do—so I knew what he was doing when he rolled up his sleeves and loosened his expensive necktie.

"Your recorded conversations with Marie Catherine Hale have been interesting."

"They have," I said.

"Shadowy figures, caped monsters in the dark—" He flashed a grin: How ridiculous were the tales of this lying girl?

"That's not exactly what she said; she said he had tricks, and that he drank the blood."

Pilson shrugged. Same difference.

"How are you going to get her to drop that nonsense?" he asked.

"My dad says maybe I shouldn't. That I should let her tell it her way and sort it out after."

Pilson smiled. It was a mean smile. No mirth at all, just condescension, and it made me feel small. He wiped his mouth with his napkin and placed it over his plate, then pushed his plate to the edge of the table. "But your dad isn't the interviewer, is he? You are."

"Yes, sir."

"Since the judge has seen fit to place the integrity of the entire case on the shoulders of a high school student."

He reached into his briefcase and produced files not dissimilar to those I'd seen fanned out across my father's desk. They were the files on the Nebraska Bloodless Murders: Peter Knupp and Angela Hawk and Beverly Nordahl. One by one he opened them on the table, before my plate of half-eaten burger and fries.

"Have you seen the photos of the Carlson family's bodies yet?" he asked.

"No."

"Don't you think you should?"

"We aren't to that part of the interview. I want the details to be fresh."

"Well," he said, and clearly he didn't believe me, "you've got to be nearly to these. So have a look." He threw me a pile of photographs.

Peter Knupp was splayed facedown. A close-up of his face showed open eyes and parted lips. The expression conveyed no fear. It didn't convey much of anything, which was somehow worse. Pilson moved the photo of his face to reveal pictures of the wounds that killed him. Cuts, deep and smooth, opened at the edges to show the layers of skin and flesh and vein. The cut to his thigh had been done through his trousers, and the edges of the fabric were stained dark. The cut at his neck was short, and narrower than the others, and the angle of the photo focused less on it than on his face, for which I was grateful.

I'd never seen a dead body before. It was nothing like I imagined, and the vanilla milkshake sat uneasy in my stomach.

"Why are you showing me these?" I asked.

"So you remember," he said.

He opened the files on the student nurses.

"I remember," I said.

"Then why are you letting her lie? Here." He moved my plate and pushed the photographs toward me so far I had to grab them to keep them from falling into my lap.

Angela Hawk and Beverly Nordahl were seated in the front bucket seats of Angela's car. Their throats had been cut, and small rivulets of blood escaped down into their collars. Beverly's head tilted toward Angela's as if she was trying to provide comfort.

"The ME estimated they died within minutes of each other," Pilson said. "They look like they were killed while they were unconscious, don't they? Except they weren't. No traces of sedatives, no intoxicants found besides the alcohol in a bottle of beer. No ligature on the throat, no signs of asphyxia. No blows to the head. And if you look close, you can see that Angela's eyes are open."

I didn't want to look close.

"They suffered," he said. "Every one. Have you ever watched someone bleed to death, Michael?"

"No, sir."

"Marie Hale was involved in this." He turned one of the photos of Angela and Beverly to look at it. "Maybe she was even in the car."

"She didn't kill them," I said. But the blood had drained from my head. I could see Marie crouched in the back of that car. I could see her leaned across the bodies.

"Maybe she didn't do the cutting," he said. "Or maybe you don't want to believe she did. She's a pretty girl, Michael."

"What does that have to do with anything?"

"Just that you're a young man. And she's using that."

"You don't know if she's using anything. Maybe she's confused. My dad says—"

"Your dad is not the most experienced interviewer, though, is he? How many murderers do you think your dad has questioned?"

"I don't know," I said, even though I knew the answer was none.

My cheeks burned. Had I opened my mouth to say something else I might have cried out of sheer frustration. Or I might have hit him. But as it happened, I didn't need to do either, because Mr. McBride had been watching and decided to step in.

"Oh, I don't know about that," Mr. McBride said. "The things our sheriff has seen might surprise you. And besides, I don't know that you have any advantage to press over him. Lincoln may be the capital of Nebraska but it isn't exactly New York City." He held out his hand. "Matt McBride. I'm the editor of the local paper."

Pilson shook it. As quickly as he'd laid them out, he swept the photos back into his files.

"I've been meaning to make your acquaintance," Mr. McBride said. "See how you're liking the place. Maybe get a quote on the case for the *Star*."

"Sure," Pilson said. "I'll stop by your offices one of these days." He never did, of course. Pilson saved his quotes for the bigger papers.

"Great. You stop by, too, Michael. Anytime." Mr. McBride waited for me to nod, to tell him I was okay. Then he tipped his hat and walked to the lunch counter for a cup of coffee.

"Friend of yours?" Pilson asked, staring into his back.

"I delivered papers for him this summer."

"That's good." Pilson smiled. "But Michael, if you speak to him about this case, I'll press charges against you faster than you can slap a fly."

"Yes, sir."

"And don't forget," he said as he gathered his things. "The man who killed these people has to pay. And Marie Hale will have to pay, too, for standing by and letting him."

"What if she couldn't stop him?" I asked. "What if she tried?"

"I need a name," he said as if that didn't matter. "I need his name, or she dies."

CHAPTER SEVENTEEN

Debunking

I NEVER IMAGINED I'd be in the position of debunking a vampire myth, but I couldn't just let Marie get away with the story. Pilson was right about that, at least. There were real people here. Real victims. I was fairly certain that Marie wasn't using the story to pull off some kind of insanity plea—but just the same, if she was determined to stick to her blood-drinker tale, she was going to have to earn it.

So I started checking out books. A whole lot of books that I had to hide inside my coat like they were dirty. It was embarrassing to even ask our school librarian, but she didn't bat an eye, no pun intended, and I thought the elementary school rumors about her being a witch might actually be true. But if it hadn't been for her, I might have gotten nowhere. Only the investigators were privy to the blood-drinking detail of the confession by then, so I couldn't ask Mr. McBride. Though I did, later on, and he found me a pretty good book on Mercy Brown and the vampire hysteria of New England.

The next time I interviewed Marie I was armed with knowledge of vampiric tradition. We met at her cell. My dad didn't have any objections to our meeting there, though I was surprised that Mr. Pilson didn't. Looking back, it's possible that my father never even asked him. In any case, when I got there, I had to haul the cumbersome tape recorder up there with me. It was such an awkward shape that I nearly dropped it, and the only thing that saved me from spending the next several years paying my father back was that I arrived when Marie had a visitor: Nancy had come up from the reception desk. She and Marie had taken a shine to each other. I think Marie reminded her of the daughter she lost in the fire.

As I burst through the two-color door Nancy rose from her chair and said, "Michael! Let me help you!" She swooped down just in time to catch the tape recorder as it bobbled from my grip. Then she helped me carry it to the table and set it up.

"I'll give you the room," she said. "If you're still at it when I come back from my dinner break, I'll bring you some cookies and sandwiches."

"That thing sure seems heavy," Marie noted when we were alone. "Nancy must be stronger than she looks."

"You two seem pretty friendly," I said.

Marie shrugged. "Did you bring me those smokes?"

"Shoot. I forgot again; I'm sorry."

"Sure."

"No, I am. Really. I keep meaning to swipe a pack from Percy."

"Don't worry about it," she said, and then slipped a cigarette out of her sock. She smiled at me and lit it with a match struck against the cement wall.

She was wearing the same blue jeans, rolled to the ankle, and a different white shirt. Her hair looked dark and glossy in its ponytail, the ends of the black ribbon nearly as long as the strands.

Inside her cell, she seemed more at ease and in control of the space, and despite the fact that I had lived in this part of the jail for many years of my life, stepping into my old kitchen felt like Marie receiving me into her parlor.

"Where'd you get that?" I asked, and pointed to the cigarette.

"Never mind." She exhaled. "You don't think you're the only boy I'm talking to?"

"I do think that, actually. Are you keeping secrets, Marie?"

"Everything's a secret until I tell you. But I'm going to tell you everything, so I guess no, I'm not keeping secrets." She watched me a minute and then laughed. "Lighten up. I got it from Nancy. Jealous, jealous."

"I'm not jealous," I said, except that I kind of was. Marie was my secret thing—an entire world separate from my usual one. It shocked me how quickly I'd begun to think of her as mine.

She took another drag and gestured to the tape recorder so we could begin.

"How have you been?" I asked, on the record.

She gestured to the walls, to the tidy kitchen, the small writing desk in her cell. "Better here than some other places." But then she seemed to regret saying so. "I am sorry, you know. That you've gotten caught up in this mess. Your mom and dad, too."

"But are you sorry for the rest?" I asked.

She shrugged.

"What good does sorry do?" she said quietly. "They're all still dead."

"Then why tell me what happened? To avoid the death penalty? To unburden your soul?"

She laughed.

"To stop your accomplice from hurting anyone else?"

Marie cast a quick look toward her window. "He won't hurt anyone else. Not for a while anyway. And when he decides to, nothing I say is going to stop him."

"Because he's a blood drinker?"

She nodded.

"No one's stopped him before," she said.

"No one?" I asked.

"He's still alive, isn't he? Sort of."

"You know he isn't really what you say he is. You know vampires aren't real."

"Believe what you need to believe, Michael. I'm just telling you what happened."

"I'm not saying you're a liar, Marie. Just that maybe he fooled you."

"Sure. Because I'm a stupid girl." She curled her lip. "Do I seem stupid to you? Because I stopped going to school?"

I paused. No, she didn't. She seemed smart. Rough, maybe.

Fast, maybe. But not stupid or like the kind of person it would be easy to get one over on.

"Tell me about him, then," I said. "How did he find you? Were you in a graveyard? Did you stumble across his coffin?"

"You're making fun."

"Of course I am, when you tell me something ridiculous."

"Were all those empty bodies ridiculous? Where did all their blood go, Michael, if he didn't drink it?"

"Maybe he moved them. Maybe the victims were killed someplace else." Except that one of the victims, Jeff Booker, found at a service station slumped over the cash register, had been seen alive by a previous customer not thirty minutes before he was found dead.

"How could he move around in the daylight?" I asked.

"With a parasol," she said sarcastically. "He doesn't burn up in daylight, all right? And he can go into churches, too, not that we ever did. Are you done now?"

"Are you?" I asked. "DA Pilson's not happy about what you're telling me. I've heard him talking about going to his governor—getting you extradited."

"I'm sure he will."

I frowned. I didn't know it then, but Pilson had already tried. And failed. The killings had seemingly stopped, or at least paused, and in the meantime no one wanted to get in deeper with Marie—they knew what it would look like if they hauled a fifteen-year-old girl to the electric chair, lickety-split.

"Marie—if he is what you say, and he has killed before, then why haven't we seen any murders like this?"

"You probably have. You just didn't recognize them."

"These kind of strange, grisly killings?" I asked, dubious. "I doubt that we'd let them just go unsolved."

"Tell that to the Black Dahlia," she said, and snuffed out the nub of her cigarette. "Or those people in the house by the train . . . the one where all the mirrors were covered and there was a bowl of blood and some bacon on the table."

I said nothing. I'd heard of the Dahlia, but the other case was unknown to me. It certainly sounded strange enough, but I searched through the newspaper archives with our librarian for hours and was never able to identify it.

"But," I said carefully, "there's never been another spree like this. Young people . . . teenagers . . ."

"He didn't need to do it before."

"So why did he do it now?"

"I don't know!" She pulled her knees up to her chest and I took a deep breath. It was hard not to scream at her—it was hard not to give my frustration away with a clenched fist or a cracked knuckle. To appear neutral when I was sure she was making it all up as she went.

"You don't have forever, you know," I said. "You only have until they catch him. Then they won't care what your side of the story is."

She laughed a little and muttered, "Forever." Then she stretched her arms.

"You're right though, Michael, about not having all the time.

You're just wrong about how much. I have until they realize they *won't* catch him. Until they give up. That's when they'll come for me."

"How long do you think that'll be?" I asked.

"As long as he keeps them jumping," she said, and shrugged. "You're the cop's son; you would know better than I would."

I didn't know anything better than she would. None of us did. Black Deer Falls, Pilson, the deputies and my dad, we were all stumbling around in the dark.

"You said he didn't need to do it," I said quietly. "What do you mean?"

She watched me, trying to see if I was serious. Then she turned her wrist over and showed me her scars.

"He doesn't always kill," she said. "Sometimes he just feeds."

I leaned forward to look at the thin lines that ran from the palm of her hand up to the elbow to disappear into her shirt. There were so many that the skin was like a patchwork, criss-crossing, some running along the length of her arm and others cutting across it, so many, but so delicate and pink that you could miss them if you weren't really looking.

"You can come closer, if you want."

I got up, and she held her arm up to the bars. I reached through and took it. Her skin was cool, and smooth until I ran my thumb over the small raised scars. Some of them seemed tentative; they were thinner, shallower. But they gained in confidence. The largest one, tucked into the fold of her wrist, looked like it should have had stitches.

"There are others, too," she said.

"Where?" I asked, but she didn't answer, and I remembered where the other victims had been cut: at their throats or the inner thigh. Marie's throat was untouched, and the blood rushed to my cheeks.

"You have good hands," she said, and I realized I was still holding her. "Gentle. You're not the kind of boy he'd want me hanging around."

"What kind is that?" I asked.

"The good kind. Good-looking. Good-hearted. Just, good."

"I thought you said the blood drinker was handsome?"

She laughed.

"No. No, he was . . . He could have been a film star."

"Who did this to your arm, Marie?" I asked, and she jerked free.

"I told you. He did."

I withdrew and wiped my clammy hands on my jeans. "It must have hurt."

She shrugged. "It didn't hurt so much."

"Where is he now?" I cleared my throat and returned to my chair. "Is he still here? Could he hide in Black Deer Falls? As a bat?" She didn't like me teasing her and I don't know why I kept it up.

"Maybe he could and maybe he couldn't," she snapped. "Your joking about it won't change what happened."

I was getting nowhere. I considered changing tactics. Confronting her, making her mad. Except Pilson had already tried that and failed, and I couldn't imagine that I would do much better.

"Someone left a snake in my friend Percy's car," I said simply, surprised the moment the words came out. The snake and the blood drinker had not been connected in my mind until right then.

"What do you mean someone left a snake?" she asked.

"We got into his car and there was a snake on the seat between us. It was only a python, I guess, and it was in a burlap sack. But Percy nearly hit a truck."

"Your friend Percy . . . does he have many enemies?"

"No," I said. "Perce is . . . Everybody likes Percy. Even when he's annoying." I smiled a little. "It was just a joke."

"Was it?" she asked, like she thought it wasn't.

"Marie, do you know where he is?"

"No. But I always thought he might stick around to watch." She looked at me seriously. "You shouldn't go off on your own, Michael."

I almost smiled. I wasn't going to hide from a make-believe monster. But someone real had killed Steve Carlson.

"You think he'd come after me? Or my family?" I asked. But she didn't answer. I suppose she couldn't have known. "Marie, why did he leave you that night after the murders?"

She clenched her teeth.

"Because the bastard wanted me to get caught."

CHAPTER EIGHTEEN

The Blood Drinker

IN THE THIRD week of October, the Upper Midwest got hit with an early snowstorm. The farmers hated it—they had to start hay-feeding their cows sooner than planned, and Percy was worried about his buck. The one he'd been tracking all summer. So one afternoon we headed into the woods behind the Valentine house to follow a few deer trails and do a feeding run. To make sure Percy's buck didn't wander off to get shot by someone else.

"He's too pretty to wind up on Martin Greenway's stupid den wall," he said.

"But just pretty enough for yours?" I asked. "We both know you're not going to shoot it."

"Well. Next year he'll be even bigger."

"And bigger and bigger," I said. "Until he turns gray and hunched over with arthritis."

I followed Percy through the silent trees, our boots sinking into soft snow, snow that was still good, not hard and crusted from melting and refreezing. He showed me the trails the deer were moving through, and the last places he'd seen the buck, in the thicket near the swamp. I watched him shimmy up trees to cut branches down, nice twiggy branches full of buds and stuck-on acorns for the deer to find and feed on.

"Gotta keep plenty of feed out," he said as he dropped another branch, then bent another to feeding height so I could tie it down with bailing twine.

I jumped up and grabbed a branch, pulling the tender bits closer to the ground.

"You know there's still plenty of leaves on the shrubs that he can paw up," I said.

But Percy just grinned. "Trying to fatten him until he's too wide to run."

"You're just spoiling him." I was a little worried about Percy, to be honest. Bow season was already on, and if that buck wandered out of the Valentine swamp and onto someone else's property after a doe or something . . . it would have broken Percy's heart.

"Percy, do you still think about the murders?"

Ahead of me, he broke the branch he'd been hanging on to.

"I try not to," he said.

"But you do."

"Sure."

"Do you ever wonder what happened to the blood?"

"Well, yeah. Everyone wonders about that." He turned to me. "Why? Do you know?"

"No," I said. "But it's so strange. Why take it? What did he want it for?"

"What do you mean 'take it'? He was taking it? I thought it was just"—he gestured to the air—"somewhere else."

I took a deep breath. "What if he wanted to drink it?"

I expected Percy to laugh. Or to shove me and tell me to grow up. But he just shrugged.

"Sure," he said. "Like the papers call it. The Dracula Murders." He turned back to the deer trail and the trees.

"You don't think that's odd?"

"*Yeah* I think it's odd. I think it's a pile of nonsense."

We went on along the trail, pulling down branches and shaking snow off the taller bushes. For being such a loudmouth, Percy didn't like to talk much on those runs—he didn't want to spook the deer. But I had too much on my mind.

"Did you know that in Europe they believed that vampirism caused the plague? They buried women with stones in their mouths to keep them from feeding on corpses in the mass graves. And they'd bury them facedown, so they'd lose their way in the dirt if they tried to dig out."

Percy frowned at me. He slapped his hands together to get the cold bits of bark off and washed his palms with snow. "What are you on about?"

I told him what I'd been reading: disturbing tales about babies being born with full sets of teeth and about Mercy Brown, whose father let her be dug up so his neighbors could cut out her heart and burn it. When I got to the part about her brother eating the ashes, Percy swore loudly.

"Why in the jumped-up hell are you reading about stuff like that?" he asked.

"I just keep thinking about the blood. How it was all missing. And I don't know. I got to wondering if someone could be so deluded, to try and kill that way. To drink it." I hesitated. "Can you even imagine something like that?"

"No, I can't imagine," he said. "And I'd rather *not* imagine. The Dracula Murders was just a name the papers made up. How much blood do you think is in a man? Or in those two girls, those nurses? You couldn't drink that much . . . no way." He was looking at me like I'd completely lost it.

"Yeah," I said as I heard the echo of Marie's words through the trees. *Where did the blood go?* A whisper, the barest brush of her lips against my ear. "You're right. I was just thinking."

"This thing's really got you turned around," he said. "Are you sure you should . . . I mean, if you wanted to quit, your dad would understand. So would everyone else. And if they didn't, well, I'd—"

"I can't stop, Percy."

He nodded. "Yeah, yeah, I know you can't. Biggest story of the century, right? When it's over, there'll be colleges . . . scholarships. You'll go on Cronkite and I'll go over to your folks' house and watch it with them." He grinned. He was proud of me. Excited for me, even though papers and scholarships weren't what I'd meant.

"Maybe you can come along," I said.

"Yeah. Maybe I'll come to college, too. Not that I could get in. But just come along to get a place."

"Yeah."

"Nothing here that won't be here anyway when we get back." He looked up into the branches. "Not like the birdseed factory is going to close down."

"Yeah," I said softly, and he went on ahead down the trail.

When I looked up again, Percy was gone, soaked up by the trees. I must've moved slower than I'd thought, but it was okay—it's nearly impossible to get lost in the woods behind Percy and Mo's place, especially since I'd been traipsing through them since I was nine. And there were Percy's tracks in the snow, headed up the deer trail.

"Perce?" I called out, and waited. "Percy?"

He might've been too far off to hear. When he finished his feeding run, he'd double back and find me. It was disconcerting to look up and realize he was no longer four feet in front of me, but it wasn't dangerous or even that strange, considering how fast Percy moved when he stripped branches. At least that's what I told myself as I stood alone in the middle of the quiet forest.

I opened my mouth to shout again. But all of a sudden I didn't want to make any noise. A strange sensation had begun to creep up my back. Like I was being watched through the trees.

I stiffened, and my boots squeaked loudly in the snow. I held my breath and looked for birds or squirrels but there weren't any. I thought of a story my dad had told me from when he was younger and answered a burglary call. The feeling he'd had when he walked through an open door and had known that the house wasn't empty.

"Damn it, Marie," I muttered into my collar, because it was her fault; she'd filled my head with stories of murderers and a blood-drinking movie monster. An hour earlier I would have laughed out loud. But in those trees I felt what a deer must feel when a hunter is on them. I was waiting for the ambush and hoping I'd be fast enough to get away.

When Percy's dark shape stepped onto the path ahead, I must've jumped a mile. The inside of my coat collar was wet with sweat.

"Percy," I said. "I lost you for a minute."

"Yeah," he replied. "I cut in toward the swamp and then back out again." He looked at my face. "What's with you? You catching sick or something?"

"Maybe. This coat's no good." The coat was fine. If anything it felt a little too warm. I wanted to shrug out of it—I was shaking all over. Percy cocked his head like he might laugh. Then he stopped short.

"What?" I asked.

"What's that?"

"What's what?" I demanded loudly. He pointed over my shoulder and I couldn't bring myself to turn around to look. He walked back and moved past me to a tree not far off the deer path.

There was a symbol marked into it, like a sun or a flower, beneath a long upside-down T. It was above head-level: when Percy took off his glove to run his fingers in the carved grooves, he had to reach.

"Is that a T or a cross?" he asked.

"I don't know."

"It's deep." He rubbed his fingers together and sniffed them. "Sap feels fresh. But who in the hell would come out here and mark up one of our trees?" Everyone knew the land belonged to the Valentines. And everyone knew that if you poached a deer on Valentine property you were prime to catch a bullet in the leg, or so Mo liked to loudly proclaim.

"Are there tracks?"

Percy looked down and around the base of the trunk. "Oh yeah." He bent down. "And they're not old either." He looked over his shoulder, quiet. Then he looked back at me. "Did you see anyone?"

I shook my head, and Percy stood back up, shoved his hand into his glove, and came back to where I stood. The strangeness was getting to him, too.

"We should have seen that on the way in," he said. "Unless they did it after we'd gone past." He chewed the inner part of his lip. "Pop's going to be pissed if someone's been out here."

"Marie said she thinks he might still be here. In Black Deer Falls."

Percy looked at me. We were teetering on the edge, the fear flying around us like bugs. If we let it land, we would run for his house as fast as our legs would carry us, like we used to when we were kids running from an imagined cougar. Or we could do something else. We'd been afraid too many times lately. In the Carlson house. By the stream with Petunia and LuluBelle.

"So let's find the bastard."

We set off. When I was alone, the killer had become something more than flesh and blood, but with Percy back my fear changed again to anger. He was just one man, and we outnumbered him. I was tall and an athlete; Percy was a little shorter but wiry and armed with a hunting knife.

Percy took the lead. He was by far the better tracker, though not even I would have had a problem following the prints as they wove around trunks just to one side of the deer trail. They were large and deep; sometimes near a tree they would become a flurry of kicked and trampled snow, and we would find another symbol carved into the bark. We'd nearly reached the edge of Percy's backyard when the tracks doubled back on themselves and disappeared.

"Aw hell, we've been going the wrong way!"

"No we haven't."

Percy kept on looking around, but I knew he was wrong. There hadn't been any other tracks leading from the first carving we'd found. And we had followed every offshoot.

"Well, they didn't just up and disappear." He ducked and turned to peer into the trees from all directions. His voice became a hissing whisper. "It can't really be him. Can it?"

Him. The man who killed the Carlsons. That feeling was back again, that we were being watched. Back and stronger than ever.

"We've got to get out of here," Percy said. "And tell your dad."

"Tell him what? That a vampire was following us on a deer-feeding run, carving symbols into tree trunks and vanishing without a trace?"

"Well, not the vampire bit but otherwise yeah."

We hurried down the deer trail until Percy's house was visible. The sight of it made us feel safe even though it was a lie—there was no one home at Percy's house that day, and no other house around for miles.

"I don't want to tell my dad."

"But you need to, don't you?" Percy asked. "If there's any chance it could be him?"

I did tell my dad, and he had men search the woods until dusk: Bert, and Charlie, called in on his day off. My dad stopped short of getting extra help from the state police, but he did let Mo lead some of his pals into the woods: Richard Wittengren and Skinny Earl Andersen, guys who knew the forest as well as we did. They found nothing. No old fires, no campsites. And they, too, lost the trail at the last carved symbol. Mo thought whoever it was must have covered up from there. They took photos of the carvings, and my dad told me it was good that I'd let him know. But I heard it in his voice. He'd have to take every last man out for beers as a way of apologizing for wasting a day on his spooked kid.

I rode home with my dad after the search ended, fingers aching from the cold, dreading when the feeling would return to my feet. When I followed him silently up the porch, I scooped up Dawn's old cat on the way. He was good and didn't scratch me, despite my never having picked him up before. He even purred against my chest.

"Dawn!" I shouted.

"Yeah?" She came bounding down the stairs. "What are you doing to my cat?"

"I'm not doing anything to him." I set him down and he stuck his gray tail out indignantly.

"Don't just throw him down!"

"I didn't just throw him down," I said as she picked him up.

"Just keep him inside for a while," I said. "Percy heard some howling in the woods. He thinks some wolves might have come down with the snow."

CHAPTER NINETEEN

Cat and Mouse

ON SUNDAY, MY mom decided to drive the car separately to church. When I asked why, she said she wanted to drop a coconut cake by for Widow Thompson, the Carlsons' old neighbor.

"You can come with me, if you want," she said when I hung around in the kitchen.

So after church, I drove the two of us out to the Carlson farmhouse along County 23. The closer we got, the tighter my tie felt around my neck, and I could tell that my mom was nervous, too—she kept fiddling with the plastic food wrap over the top of the cake, worrying the toothpicks were going to punch through and the covering would ruin the frosting.

We pulled into Fern Thompson's driveway, which was actually an offshoot of the Carlson driveway, and parked near her front walk. I got out and opened the car door for my mom, both of us stealing solemn and nervous glances toward the Carlson farmhouse. Charlie and Bert had been by to clean things up like my dad had promised, so the chalk marks were gone and the blood-stained rug had been burned. But if that had been meant as an exorcism, it hadn't worked. The place still looked empty and inhabited at the same time.

We went up Fern Thompson's cement steps and I knocked. My mom didn't wait for a reply before trying the knob and opening it up a crack.

"Fern? Hello, Fern? It's Linda Jensen and Michael!"

We stepped into the linoleum entryway just as Widow Thompson was getting up from her living room chair. Steve's old tomcat swayed a few steps ahead of her with his tail in the air. Then he jumped up onto the kitchen table to say hello. My mom gave the cat a look, but when Mrs. Thompson gave no objections, she just said, "Michael, take care not to let the cat out."

"It's all right," Mrs. Thompson said. "He won't go. Not even if I try to shove him through the door. That's a very pretty cake."

"I hope you like coconut."

"Mmm," she said. "I'll put on some coffee for us to enjoy it with."

She nodded to me and I said hello, but I think my being there made her kind of sad. Maybe I reminded her of Steve. We didn't have the same build or the same coloring, but being the same age might've been enough. She moved around her kitchen, setting out three small plates and three forks. Only two cups for coffee, figuring I was too young to drink any. She and my mother chatted, and I tried to pet Steve's cat, but it seemed shy of being touched. Not by Mrs. Thompson, though, who scooped him up with one arm and set him on the back of the sofa. I remember wishing that the old tom had been younger. So he would live longer and give her more company.

"Would you like a big slice of cake, Linda, or a smaller one?" Fern asked.

"I never say no to a big slice. I just won't have sugar in my coffee."

"Your boy will have to have a big slice, too. So I won't have so much left over."

"Yes, ma'am," I said, and wandered out to the living room while they talked about church and what my mom used to make the frosting. The Carlson house was clearly visible through the front windows, just across the small yard and driveway. Close enough to give the impression that it was looking back at me. The night of the murders, Widow Thompson would have been able to see right into the living room. Except that the curtains had been drawn closed. Earlier that evening she'd have been able to see Mr. Carlson going to and from the barns. She'd have been able to see everything they did on that last day.

When Bert had interviewed her, she'd said that Steve came home around eight thirty, which checked out—he'd had dinner over at Cathy Ferry's house that night and stayed afterward to watch a little TV.

"Come and have some cake, Michael," my mom said.

I went and took my plate and a fork, then wandered off again so they might be able to keep visiting. But when my mom excused herself to the bathroom, Mrs. Thompson asked, "Michael, how is that girlfriend of Steve's doing?"

"Cathy?" I asked. "I guess she was pretty upset. They hadn't been going out long; they weren't a couple. But I know she liked him a lot."

"I never did see him take her home that night," Mrs. Thompson said. "I must've dozed off. Like I dozed off during . . ." She looked down at her cake. But then she smiled. "She seemed like a nice girl."

"She is," I said. Then I stopped. "What do you mean you never saw Steve take her home? Cathy was never at the Carlsons' that night."

"She wasn't?" Mrs. Thompson put her fingers to her lips. "But I'm sure that she was . . . She had his jacket on over her shoulders and he took them in through the back door."

I froze. The girl she saw had to be Marie.

"Them," I said. "Who else was with Steve and Cathy?"

"Hmm?"

"You said he took them in through the back door. Who was 'them'?"

"Oh." The widow blinked a few times, like she was trying to remember. "No one," she said finally. "It was just him and his girlfriend."

But at first she hadn't been sure. That uneasy feeling crept up my collar, but she was an older lady and probably couldn't trust her memory when it came to a lot of things.

"Why didn't you tell Bert or my dad that Cathy had been here that night?" I asked.

"Oh," she said. "Well, I didn't want to bring her up. Being a young girl and out late with a boy—even a nice boy like Steven. It didn't seem like any of my business."

I would have asked more, but my mom returned from the bathroom. I turned back to the window. The Carlsons had a bright light mounted on a pole above their driveway, to light the way between the house and the barns. If it had been bright enough that night for Mrs. Carlson to see Steve and Marie and where they went, she couldn't have missed someone else. The killer must have come later, after she had already nodded off.

Except she had said, "Them." That Steve had taken *them* around the back of the house. Maybe she misspoke. But I didn't think so.

"I wish someone would move into that house," Mrs. Thompson said to us before we left. "But I suppose no one will. Come next summer, all those flowers will need to be tended."

When we got home, I told my dad what the widow had told me, and he cursed Bert under his breath and said he would reinterview her himself. My mother just stared at me, aghast that I would question Fern Thompson while she had been away in the bathroom.

"That was a sneaky thing to do, Michael," she said. But I hadn't meant to do it. It had just happened. I didn't regret it, though, because between what Mrs. Thompson had said and what Percy and I had seen in the woods, I was starting to feel like I was being toyed with.

*

That Monday I went back to the jail to see Marie.

"What?" she said, and I pulled out the piece of paper I had stuffed into my pocket.

I'd crudely sketched the markings we'd seen cut into Percy's trees. I've never been much of an artist and I kept messing it up—I must've drawn it thirty or forty times. In the end my bedroom was littered with symbols staring up at me in furious black ink, large and small, over and over and over.

Marie studied it, her eyes lingering on the inverted cross.

I'd already tried to explain it to myself: Percy and I could have missed those carvings on the walk out. We were distracted. We could have covered over the other footprints with our own. But none of that really stuck. And I couldn't stop thinking about something that Percy said, right before I left to go home with my dad.

"The carvings were deep," he said. "So deep those trees might never heal."

I didn't know how strong someone would have to be to stab that far into the wood; I just knew that I wouldn't have been able to do it, not even if I'd been leaning over a log on the ground.

Marie handed the paper back to me.

"They're only games."

"Games?" I asked.

"Yeah," she said. "He's just showing off. It must be quite the novelty having me locked up. I suppose he didn't figure it would take this long. I suppose he's enjoying watching, knowing I didn't get away."

I studied her quietly. The things she said about the blood drinker didn't always make sense; she made her incarceration sound like it was planned and also a fortunate surprise.

"Does he want to hurt me, Marie? Does he want to hurt my family?"

"He might want to. But he wouldn't dare."

"What do you mean?" I asked.

I assumed she meant that attacking me would be too big a risk. But the way she said it seemed to imply something else. Like she had forbidden it. Like she had that power over him.

That thought only occurred to me later. It was only when I was away from her that I could consider what she was and her role in the murders. I know everyone thinks I thought she was completely innocent. A victim. A hostage. But Marie was never as simple as that. Victim. Killer. One thing or another.

"Are you afraid of him?"

"Of course not," she said. "Why would I be afraid of him?"

"Because he killed people," I half shouted, frustrated. "Or was he ever there at all?"

Marie's eyes widened.

"How did you get to the Carlson house that night, Marie?"

"Your friend Steven picked us up. We were walking along the road and he stopped to check on us."

"We?" I asked. "Widow Thompson said she saw you go into the house with Steve. And only you."

"Widow Thompson doesn't know what she saw. I never killed anyone."

"You can't do this, you know," I said. "Tell me a killer is in my town and not tell me who he is, give me no way to protect myself besides hanging garlic in my window."

Marie laughed. "That wouldn't work."

"I know it won't. Not any more than holy water or a wooden stake. Because he's just a man."

"If he's just a man, then why didn't any of them run?" she asked. "Why didn't they fight? He never tied any of them up. Doesn't that seem odd to you, that they just lay there and let the life drain out of them?" She licked her lips. "Almost like someone had convinced them it wasn't happening."

I glanced at our old kitchen table, where the tape recorder sat, whirring. I hadn't brought my pen and paper, but I'd switched on the recorder the moment I came into the room.

"But that wasn't always true," I said. "Sometimes they ran." The truck driver, Monty LeTourneau, and the hitchhiker who was found with him. Their bodies had been found almost a mile apart. One of them must have run.

Marie shrugged and I sat down on one of the kitchen chairs. It was strange, but talking about the murders put me at ease. They were as real as the graves and the photographs in the files. They weren't an imagined monster stalking us through the woods and leaving me presents of snakes on the bench seats of cars.

"What about Stephen Hill?" I asked. "The other service station worker who was found in the field across the highway? He had run."

"Sometimes he let them run," Marie said.

"Why?"

"So he could chase them."

"What about the way Stephen Hill was found?" I asked. Stephen Hill was presumed killed on August 18, in the same attack as Jeff Booker, though his body wasn't found until a day later, abandoned in a field across from the service station. His corpse had been in a different state than the others: lying on his back with his pants around his ankles, the deep bloodless cuts in his thighs laid open to the Iowa sky. "The investigators," I said, and cleared my throat, "thought it might indicate a sexual element."

"The investigators are disgusting men," Marie spat. She lay down on her bed and rolled onto her stomach. "Are you thinking about that?"

"No."

"Sure you are. You're thinking about it and those pretty nurses. You're thinking about the other marks on me." She pushed up onto her elbows. "Have you ever gone all the way with a girl?"

"What does that have to do with anything?" I asked.

Marie rolled over again and sat up.

"You haven't. When you do, you'll realize that there are lots of other things to think about."

"So those investigators . . . you don't think they've slept with a girl either?"

Marie laughed. "You've got me there. I guess maybe men just never stop thinking about it. The way they pursue . . ." She trailed off. "My stepfather wasn't young when he met my mother, but every time he showed up at our door, you'd have thought it was to go to the senior prom."

"I thought you said he was terrible?"

"He wasn't at first. At first he was good. Kind of stupid. He used to brag that he had an ancestor who was a cowboy. One of the famous ones from those parts. But my stepfather was the least cowboy-looking man I'd ever seen. Always in a suit. Always shined shoes."

"What about your father?" I asked.

"We lived by a train yard. He was one of those railmen. Left before I was seven."

"Was he a transient?"

"No. He just had someplace else to go. He was just smart enough not to put down roots."

But you were a root, I wanted to say. You and your mother. But before I could, Marie asked, "Do you think I should die?"

"You didn't do the killing," I said quietly.

"But if I let them die, does it make a difference?"

"That's not for me to say."

"Well, it's for someone to." She reached down and touched her scars. "I cut my hand the first time he saw me. I think that's why he noticed. It was at the roadhouse where I worked. I'd been washing glasses. Sharp glass in warm water."

"Why did he pick you?" I asked. "Why did you go?

"I don't know. He said he loved me. Said I was special."

"What was special about you?"

"I don't know. Maybe he thought I'd be willing to go along with it. That would make me pretty special."

"But you didn't go along with it?"

"No, I already told you. I never killed anyone."

"Who was he, Marie?"

"I told you."

"But what was his name?"

"His name doesn't matter," she said, "because it wasn't his real one."

I sat back and eyed the tape recorder again. In the months to come I would sometimes forget that it was there and we were being recorded. I have an almost vitriolic resentment for it now and its mechanical intrusion on some of the most intimate moments of my life.

"All right," I said, "then why him? It couldn't have been just because he looked like James Dean."

"I never said he looked like James Dean. I said he looked like a film star."

"Yeah, well. Same difference."

"He was charming," she said. "I wouldn't say he was kind, but he was kind to me. And his smile was—"

"Full of fangs?" I prodded, and she gave me a look.

"If he had fangs, what would he need the straight razor for?" She pursed her lips, and I resisted the urge to mutter about what kind of a vampire didn't have fangs.

"But even if there was some kind of attraction—after you saw him kill, how could you go on with it? Did he threaten you? Promise to protect you?"

"He promised that after it was over, I would never need to be protected again."

I sat back. "Because you would be like him."

"A blood drinker like him," she said. "The Carlsons were supposed to be mine. My first. But I didn't want to do it. Only he had the baby and he kept saying—"

I shook my head and stopped her. Mr. McBride said I should let her talk, but it wasn't right.

"This is grotesque, Marie," I said. "It's indecent. These were real people. They were my friends. Stop with the monsters. Tell the truth."

Marie just sighed.

"All these bodies without blood," she said. "And you won't believe in vampires. Yet you believe in God."

"That's different."

"How?"

"Do you believe in God?" I asked her.

"I guess," she said softly. "And I'm still not scared of Him. What about this"—she held up my scrap of paper—"cut into a tree? What about everything I've told you? The tricks to fool them into not struggling? What about me, covered in the Carlsons' blood?"

"There has to be an explanation," I said.

"And I gave it to you," she said. "We didn't just slash people and leave them to bleed. Why would we do that?"

"You were fleeing. You panicked and stole cars and hitched a ride with Steve on your way to Canada."

"Who chased you and Percy through the woods?"

"Maybe no one. Maybe we mistook it all."

"Where was the blood?" she asked, and I looked away.

"You still don't believe me," she said quietly. "But you're starting to."

CHAPTER TWENTY

Black Deer Falls, November 1958

I STAYED AWAY from the jail for a while after that—for nearly a week. If Marie believed what she said, then she was deluded. But deluded or not, I knew what Pilson would eventually make of it: it was motive. She had gone along with the killings in exchange for what she thought would be eternal life.

Then again if she was making it up as she went . . . I didn't know why she would choose to tell that story. I only knew she was doing a damn fine job.

Marie and the murders had taken over my entire life. I walked through my days with my mind on nothing else—more than once I crossed the street to nearly get flattened by a passing car. I'd been speaking with Marie almost every day since the interviews began and was still no closer to finding the truth—she'd given me a description of the killer's home ("not a cave or a castle or a bur-row dug into the ground if that's what you're thinking, Michael") but left out anything that would allow us to locate it. Sometimes when she talked about him she sounded dreamy. Other times her words were clipped and bitter. She had called him a bastard once, when he left her at the Carlson farmhouse. "The bastard wanted me to get caught."

All the while the search for the killer continued. Authorities were still certain of catching him. He was flustered now, the papers said. He had to be, when his flight from the Carlson house had been so fast and sloppy that he'd left his accomplice behind.

Early in the month, the FBI came in and conducted a very embarrassing series of interrogations where Marie shouted at them and called them all no-good cheats. They kept her under the lights for almost thirty-six hours, but according to Charlie, when it was over she bounced out of there like she was fresh from a feather pillow. The agents, on the other hand, looked like they'd been hit by a truck.

A reporter from the *Times* would say later that it was like Marie had us under her spell. That the heartland had been held captive by the murders all summer and now were held captive by the murderess. It was a nice turn of phrase. Made for a good story. But he was an idiot. I don't think he ever set one foot in Black Deer Falls, and if he did, he didn't spend his time talking to any of us.

On my way to the jail one afternoon, I ran into our neighbor, Mr. Vanderpool, who had managed the Buy-and-Bag before retiring a few years ago.

"How's it going over there," he asked, "at the jail?"

"I don't think I'm allowed to discuss it, sir. My dad would tan my hide."

"And right he should! But I won't lie; there are plenty of people who'd have preferred your dad had turned her over, and let that prosecutor from Nebraska handle the mess. Having her here, lingering . . . it isn't helping anyone to move on from the Carlsons' deaths."

"Yes, sir," I said, even though that was the very reason she'd had to stay. The Carlsons were ours. If my father had given up and let her go, we might have never gotten the answers we deserved. They'd have called him a coward and accused him of passing the buck.

"How much longer do you think it'll be?" Mr. Vanderpool asked.

"I really couldn't say, sir."

"I see you coming and going from Matt McBride's office over at the *Star*. . . . This'll all be written up for us, then? Everything she said? Everything she's done?" He smiled harder when he asked that, a forced smile that stretched across his face.

"I'm not sure what will be released to the papers," I said. "It's not really my story. It's Marie's story. I'm just taking it down."

"Marie's story," he said, and the corners of his mouth fell, though his teeth continued to show. "Well, you can hurry her up, can't you? And then send her on to the chair."

He tipped his hat and went home. Black Deer Falls was not under Marie's spell.

Neither was the rest of the country. The headlines that had

sprung up in the wake of Marie's arrest were in black ink and bold letters. They declared her the Blood-covered Demoness of the Bloodless Murders. The articles said she was coldhearted, an accomplice who refused to give up her man. And of course there was the picture. Always the same picture on the steps of the court-house in the capital—the one snap, the one instant, where she appeared to be smiling, with my mother's lipstick darkly crimson on her upturned mouth.

I don't know how many times I went back over my notes, over and over them, wondering if the story I would write would show a different side of her or if it would turn out the same.

Mr. Vanderpool's words rang in my ears as I walked to the jail that day. *Send her on to the chair.* I didn't know if I could face her. If I could look at the bars and the painted door. The small square of sky through the window. Suddenly everything seemed over already. And it seemed like such a waste, that she would spend the rest of her life in that cell.

I made it through the doors of the station, but I couldn't go up. Nancy saw me sort of standing there.

"Come with me," she said. "For a breath of fresh air."

She took me out around the building and I leaned against the brick wall as she lit a cigarette.

"Some breath of fresh air," I quipped. "How many packs do you think you've given to Marie by now, anyway?"

She held the pack out to me and I took one. Just one, the way I did sometimes after a few too many beers with Percy.

"Don't tell your dad," she said as she lit it for me.

"They shouldn't have made you do this," she said. "It's too much for someone your age."

"Marie's younger than I am," I said, and she took a long drag. Nancy was so pretty: bright blond hair and ruby lips. "How's Charlie?" I asked, and she shoved me lightly.

"Mind your own business."

We smoked for a while in the cold quiet.

"You've taken a shine to Marie," I said.

"I guess I have. I guess you have, too." She ashed onto the pavement and smudged it with the toe of her low-heeled shoe. "People probably think we're crazy. But she's just a kid. I don't want to see anything worse happen to her than what already has."

"You don't think she did it, then?" I asked.

"She says she didn't. And she doesn't seem like . . ." Nancy trailed off. "She just seems lost. Tough and lost."

Images of the murder victims flashed through my head. That was the week I'd finally looked at the photos of the Carlson murder—if you could call it looking. I'd sat at the desk in my room and held my breath while I flipped through the pages. When I got to the shot of Steve's body lying curled on the rug, I shut the file and sat there with my face in my hands.

"Why didn't they fight?" I asked Nancy. "Do you ever wonder about that?"

"Maybe they were afraid. Maybe he told them he was going to let them go if they didn't."

"But when he cut them—why didn't they fight then?"

Nancy shrugged. "Have you ever felt the difference between

a shallow cut and a deep one? There isn't much. Just a sense of panic. Remember William Haywood, how he died?"

"William Haywood the movie star?"

"He hit his head and cut it deep and then sat down drinking gin until he stopped breathing. Just sat there on his bedroom floor, not knowing he was bleeding to death." She stubbed out her cigarette and picked up the butt to toss in the trash. "Maybe none of the victims knew either, until it was too late. You coming in?"

"I think I'll stay out here awhile longer. Thanks for the smoke, Nancy."

"Just get the smell off before your dad sees you," she said, and went back inside.

I stood there in the cold and thought about Marie. I thought about the scars on her arms. The shallow and the deep ones. And I thought about Nancy and why she knew what they felt like.

Nancy had moved to Black Deer Falls five years before, from one of the small states out east. Looking at her now, so pretty, flirting with Charlie, you'd think she was never sad a day in her life.

The fire that had killed her husband and baby had been an accident. A freak thing. Sparks from the flue had caught on the rug, and when she woke coughing, Nancy had run out on instinct. By the time she realized what was happening, the blaze was too high for her to go back in. So she just stood in her yard and screamed and screamed until the fire truck came.

We never would have known about that, except when she first came to town she used to have drinks at the Rusty Eagle, the old army bar between the butcher and the bus garage. And when she'd had enough, the whole story came out. How much she'd lost. How much she hated herself. It wasn't her fault, of course. It could have happened to anyone.

But there are women in town who to this day refuse to speak to Nancy. They think it's indecent that she could dare go on. That she smiles. That she flirts with Charlie. I used to think they were just being ugly. Now, after knowing Marie, I just think they're mistaken.

The woman they condemn doesn't even exist. The mother, the young wife, she died in the fire with her husband and baby. Whoever Nancy is now had to leave that all behind.

Since the carvings in the woods behind Percy's house, there had been no further signs of the blood drinker, and I had almost begun to believe we had imagined the whole of it. Weeks had passed, and Mo had finally stopped sitting by the fire in his backyard pit with a pile of beer cans built into a pyramid and a rifle in the crook of his arm, and Percy said they hadn't seen anything but does and squirrels in their woods since the day of the search. He also kicked slush at my shoes because I'd scared off his buck.

But if the buck had moved on, all the better for it. Those woods weren't safe.

For my part, I wasn't taking any chances. I still made Dawn keep her cat in, and I still walked her home from school.

"Can we stop and get an ice cream soda?" she asked as we cut down Main Street.

"Only you would want an ice cream in November," I said. Dawn was made for Minnesota: she kicked her blankets off year-round. She'd been that way since she was a baby. My mom said she'd had a real time of it, keeping her tiny feet in socks.

We started up the block to Anderson's Drug Store, where the soda fountain was. Dawn wanted a chocolate soda topped with a scoop of butter brickle. I was after a hot dog with extra mustard and a root beer float. The streets were busy for a weekday afternoon—probably because the sun was out and made town look warmer, even though it wasn't—and full of unfamiliar faces. Black Deer Falls was never so small that I knew everyone, but lately, the people I didn't know seemed to know me, and that was an uncomfortable feeling.

"Maybe not today, Dawn, okay?" I said, and stopped walking.

She frowned, and when I looked up the street again, I saw Mr. McBride and his wife. They were arm-in-arm, and brown paper bags of groceries were tucked in each of their outer elbows like bookends. Mrs. McBride saw us first and whispered, and Mr. McBride looked up and shouted hello. He gave a little wave with the hand holding his groceries and almost spilled them in the process.

I took my hand out of my pocket and waved back, then put my arm around Dawn to hurry her along home. I felt guilty repaying his warm greeting with something so brief, but I wasn't up to talking. I thought about it the rest of the short walk to our house, wondering whether he'd taken it personally or if I'd just flat out hurt his feelings.

"What's that on our door?" Dawn asked.

"What?"

She pointed with a red mitten. Something was hanging on our front door, like a wreath hung for Christmas—except whatever this was hung straight down. It was three-feet long and narrowed at the bottom. And it was dripping.

I knew what it was before Dawn did, but my legs kept moving forward like in a dream as I tried to make sense of what it was doing there. I kept on walking toward it, like a fool, until Dawn finally put her hands to her face and started to scream.

"Dawn, Dawn!" I shouted, and bent down to take her by the shoulders. I tried to pull her in close but she fought me. She wouldn't stop screaming. In the corner of my eye I saw our neighbor's door open up and Mrs. Schuman step out to see what was wrong. Others would join her soon enough—Dawn's screams must have been audible for at least two blocks. But all I kept thinking was that my mother was inside. My mother was inside, and I didn't want her to open the door.

It was a snake hanging down the white wood. The same snake that someone had left in a sack on Percy's front seat. Someone had taken her and nailed her to our front door, right below the brass door knocker.

"Good God."

I heard Mr. McBride's gasped words as his running footsteps came to a halt. Mrs. Schuman approached on the other side, hands over her open mouth. Mrs. Spanaway and the Misses Monson—the spinster sisters who live two houses down—crept toward us with wide eyes. They made me sick to my stomach,

172

those eyes. They made me cold all over. The snake was terrible, and here we were, my family, in the middle of it again. And then my mother came to the door.

"What's going on?" she asked. The door swung in, and as it did, the snake's dead body swung in toward her like a fat length of rope. Her mouth made a surprised O and she screamed and slammed the door back shut, disappearing from view to shriek inside the house while the snake thumped heavily against the wood.

"Someone call Sheriff Jensen," Mr. McBride said to the growing crowd of neighbors. He looked down at Dawn and placed a hand on top of her red knitted hat. "It's all right, sweetheart. It can't hurt you."

At his words, Dawn started to cry. Dawn never was afraid of snakes. That wasn't why she had screamed. She had screamed because someone had killed the poor thing.

"Tell him not to bring Bert," I called to Mrs. Schuman, who was hurrying back to her house to call my dad. "Tell him that no matter what, he needs to keep Bert away!

"It was Bert's snake," I explained to Mr. McBride. "He took it in after someone left it in the front seat of Percy's car."

He blinked at me and looked at the snake. It had nearly stopped swaying after being disturbed, but the movement had made the scene more gruesome; she had slid and rolled through her own dripped blood and smeared it in an arc.

"How do you know it's the same one?" he asked.

I didn't respond. I couldn't be sure, not then. I just knew that it was. Later, poor Bert would confirm it when he found her tank empty, though he couldn't say how she'd been taken. There was no evidence of forced entry. He figured that one of his window latches was faulty or that someone had picked the lock to the back door. Poor Bert. He hadn't had her long, but he loved that snake.

While we waited for my dad, Dawn and I lingered on the lawn with our backs to the door. My mom chose to remain in the house on the other side of it. I don't think she wanted to face the crowd. I saw her peering out at us through the curtains in the kitchen and gave her a small nod. Then I tugged Dawn closer. I had her. My mother didn't need to worry.

Behind us, I heard a familiar click and whir and caught the light of a flashbulb. Mr. McBride was kneeling at the base of our front porch steps and taking photographs.

"I didn't know you had your camera," I said.

"I asked Maggie to get it from the car." He gestured back toward town. "We're parked not far up Pine." He snapped off a few more photos and changed the angle, stepping up onto the porch like I had given him permission.

"Are those for my father?" I asked.

He lowered the camera. "Well, yes. He's welcome to them. But they're also for the paper."

"The paper? You'd publish this—our house—in the paper?"

He looked down.

"Mr. McBride, Dawn's already having trouble at school because of the case, and if I get one more suspicious glance from my neighbors, I'm going to turn to salt."

"Lot's wife was turned to salt for looking," he said with a small smile. "Not for being looked at. But I know what you mean, Michael. I know what you've been going through." He put the camera away, slinging it over his shoulder by the leather strap.

Not long after that my dad arrived. He pried the nail free of the door and placed the snake into a sack to bring to the station. Then he broke up the crowd and brought Dawn in to my mom around the back. After that he came to stand with me and Mr. McBride.

"Do you think this was a prank, Sheriff Jensen?" Mr. McBride asked.

"One hell of a nasty prank," my dad replied.

"Too nasty for those same folks who came to the jail the other day?"

"What folks?" I asked. My dad hadn't told me that there had been a group at the station, protesting Marie being kept there.

"Hard to say," he said, ignoring me. "Hard to judge the limits of anyone, after the things we've seen lately."

Mr. McBride asked a few more questions, but my dad wouldn't comment further. So he nodded and tipped his hat. "I hope that little girl of yours is okay," he said, and walked back to his wife, slipping his arm around her thin waist. I hadn't noticed before, but she looked near frozen to the bone, and they broke into a jog as soon as they were back on the sidewalk, in a hurry to get to their car.

"Do you want me to scrub the door?" I asked.

"It's too cold. Let's go inside. I'll get a bucket of soapy water and come back out while your mom finishes up supper."

"He was taking photographs," I said when we got into the warmth of our mudroom. "Mr. McBride, I mean. He said you could use them for the investigation."

"So I can use them. And so he can use them."

"He said he wouldn't," I said, though looking back, I guess he'd said no such thing.

"Listen." My father grabbed my shoulder. "I like Mr. McBride. I really do. I know some folks think he and his wife are a little strange but I've always found them pleasant enough. But his obligation is to that newspaper. His loyalty is to that newspaper. Not to what's decent. And don't you forget it."

Before the events of that fall and winter, I would not have understood what my father meant. How could an obligation to the truth be anything but decent? But now I know. Matt McBride ran the photographs in the *Star* a week later. When I confronted him about it in his office, he said he'd held them back as long as he could. But too many people had seen him take them, and he was beholden to them to write the story. Because it might have been a prank, sure. Or it might have been a threat, and if it was, the public had a right to know. He said he wished he hadn't had to run it. Or that it hadn't been my house. He wished it hadn't been the same snake that had been left once for me already. But I was still angry. And I still felt betrayed.

"You're a journalist, Michael," he said to me. "You understand these choices."

I did understand. And his running the story didn't stop me from thinking of him as a mentor. But it did change things between us, and I knew he regretted that even if he didn't regret printing the photographs. Sometimes choices bear a price. Even the right ones.

One day a long time afterward, I told him I still thought he was a good man. "So does my sister," I said. "She says she knew it the day we found the snake. Because when you waved to us in the street you did it with your hand full of groceries even though it would have been easier to let go of your wife's arm. She said she knew it then."

I remember thinking once that I wasn't sure if the McBrides were happy together. I remember I thought of them as distant. But I must not have been paying very much attention.

CHAPTER TWENTY-ONE

The Carlson Graves

MY DAD ASKED around to all of our neighbors about the snake, but no one could say how it got there, despite it happening in the middle of the day and the fact that my mom had been home the whole time. She had been in the kitchen, yet she swears she didn't hear anyone come up the walk, and she certainly didn't hear a nail being driven through our front door.

I stood with my dad in our backyard, beside the fence and winter shrubs. He was holding the nail we'd removed from the snake's head. Her body he'd given back to Bert, who would keep her in the freezer until he could bury her in the spring.

"Someone must have seen something," I said, eyeing in particular Mrs. Schuman's front windows that lined up nearly perfectly with ours right across the street.

"If they did, no one's talking." He rubbed the nail back and forth between his fingers. All the blood was gone; it looked like a brand-new nail. "If you hear anyone whispering about it at school, you let me know."

"We should have dusted the door for prints. But I was just so eager to—"

"It was only a prank, Michael. I wasn't going to pull prints for a prank."

"How did they get it out of Bert's house, though? How did they keep from being seen?"

My dad looked at me, thinking I was getting spooked. And worried I was starting to buy into everything Marie was telling me.

"He was seen," he said. "Whoever saw him is just lying about it. And I don't know why."

"It must've been someone from school," I said. "Or there are plenty of people around town, I guess." I glanced at him. By then my dad walked around with a slight hunch, like he was ready to fend off something thrown at him. Dawn, who had always loved school, didn't want to go anymore because of the things the other kids were saying about us. And Steve and his parents were lying cold in boxes under the ground.

"We'll be all right," my dad said. "This will pass, and everything will go back to the way it was."

Except that was the problem. The hostility had taken hold of Black Deer Falls so fast and with such ease that it was hard to pretend that it hadn't always been there.

On the way to the jail to see Marie, Charlie rolled past me in his patrol car. He nodded from behind the wheel, but he was grim. Because he wasn't just driving by on the way to see my dad. He was on duty and keeping an extra eye on our house.

I'd thought the interviews were my ticket into any journalism program in the country, but that ambition had started to feel foolish. I'd been thoroughly humiliated and made to look like an idiot—chasing symbols through the woods, reading about vampires. My family was being harassed. By the time I knocked at the door to the women's cell I was angry, and I threw open the door.

"It's not a game now," I said. "What's he playing at?"

Marie stood, fists clenched. She looked at the door still banging against the wall.

"I don't know! I've been stuck in here, if you haven't noticed."

"You're going to be stuck in here for the rest of your life if you don't start telling the truth!"

"They can't keep me forever," she said. "Not when I didn't do anything."

"Even if you didn't kill them, you were there."

"Only because he made me! Because he said I needed to if I wanted to—" She cut off abruptly. I was mad but so was she. I could tell by the bright shine in her eyes and the way her chest rose and fell under her sweater.

"If you wanted to be like him," I said, disgusted.

"What's gotten into you?" she asked. "I mean, I heard about what happened to Bert's snake . . . but that could have been anybody who did that."

"But it wasn't just anybody, was it?"

"I told you, I don't know."

"Sometimes I wish you'd never come here," I said.

"Only sometimes?"

"They hate you, you know. Everyone. And they hate us, too—me, my dad, my little sister—because they think we're . . . we're—"

"They're going to think what they want to think. They don't *know*."

"They know what you brought with you," I said. "All this mess."

Marie relaxed. She slipped another cigarette out of her sleeve and lit it, even though she'd been smoking one just before I came in. I could still smell it hanging in the closed air.

"Not everyone hates me," she said, and puffed. "Nancy doesn't. You don't."

"What would you do," she asked, "if someone told you you could live forever?"

"That's not possible."

"What if it was? What would you do for it? What would you give?"

"Nothing," I said. "I only want the life God gave me."

"That's only because He gave you a good one," Marie whispered.

"Marie, I just want you to—" I stopped. Standing there, watching her smoke, the anger just dropped through my feet. I couldn't say all the things I wanted. I wanted things I couldn't even admit to myself. And I wanted for her to be innocent.

"I just want you to tell the truth. I just want him in the chair where he belongs. If he comes near my family, I'll take him in myself."

"Don't do that," Marie said.

"Why not? I'm not afraid of a knife, Marie. I'm not afraid of a straight razor."

"Don't be stupid, Michael!"

Marie was tough—tougher than most, boys or girls. But she was so frustrated with me, she could hardly speak. "Look, I don't want anything to happen to you, okay?"

"Nothing's going to happen to me," I said, and left.

That night, Percy dragged me out. Away from my notes, away from Marie. "Just come and have a few," he said. "A bunch of us are going down to the lake. It'll be fun."

We drove down the dirt roads that edged Eyeglass Lake and stopped when we got to the row of cars parked along the shoulder. Then we got out and made our way down to the boat landing.

"This doesn't sound like a small party," I said.

"I never said it was," said Percy.

The road was hard-packed with snow, and the air was crisp and clean. Orange light flickered in the trees from the fire someone had started by the shore but we'd have been able to see without it: out there the moon reflected off all that snow and made it bright enough to see the happy grin on Percy's face. The night was warm, all the way up to the low thirties. Which may not sound like much, but when temps drop regularly into the single digits, twenty-five starts to feel downright balmy.

We were late, or so it seemed, though it couldn't have been past ten o'clock. When we reached the party, Percy asked me for a few dollars and headed off; when he came back, he had two six-packs tucked under his arm. He popped off two cans and put one in each of my hands. To catch up.

I don't know who put the party together. I never asked. Percy always seemed to know about those kinds of things, what was happening where and who was going. I saw a few guys from our baseball team, mostly the ones who played football, too. And a few of the girls were there: Sandy Millpoint and Jackie and Violet Stuart, Rebecca Knox and a few of her friends, standing by the fire, looking nice with scarves wrapped over their ears.

I did as Percy asked and drank a few, and then I drank a few more. I helped the guys unload more firewood. Nobody seemed to mind that I was there, and if they looked at me funny, after the first four beers I didn't notice. I sang the school fight song with everyone but mostly I kept to myself and let Percy do the entertaining. He'd had quite a bit to drink but he kept on looping back to me.

"You feeling okay? You out of beer?"

"Nope, I'm fine."

"Jackie Stuart looks cold. Maybe you should go see about warming her up."

"I think Morgan's doing a good job of that already." I gestured to a car parked near the road with the taillights on and the rear window all fogged up, and Percy made this disappointed face, like he hadn't known she'd gone in there.

After a while it got pretty late, and the girls went home, and the guys started horsing around on the ice. Sliding around and snowball bowling, but everybody was too drunk to be any good. I was pretty drunk, too, so when the fire died down and someone said they had an idea, Percy and I didn't ask questions.

We got into our cars and drove along the snow-packed dirt roads, too fast and too loud. There was a bunch of us but I can't say with certainty who was there. Morgan, for sure. He and Paul Buell rode in Percy's car. I thought I'd seen Joe Conley earlier, but I think he'd gone home by then.

There weren't any houses out that way so we turned our radios up and rolled down the windows. One of the guys in the car in front of us pulled down his pants and flashed a full moon through the back; Percy hung his head out the driver's side and howled at it. By the time we stopped we were out of breath from laughing. I don't think Percy even knew where he'd driven us. But we'd wound up at the Methodist cemetery.

The Methodist cemetery isn't very big, and it's pretty far out. The parking lot only had enough space for four cars. Funeral parties had to pull off and park along the ditch down the road.

"What are we doing here?" Percy asked. But I think he knew. The Methodist cemetery was where the Carlsons were buried.

A few of the guys tugged open the short iron gate. It had been half ajar already, and even if it had been locked, we could've jumped it. I hadn't noticed when we left the lake but the only boys who'd come with us were Steve's friends. His best friend, Rudy Bartholomew—who everyone called Bart or Rudy Bart! when he came onto the football field—tossed me a fresh beer and said to come on.

"You wanna go home?" Percy asked.

I looked at the guys. They were still laughing, maybe swaying a little on their feet. I didn't feel like going home. It felt like I should go in, like I should've gone already.

They led us through the cemetery, up the little hills, past the grave markers—most of them small, some of them old and leaning crookedly, partially sunk into the dirt. Some clouds had rolled in and it was darker there than by the lake. I tucked the beer into my coat pocket and pulled my collar up. Ahead, the guys were shouting. They shouted "RUDY BART!" all at once, like they did when he took the field during home games. "RUDY BART!" like "TEN HUT!" in the army.

Percy tripped over something and swore.

"Someone got a light?" he called, and ahead, one of them switched on a flashlight.

"Don't yell in the cemetery!" someone whisper-hollered, and we heard them laughing.

"This doesn't feel right," Percy said. "Let's go back."

"What about Morgan and Paul?"

"They can pile into one of the other cars. They'll be all right."

But it was too late. They'd stopped at a flat patch of ground, under a copse of bare winter trees. The Carlsons' graves.

Their headstones weren't like the others in the cemetery. The town had taken up a collection and purchased all three: large rectangular monuments in white granite. They sat in a row: Bob, and Sarah, and Steve in between them, and against the snow, the white of the granite looked dirty and gray.

I crept closer, shoes sinking into the snow. It was different seeing them there than seeing their caskets. Buried under all that dirt, and all that snow, resting beneath the heavy headstones, the Carlsons felt like a memory.

The first full can of beer hit me in the back, between the shoulder blades. The next one caught me in the side of the head, by my ear. I barely felt the cold of the snow on my hands when I fell.

"Hey!" Percy shouted.

The hit near my ear made my head ring, but I could still see two guys grab Percy from behind. They yanked his arms back hard enough to put him up on his toes.

"Knock it off, you guys; that's not funny!"

"It's not supposed to be funny," said Paul, and threw another can. It was open already, and half-gone. It hit me in the chest and splashed beer up onto my chin.

"Hey, let go of him," I said, and got up on my knees. In the fog of the beer, I thought they were going after Percy. But they were just holding him back.

A few more cans hit, catching me in the face. Or maybe someone hit me. I'd never been in a real fight before, and I suppose that wasn't much of one either. I just knew the blood was warm coming out of my nose and tasted bad, and my split lip was stinging already. I knew I'd had too much to drink, and I thought if I laid down a while whatever was happening would stop.

"Cut it out," Rudy said. "It's a waste of beer."

The cans and hits stopped. It was just Rudy standing there with his dad's pistol.

"You better leave off!" Percy shouted. "He's a Jensen and you'll catch hell!"

But they knew that already. They'd known that before they started.

"You planned this," I said, and Rudy pointed the gun in my face.

"Shut up," he said. "You've got this coming."

I was on my knees in the snow beside the Carlsons' headstones. Percy was screaming, asking them what they were doing, warning them off. I was going to let her get away with it, they said. I was a traitor.

"Don't," I said. "Rudy, don't."

"You think you're so smart," he said. Then he screamed in my face, and I shut my eyes.

I knew that they meant to do it. That they would lose the last of their tempers and pull the trigger. I knew they'd kill Percy, too.

"Keep the light on him," Rudy shouted. Then he pointed the gun at Percy, who had started to call for help.

"Leave him alone!" I screamed, and straightened up, still on my knees in the snow.

The gun swung back, and Rudy rushed forward and pressed the barrel against my forehead. I closed my eyes again.

"Keep it on him," I heard him saying. "Keep it—"

He stopped.

"What is that?" I heard him ask.

"I don't know," said Morgan.

"Give me the light!"

I opened my eyes and looked at Percy as the beam of the flashlight moved behind me. The guys holding him had let their arms go slack, and Percy had nearly sunk down to the ground. They looked less certain.

"What is it?" Paul asked. He went around with Morgan to Rudy. They were behind the graves, the flashlight trained on the back of Steve's headstone.

"What is that?" Morgan asked. "Jesus Christ, what is that?"

The guys holding Percy let go as the flashlight beam swung wildly into the trees, like Mo's had the night of the search party, and Percy scrambled over to me.

"Let's get out of here," he whispered. "Let's go!"

He started to help me up, but Paul and Morgan started screeching the same thing.

"Let's get out of here, Rudy! Come on!"

Then they ran off and took the flashlight with them, leaving Percy and me in the dark. After a few minutes we heard their cars start up and their tires spin as they drove out of the parking lot.

"You okay?" Percy asked. "Christ, you're bleeding."

"I'm okay."

"Christ, let's get out of here."

But I was looking at Steve's headstone in the scant moonlight. They'd seen something there. Something had stopped them.

"Hang on," I said.

"*Hang on*? For what?"

"Percy, give me your lighter."

He grumbled and handed it over, and we moved around the

graves. I flipped the lighter open, and flicked it on. "What in the jumping hells," Percy whispered.

The same symbol that had been carved into the trees in the woods had been cut into the back of Steve's headstone.

I held the flame closer. It wasn't just one symbol this time. It was dozens, etched into the granite, so tightly packed that one bled into the next, large and small, some so shallow it could have been done with a penknife, others so deep it was a wonder that the whole headstone hadn't cracked into pieces.

I cast the light out into the trees, just like Rudy had with the flashlight, and Percy jumped. Whoever had done it wasn't there anymore. The marks had taken time, and could have been done any night after the headstones had been installed. Just the same, I expected to see that pale face.

"Hey," Percy said, "can we just go now? Can we just go?"

"Yeah. Let's go." We backed away from the graves and walked out of the cemetery, and I didn't flip the lighter shut until we were inside his car.

We spent the night at Percy's place, in his room with the lights on and pretending to read comics after I'd washed all the blood from my face.

"What are we going to tell your dad?" Percy asked.

"The truth, I guess. Just . . . not all of it. We were fooling around at the lake and decided to visit the cemetery. We saw the marks on the headstone and got into a fight."

"With who?" he asked.

"With everyone. We were all upset. It all happened fast."

"You're just going to let them get away with it? Morgan and Rudy Bart and those guys—"

"They didn't mean anything by it," I said.

"They had a gun."

"They weren't going to use it." But they were. And he knew they were, too; I could see it on his face.

"I guess it was lucky for us the killer decided to mark up Steve's headstone," he said. "That's a strange thing to have to say."

"Yeah," I said. But I knew what he meant.

The blood drinker, or whoever had carved up Steve's headstone before we got there, had saved us by accident. Over the next few months, I thought about that a lot. I wondered if there were other symbols just waiting to be found.

"Well," Percy said, and sighed. "You want to punch me in the eye? Mo's going to do it anyway, when he hears you got beat up and I came out with not even a scratch."

Mo would never do that, of course. But I told Percy I would hit him with a board before we went to school, if that would make him feel better.

CHAPTER TWENTY-TWO

Lasting Cuts

PERCY AND I reported the defacing of Steve's headstone to my dad, and it didn't take long for pictures to be splashed across the papers. The photo that Mr. McBride took of it was reprinted nationally, and the interstate manhunt refocused on Black Deer Falls. For a few days the town was once more swarmed by state patrol and federal agents, knocking on doors and searching attics and storage sheds. And they inspected every inch of our cemeteries, looking for more marks.

When I went by the women's cell, Marie was up on her toes, staring down through her window. She was watching the extra patrol cars come and go from the parking lot.

"Dummies," she said. "Driving all the way out here, guns blazing, like they don't know that headstone could have been carved up as soon as it went in."

That's just what I had thought, but I just said, "You must be pleased. He's keeping them jumping." The headlines were all about the killer again, and for a little while she would be forgotten. He'd bought her more time.

"Why would he want to?" I asked. "I thought you said he wanted you caught. That he wanted it over."

"I said I didn't think he figured it would take this long. But as for what he wants . . . I don't always know." She turned and saw my face, covered in bruises with my lip scabbed in the middle.

"What happened?"

"Just some guys from school."

She came to the bars and wrapped her fingers around them. "Tell me."

So I did. I played it off as a joke. As a scuffle.

"They were just fooling around," I said.

"They pointed a gun at your face," said Marie.

"It wasn't like that. I'm okay. Percy's okay."

"They're bullies," she spat. She let go of the bars and dug her fingernails into her palm. Then she let go and did it again.

"Rudy Bartholomew," she said. "Morgan Todd." She repeated the names I'd told her and dug her nails into her fist.

"Marie," I said.

"I don't want to talk today, Michael."

"Marie." The tips of her fingernails had broken the skin; they came away red. "Marie, stop that." I opened the door to the rest of the jail and called for Nancy.

"Everything's fine," Marie said.

I left when Nancy got there. Later she told me that Marie

willingly stuck her arm through the bars and let her clean and bandage the wounds. And Nancy trimmed Marie's nails down on both hands, to the quick.

"She did that?" Percy asked when I told him. "Christ."

We were sitting in the school parking lot, the Monday after the cemetery. As had become usual, we were in no hurry to go in. My face was still bruised, and you could still see the cut on my lower lip. We'd seen Morgan go in earlier and he'd seen us. He sort of looked scared, and maybe a little sorry. Percy said he didn't look sorry enough.

"Is she—" Percy asked, and twirled his finger beside his ear to ask if she was crazy.

"No," I said. "She was just upset." But her reaction had disturbed me, too. I'd never seen anyone behave that way.

"Well she's not the only one," he said. "They'll get their payback."

"No. Let it go, Perce."

"You can't be serious."

"I am." But inside, I was boiling. If I could have whisked my classmates away with a thought, they would have disappeared. Morgan. Rudy Bartholomew. Even Carol. Those guys had done what they did because they were angry. Because they were scared, of the killer and of Marie. But they'd been able to do it to me because to them I *was* Marie. I was an outsider. I'd never quite fit in. Never found my place, except with Percy.

"I'm not staying here, Percy," I said. "After this is over, after graduation, I'm getting out."

"I know," he said. "I always knew that." He stared out the window, watching the last of the students hurry inside, wrapped up in their coats, their books clutched to their chests as they ducked against the cold morning wind. "It used to make me mad, you know? You always had one foot out the door. On to bigger and better things. Better than this. Better than me."

"Not better than you."

"Well, this town is me," he said, and pointed to himself. "So how was it supposed to feel? But now I think I really would go with you. Now it feels like Black Deer Falls isn't such a good place.

"He must like it," Percy said, and I knew he wasn't talking about Morgan or Rudy. "He must like what he's done to us."

Sometimes it was hard getting Marie to talk about the murders. She would wander off or daydream. She would ask about Percy or Nancy or Dawn. Other times it was easy. I'd ask, and she'd answer.

"My mother and stepfather. Peter Knupp. The student nurses. The Taylors. The truck driver and his hitchhiker. The guys at the gas station. Cheryl, the waitress at the truck stop. The students, Stacy Lee and Richard. And the Carlsons."

"So that's everyone," I said. "And no undiscovered victims in between?"

"Nope," she said, and looked at my empty pockets. I'd yet again forgotten to bring her any cigarettes.

"So the Taylors were killed right after the nurses?" I asked for clarification. Because they lived alone and kept to themselves, the Taylors' bodies hadn't been found until after the discovery of the next victims: the truck driver Monty LeTourneau and his unidentified drifter.

"Yes. It was August eighth."

"You're sure?"

"I'm sure. He was careful about dates. I thought it was dumb: when you had forever, what did the date matter?" Marie rolled her eyes. "But he said that was precisely why it did."

"And it was after the killings at the Taylor house that you came upon Monty LeTourneau and his hitchhiker?"

"Monty first. And he picked up the hitchhiker later."

"Who? Monty or . . ."

"The blood drinker," she said, and her eyes widened when I grimaced. "What? You gave him that name."

"All right," I said. "What happened with the hitchhiker? How did his and Monty LeTourneau's bodies wind up so far away from each other?"

"Because they ran."

"Like Stephen Hill ran. Why them and not the others?"

"Maybe he let them," Marie said. "I don't know." She fidgeted sometimes, running her fingers through the ends of her long brown hair. "He liked Stephen Hill. Stephen Hill was good-looking. Better-looking than he was, even."

"Is that why he was stripped?"

Marie shook her head. "It was just a game."

"What kind of game?"

"Like a cat with a bird," she said, and looked up. She seemed a little angry, frustrated with me.

"So he liked it? The running?"

"And the screaming. They were all quiet at first. Peter Knupp, the Taylors. Those nurses were like two swoony church mice. But by the time he got to Cheryl . . ." Cheryl Warrens, the waitress at the truck stop where Monty LeTourneau's truck was found abandoned, "Cheryl screamed so loud my ears hurt."

For a moment, Marie's eyes clouded, and we sat in silence. On the tape it goes on for fifty seconds.

"It didn't seem so bad, you know? Not at first. Some of them even smiled. Peter Knupp was smiling until he was dead."

"Smiling," I noted, and jotted it down.

"Listen," Marie said. "I'm going to tell you this, but I don't want you making fun. I need you to believe that everything I say is true, even if you only keep on believing it until I'm done. Got it?"

"I got it. I won't make fun."

When Marie had seen the picture of Steve's headstone, she wasn't surprised. But no one else knew what to make of it. In the end they called it unexplained. An unexplained prank. But I'd had enough of the unexplained. I was ready to believe.

"I told you he had tricks," she said. "To make people see what he wanted them to see. He used them all the time, if there was something he wanted. He said all kinds of things to get people to invite him in. He told Walter and Evangeline Taylor that we were their grandchildren. Evangeline kept saying how sorry she was—that she didn't have any sweets for us or any presents. And she said her house was a mess—but it wasn't.

"Are you close to your grandparents, Michael?"

"I was."

Marie nodded. "I never knew mine. Not even my mother's. She had an older sister, but I never met her either."

"So you tricked them," I said, putting her back on topic. "But how did you kill them?"

"I didn't kill them. I never killed anyone."

"Then how did he?"

She took a deep breath.

"We stayed with them all night, playing the game. Then we put them to bed. Into their nightclothes. I shaved Walter's face with the razor."

"The same razor?"

She nodded.

"He drank Walter first. He slit his wrist. Evangeline didn't even notice. She just kept looking at Walter like he was talking to her."

"And you never considered letting them go?"

"He wouldn't have let them."

"But what about you? Why didn't you run? Did he carry a weapon? Did he have the razor in his hand the whole time?"

"No."

"Then why didn't you go for help?"

But Marie didn't answer. "You can check everything I told you against what they found. It'll match."

"Marie," I said. "Why did you go with him? Was it really just because he was good-looking? Was he so good-looking that it made it okay?"

"No!" She looked at me sharply. "You wouldn't understand.

"Everyone said I was a bad girl. He said that I wasn't."

CHAPTER TWENTY-THREE

A Welcome Departure

AFTER MARIE RECOUNTED the murders of the Taylors, I tried to do what she asked and believe that her story was true. That the blood drinker was real and everything occurred just the way she said. But I couldn't. The idea of the blood drinker was a block—a blank spot. So instead I imagined it in all the different ways it could have happened.

I imagined the Taylors terrorized and slaughtered. Trying to run and dying in fear, still slightly alive as they were placed in bed and the scene was staged. I imagined Cheryl's screams. I imagined the smile slowly relaxing off Peter Knupp's face.

I was starting to worry that something was wrong with me. It was odd how detached I could be, how detached we could both be when she was talking about the killings, as if we were older and harder boiled.

"It's a coping method," Mr. McBride said to me. "A tactic.

Every good journalist has to have it."

"I still care about them," I said. "About the victims. About the Carlsons, and Steve."

"But you care about her, too."

We were sitting in his office at the *Star* with his crowded desk between us. Since the murders came to Black Deer Falls, he'd gotten messier; practically every surface was covered in coffee-stained papers and photographs, editions of other, bigger newspapers. There was so much that the picture of his wedding had been moved to the top of a filing cabinet.

"It's fine if you do," he said. "You can't spend that much time with a person and not see their humanity."

I reached out and dug around in the mess until I found a paperweight. It had a similar heft to a baseball and I tossed it back and forth between my hands.

"I do care about her," I said. "And I care about the story."

"That's okay, too." He smiled with closed lips. "She chose you to tell it."

"She chose me to hear it. I don't even know if she understands that I want to use it. Write it."

"She seems too smart to me," he said, "not to. Does she care about you?"

I looked at the wall behind him, at the framed diploma from the University of Pittsburgh School of Journalism.

"Why did you come out here?" I asked. "When you could have stayed and written out there?"

"I see you've learned the art of deflection."

I sighed.

"Yes. I think she does care about me."

"Then she's probably glad."

But I wasn't sure. I was no longer sure about anything. I only knew that the interviews were almost over. Soon she would tell me what happened the night that the Carlsons were killed, and after that she would go to trial or jail—and it would be up to me to put it all together.

"Don't be afraid of your involvement in the story," said Mr. McBride. "Don't be afraid to show your heart."

"What does heart have to do with the truth?" I asked.

"More than you'd think. You'll know what I mean, when you're writing."

"I don't know why you're so confident," I said, and he grinned.

"Call it a reporter's instinct."

It was a day toward the middle of December that I went by the jail and Bert told me I had to wait.

"Wait for what?" I asked.

"Mr. Pilson is up there with her and Ed." By Ed he meant Mr. Porter, Marie's defense attorney.

"What's Pilson doing up there?" I asked. Benjamin Pilson had been in Black Deer Falls all that time, through all those strange occurrences and wild tales that must have infuriated him. He'd still been there, plotting, huddled over a pile of Marie's taped sessions in his room at Mrs. B.'s. I really don't know why he'd stayed. He had almost never interfered.

"Nancy, do you know what he's up to?" I asked. But before Nancy could guess, we heard Marie's shout, carrying from all the way upstairs.

"You can't do that!" she hollered. "You can't kill me if I'm not the one who did it!"

I bolted for the women's cell, and raced through the station in what seemed like three strides. I burst through the door to our old kitchen just in time to hear Mr. Porter say, "You'll never get the death penalty for an accomplice. Not for one who didn't do the killing. And who's a fifteen-year-old girl!"

"Sixteen, isn't she?" Pilson said, and looked at Marie. "Sixteen, now that December's here. And yes I will. That little nurse they killed? Angela Hawk? She wasn't just anybody. She was the niece of the governor's wife." He picked up his briefcase and turned to go. "Felony murder, Mr. Porter. Look it up. In the state of Nebraska you do not have to wield the knife to be found guilty."

He strode out of there, leaving Mr. Porter to try and calm Marie, who looked like she might climb up the bars.

"Mr. Pilson, wait!"

I chased him all the way through the station, out into the cold parking lot where his car was idling. The entire back seat of his sedan was full with boxes of case files, satchels, and suitcases, dress shirts hung ingeniously from hangers hooked onto the edge of a cracked-open window.

"You're leaving?"

"I'm going back to Lincoln until the trial."

"You can't," I said. "You can't do this. You can't just kill her!"

"She was there and she's protecting him," he said. "Yes, I can."

"But she's telling the truth!"

He stopped, and looked at me like I'd gone crazy.

"She's telling the truth," I said again, more quietly. "I know how it sounds. But I've seen things, and what she's told me—"

"I knew this was a mistake. You're just a kid." He opened his door and threw his briefcase inside. "Marie Hale was advised of the potential consequences during the district court hearing. And so were you. Yet for months you've let her play out this fantasy. When she goes to the chair, it'll be your fault as much as her own."

"Wait, Mr. Pilson—"

"You just have to look at the facts—"

"I am looking at the facts," I said. "And all the facts that you can't explain." He opened his door and made to get in but I cut him off.

"The fingerprints found at the scene. The footprints. Why are they only hers? The people you've shown her picture to in Loup City, in Norfolk, in Grand Junction—why is hers the only face they remember? Unless you think she did it alone?"

He turned away and put his hands on the hood of the car. I could see him thinking about it, that she was the one, and I regretted floating the idea. But a moment later he shook it off: no jury would buy that once they saw Marie, so young and so little. So female. A woman couldn't commit murders like that. She could only help a man do it.

"She doesn't deserve to die," I said quietly.

"It's not for you or I to decide. But the judge. And the governor. And the Lord."

"But it is you deciding. If you ask for mercy, they'll listen to you."

"So I guess it's true," he said. "About how close you two have become. You do know she never really wanted to confess? That if you hadn't been there, all of this would have gone another way. But a nice-looking boy like you? From an upstanding family? Marie Hale has never been alone in a room with someone like you, let alone have him listen to her. Part of her probably even believes that if she can convince you she's innocent . . . then she really will be innocent."

"That's not what she's doing, Mr. Pilson."

"I know you're not recording everything," he said. "Sometimes the tape will start and you're already in the middle of a conversation."

"Sometimes I forget to start it," I said. "But I'm not missing anything important. Just shooting the breeze. She'll ask me for smokes, things like that."

"Smokes," Pilson repeated. "And maybe things of a more delicate nature? Things you might not think are appropriate to record on tape?"

I stared at him blankly.

"Like sexual things?"

"I—"

"Do you know if they had sexual intercourse? Do you know how many times? How about if they engaged in deviant sexual behavior? Did she maybe let him put it in her mouth?"

"Why does that matter?" I asked.

"Insight into her level of involvement." His eyes had gone mean—he was enjoying how uncomfortable he was making me. "Come on now, you don't think that she's a virgin?"

"I guess I don't. But I still don't see why it matters."

"It matters because she's got you fooled."

"Where was the blood?" I asked as he got inside the car. "Where was the blood, Mr. Pilson?" I raised my voice over the sound of the shutting door, the revving engine. "Where was it, if it wasn't like she says it was?"

"I have a lead on something, Michael," he said. "I didn't want to say so in there in case it doesn't pan out. But if it does, I'll be back. And then everything is going to change.

"You know, most of the so-called mysterious anomalies of these cases can be explained by institutional foul-ups. You say they never tried to get away? Never tried to call for help? Except the Covey kid in Madison did try to call for help."

Richard Covey, the graduate student who was killed in an abandoned house with his fiancée, Stacy Lee Brandberg. The last killings before the Carlsons were murdered in Black Deer Falls.

"What do you mean?" I asked.

"He dropped textbooks out the window of a car with his name and messages to police written in them. Someone even picked them up and reported them. Only no one made the connection until after the bodies were found. Madison PD kept it out of the papers." He looked at me one more time. "Just get her to tell the truth," he said. Then he put the car in gear and drove away.

That evening, my dad stopped by the jail to give me a lift home for supper. On the way he looped around to the service station and the small store across the train tracks, and left me in the truck while he went in and bought cherry-vanilla pipe tobacco and some bubblegum for Dawn. He got back in and tossed me a box of Mike and Ikes.

"Toxicology reports came back on the Carlsons," he said as I opened the box and he backed the pickup out of the parking lot, sliding a little on the ugly, half-melted ice. "They came back clean.

"I'd hoped," he said softly, "since they did the autopsy so fast, that they'd be able to find something. But if there was poison or sedatives, it was nothing that could be identified."

"Why weren't they bound?" I asked. "Wouldn't it make more sense for them to be bound? It wouldn't be hard to do it if there were two perpetrators. One to hold the razor, the other to tie them up?"

My dad shrugged. "Maybe he didn't trust her knots."

"Or maybe she was unwilling."

I caught his glance at me from the side of my eye.

"Maybe."

"Pilson thinks he has something," I said.

"*Mr.* Pilson," my dad corrected, even though he thought about as much of him as I did. "And what's that?"

"He wouldn't say."

"That why he's going back to Lincoln?"

I shrugged.

"Richard Covey tried to signal for help," I said. "He dropped textbooks along the highway with his name on them."

"Where did you hear that?"

"Mr. Pilson."

My dad glanced at me.

"Michael, do you want to stop?"

"I can't stop, Dad," I said. "Even if she did what she did, I don't want Marie to die. I don't even really want her to be gone." I shoved Mike and Ikes into my mouth to keep from crying and my dad shifted in his seat and let me chew.

"I'm sorry, son."

"I don't know how to help her."

"There's only one way to help her," he said. "Pilson doesn't really want Marie. He wants *him*. She has to give him up."

"What if there's no one to give up?" I asked.

But he shook his head. "There has to be. I don't believe that little girl ever hurt anyone."

CHAPTER TWENTY-FOUR

Winter

PILSON WAS GONE from Black Deer Falls for the rest of December, and all the blessed month of January. And for a while it was as if his leaving had freed us—in the absence of him peering down the backs of our necks, we forgot where we were. We forgot, for a little while, why we were there and that our time was borrowed. We refused to believe that it wouldn't just go on that way forever.

But when I was away from Marie, I knew it was almost up. The blood drinker was no longer keeping folks jumping. The roadblocks, the extra patrols and searches still went on, but in fewer and fewer numbers. For weeks, there had been no new trace, no new clue. There had been no trail to pick up, not so much as a gas station knocked over for cash. And there'd been a subtle shift in the dwindling number of newspaper articles, too: just a few carefully placed questions about what Marie knew and what she could have done.

The day after Christmas, I brought Marie a few gifts from my family, and a plate of leftover Christmas dinner: roasted goose and mashed potatoes and my mom's wild-rice stuffing. I figured we had at least through the holidays before I had to push. But after she'd opened the card Dawn made, and unwrapped the skirt and the length of green ribbon from my mother, she asked,

"How long do you think we have left?"

"I don't know. Not long. To be honest I thought we'd have heard from Pilson already." I reached through the bars of her cell and picked up the ribbon. "What do you think he knows? What lead was he following?"

"He can't know anything," Marie said. "He's bluffing."

"Do you think he's bluffing about the death penalty?"

I didn't want to talk about it that day. It was Christmas, and I figured it would upset her.

"No," she said. "That was always what he hoped for. He's so damned lucky that Pilson showed up."

I was confused. I'd thought she was talking about Pilson.

"You mean the blood drinker," I said. "He wants you to die?"

"Has to happen somehow. If he can't do it himself."

It took me a moment to figure out what she meant: to die and be raised from the dead. That was how it went in the legends and the lore.

"Oh," I said. "Because of the vampire stuff."

Marie's mood lightened, and she smiled.

"Right. Because of the vampire stuff." She smoothed the skirt where it lay across her knees. "This is really nice, Michael. It's the nicest Christmas I ever had."

I want to recount one more thing that happened before Pilson returned in February.

It was a night in January. A school night, but I was up late, and the rest of my family was fast asleep. I'd been up in my room, looking over a book on vampire lore or maybe just reading a comic, when something hit my window. A pebble, like I was a girl and someone had come calling. At first I took it for a branch from a tree or a leaf, even though it wasn't windy out. Except it kept on. One pebble. Then a second. Then a third, and that one hard enough to leave a chip in the glass.

I got up and looked, expecting to see Percy, or a friend of Dawn's. But there was no one. No one below my window. No one on the front porch or standing in our driveway.

He was standing in the street. Hidden mostly in shadows, only his lower half and left shoulder illuminated by the Schumans' outdoor garage light. For a minute I thought I was seeing things and blinked hard—but when I opened my eyes he was still there. Looking up at my window.

I was scared at first. Then I filled with jittery excitement. It was him. The one who'd dragged Marie into hell. Who had murdered Steve and his parents and a dozen others. And he was right there.

My dad was asleep down the hall and he kept his service pistol in there with him, hung up in the closet, but it had been locked since I was a kid. So I grabbed my baseball bat instead.

I don't know what I was planning. I would run him down and break his legs. I would hit him until he didn't wake up. All of the odd things that occurred to me later—that he had managed to throw rocks at my window from the street, that he was standing in the middle of the night in the dead of winter with no coat on—didn't occur to me then. I just wanted to catch him.

I would've been a hero. Marie would've been safe. And it would have been over.

The time it took to turn from the window, grab the bat, and run downstairs couldn't have been more than five seconds. I know my front door was locked and that I didn't hear the knob or the heavy jangle of the holiday wreath. But when I charged off the last stair, the door was already open.

He was standing in the middle of our living room. The exact same shape he'd been in the street, as if he was a statue that someone had moved. And despite our living room being lit by the moon and the clean white snow—I couldn't make out anything about his face.

I raised the bat.

"Ask her how much she drank," he said.

I started screaming at the sound of his voice. It wasn't like any voice I'd ever heard. And his face hadn't moved with his words.

I screamed for my mom; I screamed for my dad. Maybe I even screamed for Dawn. I was still screaming when my dad came down the stairs, half stumbling from sleep, and flipped on the lights.

"Michael, Michael! What's going on?"

I was standing in the entryway in front of the open door. The living room was empty.

They were scared. They said I'd been sleepwalking. I got a short lecture about how my dad could have shot me even though he hadn't brought his gun. And another after my mom had to field phone calls from nearby neighbors whom I'd woken.

"It's that girl, isn't it?" she said.

"No. It wasn't her at all."

"She's manipulating you, Michael. All those days the two of you alone. A girl like that knows how to get what she wants."

"Is that what people are saying?" I asked. "Is that what you think?"

"All I know is that before you met her, this would never have happened."

People blamed Marie, they suspected her, they even hated her. Those who were kind pitied her. But no one believed her, and maybe that's why I had to.

We found no trace of the intruder—no snowy footprints or wet spots on the carpet, nothing out of place. By the next afternoon, my family had all but forgotten about it. My mother apologized for what she'd said and made me some meat loaf sandwiches to take to the jail.

But there was still a crack in the glass of my window. And I have never been a sleepwalker. I asked Marie about it, in a roundabout way, but even she said I was imagining things.

"He couldn't have come inside your house unless you'd invited him, Michael. And you didn't invite him. Did you?"

I hadn't. But it was funny how the bastard only followed

vampiric rules when following them made me look crazy.

A few days later, my dad came up to my room and made me get rid of everything vampire related. The books went back to the library, and he confiscated a few of my notebooks. He pulled down the sketches of the symbol Percy and I had seen in the woods.

Maybe it worked. Maybe it was all in my head. In any case, the blood drinker never tried to contact me again, in my dreams or otherwise. And then, a week later, Pilson returned with news.

CHAPTER TWENTY-FIVE

The Discovery

I BET WHEN Benjamin Pilson first heard about Marie, he was excited. A young girl like that at the scene of the crime? I bet he thought he'd lucked out. She would be easy to lean on and easy to fool—the entire case had to have felt like a golden egg cracked right onto his plate.

I remember the day he came back: walking into the station smiling like a game-show host.

I was on the main floor, helping Bert clean up his desk. It was always a mess—food wrappings and napkins from hurried lunches, coffee rings everywhere—and my dad harped on him sometimes, so I wanted to help. We all still felt bad about what had happened to his snake. Later that spring, as soon as the snow melted, my dad drove to the big pet shop in Brainerd to get him a new python, a trip that made for a few rare moments of levity: my dad had never looked so nervous during any prisoner transport as he did driving around with that snake.

Pilson came in as I was carrying out the trash. He glanced at me and I just sort of nodded, surprised to see him. He didn't bother nodding back and went in to speak with my dad. They must have made some calls because before long our prosecutor, Mr. Norquist, arrived, and then Mr. Porter a few minutes later.

"What in the world's he starting now?" Bert asked as we stood beside his desk.

Pilson wanted everyone to march up to Marie's cell.

"She's just finishing her lunch, Rick," Bert said. "Why don't you let me go up and fetch her?" My dad nodded, and Bert got up with the keys.

"What's going on, Dad?" I asked, but he motioned for me to be quiet.

Bert brought Marie down uncuffed. He kept a hand on her shoulder.

"Into the interrogation room, please," Pilson said.

Marie frowned. "It'll be pretty damned crowded. Can't you just tell me out here?"

At first Pilson seemed annoyed; the line in his forehead creased deep. Then that smile came back, and that was even worse.

"If that's what you want, Miss Hale," he said. "Or should I say, Miss Mewes?"

"Miss Mewes?" my dad asked.

"Her name isn't really Marie Catherine Hale," Pilson said. "It's Marie Catherine Mewes. She was born in Greeley County, Nebraska, to one Audrey Cody—formerly Mewes—of North

Platte. Mrs. Cody was reported missing some months ago. Along with her husband, Nathaniel."

I looked at Marie. I'd never seen her afraid, not even when she was drenched in the Carlsons' blood. But every time Pilson said the name Mewes she flinched like he'd hit her.

"Isn't that them?" he asked. "Your parents? Audrey and Nathaniel Cody? Missing since early summer. And dead, according to you."

"Yes," Marie said. "They're both dead."

"But they aren't, are they? Or at least he isn't."

"What do you mean he isn't?" I asked.

"I mean that Nathaniel Cody is our killer." He told us how he'd found them. It was a clue from the taped interviews. He'd been trying to trace Marie for months, calling orphanages and halfway houses and combing through reports on missing girls. Then one night he was listening to the interviews and heard Marie say her stepfather claimed lineage to a famous local cowboy. It didn't take long for him to learn that Buffalo Bill Cody's Wild West Show had been founded in North Platte. And once he had the name Cody, the rest was easy.

"Mr. Cody's employer had thought it odd when he failed to report for work on a Monday morning, but after he asked around and discovered that his wife and stepdaughter were also nowhere to be found, he assumed that the family had picked up and moved on, as some folks do. It wasn't for another week that the landlady went by the house and noticed that nothing had been packed. Clothes still in the dresser. Jewelry and family photographs all left behind.

"I always thought it was strange," he went on, "that no one came forward to claim you after your picture was all over the papers and shown on the news. But you looked a little different back then. Meeker, and your hair longer and dull. Flawed skin. And no smile, even for a photograph." He pulled a photo out of his jacket and flashed it at us: it was taken not more than a few years ago and in it her hair was lighter and thinner. Dark spots marred her forehead and chin. It was different, but it was her.

Marie looked like she wanted to claw his eyes out.

"Is that true?" I asked.

"I already told you it was," she said. "I already told you they were dead."

"They were dead," Pilson went on. "Isn't that what you said? *They*. But people in North Platte had a lot to say about your step-father after they found out you were the one being held up here. Troubling things."

"You shut your mouth."

"What kind of troubling things?" Mr. Porter asked.

"Nathaniel Cody had a proclivity for young girls."

Marie's jaw and fists clenched. My dad caught on sooner than I did, and whispered, "Good God."

"He made a sort of pet of you, didn't he, Marie?" Pilson said. "Buying you little presents. New outfits. You were plain and he spruced you up. Maybe it was innocent enough at first. But then it changed. That's what your landlady said. Mrs. Marshall. She said maybe it was never your mother he was interested in in the first place."

"Shut up."

"Looking at you now, I can hardly blame him."

"Shut up, shut up, shut up!" Marie lunged for Pilson with hooked fingers. Bert had to haul her back. He and my dad had to pin her to the floor and put her in cuffs. And she kept screaming, these awful animal screams.

"Put her in the interrogation room," Pilson said. "I'm not done with her yet."

"No," Mr. Porter said. "You are. You're done."

"Take her back up, Bert," my dad said. "Keep the cuffs on and stay with her until I tell you different!"

Bert nodded. He looked terrified, wrestling her toward the stairs. She was furious, screaming and kicking.

"Did you seduce him?" Pilson called. "Did you help him kill your mother? Tell us where he is, Miss Mewes! Don't you want her body found? Don't you want her to have a Christian burial?"

He smiled the same smile he had on when he came in. Until my dad put an arm across his chest and shoved him into the wall.

"That is enough out of you, Mr. Pilson."

"Get your hands off me!"

"You come into my station and let all hell out?" My dad shoved him one more time. Pilson's tie hung askew and his top button had come loose; he straightened the tie angrily as my dad pointed for him to go through his office door.

I followed them inside.

Pilson slapped a thin file folder onto my father's desk. My father picked it up and leafed through the pages.

"Once we found her, everything fell into place," Pilson said. "She and the stepfather embarked on some kind of affair that resulted in the death of the mother. From there things spun out of control."

My father cast him a disgusted look. "Around here, when a grown man takes up with a fifteen-year-old girl, we don't call it 'embarking on an affair,'" he said. "Where is he? Have you found him?"

"Not yet. We've put out a bulletin. The Federal Bureau is sending men. Now that we know who we're looking for, he won't be able to hide for long."

I stood to one side like wood. I had never heard the name Nathaniel Cody but now I couldn't stop hearing it, and imagining what he looked like: tall and dark, handsome like a movie star.

My dad closed the folder.

"It's disturbing," Pilson said. "But at least it's an explanation."

But it wasn't the real explanation. Everything about it was wrong, even her name: Marie Catherine Mewes. It was like they were talking about a different person.

"Listen, Rick," Pilson said, "you have to give me another run at her. Now, before she comes up with something new. We've already lost too much time."

They glanced at me. They were embarrassed at having let the interviews go on for so long and listening to all that silly vampire talk. Only it wasn't silly. Nathaniel Cody hadn't been standing outside of my window. He hadn't been scaling trees and carving symbols into them.

But my dad gave in. "Mr. Porter will need to be present."

"Dad," I protested.

"It'll be all right, Michael."

"It won't be," I said quietly. I could've slugged Pilson in the gut. Yet he still had the gall to look at me with sympathy, and to give my shoulder a squeeze. Then he went into the interrogation room.

Pilson questioned Marie for two hours. She shouted through most of it. But it was worse when she was quiet. I didn't want to think about the questions he was asking, filthy questions like he'd put to me before he'd left town. And I didn't want to think about the answers.

When it was over, she came out looking like a ghost. I said her name but she just walked through the station with Bert back up to her cell. To be fair, Pilson came out not looking much better: he'd taken off his suit coat and his underarms were dark with sweat.

"So?" my father asked. "Is it like you said?"

He nodded, and wiped his face. "But she's not cooperating. She won't give him up."

"It's been months," I said. "She doesn't know where he is."

Pilson looked at me, annoyed. "The interviews will stop. There's no need for the expense of the tape recordings. And we can arrange for transport to Lincoln as soon as next week."

"Hang on," my dad said. "There's been no new hearing."

"And she's not finished," I said. "There's still more—"

"If she needs to confess more," Pilson said, "she'll have a priest."

"You can't just take her."

"With this new information—her identity, the main suspect—Nebraska has the better claim."

"With all due respect, Mr. Pilson, that's for a judge to say. And the people of Black Deer Falls will disagree. We still don't know what went on in that farmhouse that night."

Pilson sighed, but then he nodded. "You're right. You do need answers. I know that I'm not the only one with an election to think about."

CHAPTER TWENTY-SIX

The Dracula Murders

SHORTLY AFTER MR. Pilson returned to Black Deer Falls, he leaked the details of Marie's confession to the press. In the interest of journalistic integrity I can't say for certain that it was him, but who else would it have been? He'd kept it quiet all this time, fearing ridicule, but he didn't need to now that he had a "reasonable explanation." So he let it out: about the blood drinker, and about the nature of Nathaniel Cody and Marie's relationship. Cody instantly became the most wanted man in America. Marie became a joke.

The papers took to calling the murders the Dracula Murders again and this time as farce: they ridiculed Marie for girlish silliness in the same article that condemned her to death.

My father and I weren't spared either. They called us rubes. They said we'd rushed through our forests armed with rifles and wooden crosses, hunting monsters, too stupid to realize that Marie probably took the idea from their very own headlines. Hadn't they coined them the Dracula Murders all the way back in August?

The reporters took the explanation of Marie's stepfather and ran with it, forgetting all about the missing blood, the missing prints, the symbols carved into Steve Carlson's headstone, and the other questions about the case that still remained. To the public at large, the mystery of the Bloodless Murders had been solved and attention turned to other things. In Black Deer Falls that meant things like transferring Marie out of our jail for trial and sentencing, and holding a special recall election for county sheriff. The whole town was ashamed of us for listening to her story. And my father didn't defend himself. He didn't tell them why he thought it was worth listening to. I guess it just wasn't his way.

At school, kids laughed at me. They threw things. They'd trip me in a crowd, or someone would run up from behind and shove me before running off again. And Percy showed up in the cafeteria with a blackening eye.

"Never mind it," he said before I could ask. "It was a fair fight. You could even say I won."

"Who was it?" I demanded.

"Never mind, I said. Just keep your head down. Let me take care of it."

"*I* can take care of it."

"No you can't. If you did, they'd say . . . I don't know. But you'd be the one in trouble, and your dad, too. They're all watching you."

He didn't say who he meant by "they." There were eyes

everywhere again, reporters gathering like crows, in dark winter coats and hats, freshly purchased scarves and gloves that weren't warm enough for our winters. Over on 9th, Mrs. B.'s was full to bursting, and so was the motel out by the highway. The diners and bars were crowded every night with "nosy reporters" and Charlie had started to grumble that it was hard to get in and out of the Sportsman's Café for his lunch break.

I sat at our table in the cafeteria, tray untouched as Percy ate his meat loaf and cottage cheese. Around us all was quiet. No chatter. Only whispers. I felt eyes in the back of my head and wished I could be more like Percy, still able to fake a good appetite with his face swollen. I even wished I was more like Pilson, who stood in the center of the reporters ever ready with a quote or a quip, every photograph taken a portrait of a grim man of the law, the crease in his forehead nearly too deep for the ink to capture.

"He says it brings him no personal joy," I said, and Percy stopped eating. "That Marie will face the electric chair. He says it's his responsibility as a prosecutor to the victims and their families. To us, the good, honest citizens afraid to turn off our lights."

"Did he say it with a straight face?" Percy asked.

"I don't know. It was in the paper."

I chanced a glance around the lunchroom and caught Carol's eye. She was sitting with her friends. The other girls were a gaggle of furtive glances and murmurs, but Carol simply looked at me, and I imagined for a second that I could lay my head on her shoulder until the reporters left. Until Marie was gone. Until everybody forgot that it was me in that room taking shorthand about vampires.

I stood.

"Where you going?" Percy asked.

"Not hungry."

I took my lunch tray and dumped the food into the trash, and Rudy Bartholomew yelled, "Going back to the jail?"

"I'm going back to class," I said without turning around.

"Steve's murder gave you a heck of a story, I guess."

I made a pair of fists and looked. Rudy Bart stood near the center of his table, wearing the letter jacket he never seemed to take off. I was a little surprised he had the nerve after what he'd done to us in the cemetery. But that was our fault, I guess. We'd kept quiet, so we'd been the ones to teach him that he could get away with it.

Percy jumped up and came over to stand with me.

"You think Michael wants to be in the papers? He's not the one following the reporters around, constantly combing his hair in case one of them wants a picture. I've seen you all do that." Percy pointed around the cafeteria.

"He's going to make everybody feel sorry for her! Don't you care?"

"I suppose you'd kill her with your bare hands," I said, a little louder than I meant to. I looked into their eyes. I glared at them. Kids I'd grown up with. Kids I knew. But I didn't know any of them as well as I'd come to know Marie. I bet if I did, they would have their secrets, too.

Percy and I walked out. Behind us the cafeteria ladies found their voices and told Rudy to sit down and go on eating.

"I don't know what your old man was thinking, making you keep on coming to school," Percy said. "Mo's not the best dad but even he would have me locked up at home with the curtains closed until this blew over."

"This isn't going to blow over."

We walked though the halls, feeling lousy, and someone shoved a newspaper in my face. Marie's photograph was on the front page—the picture of her at the courthouse in my mother's red lipstick—beneath the headline "16-year-old Lolita or Bride of Dracula?"

The kid holding it was Nick Clinton, a decent enough fellow and a sort of friend of mine. It wasn't his fault. He'd just had bad timing.

"My mom's making a scrapbook," he said. "Of the articles. She says someday we'll want to remember the days when Black Deer Falls was famous."

I hit Nick in the face. Then I hit him again when he fell, over and over, so when Percy finally pulled me off, his face was marked red and his lip was bleeding.

"Have you lost it?" he cried as he struggled to one knee. He had his hands up to catch the blood dripping down his chin.

"I'm sorry," I said numbly, and let Percy pull me away before I could throw up all over the linoleum floor.

"No one'll blame you," Percy kept saying. "But we should cut for the rest of the day just to be safe."

"I don't want you to get in trouble, Perce."

He waved his hand. "I won't get into any trouble. This my old man will understand."

Percy slowed the car to a crawl as we approached the parking lot of the sheriff's station. The lot was peppered with strange cars, most of them running to stave off the cold, and inside each was a reporter or a pair of them, ready to leap out at the first sign of movement.

"Are you sure I shouldn't just drive on by? We could hide out at my place or head over to the bowling alley in the Rapids."

I shook my head. I couldn't avoid it forever, and there was really nowhere to run. He pulled in, and I looked at him gratefully as he parked.

"You haven't asked me anything since the story about the confession came out."

"I figured you'd been questioned enough."

"But it's different," I said. "You're my friend. I don't mind you asking."

He sat and considered it, his eye shifty over his swollen cheek.

"Do you believe it?" he asked. "What she told you?"

"I don't know," I said. "Should I?"

He shook his head. Of course I shouldn't. But what he said was, "I just keep thinking of the marks in our trees and on Steve's headstone. What it felt like out there in the woods." He looked at me. "That thing you said, about that girl in New England. Those people digging her up and cutting her heart out. Was that true?"

"Yeah," I said. "That was true."

He gave a big sigh.

"Then I guess I wouldn't put anything past anybody." He looked out the window Three reporters had gotten out of their cars and were headed our way. "Here they come," he said. "Good luck."

"Thanks, Perce."

I kept my head down and said nothing as I made my way inside. Not even so much as a "no comment."

Inside the station, Nancy sat behind the booking desk, typing.

"You should have called first," she said glumly. "I'd have had Bert go out and order them to stay in their cars."

"Would that have worked?"

She shrugged and went back to typing.

It was oddly quiet inside compared to the commotion in the parking lot. My father had gone home for lunch and Bert was at a loss about what to do with the reporters; he peered out at them from behind the deputy's desk like he was trying to decide how he was going to get to his patrol cruiser. As I passed the hallway that led to the jail, I got a heavy feeling, like I sometimes got when the cells weren't empty.

"Just a few drunk and disorderlies from last night," said Nancy. "Charlie had to bring them in after a fight broke out at the Eagle. They were scuffling with the out-of-towners."

"Has anyone been up to see Marie?"

"No one but me, and I've been here since nine."

I went up and knocked on the door that led to our old kitchen and the women's cell.

"Come in," she said.

"You should've asked if it was me. It could have been anyone, with so many folks in town."

"No one else would've knocked."

"How are you?" I asked.

"I'm fine." She was seated on her cot like normal, her dark hair tied back with black ribbon. A lunch tray sat on her writing desk, the food untouched. It wasn't much, just a sandwich and a macaroni salad. But it was uncommon for Marie not to eat.

"What are you doing back here, Michael? I thought they'd keep you away now that they've got their story."

"Is it true what he said?" I asked.

"What who said?"

"What Pilson said. About your stepfather."

For a moment she seemed angry, and her jaw tightened. She curled her lip. "Which part?"

"That he's the killer."

"Of course not." She made a dismissive sound. "He lacked the nerve, among other things."

"You sound like you hate him."

"I do. He deserves to be hated."

"When you spoke of him before, you didn't seem to care much one way or the other."

"Well, that was when he was dead. Now he's back and ruining everything." She cast her eyes to the empty table in the kitchen, where the tape recorder usually sat. "They took it yesterday morning."

"So what?" I held up my notebook and pen. "The tape was never for us anyway." I drew my usual chair away from the wall and sat down.

"Why do you still want to talk to me?"

"If you say he wasn't the killer, then I believe you."

She smiled with such relief that I felt bad about what I had to ask next.

"But what about the rest of it?"

She tucked her knees up to her chest. She seemed so young, all of a sudden. I remembered how I had thought she was a fast girl. I remembered thinking that she seemed older, and felt disgusted with myself. And I felt guilty for thinking about her the way I sometimes did when we were alone. There was only a year difference between our ages. But she didn't need anyone thinking about her like that.

"Nathaniel Cody," she said, "was a filthy bastard."

"So it's true."

"No, it's not true. Why does it matter?"

"Because it matters."

"It doesn't. I told you."

But I knew that she was lying. She wouldn't look at me. She hunched her shoulders.

"Tell me the truth."

"I am."

"What have you left out?"

"What does it matter?" Marie shouted, the only time she ever raised her voice to me. "Even if it was true it doesn't mean the rest of it's a lie! I told you he was terrible and you were happy enough. But now you want to know it all. Every dirty detail. As if that's the only part that's important."

"Marie, what he did—it is important."

"No it isn't. It only is if I say it is. And I don't."

I sat back quietly. I didn't understand. I still don't, and I suppose that I never will. But I did understand this: if she gave them anything on her stepfather, they would let her live. But everything she had told me—her story—would be erased as if it never was.

"Okay," I said. "Then keep going. Finish it."

"I can't. He's tainted it," she said, and I couldn't tell whether she meant Nathaniel Cody or Benjamin Pilson.

"Well, isn't there a way to 'untaint' it?" I asked. "If Cody didn't do it, there must be a way to prove that he didn't."

She looked down and toyed with her shoelaces.

"Marie? There must be a way."

"There is," she said. "But I don't want to ask you to do it." She took a deep breath, and I leaned forward so she could tell me what she wanted me to do. When she was through, I won't say I wasn't nervous. But I agreed.

"Okay, then," she said. "Go get Pilson. Tell him I'm ready to tell him where my stepfather is."

I rang Pilson and caught him at Mrs. B.'s. He said he would be there within the hour but he showed up not ten minutes later, storming through the station like he owned it—which he only got away with because my father wasn't there. When I heard him on the stairs, I made sure to step back to avoid catching the swinging door in my face.

"Miss Mewes," he said.

"Don't call me that," Marie said, and scowled.

"It is your name, isn't it?"

"So is Marie."

"How about I just call you 'Miss,' then?"

Marie shrugged.

"Well, then, what did you want to tell me?"

"I wanted to tell you that Nathaniel Cody didn't kill Peter Knupp. Or Angela Hawk or Beverly Nordahl, or any of the others. He never even met them."

"I think we both know that he did."

"He didn't. He wasn't innocent of much, but he's innocent of that."

"That story won't hold up for much longer. I'm circulating photographs of your stepfather around Grand Junction and Loup City, even around the University at Madison."

"It won't amount to anything."

Pilson looked at me and laughed. A short bark. "We'll see."

"We will see, you horse's ass!"

"Marie," I cautioned, and she clamped her mouth shut.

"Why don't you tell me where the blood went," she said, "if you're so set on things?"

"Cody will tell me himself when we catch him."

"No one's going to find Nathaniel Cody unless I tell you where he is."

"We're broadening the search daily."

But so far they'd come up with squat. Pilson's eyes hardened. He wanted Marie to fear him, but the truth was that he feared her: Marie was someone he couldn't intimidate. No matter which of his many faces he presented her with, Marie remained the same. Unflappable and threatening.

"All right, then. Where is he?"

"He's just where I said he was." Marie crossed her arms. "He's dead and buried with my mother. And since there's no other way to make you believe me, I'm going to let you dig them up. I'm going to tell you where they are."

Pilson shifted his weight, impatient or maybe nervous. If she was lying, she was getting better at it.

"And where is that?"

"Oh, I'm not telling you," Marie said. "But as usual I will tell Michael."

CHAPTER TWENTY-SEVEN

Hatching a Plan

MARIE'S PLAN WAS for me to go with Pilson to find the bodies. Pilson agreed to it, because what choice did he have? It took only a few hours for him to assemble a team of local police officers and even federal agents to aid in the recovery of the bodies of Marie's mother and stepfather. I would be with them all the way. I would show them the route to take. And not even I would know exactly where we were going—Marie wanted to be sure they couldn't shake it out of me and go ahead on their own. She gave us the name of the town, and when we got there, I would phone her at the jail for the final location.

We were to leave that afternoon. I had only to go home and pack a bag—and get permission from my mother.

"Pot roast with carrots," my mother said when I walked through the door. She often did that—announced the evening meal in lieu of an actual greeting. "I didn't expect you home so early." When

I didn't say anything and hovered near the door, she turned and asked, "What is it? What's the matter?"

"I can't stay for dinner," I said. "They need me to go to Nebraska."

"Nebraska? For what?"

"Marie's going to tell us where some bodies are buried."

She blinked. "What's your father say?"

"He says I need to check with you."

"Then no. Of course not. It's too far. And on a school night."

"Mom—"

"And it isn't right. It's . . . morbid. You're not even eighteen yet."

"But—"

"I said no, Michael. Now set the table and call your sister. There's Jell-O for dessert."

I pursed my lips, but I called Dawn, and we sat down to eat, even though it was more than an hour early and the roast was still tough. It was an awkward meal, cuts of meat slapped down on my plate and sloshed with gravy, extra carrots because she knew I wasn't fond of them. Dawn giving me wide eyes and mouthing, "What did you *do*?" And I did not get any Jell-O. I figured I would take the matter up again while we did the dishes. After she'd had more time to think it over. But as luck would have it, I didn't need to. Because before we cleared the table, my dad came home with Pilson.

When they came in, I stood up hopefully, and was immediately ordered upstairs. But I heard everything they said.

"Absolutely not," my mother said. "It's not right to take a boy his age. Dead bodies? After a killer?" She kept on like that for a long time, even speaking over my dad. So I crept back downstairs.

"I have to go. Marie won't have it any other way."

"I don't see why she has to get her way. It seems like she's always getting her way."

"She's sitting in a jail cell," I said. "And this isn't just a body. It's her mother."

My mom made a sad, frustrated sound. In the end both Pilson and my dad had to swear that I would be in no danger and wouldn't be there for the actual discovery. They were lying on both counts, as it happened, but they didn't know that at the time.

Back at the jail a caravan was waiting to take us to Nebraska and the city of North Platte. For reasons of jurisdiction, it was decided that my father would stay behind, so I would be on my own.

"Can I talk to Marie before we go?" I asked.

"No time," Pilson said. "You can speak to her on the phone when we get there."

He didn't want us cooking up any more schemes. Despite having access to all of our recordings, he'd become paranoid. We rode together in the same car all the way to Nebraska and he stopped to eat supper on the way. But there were no more milkshakes and easy smiles. Pilson scrutinized my every movement like he was trying to crack a code.

We stayed in a motel near North Platte, off the interstate—the kind with a detached lobby where an old woman parsed out room keys from a wooden pegboard and offered you a warm-up from an hours-old pot of coffee. Our cars filled up the otherwise empty parking lot, but the woman who ran the place didn't snoop, as if she saw a troop of investigators and federal agents pass through every month. When I asked her about it, she squinted at me.

"Government workers. They're clean and their money's always good. Some of them even make the beds up before they check out, tight enough to bounce a quarter off."

"Yeah," I said. "Every one of them is tight enough to bounce a quarter off."

She chuckled. "I won't ask," she said, "but I imagine this is something to do with those murders last summer. I can't guess what you're doing caught up in it."

"I'm Michael Jensen," I said, and shook her hand. I could tell she recognized my name. "I'm taking Marie Hale's confession up in Minnesota."

"Well, I'm not asking. But you'll tell me, won't you? If I need to start keeping my shotgun behind the desk again?"

I couldn't think of what to say. During those weeks when bodies were showing up in Nebraska, she must have been terrified. A woman alone, right off the highway.

"Maybe I ought to just keep it out from now on," she said.

I went back to my room, a room that I shared with—of course—Pilson. I kept expecting him to try to get at me about Marie, or to change tactics and sweet-talk me again, but he barely said a word. In fact I don't think our sharing a room was part of his strategy at all; I just don't think anyone else would have me.

In the end, though, I was sort of glad. I was nervous that

night and couldn't sleep. Had I been in a room with anyone other than Pilson I might've spilled my guts just for someone to talk to. Instead I lay on my side, facing the wall, and thought about the bodies lying dead somewhere nearby. Bodies that Marie had buried or helped to bury. Sometime before dawn I must've fallen asleep, because the next thing I knew Pilson was shaking me awake, saying it was time to get dressed and call Marie.

The man in charge of the operation was with the FBI: Agent Daniel McCabe. He was a slender man of medium height and wore the same dark suit as the others except that his necktie was oddly thin. He had dark hair, speckled but not yet peppered with gray. He never smiled, and despite his diminutive size it was obvious that he was in command. I've described him as slender but really he was a twig, skinny but skinny in the mean, dangerous way, like a winter wolf. By the time we'd assembled in his room that morning to make the phone call, twelve agents and three cars of local police had joined us at the motel. They stood around drinking coffee from paper cups and watching me curiously. Pilson moved the phone from the bedside table onto the bed and pointed at me to sit.

"Is this normal?" I asked. "This many men"—and more to join us at the location (I had overheard a few of them speaking)—"for a body recovery?"

"We can't know for certain what we'll find," Agent McCabe replied. "Or what we're being led into."

"Nothing, is my guess," said Pilson. He picked up the receiver and dialed the jail back home. His jaw was tight, and after having shared a room with him and lying awake half the night, I knew that he hadn't slept much either.

"What will you do after we find him," I asked, "long dead and just where she says he would be? Then who will you blame?"

He glanced at me, irritated. Then my dad must have picked up.

"Sheriff Jensen," Pilson said. "We're ready when you are. All right. Put her on." A pause. "Miss Mewes?" Another pause and a grimace. "Miss Hale. I have Michael here, as requested."

He handed me the phone.

"Hello, Michael," Marie said.

"Hi, Marie." I looked at Agent McCabe, who gestured for me to hold the receiver away from my ear so they could hear both sides. I did it, and he nodded. "We're in North Platte."

"Where?"

"The Sunshine Motel and Motor Lodge off the interstate."

There was a pause.

"Good," she said. "That's not far."

"Where are we going, Miss Mewes?" Pilson asked loudly, and received a roomful of dirty looks.

"Follow Highway eighty-three down to the lake," she said, and at a snap of Agent McCabe's fingers, three men fell over themselves trying to get him an unfolded map. "Take a right and follow the lake road until it turns off from the river, then go right again heading north. After three miles there will be an unmarked dirt road on your left. Take it. The house sits off in the middle of a field. There's a bright red mailbox and an oak tree in the side of the yard taller than the house."

"Is there a house number on the mailbox?" Agent McCabe asked.

"No."

"What color is the house?"

"Gray."

"Where will we find the bodies?"

"Have Michael put the phone back to his ear."

McCabe frowned and backed off—he'd come so close listening that he could've puckered up and given me a kiss. He gave me another nod, and I placed the receiver back securely against my ear.

"They still listening?" Marie asked.

"They're still listening but I don't think they can hear," I said.

"I'm surprised they didn't try to hook us up to one of those tape recorders."

"So am I."

"I'm going to tell only you where the bodies are buried," she said. "So they'll have to bring you with."

"They could just search the property themselves," I said, and she chuckled.

"Don't give them any ideas. But they won't. The property's too big."

"All right. So where are they?"

She paused.

"Listen, Michael. I want to say that I'm sorry."

"About what?"

"About you having to see them. My mother and stepfather, I mean."

"It's okay." I swallowed. I didn't know if it was. I'd never actually seen a dead body up close.

"Can you do something for me?"

"What's that?" I asked.

"I need you to tell me if my stepfather's body is unmarked."

"Unmarked?"

"Uncut. Full of blood."

"Sure," I said, and licked my lips nervously. "Sure, I will. But why?"

"Because I made him swear to leave just that one alone. Will you make sure? Will you promise?"

"I will. I promise."

She sighed, heavy, and lowered her voice. "The bodies are in the basement. Near the west wall. It will be work, to bring them up. Will you call me when it's finished?"

"I'll try, Marie."

"Okay. Goodbye."

We hung up, and I looked into the faces of a dozen waiting agents.

"I'll take you to them when we get to the house," I said.

Pilson might have groaned; I know he made a face. But Agent McCabe just asked, "But the bodies are inside the house?"

When I nodded, a ripple of relief passed through the men. If they'd been buried elsewhere the whole operation might have stalled until the spring thaw.

"Very good," he said. "Let's get the warrant."

Not an hour later, we loaded into our caravan of cars and police cruisers and I did my best not to compare the precise, practiced movements of the agents to the slow and often haphazard antics of Charlie and Bert. Still, I couldn't help but be impressed by the efficiency with which the agents moved: Agent McCabe coordinated with the local authorities in the span of two or three sentences and within minutes we were pulling out of the motel parking lot as smoothly as floats in a parade.

Pilson and I rode in the lead car with Agent McCabe and another agent whose name I didn't get. We sped down the highway and turned off at a lake, where the pace slowed as McCabe tried to follow Marie's directions. A few times we had to stop and McCabe hung his arm out the window with a *what now?* gesture, and an agent in the car behind us had to hang most of himself out to shout whether he thought this was the turn or that was or that we hadn't gone far enough. But once we reached the unmarked road, the house itself was easy to find: it stood in the middle of not just one field but many—huge stretches of unplanted and untended land. Huge stretches of nothing, and beside the house a bare winter oak. As we passed the red mailbox, I shivered and pretended like a draft of wind had snuck down my collar. But it wasn't that. It was the house: flat, gray paint and white, peeling trim and obviously abandoned. And it looked to me like nothing but a grave.

We parked in the area that should have been a driveway, though it was clear that no car had come through all winter; our car floundered and spun tires a few times. We got out and stared up at the house. Our breath rose white in the still. It was cold, bitter cold even without any wind, and as the men unloaded, thermoses of hot coffee came out with the picks and shovels. Agent McCabe looked around uneasily. Our party had descended upon the house like a cluster of flies and we were out in the open. Our presence wouldn't go unnoticed for long.

"Well, Mr. Jensen," he said. "Where do we begin?"

CHAPTER TWENTY-EIGHT

The Bodies

"AFTER YOU, MR. Jensen." McCabe gestured to the porch and I stepped up. I wasn't the first one in; two other agents had been inside already and done a sweep before emerging and calling, "Clear!" A small crowd of men followed Agent McCabe and me into the house. Mr. Pilson stayed behind, looking cold and out of place, and I'm unashamed to say I did not feel sorry for him.

The front door of the house opened directly into the main room. It had indeed been abandoned, but it had been abandoned with care: the sofa, chair, and large dining table had been covered over with sheets, by then lightly coated with dust. And though the main furnishings were spare, the rest of the house was littered with possessions. Over the mantel was a long row of books, with more stacked along the wall. There were shelves and glass cases filled with all manner of things: figurines and ceramics, jeweled hat pins and jewelry boxes—one box held a fancy, painted egg. The glass cases lined the entirety of the dining room and the far wall of the living room. One shelf was nothing but piles and piles of silver spoons, tiny and ornate, the kind that were never meant to be eaten off. The house felt, oddly, like a shrine or maybe like storage. I couldn't help wondering whether Marie had ever been there. Whether she had touched some of the strange objects. Whether some of them were hers.

"Send somebody outside down to the clerk's office," said McCabe. "See if they can find the owner of record."

A few of the agents frowned. Not a man there thought that the owner of record had been the last person in residence. Or that they were still alive. We wandered the ground floor for a few minutes more, studying the items here and there—a typewriter resting against the wall of the hallway, a doll in a dress of blue silk—and I paused before a dark red door, nearly the same shade of red as the mailbox.

"Tell us where to go, Mr. Jensen," said McCabe loudly, startling everyone. "And then, if you like, you can go and wait in one of the cars. Or an agent can take you back to the motel."

"Aren't Mr. Pilson and I driving back tonight?" I asked.

"Yes, but I think the federal government can afford to pay for another day's room."

I hesitated.

"Marie asked me to be there. She wants me to verify something about her stepfather's body."

"What did she want you to verify?"

"I'd rather not say. Or I guess, I'd rather tell you what it is when we find him."

"Fair enough." He held out his hand again, like he had when he was motioning me to step into the house, so I walked past him to a second set of stairs that led to the basement. The door had already been opened by the agents who conducted the sweep.

"They're down here."

We walked down single-file. The light from upstairs illuminated an eight-by-six-foot patch of plank wood flooring, which was lucky—I'd expected a lot of frozen dirt and agents toiling away with pickaxes. We stepped onto the floor and our feet rang out against hollowness. The corpses had been sealed up beneath the floorboards.

"Near the west wall," I said.

The agents commenced with the recovery at once, nearly trampling over me as they carried down tools and hung lamps from the low ceiling. In contrast with the crowded floor above, the basement was almost entirely empty, the walls an amalgamation of stone and dirt, supported by thick wooden beams. It did not run the full length of the house—only a forty-by-twenty rectangle, crudely shaped—and the only thing in it was a broken rocking chair huddled like a ghost in the corner.

With so many men in the small space, the air began to warm and give rise to all of the smells that the cold had made dormant. I hung back near the stairs to stay out of the way but also to keep from being too close when the first of the boards was pried up. The bodies would be frozen now, or nearly so, but the corpses would have been decaying in the basement all through the long hot summer. I feared that they would have a scent and that it would make me turn away, or get sick all over my shoes.

"It's coming loose," one of the agents said. He'd been at the board with a pry bar and reached down to lever his fingers into the opening he'd made. The board came up with a dry creak. Every head in the room craned forward as he stepped back, one hand covering his mouth and nose seemingly out of habit.

There she was. Marie's mother. I couldn't see anything besides a flash of her dress—white cotton with a pattern of small brown flowers—but when I rose up on my toes, I saw that the removed board had revealed her lower half and her left leg. The skin of her calf was gray and withered, shrunken down to a foot that looked like it could never have filled that dusty black shoe.

The mood in the basement had been irritable at first; it changed immediately to one of practiced grimness. The agents had been through all this before.

"Get the cameras," McCabe ordered. More boards came up. Within minutes the whole of Marie's mother's corpse was exposed. Her hands had been folded on her chest, the fabric underneath stained dark from the last trickles of blood from cuts at her wrists. Her hair had been a deep brown, like Marie's, and in death it had been laid out over her shoulders. I looked into her face to find traces of the girl I knew. But it had been altered too much by decay.

"Not much blood," said the agent leaning over the body. Not even on the dress. But at least in this case that was expected. We knew that Marie's mother had been killed somewhere else and brought here to be buried.

Bursts from flashbulbs cut through the yellow light of the lamps. Then the photographer stepped back so the agents could resume tearing up the floor. I waited, tensing as every new board was pulled away. Marie's stepfather would be there, right beside her.

"Another body," an agent said. "It's not the stepfather."

I broke through the barrier of agents and looked down. Marie's mother's body was tucked perfectly between two support beams. On the other side of her, where Nathaniel Cody should have been, was instead the corpse of an old woman.

"Who is she?" McCabe asked me.

"It was supposed to be Nathaniel Cody."

"Pull up more boards," Agent McCabe ordered.

"Seems like a waste," said one of the men. "These are the only new boards. See here—" he held one up. "Different wood." He pointed at the exposed edges of the adjoining floorboards, which were noticeably different, warped and weathered.

I kept on staring. The body beside Marie's mother looked like it had been dead longer. The skin was tighter, more wrinkled. I couldn't see any bloodstains, but she was wearing black, kind of like Widow Thompson, who still wore only black after all these years.

"Pull them up anyway," McCabe said, but his voice was dull. "Kid, why don't you give us some space."

"But—"

"If we find anything else, we'll call you back down. You have my word."

I looked back at the opened grave. More men came down with bags to transport the bodies out of the house.

I went back upstairs feeling dazed. I'd been so certain that we would find him. Why had Marie sent me so far on a wild-goose chase? Why had she been so triumphant with Pilson if she'd known she would only be proven a liar?

I couldn't bear going outside and seeing Pilson's smug face, so I wandered around the house, continually returning to the closed red door. It seemed odd that it would be closed—that the agents would shut it again after doing their sweep. But I figured there was no reason I shouldn't open it and go through.

The red door was unlocked and came open with a soft sound, barely a creak. I looked over my shoulder, through the main room to the agents walking back and forth through the kitchen, but none seemed to notice. The agents in the basement were bound to be a while, and I'd be able to hear them if they called. Sound carried through the house like it was made of paper. So I walked down the hallway that had been blocked by the red door, listening to the house creak and trying to figure out what Marie had been up to, sending me there.

I wondered why she had lied and what else she'd lied about. Had she lied about everything? Maybe Pilson was right and it was in her nature. Maybe she couldn't even help herself.

In the creaking house, with the smells of dirt and death fresh in my nose, the unreality of her story landed hard. Seeing those bodies had been like turning the lights on after a nightmare; I was far from home, far away from carved symbols and spectral figures in the night. Far away from Marie and her strange, steady voice. Of course there was an explanation for the missing blood. Just because we didn't know what it was didn't mean an explanation didn't exist. And it certainly didn't make it a vampire.

The late winter sun had begun to slant, and I followed it west into a bedroom. It had soft blue walls, and the floorboards had been painted white. There was one large window, and above it a brass curtain rod hung bare. The bed beside it was still covered in a blue-and-green checkered quilt, while in the corner a vanity dressing table sat idle, missing its mirror. There was a large walk-in closet full of women's clothes: dresses in plain colors of yellow and gray, the style a little old-fashioned.

As I walked around, making lines through the dust with my fingertips, I heard a voice from the main room note that the floors seemed too clean.

"Like, freshly cleaned," he said, and a chill crept up the back of my neck. I hadn't noticed anything odd about the floors. But once he mentioned it, I realized he was right: the floors in the main room and the kitchen had shone. They'd been completely free of dust. Yet the rest of the house looked like no one had been there in a year.

"Did you check the entire house?" an agent asked.

"Wasn't that red door closed?"

The red door, I thought. The red door I was currently on the other side of. I walked out of the bedroom and back into the hall. The door had drifted mostly shut again, and I was about to say it was me, that I had opened it, when I took a step, and the floor squeaked. The next thing I knew, the door was thrown open and a gun swung into view. I ducked, right before it went off and shot two holes into the wall.

"It's me, it's me!"

"Shit! Goddamn it, kid, are you okay?"

The shots had been so loud that my ears felt stuffed with cotton. More agents crowded into the door with their guns drawn and I put my hands up.

The guy who'd shot at me—a local police officer, not an agent—was shaking all over. He came and helped me to my feet.

"Kid," he asked, "are you sure I didn't get you?"

CHAPTER TWENTY-NINE

The Findings

"KID, ARE YOU sure I didn't get you?"

Even now, what that officer said almost makes me laugh. *Are you sure I didn't get you?* Are you sure you're not shot plain through?

The bullet holes in the wall where I'd been standing were at head level. Yes, I was sure he didn't get me.

After the agents had completed the search of the house—and after my brush with danger courtesy of the nervous deputy— Agent McCabe designated the house a crime scene and ordered it processed: more photos taken, every item cataloged, and an extensive search of the grounds once the snow cleared and the dirt softened. The body of Marie's mother was transferred to a coroner for examination. After that it was released to the next of kin: not Marie but an aunt, Marie's great-aunt, some sixty years old. Marie had never met her.

The body discovered beside her was later identified as a

previous owner of the house but not the current one: she was a woman named Lorraine Dusquene. Five years earlier she had sold the property to a man named Peter Quince. As of this writing, no other records of Peter Quince have been located, and I do not believe that any will be. Nor does Mr. McBride. When I mentioned the difficulty in finding him, he wasn't surprised.

"When you told me the name I thought it sounded made-up," he said. "Peter Quince is a character in a Shakespeare play. *A Midsummer Night's Dream*."

And of course, poor Mrs. Dusquene was just like all the others: cut at the neck and emptied of blood. The medical examiner stated that she had been dead for a number of years. I could guess that number was five.

Pilson couldn't wait until we got back to the jail to tell Marie that we hadn't found her stepfather's body. He called her to gloat as soon as he found a telephone, and he did it in front of everyone. I heard only one half of the conversation at first.

"He wasn't where you said he was." A pause. "Oh, there was a body; it just wasn't him. Your mother was there, buried in the floorboards beside an older woman. Who was that older woman, Miss Mewes?" A longer pause. "He wasn't there, I said. The entire house was searched. Come on, Miss Mewes. You knew all along what we were going to find."

That's when Marie started shouting, and he pulled the phone away from his ear. He feigned a wince but really he wanted us to hear what she said, how unhinged she sounded.

"I don't know about any woman! Just my mother and him,

Nathaniel Cody, right there under the boards, in the dirt, so you look again, you son of a bitch! You look again!"

Pilson grinned at us, at me and the FBI agents, before he hung up the phone.

"She may be a liar," he said. "But she's a committed liar, I'll give her that."

Days later, when she was transferred from our jail to the one in Lincoln for her trial, Pilson was her escort. As she was loaded into the police car, she resisted a little. Her eyes moved over the walls of the sheriff's office to the window where she'd spent so much time looking out. She lingered with us as long as she could, until Pilson finally snapped that she'd stolen enough time, but she wouldn't be stealing away with her life.

"I was never trying to 'steal away with my life,'" Marie said. "I was trying to steal away with my soul."

I told my father later that she had almost gotten to Pilson, that I saw his brow uncrease at those plaintive, Christian words. But my father only frowned and said the truest thing I'd ever heard.

"Benjamin Pilson is no real Christian."

CHAPTER THIRTY

The Things We Have to Do

THE DRIVE BACK to Black Deer Falls with Pilson was tense. I couldn't stand the man, how he kept humming along to the radio, and how friendly he'd become again now that things had gone his way. He'd even seemed truly concerned that I'd almost gotten shot. Though maybe he really was—I guess if I'd been killed he'd have been in a heap of trouble for bringing me along.

"Mr. Pilson," I said, and the humming paused.

"Yes, Michael?"

We'd just passed a highway sign saying we were thirteen miles from St. Cloud. There were only two more hours left in the trip.

"You have to change your mind."

"About what?" he asked.

"About asking for the death penalty."

"That is what the State will ask for. I've already spoken to the judge, and he's amenable."

"But she's just a kid," I said quietly.

"And who were the sixteen people she killed? They were also someone's kids. Marie Catherine Mewes murdered her own mother. No one will weep for this." Then he sighed. "But I am sorry for you, son. I know you care about her. Maybe foolishly, but I can't say that the same thing has never happened to me."

I stared out into the darkness past our headlights. I didn't believe for one minute that the same thing had ever happened to him.

"I don't understand why she has to die. I don't know why you won't believe her."

"Why I won't believe her?"

"There are too many holes in your story," I said. "If Nathaniel Cody was the killer and they killed her mother, then what? It's weeks from the Codys' disappearance before the murder of Peter Knupp—"

"So they were hiding. Honeymooning."

"But why kill him at all?"

"Their interaction with Knupp went wrong. They panicked. Then they go right on killing as they run to Canada."

"None of the victims were robbed."

"Witness disposal, then. Or they'd just acquired a taste for it." His cheek tensed. "Your theory is a campfire story. A monster that drains people of blood and flaps away into the night."

I gritted my teeth. I wanted to say that I never said he turned into a bat, but that seemed counterproductive.

"What about the blood?" I asked. All those murders, whether

the victims had lain nice and docile or whether they had run and been chased down—all of their blood had been missing. Exsanguination. Severe loss of blood. It's what had killed each and every one. Yet there were no pools or stains around the bodies. No arterial spray across the dash and steering wheel of Angela Hawk's car.

"She was there," Pilson said. "She knew what would happen, and by her own admission, she helped Cody carry out these crimes."

"You say Cody like you know for sure, but you don't. Where was the blood?" I asked, and he looked away. "What about her fingerprints? Why were they the only ones?"

"He was careful," Pilson said. "He directed her."

"And the blood on her the night of the Carlson murders. Soaked through every inch of her clothes, like it had been poured over her head—how do you explain that?"

"It was collected. And poured over her, just like you said."

But I was barely listening anymore. I was running roughshod over the top of him and his unanswered questions.

"The house in North Platte. The cleaned floors. Someone had been there before us. Someone could have moved Nathaniel Cody's body—"

"Who?" he demanded. "How would he have known to move it? No one knew we were coming. How would he have beaten us there?"

"Maybe he went back and moved it when you released Cody's name to the press."

"And why would 'he' do that?"

"Because you gave him someone to lay it on. And moving the body would make sure Marie couldn't disprove it. It made Marie look guiltier."

Pilson barked laughter. He bore down on the accelerator.

"There's doubt," I said. "I'm just saying there's doubt."

"Not *reasonable* doubt. And Miss Mewes has only herself to blame for that."

He dropped me in front of my house just past eleven p.m. and didn't go inside to speak to my father, despite seeing the lights on in our living room. My dad opened the door to let me in and gave a half-hearted wave to Pilson's taillights.

"Are you all right?" my dad asked.

"How's Marie?"

"That's not what I asked." But when I didn't budge, he said, "She's fine. She's resting. We had to bring the doc in—"

"The doc?"

"After Mr. Pilson's phone call she wouldn't calm down. She didn't believe that the body hadn't been found. So eventually Dr. Rouse came in and gave her a little something."

"It should have been me who told her," I said. "Not Pilson."

"She might have taken it better," he said.

"She was upset."

"She was angry. Almost like she really believed that his body would be there."

"She did believe it, Dad. She did."

"Michael." He looked at me with a kind of pity and seemed to search for his words for a while. "Sometimes . . . when something is really bad . . . like what happened to Marie, a person will—"

"Make something up?"

"Not because they're a liar. Just so they won't have to face what really happened."

"You think that's what Marie's doing?" I asked.

"I think so."

"Do you think the judge will understand that?"

"I don't know. I'm not a judge. Or a jury."

"I want to see her. I want to see Marie."

"You can see her in the morning," my dad said, and squeezed my shoulder. "She did lead them to a body. Maybe that will be enough."

But I knew it wouldn't be. And I knew that with the Cody story, Pilson would be able to avail the judge to move the first trial out of Minnesota and into Nebraska. Marie had bought herself a few days, with the body search, but Pilson would be at the court as soon as he'd had enough sleep to get up and type the motion.

I went up to my room and set my bag on the floor, then lay on my bed. They would never catch the one who really did it—he was gone, disappeared like smoke—but they would make someone pay. And I couldn't let them do that.

She wasn't innocent. But she wasn't alone in the crimes. And I never believed she was a killer.

I waited until I heard my dad go to bed and then waited another hour after that. I'd never snuck out of my house before. Never tried to go out through the window or creep through the downstairs without making noise. I thought about that before I did it, how my parents would never believe I had broken the rules. When they found my bed empty in the morning, they would probably check underneath it first. And they would be scared. And disappointed. But there was nothing I could do about that.

Considering my lack of experience and the light sleeping habits of my father, it was a wonder that I made it out the front door. But I did, with a fresh bag of clothes and some food from the pantry and all of my savings folded into my wallet. In my right hand, I had my father's keys.

I unlocked the back door at the jail and went up to find Marie in her cell. But she wasn't alone—Nancy was sitting on the bed holding Marie's head in her lap.

"Michael," Nancy whispered. "What are you doing here?" She saw my coat and my bag—the keys. "Oh no. You can't do this."

I unlocked the cell door.

"I can't let her stay."

Marie stirred. When she saw me, she came awake all at once, her eyes a little glazed, probably from the effects of what the doctor had given her. But when she saw my bag, she turned over and got up.

"You'll get into trouble," said Nancy. "You'll get caught; you'll never make it."

"We'll take one of the cruisers. Drive until dawn. Then we'll hide it and go on hitching. Come on, Marie."

"You mean it?" Marie asked.

I held out my hand and she smiled and came to me. She wrapped her arms around me and buried her face in my shoulder.

She felt cold and small.

"Nancy, do I need to tie you up?"

"I guess not." She looked at Marie sadly. "I'll just say I never saw you."

I tugged Marie out of the cell. She was going to need a coat and better shoes and I had no idea where to get them.

"Michael, wait," Marie said.

"Wait for what?" I asked.

She slipped her fingers down my arm and held my hand. She looked around at the same walls she'd stared at for months.

"You would really do this," she said. "For me."

"I have to," I said. "So let's hurry and get it done." She still had a hold of me, so steady. I was trembling like a leaf.

"I can't go," she said quietly. "But I appreciate the gesture."

"Marie—we have to. They're going to kill you."

She didn't let go of my hand, but she gave it a little shake, like she was trying to wake me up.

"I have one more thing I need to tell you, before they come to take me away. Since you're here anyway, would you mind taking it down?"

CHAPTER THIRTY-ONE

The Murders of Bob, Sarah, and Steven Carlson: September 18, 1958

THE TAPE RECORDER was gone, but Nancy brought me a pen and one of my dad's notebooks. She said since it was only us there we could move down to the interrogation room, or I could sit with Marie inside the cell. But Marie joked that she would miss the bars and wouldn't recognize me if she could see all of my face at once. I don't think she wanted anything to change. It's difficult to explain. She hadn't been free for a long time. But at least her incarceration with us had been on her own terms, and I'd like to think that it wasn't all terrible.

So we sat like we always had: her on her cot and me at the kitchen table, though we left the cell door open and Nancy brought us cups of coffee. It didn't feel official, without my father there and without the tape recorder. Without Pilson looking over my shoulder. But I was glad that it happened that way. This part of the story belonged to Black Deer Falls—it was ours the way that Steve and his parents had been ours, and it was right that we would know it first, before the rest of the world.

Marie's accounting of the events of September 18 were difficult to hear. Her story was at times disjointed. Some parts she narrated as well as any storyteller. Other times she got stuck and needed me to nudge her along with questions. She repeated the conversations of that night like she was reciting lines from a play—I had to stop her a few times and ask who was speaking. But I took everything down.

This is what she told me.

They had begun to quarrel on the road. It started in Madison, Wisconsin, when Marie had refused to kill Richard Covey and his fiancée, Stacy Lee Brandberg. They were supposed to be for her: Marie's first kills. Carefully selected. So when she refused, he got angry.

"They seemed so resolute," she said. "Holding on to each other in that empty house. They'd heard about us on the radio and read about us in the papers. They knew what was going to happen. But still they didn't scream or try to run. They didn't panic.

"I said it wasn't like he'd promised. They knew what we were going to do; he hadn't used his tricks on them. But he said, 'The first time can never be easy. The first time you leave everything behind.'

"But I wouldn't. So he did it himself.

"And he did it mean: he made the boy watch when he cut her

throat. Made him keep his eyes open. Then he cut him twice in one wrist. Made him bleed out slower."

How long did it take Richard Covey to die?

"At least a half hour. Much longer than the rest.

"He was mad all the time after that. He said I'd been lying to him, playing a part. That I lacked courage and he'd made a mistake. I said he could go ahead and kill me then and start over, but he said we'd already come too far. My mother was already dead. He'd killed her for me, and he'd killed Nathaniel, and as much as I wanted Nathaniel dead, I loved my mother and cried and cried."

Do you want to tell me more about what happened to your mother? How she died?

"No. But I wish I hadn't told you where she was buried. She didn't deserve to be dug up like that. Photographed."

She paused for a long time here and then spoke at length about how they came to Black Deer Falls.

They came into Black Deer Falls on foot and wandered the back roads through dusk, until the sun went down. There had been no hunt, no plan until the headlights of Steve's Chevy caught them walking on the side of the road. It had all been by chance; it could have been me in my dad's old truck, or it could have been Percy. Steve hit the brakes and pulled over, and Marie and her companion walked in the red of his taillights right up to the passenger door. I can imagine it as if I had been there: Steve, leaning over to get a better look and then reaching to pop the door open. He'd have been in his varsity letter jacket, but it wasn't cold yet, so it would've been unbuttoned. He'd have smiled and asked them where they were headed.

"It was easy to tell him our car had broken down and ask if we could use his family's telephone. He was nice—so nice—and I thought, He'll never try to make me kill this one, when he's so similar to Richard Covey. But when we got to his house and spoke with his family, I knew I was wrong."

Steve parked the car in the usual place in the empty side of one of the large red barns, and walked them inside. I stopped here to ask if Marie was sure.

Widow Thompson saw you walk into the house together but only you and Steve. Are you sure it was the three of you?

"I am."

You're sure he didn't go on ahead or trail behind?

"He was right there, on Steven's other side."

I let her go on.

Inside the house, Mrs. Carlson had just finished cleaning up the kitchen from supper. Mr. Carlson was in the living room, settling down with a newspaper. Steve said he'd been at his girl-friend's house, eating dinner and watching television with her family. Cathy Ferry, though they had not been going steady and she didn't call herself his girlfriend after he died.

The house was warm and lived-in—the rich smell of that evening's stewed beef and potatoes hung in the air and permeated every room. Mrs. Carlson said there was still some left, if they hadn't eaten yet.

"You look like you could use some color in your cheeks," Sarah said. "How about some coffee? Or I could get a pie into the oven.

It's no trouble: I can make a crust with my eyes closed, and there are a dozen jars of filling in the pantry."

"Just coffee, please," said Marie. "Thank you."

Sarah poured a cup for Marie and set it on the table. Marie heard Steve and his father in the living room, conversing with him and laughing.

"I knew it was a trick, to keep them from being put off by his appearance in the light."

Sarah decided to start a pie anyway and asked if Marie was partial to apple or cherry.

"She didn't think anything of getting bowls out and flour and making a mess of her kitchen, even though it was plain that she'd just finished tidying up. She said she thought I looked like an apple girl. That's when I heard the baby. She started to fuss from her crib in a room just off the kitchen."

"You have a baby?" Marie asked.

"Yes, ma'am." Sarah fetched the child up out of the crib. "Patricia. A surprise for everyone, believe me, after all those years of hoping when Steve was little. But here she is. Our little Patty. Steven," she called, "come and get this pile of folded laundry and bring it up to your room before the pie's done!"

He came and took it, and from the living room Marie heard a voice: "Don't go up the stairs. . . . That will be fine. Set it just there." And Steve set the laundry on the step and went back to sit on the couch.

"I got up and went in there—they were all sitting around, chatting, chuckling at nothing like they had known each other for ages. I said, 'There's a child. A baby.' And he said, 'Crueler to leave her alive, don't you think, than to send her along with her family?'"

Steve and his father, his mother, didn't seem to hear this exchange at all. Neither man had looked up when Marie approached, and in the kitchen Sarah had put Patricia into a high chair and gone back to making the dough.

"He had this look in his eyes and it made me angry. I don't know at what. I didn't want to do it, but I felt like I needed to prove it to him that I could. I was mad about the baby. I was angry that they were such nice people."

"Well, if you're going to do it," Marie said, "don't make her go to the trouble of a whole goddamned pie."

"I was shaking. I was shaking all over, and he said, 'Sarah, will you and the child come in here, please.'"

He called, and she obeyed, even with a smile on her face, and the baby on her hip. He took the straight razor out of his pocket and opened it.

"What's that there now?" Bob asked.

"Nothing you need to worry about," he said. "Nothing at all. It's just something for her." He held it up, the blade shining in the yellow light cast by the two humble lamps.

"I stared at it and then noticed the curtains had been pulled shut, and I asked him if he'd done it."

"No, dear, I did that," said Sarah. "Our neighbor lives alone and likes to look in on us. She's a sweet old thing, but sometimes we need a little privacy." Then she went back to cooing at the baby.

"I walked over to him and took the razor. I asked him if we needed all three; it seemed like a lot. And he said, 'You could have had two, back in Madison.'

"So I looked down at Steve, who was sitting next to him on the couch. I asked if they had to be looking."

"Look away," he said, and Steve did. Marie turned away from him, though, and went to his father. Slowly, she touched the razor to the skin of his throat.

"I kept expecting him to leap up. To realize what was happening. The blade had to feel cold and strange, but he didn't even flinch. He didn't seem to notice at all. So I just leaned down and did it."

You did it?

She didn't answer me. She wasn't looking me in the eye; throughout the recounting she'd looked over my shoulder or toward the floor. Sometimes she watched the movements of my pen.

"It was easier than I thought, but I went too deep and it got on me. I tried to drink it but there was a lot. He tried to help. Moved my head, and that was better."

When she couldn't do any more, he got off the couch and nudged her aside to clean up her mess. Then he let Bob Carlson slide down from the chair and onto the rug.

"Mrs. Carlson . . . she didn't know, really, what was happening. But just the same she had started to shush the baby like she was fussing something awful, even though she wasn't making a sound. She just kept shushing her and bouncing her, and not looking at her husband on the floor. I said, 'That's enough, that's plenty,' and he said, 'It's not. You need more.'"

"I'm full."

"You're not."

"He told Steve to come and take the baby. Then he went to Mrs. Carlson and—and he did it and I just went along, I guess, like in a dream. It all felt like a dream by then and there was so much and the *taste* . . . But that was it. That was all I could do."

What do you mean, Marie?

"I mean I knew the boy and the baby would be next. So while he was finishing off Mrs. Carlson, I clenched my stomach until I threw up. I didn't think it would ever come out. I thought, Out, out, out, and I knew it wouldn't, but I threw my head back and all of a sudden it did, right out of my mouth."

It bubbled up over her face, and over her hair—so much that it soaked through her clothes and ran down all the way down to her shoes. I remembered how she looked, sticky and red from head to toe.

"I told Steve to run, to take the baby and get out of the house, but he didn't move. The baby started to cry and he set her down on the rug. I yelled, 'Get out now! You have to!'

"But he said, 'He won't.' So I said, 'You go, then. I'm not coming with you.'"

Did he seem surprised? Angry?

"No. He didn't seem surprised by any of it, not even the sight of me like I was. I thought for a minute he might just kill me, too. Kill me and disappear, and I would become part of the mystery.

But he didn't. I stood between him and the baby and then he left. But not before he shot past me and killed Steve."

Marie said she stayed between him and Patricia after he dropped Steve to the floor, and I pictured her there: teeth bared, covered in red.

"And that's how Charlie and your dad found me: standing on the rug with the baby. She had nearly cried herself out by then. But I couldn't pick her up and comfort her. It wouldn't have been right."

It was late by the time we finished. Our cups of coffee were empty. It was quiet in the jail. Still. Outside the window the sky was black.

"So Mr. and Mrs. Carlson," I said. "You killed them."

"I killed them," she said.

She reached her hand through the bars, and I leaned forward and took it, and she closed her eyes and cried.

CHAPTER THIRTY-TWO

Leaving Black Deer Falls

THE NEXT MORNING, my dad burst in and found me asleep in his office. He looked pretty relieved to see me, even though I don't think he really believed that I would help Marie break out of jail. He let me clean up in the bathroom and got Charlie to bring in fresh coffee and some donuts from the diner. Nancy came in, too, even though her shift was over and it was her day off. I told them what had happened, and what Marie had confessed.

"Why would she say that?" Nancy asked after I'd finished. "She couldn't have. She always said she never hurt anyone."

"What does her story matter, anyhow?" asked Charlie. "If it's not true? If she's still going on with that blood-drinking nonsense?"

"Because it was the truth," my dad replied. "Take out the wild tales and I reckon it is just what happened. The Carlsons still have family here, and they deserve to know everything there is to know, if they want to."

He looked at me. The fact that Marie had killed circled in the air, along with the knowledge that this strange story was nearing its end. Soon there would be no more letters to the *Star* about our mishandling of the case. No more phone calls to my mother about how ashamed I should be for cheapening the Carlsons' memory. No more Marie, sitting quietly upstairs.

Later that day we got word that Pilson had petitioned to have Marie brought to Nebraska for trial. Now that he had her identity and the body of her mother, his claim was at least as strong as ours. So the lawyers came and got her again and brought her back to the capital. This time I wasn't allowed to attend. I was sick all that day, thinking I would never see Marie again, that she would be given over immediately and moved to Lincoln. But she came back that night.

"What are you doing here?" I asked. "You won?"

But they hadn't won. It was plain in Marie's sad smile, on the defeated, exhausted faces of Mr. Norquist and Mr. Porter.

"They're trying her in Lincoln for the murder of Audrey Cody," Mr. Norquist said. "They're coming to transfer her in two days."

"Then why are you back?" I asked. "She's here just long enough to plead guilty to the Carlson murders," Mr. Porter said. "And she's here because the judge didn't care for Mr. Pilson."

I didn't know what to say. Neither did Marie. I think she figured there was never any other way it could go.

The State of Nebraska didn't charge her with the murders of Peter Knupp, Angela Hawk, or Beverly Nordahl. Pilson didn't have the evidence, I guess, to feel confident about prosecuting the rest. Or maybe he figured that her mother would be enough. People were mad at first. They wanted justice on all counts. But eventually they resigned themselves to his decision. It was, after all, like I heard some say: you could only electrocute her once.

I didn't go home much in the two days before Marie was taken away. I ate my meals with her up in our old kitchen. When I had to, I would go home and get cleaned up and come right back. School was forgotten. At night, Nancy or Bert would let me into Marie's cell, and I would sleep curled against her on the narrow cot. When I woke in the morning, I would find her arm around me, gripping my shirt, the fabric wrinkled between her tight slender fingers.

The morning of the day that Pilson was to arrive, Marie asked if my mom would come and cut her hair into a bob, so my mom came with her scissors and did it while Marie was seated at our old kitchen table.

"Perfect," my mom said when she was finished. At that length the waves in it stood out more, and truthfully it looked less perfect than wild. My mom tried to tie it back with green ribbon and then immediately pulled it out again. It wouldn't all stay, and the ribbon made Marie look too young for any of us to bear.

"I'll keep the ribbon anyway," said Marie.

My mom smoothed Marie's hair back and tucked it behind her ear. Then she left, and Bert came up to put Marie back into her cell.

"You know I'd let you stay out," he said.

"It's all right, Bert," she said, and he swung the cell door shut between us and left us to ourselves.

"Are you afraid?" I asked.

"I suppose."

"Do you want me to be there? I'll come, to the trial and to what happens after, if you want me to. I'll have my dad—"

"No." She knew what was going to happen. She knew she was going to lose. "I don't want that. You have to promise me that you won't."

So I promised. Much of that last day together we spent in silence. We sat in our quiet, familiar place and listened to the clock tick away the minutes. I listened to her breathe and knew I would remember the sound.

"You don't have any more questions?" she asked.

"What do you think is left to tell?"

She leaned back against the bars, and her new shorter hair made her neck look bare and long.

"Nothing, I guess," she said. "But anyone but you would be asking for more."

She looked at me and smiled a little.

"I wish I'd met you first," she said, and I wished for that, too, even though I knew it could have never been—it was the murders that had brought her to me and without them we never would have met. It was a terrible thought, and it was terrible knowing that I didn't entirely regret it.

Pilson came to collect her with a caravan of state police. Reporters swarmed the station—even Mr. McBride had staked out the building since morning, not wanting to miss the moment she was brought out. My dad put the handcuffs on her and walked her down, and he let me walk with them.

"I don't know what there is to be done," he said to her, "but I think you could still save yourself if you just told them where he went. And I really wish you would."

We walked through the station and through the front doors to the parking lot, where Pilson waited. Charlie and Bert were on hand to keep the reporters at a respectable distance, and the state patrol that Pilson had brought did their best to help out. When Pilson saw Marie, he nodded grimly and said, "You've got a moment." Then he ducked into the front passenger seat of the car.

Marie took a deep breath and looked around. It was the first time she'd been allowed to linger outside in months, the most fresh air she'd breathed. I was glad the day was warm—it wasn't spring yet but it was one of those early days where the scent and the feel of it were in the breeze.

She turned to me. I searched for something smart to say. She was wearing her familiar blue jeans, rolled at the ankles, and her white buttoned shirt. Instead of her usual green sweater she wore a blue one that Nancy had gotten for her—Nancy, who stood to one side with Charlie and quietly cried into a handkerchief.

Marie lifted her cuffed hands and looped them over my head. She pulled me close, and I hugged her gently, and she whispered into my ear, her voice too low and close for anyone to hear.

She whispered what she felt. She whispered her regrets. Then she took her hands back over my head and pressed them flat against my chest.

"You never did bring me those smokes," she said.

And then Pilson got back out of the car, and they pulled us apart, and the reporters closed in like a flock of crows.

And then Marie Catherine Hale was gone.

Marie's trial lasted for two weeks. As expected, she didn't change her story, and the headlines blazed. Doctors and psychiatrists were brought in to evaluate her, and she was found to be competent. They said that she was willfully making it up.

The papers said that the jurors were released at 5:25 p.m. on Thursday night to deliberate. They broke for supper at 6:30 and would not bring back a verdict until Friday evening. They found her guilty, with a recommendation of death.

According to witnesses in the courtroom, Pilson had been right. There were several gasps of shocked surprise, but no one wept.

After Marie's sentencing, the mood in Black Deer Falls—and across the nation—shifted. Groups came out in support of her, asking for mercy; those same people who for all the weeks and months before had called her a seductress now said she was a child. Mr. McBride published a Letter to the Editor in the *Star* titled, "Who but God Has the Right to Vengeance?" submitted by one Mrs. Veronica Macready, who my dad said had once come to the station to complain about Marie being held there.

Even in Nebraska, the outcry was such that Pilson held a press conference. It was unprecedented, reporters said, sentencing a girl to death who would have been in the tenth grade. And Pilson's reply made headlines of its own.

"Even fifteen-year-old girls must realize that they cannot go on sixteen-victim murder sprees."

After the furor had settled down, Agent McCabe quietly suspended the search for Nathaniel Cody. He'd not been seen or heard from since the murders ended, and it was reasoned that he had long gone over the border to Canada.

Marie Catherine Hale was set to be executed by hanging in Lincoln, Nebraska, on May 8, 1959. It was expected to go on as scheduled, as she had no intent to file an appeal.

After the trial, everyone seemed to forget all about Marie's blood-drinker story. In the same way that they forgot about the missing blood and the symbols carved into the trees and Steve Carlson's headstone. The same way they forgot about the snake nailed to my door and the man who stood in my family's living room in the middle of the night. That was just a hallucination anyway. A bad dream. Even Marie said so, since he couldn't have come in without being invited.

But I never had the chance to tell Marie about a conversation I had with Dawn.

About a week after Marie left for Nebraska, I asked Dawn if she'd seen anyone strange around town.

"No," she said. "Except for the man who was lost."

"Who was lost?" I asked.

"He came by the house one afternoon. He looked cold so I

asked him to come in and made him a cup of coffee and let him use the telephone."

"You invited him in," I said. "Dawn, what was his name?"

She couldn't remember, even though she'd sat right by him and called him by it.

"Was it before or after I'd been sleepwalking?" I asked.

"Before."

She wasn't bothered by her lapse in memory. And when I asked her what he looked like, she smiled and said, "Like a film star."

Like a film star. Not "like a movie star" or "a handsome prince" or any other phrase she might have been more likely to say. But those exact words, the same words that Marie had used, like they had been planted in both of their heads.

In the days leading up to Marie's execution I thought often about the other victims: Cheryl Warrens, Richard Covey, and Stacy Lee Brandberg. I thought about the woman buried with Marie's mother in the abandoned house: Lorraine Dusquene. I thought about the made-up property owner, Peter Quince. Five years he had owned that house, according to the county records. Five years of not living there, of coming and going from other places. Five years of filling it with strange objects. I wondered if they had come with the house. I wondered if he had known Lorraine Dusquene before he killed her.

But there will be no answers to those questions. The investigations have stopped. This is all there is. Marie's accounting of the events. We can only know what she knew and what she believed to be true.

Maybe it doesn't matter. The people who were killed will remain dead. Steve and his parents, Peter Knupp—there is no bringing them back, no matter what answers we think we find or what mysteries we think we solve.

The vampire got away.

The vampire never was.

Dear Mr. McBride,

Dear Matt,

I hope you don't mind my calling you that. You always said I
could, but I could never tell if that was just you being friendly.
I know I never felt comfortable doing it, and even now, after all
that's happened, I can only do it on paper.

In the package that accompanies this letter you'll find
everything I have compiled about the Bloodless Murders, and
about Marie Catherine Hale. Pages and pages chronicling the
interviews and our time together. I took it down, just like you said
to. And I did my best to tell it like she would have wanted.

I hope it's all right that I turn it over to you now. Take it
and run. Make what you can out of it. I know that's what I was
supposed to do, to sift through it all and find the truth, but I guess
I don't have the heart for it anymore.

The story I wrote isn't the story you figured on, and after you
finish reading it, I'm sure you'll be disappointed. I'm sorry about
that. And I don't want you to think that I'm not grateful for all
your advice or that I wasn't listening. You're a great reporter,

Mr. McBride, and a better mentor than I could have ever hoped to find, in Black Deer Falls or anywhere. Last summer when I was delivering papers for you, I took your diploma down off the wall and the nail got stuck—I scratched the hell out of the paint behind it so I'm sorry about that, too. I just wanted to get a better look at it. The ivory paper and the stark black lettering. The school seal from the University of Pittsburgh. I imagined it was my name on it instead of yours. I really did want to know what brought you out here to us from there, but I should have asked sooner. I guess I never was much of a journalist.

By the time you get this package, I'll be headed out of town. I got a letter from Marie, you see, and it contained a sort of last request. She'd carefully timed the sending of it, and I like to imagine the determined look on her face when she wrote it, and how she must have hidden her nerves, worrying about whether it would reach me or be intercepted by my mom or dad, or even picked off by a prison guard looking to make a buck by selling it to the national papers. I kept the original for myself, but this is what she wrote.

Dear Michael,

I'm writing to you now to ask you what I couldn't ask then. Because I lacked the nerve. And because I was afraid you would say no. So I waited until it's almost too late, hoping that will mean you won't.

Do you remember the story of Mercy Brown? Do you

remember what they did to her?

Those first days, I bet you can't read that shorthand, your pen was shaking so bad. I imagine you looking back on those papers and seeing nothing but wavy lines. But I know you were listening.

And I know this is a lot to ask. But I don't want to come back. So I need your help. I know you remember what to do.

So I'm asking. If you ever cared about me. Like I cared about you.

I'm sorry, Michael. I want you to know that I'm not the same as I was then. But it doesn't matter because I did what I did. My confession was for who I used to be. Do you believe that? That I could change? I hope you do. And I hope that you believe me.

xo,

Marie

Once upon a time, there was a girl named Mercy Brown, who they thought was a vampire, and whose grave they unearthed, whose head they severed and whose heart they burned to ashes upon a stone. Of course I remember that. And I know what it is that Marie wants me to do.

By the time you read this it'll be too late to stop us. We'll already be there.

The cemetery of Nebraska State Penitentiary is located in southwest Lincoln, on a slowly sloping hill that rises above the prison grounds. Grasshopper Hill, they call it, on account of the locusts in summer. The main prison is a ways away, but there are still lookout towers, and even at night guards will be making their rounds. We'll be lucky if we don't get shot.

Funny, my mother always thought that journalism was the safer choice. She was never wild about my dad trying to get me to follow in his footsteps. Before the murders, he used to ask me about it at least once a month. Now I doubt that he'll ever ask me again.

I know this sounds like a goodbye letter, but it isn't. I don't know what I'm going to do. I just know she asked me to do it, so I have to try. I guess I'll decide when I get there.

So I guess we both have some decisions to make. I trust you to decide what to do with this story. It was never really my story anyway.

You know, before Marie left I asked her why it was so important that the killer not be her stepfather. I didn't understand why she wouldn't just take the out and lay it all on him. Save herself. Then the papers started to run stories about him being the killer and them being on the run.

"They're saying I was abused," she said. "They're saying I was raped, I was molded, I was a victim." She was angry. And angry at me because I couldn't see how that was worse. But I think the whole reason that Marie wanted to confess was so she would have the final say. Marie would not be defined, not by the reporters, not by the blood drinker, or Nathaniel Cody. Not by me.

If the articles are to be believed, she didn't give any last *words at her execution. And she didn't pray, unless you count telling the priest to "go ahead if it makes you feel better." Marie Catherine Hale. Tough to the end.*

I'm going to miss her voice. I'm going to miss her. I suppose you'll think that's strange, but it's the truth.

Tell the truth and shame the devil. When I started that seemed like an easy enough thing. Find out what really happened, Michael, because the truth is the truth. Except it isn't, is it? Facts, maybe. But the truth is our own. It's tied up with belief. And belief is harder to hold down.

I want to thank you for everything, Matt. And if something goes wrong at the cemetery, I hope you'll give this to my parents and let them read it so maybe they'll understand.

Yours Truly,
Michael Jensen

May 9, 1959

When I asked Percy to drive me down to Lincoln, he didn't seem surprised. He just snuck out early and picked me up, as if we'd done it a hundred times.

"I guess I don't have to ask you why," he said when I got in. "I guess I've known for a while. But she was a killer, right?"

"Yeah," I said. "She was a killer. But that's not all she was."

We drove out of town down Main Street, watching lights turn on as the shops opened up, the sidewalks still dark and empty.

"You know I do love this place," I said. "Just because I think I might wind up somewhere else, it doesn't mean I don't. It doesn't mean it isn't home."

Percy looked at me. Some people say the Valentines aren't the cleverest of people, but I find them downright intuitive.

"Yeah," he said, and smiled. "I know."

Hours later, outside the car window, a whole lot of nothing

breezes past as Percy carefully drives the byways. We've crossed well into eastern Nebraska and the springtime remnants of tall-grass prairies. As I stare into them, the pale tops rustle in the wind and in my mind, I see Stephen Hill, running for his life as the grasses snarl around his legs. In my mind the grass is green—high summer grass to his waist, and behind him the dark shapes of Marie and the blood drinker dart through it like fish through underwater weeds. I can almost hear his panicked breathing. I can almost hear her laughing.

Only that isn't the way it happened. Stephen Hill was killed far away, in a regular flat field next to a service station between Grand Junction and Mason City, Iowa.

"Can you reach back and grab Pop's atlas?" Percy asks. "I think our next turn is coming up."

I reach back for the atlas—which is really not an atlas but a collection of individual maps secured with a tie—and unfold the map of Nebraska.

"About how long?" he asks.

"Ten miles to the turn. We should be there before dark."

We drive past the cemetery just before sunset, when it's still light enough to see the rows of white grave markers and crosses. We park down the road and wait until the sun goes down. We wait until after the prison will have called lights-out.

"You shouldn't come with me," I say. "This isn't like just ditching class or swiping beers from Mo."

"Come this far, haven't I?" he says. "Can't very well let you go the rest of the way alone."

We get out of the car and he opens the trunk—there are things inside we need: shovels, a sharpened hatchet. They all feel cold in my hands. The moon is out, and the night is brighter than I would like. I tell Percy to button his jacket up over his white shirt.

We go quick and quiet along the dirt road until we reach the edge of the cemetery. Ahead in the blackness I can just make out the ghostly shapes of the crosses in row after neat row.

Percy touches the fence, and wraps his hand around the strand of barbed wire hammered into the old wood posts.

"Stay low," I say. "Stay covered."

"Not much cover to be had."

"I'm sorry about this, Perce."

"I don't know why you're doing this," he says. "I don't believe you're really going to do it."

I tighten my grip on the hatchet.

It takes some time to find her grave, stumbling around in the moonlight, sometimes on our hands and knees and feeling our way across the ground for fresh dirt. But it takes even longer to dig her up. Percy helps, and we work side-by-side until our shovels strike something firm, of wood, and he looks at me before climbing out. This part I have to do alone. The top half of her casket is exposed. It's just a plain pine box, and above it in the grass the small rectangular stone bears no name, only the date. I don't know if I have the nerve for this. If I can pry open the casket and look upon her face. If I can cut out her heart.

I kneel down. She hasn't been in the ground long. I lean in close.

"Come back, Marie. I want you to come back."

I wait.

Against the wood, the hatchet in my hand shakes.

AUTHOR'S NOTE

Though the character of Marie Catherine Hale and the killings known as the Bloodless Murders are inventions of fiction, they were inspired in part by actual events. In 1958, nineteen-year-old Charles Starkweather and his fourteen-year-old girlfriend, Caril Ann Fugate, embarked upon a murder spree that left eleven people dead throughout Nebraska and Wyoming. Eventually apprehended, Charles was convicted and executed for his crimes on June 25, 1959. Though Caril Ann's level of involvement in the killings has come into question, she was also convicted and sentenced to life in prison.

The murders of Michael's friend Steve Carlson and his parents were inspired in large part by the murders of the Clutter family in Holcomb, Kansas, on November 15, 1959, which were famously profiled by Truman Capote in his novel *In Cold Blood*.

Any quotes taken from the actual investigations have been paraphrased and otherwise altered for the sake of Marie's story, and though some of the criminal justice elements are similar to the real cases, Marie's case is different and fictionalized. All inaccuracies and liberties taken with procedure are mine.

ACKNOWLEDGMENTS

This book owes many things to many people, but let's start at the beginning, with my agent, Adriann Ranta Zurhellen, at Folio Literary Management. She kindly listened and kept an open mind as I pitched her this weird story. She also wisely told me I should write the Three Dark Crowns series first.

As usual, I am completely indebted to my editor, Alexandra Cooper, at Quill Tree Books. I handed her a painstakingly crafted birdhouse made of words, and she deftly pointed out where I'd meant to put the door, and where it needed more paint, and how to shore it up so the words wouldn't collapse and murder every bird inside.

Thank you to Rosemary Brosnan, Jon Howard, and the entire team at HarperCollins/Quill Tree: art director Erin Fitzsimmons, who designed the cover; the talented artist Miranda Meeks; the publicity dynamo Mitchell Thorpe; copyeditor Robin Roy; and of course the amazing marketing stylings of Michael D'Angelo.

Eternal high fives to Allison Weintraub and Marin Takikawa, who keep me in line and in the know. Big heart eyes to power-house publicity trio Crystal Patriarche, Keely Platte, and Paige Herbert at BookSparks.

Thanks to my two dogs and two cats for taking long naps so Mama could work. Thanks to Susan Murray, whose Father (capitalization deliberate) was a small-town detective and whose expertise in criminology, forensic psychology, and criminal justice really came in handy. Now if you would be willing to obtain an advanced degree in ancient warfare before my next book that would be just aces.

Thank you to the talented writers Marissa Meyer, Lish McBride, Sajni Patel, Rori Shay, Alexa Donne, Kaylyn Witt, Alyssa Colman, and Jessica Brody for camaraderie, good food, brainstorms, and wine.

And thank you to Dylan Zoerb, for luck.

ABOUT THE AUTHOR

KENDARE BLAKE is the #1 *New York Times*-bestselling author of the Three Dark Crowns series. She holds an MA in creative writing from Middlesex University in northern London and is also the author of *Anna Dressed in Blood*, a Cybils Awards finalist; *Girl of Nightmares*; *Antigoddess*; *Mortal Gods*; and *Ungodly*. Her books have been translated into over twenty languages, have been featured on multiple best-of-year lists, and have received many regional and librarian awards. Kendare lives and writes in Gig Harbor, Washington, from under a pile of dogs and cats. Visit her online at www.kendareblake.com.

THREE DARK QUEENS ARE BORN IN A GLEN, SWEET LITTLE TRIPLETS WILL NEVER BE FRIENDS

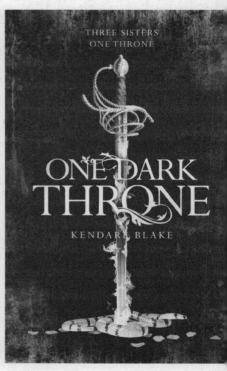